The Red Coat

A Novel of Boston

DOLLEY CARLSON

LETTERMULLEN PRESS

Edited by Candice Davis-Williams
Cover art © Dan McCole, www.danmccole.com
Book design by Jera Publishing, www.jerapublishing.net

ISBN 978-0-9862238-0-8

Library of Congress Control Number: 2014920095

Published by:
Lettermullen Press
Irvine, CA

To Tom Carlson
My love

ACKNOWLEDGEMENTS

Thank you to my friends and family, who loved me through and encouraged every word. Tom Carlson, Candy Carlson, Katie and Joe Rider, Connie and Dave Hanson, Rita Horsley, Joni Larson, Marie Carlson, Jim and Jane Hayden, Ken and Lorayne Carberry, Jeanne and Bob Peck, Gail and Peter Ochs, Anne Storm, Mary Hendricks, Sandra Cornejo, Susan Gaffney, Rosemary O'Day, Teri Gundlach, Carol Timmons, Susan Yates, Cheryl Perez, Diana Brown, and Karen Wilson.

Thank you to all of my dear cousins, who blessed the book with their whole-hearted enthusiasm and prayers.

Thank you to my amazing writer friends, without whom this book would never have happened. And who edited, proofed and blessed the work with their un-daunted support and joy. Candice Davis-Williams, Mary Rakow, Dianne Russell, Marrie Stone, Susan Bernard, Hilary Katersky, Michael Friedrich, Lynette Brasfield, Barbara DeMarco Barrett and Gail Roper.

Thank you to the city of Boston, home of my heart, and its citizens, who so generously assisted me in research with keen interest and "best to you" for the work; especially to Margaret Sullivan, Archivist for the Boston Police Department, Rick Winterson of South Boston Online, and to the Archdiocese of Boston.

Thank you to Jimmy McCarthy, of Ireland, who kindly granted me permission to quote lyrics from his heartfelt "Diamond Days" song.

Thank you to Kimberly Martin, Stephanie Anderson, and Jason Orr of Jera Publishing for so skillfully ushering this book into being.

PROLOGUE

EVERY TIME I RETURN TO Boston, I realize now, I am looking for my parents. Will he come quickly around the corner? That handsome young copper with the brilliant blue eyes and confident swagger? Will I, in some mystical way, time frozen in 1953, see him again? Daddy.

Will the wished for dream continue as I catch one more glimpse of the pretty mother of three pushing her baby's carriage along the Strand in South Boston? Will I see the darling little boy who always held on to the carriage handle? And the little girl who loved to lead the way just a few-skips ahead? Does she dream of seeing me too? Mummy.

There really isn't any reason for me to walk and walk through the city of Boston, up and down the upper-crust streets of Beacon Hill and across the vast Common, which was my father's beat when he was a rookie policeman. Or stroll working-class South Boston's tight-knit Irish neighborhoods and treasured beaches and stop to light candles at Saint Augustine and Gate of Heaven churches, in memory of my loved ones. No reason, other than to say, I miss them and I miss the diamond days.

"Diamond Days" is an Irish song that refers to cherished times, and that is how I remember my Boston Irish Catholic childhood's bygone days of love and promise.

And then there's the red coat—an enduring legacy from both sides of the city . . .

And I'll love the memories of the diamond days.
I'll keep a candle burning, 'til we sing again, the diamond days.
JIMMY MACCARTHY

I

PART I

CHAPTER I

Norah King stood straight in her black stockings, black, low-heeled, laced work shoes, navy-blue skirt, white blouse, and full, starched white apron, her thick, auburn-gray hair piled neatly on top of her head in a bun. "Mrs. Parker . . . may I please have a moment of your time?"

Caroline was stunned to hear one of the floor washers say her name, and surprisingly pleased by the soft Irish brogue in which it was said.

"Mrs. Parker, first of all I want you to know it isn't my way to be listenin' to the conversations 'round about me . . . still, I couldn't help but overhear you're givin' that fine red coat away to the poor. And isn't that a good heart you have now, to be thinkin' of others?"

Norah and Mary had been keenly eyeing the elegant garment all morning long. Both knew it would be out of place for Norah, a domestic, to request the coat for her daughter, and doing so could possibly put an end to any future work in the brownstone mansion. However, Norah deeply loved her firstborn; so grateful was she for the girl's uncomplaining nature and helping ways that maternal love overtook propriety. And when Mrs. Parker hurried across the damp entry floor on tiptoe, carrying a vase of fresh flowers from the kitchen to the parlor, Norah stood, wiped her rough, wet hands on her apron, and stepped forward.

The mother of nine had a lump in her throat for what she was about to ask, but self-respect brought her shoulders back, while resolve took a breath, and pride held her chin up. "If it would be all right with yourself, could I please have that beautiful red coat for my daughter, Rosemary?" Norah put her right hand in her apron pocket, placed her left hand over her wrist, and waited.

♦

It was early April, and Caroline Adams Parker busily ordered her housekeeper, caretaker, and cook about the task of spring cleaning with the goal of having everything in order by tomorrow, Palm Sunday. Earlier in the week, curtains and drapes were removed from every window—even the one in the small cellar door—laundered and pressed, or sent out to the drycleaners. Each multi-paned window upstairs sparkled after being washed the day before by Palowski & Son's—Best Window Cleaners in The Commonwealth, as the sign on their paneled truck advertised. They would finish the job this morning.

Caroline firmly believed in hiring skilled help for specific house maintenance jobs: gardeners, window cleaners, painters, and now floor washers, two Irish women who usually scrubbed the floors of her husband's company, Parker Shipping, after hours on weeknights, had come in from South Boston for the day. Norah King and Mary Callanan both had large families and saw the opportunity to work on Saturday as heaven-sent and a chance to earn a little something extra to help with the children's Easter clothes.

The Parkers' live-in help, husband and wife, Rolf and Hilda, were immensely grateful for their employer's delegation of heavier tasks, so unlike the fate of many other live-ins on Boston's Beacon Hill, most of them European immigrants. There was prestige in hiring German, French, and Swedish. But not the Italians, unless one needed marble work or fine woodcarving, nor the Irish, though everybody knew no one did laundry better than they did. Years ago, Caroline's mother, Rebecca Meriwether Adams—proper and kind-hearted, diminutive in stature but enormously particular—had a white, Chinese rice-linen tablecloth that had been badly stained with red wine. The predicament birthed a favorite family story, which Caroline repeated to Hilda as they sat at the dining room table slipping damask napkins into ivy-embossed silver rings for that evening's dinner party. The Irish women, working nearby but unseen, heard every word.

"My mother was absolutely convinced she'd never be able to use that cloth again. Then Pru Walker suggested she borrow their laundress, Mrs. Finnerty, who wasn't a bit worried about getting that stain out. And she did. It's perfect. The Irish are positively magical at bringing lost causes back to life."

Norah and Mary shook their heads.

Hilda, aware of the scrubwomen's location, felt the need to redeem Mrs. Parker's somewhat patronizing account.

"Ya, Mrs. Parker, your mother, she was right. Those Irish ladies have already begun their magic. The entry floor shines like the State House dome."

From time to time Boston's gleaming State House dome received a fresh coat of 23.5k gold leaf. Despite canvas-draped scaffolding tiny golden flakes would whirl down Beacon Street. Legend has it, that at the turn of the century, and within hours of his arrival in Boston, a hopeful Italian immigrant thought he saw gold floating in the air. And when he walked into a North End boarding house, the young widowed owner interpreted his "golden hair and shoulders" as an answer to her prayers and a sign that he would be her next husband. They were wed within weeks.

Kitchen cupboards, even the pantry, and every single closet in the house, were cleared of anything Caroline considered clutter, including her daughter's red wool coat.

"Imagine, Hilda, the girl only wore it for a season, and that was two years ago. No sense in having it take up space." With that she handed the coat to her trusted, long-term housekeeper. "And Hilda, put this on the entry settee with the other things, will you, please?"

After the coat had been placed on the settee, just three feet away from where Mary and Norah were on their hands and knees, scrubbing the black-and-white-marble entry floor, Norah whispered, "And wouldn't that beautiful red coat look grand on my Rosemary?" She dipped her scrub-brush in a bucket of suds and back again to the floor. "Sure and you've seen her wearin' the dull brown tweed for years, and now it's so threadbare we won't be handin' it down to her sisters.

And haven't they said so themselves?" Picturing the pretty faces of her Kay and Rita, she smiled and kept scrubbing. "Oh, God in heaven, wouldn't I love to be bringin' that fine coat through me front door for Rosemary."

Earlier that day, just as the window washers were arriving, Caroline happened to gaze across the street and saw her neighbor, Eleanor Brewster, standing by the elm tree in front of her own house.

"Hello, Eleanor. My, you're up and about early this morning."

"Hello, Caroline. I needed a breath of fresh air, and perhaps a little conversation, but it appears you're rather busy."

"Simply spring cleaning. I stepped out for fresh air as well. The house positively reeks of pine, which will, of course, be lovely once it calms down. Please, come in for a cup of coffee. Everything's in such disarray, but we'll have at least twenty minutes before they get to the kitchen floor and windows."

"Perfect. Nanny should have the baby dressed and ready for our walk by then. Are you sure you can spare the time, Mrs. Parker?"

"For goodness sake, Eleanor, you must call me Caroline. Every time you say Mrs. Parker, I look for my late mother-in-law." Caroline smiled. She took her young neighbor by the hand and led her up the front steps. "Actually, you're doing me a favor. I'm exhausted already, and the day's only begun."

Eleanor pulled a chair from the sizable kitchen table, and faintly sighed as she sat down. Caroline set two china cups and saucers on the bare wood, and two plates as well, each with a blue-and-white plaid cloth napkin, butter knife, and teaspoon on top. "I have some homemade raisin brown bread. Why don't I toast a couple of pieces for us?"

"Thank you, but the baby's eight months old, and I still look like I'm in a family way." She took a breath. "I'm so blue. I went shopping for an Easter outfit, but nothing fit properly." The young mother began to cry.

Eleanor Brewster had gratefully squeezed into her non-maternity spring best for yesterday's shopping expedition, only to have a saleslady at R. H. Stearns Co. inquire, "When is your bundle of joy expected, madam?"

"Eleanor, you have made an entire person. Your body has done a remarkable feat. The weight will be gone in no time." Caroline pulled a hankie from her smock pocket and handed it to her and then presented a serving dish with an apple-shaped knob on top and lifted the lid. "May I present for your morning pleasure, prunes? And they're still warm. Price so enjoys warm prunes. Let's have these instead."

"Thank you, Caroline," Eleanor said with a budding smile.

"So tell me, do you have any special plans for Easter Sunday? If not, your family is certainly welcome to join us."

Eleanor placed two more prunes on her plate. "Sinclair's parents usually host Easter dinner, but they're traveling this year. His sister offered, but she lives all the way out in Concord, and the baby doesn't do well in the car. Motion sickness, I'm afraid. We'd love to join you."

"I'm delighted." Caroline raised her coffee cup. "Absolutely delighted."

Just then Zingy Palowski tapped on the window and waved his index finger, mouthing, "Is it okay to wash these windows now?"

Caroline walked Eleanor to the door and quickly returned to her spring-cleaning effort.

As was her custom when there was housekeeping to be done, Caroline held her dishwater-blonde-gray hair back at the nape of her neck with a tortoise-shell barrette and wore a full smock over her clothing. Today's was a deep blue Oriental print, which covered most of her tall, slender frame.

Glancing toward the dining room, Mary caught sight of Caroline coming from the kitchen and whispered to Norah, "Will you look at the Missus, glidin' about like a swan? Sure and there's not a bounce in her. Oh, it'd be grand to move like that, but I think you've got to be born with it."

Mrs. Parker approached the two women. "Of course we'll have a hot lunch for you, about noon. And dessert, there's just enough bread pudding and cream for two."

"Thank you, Mrs. Parker," they said, the unspoken clearly understood between them: *Can you believe she's feedin' us as well?*

Waiting until the lady of the house was out of sight, Mary directly addressed what needed to be said. "And don't I know what you're thinkin' Norah King, that the two of us gave up sweets for Lent? Don't be worryin' about eatin' that bread puddin'. For isn't it only bread and cream we'll be eatin', and not a true dessert, say, Boston Cream Pie with the chocolate and all? And wouldn't our Lord be disappointed in the two of us if we showed the least bit of ingratitude by declinin' Mrs. Parker's Christian hospitality?"

Norah whispered, "Sure and your smooth tongue will talk us right into heaven when Saint Peter asks why we went back on our solemn promise for Lent 1941. I'm dependin' on it, Mary. You'd best practice that Christian hospitality bit so you've got it down pat for Saint Pete."

Hilda followed closely as Mrs. Parker went throughout the house from one room to another. Presently they crossed the entry hall, and walked right past the settee that held all the items to be given away, including the red coat.

"Imagine, Hilda." Caroline Parker's sentences lacked endings, even pauses, and she often drove home a point by repeating it once or twice. Consequently, Hilda seldom knew when she could leave the room and spent a great deal of time shifting from one foot to the other while waiting for an opportunity to escape.

"Imagine," Caroline said again, looking back at the crimson garment, which lay on top of the pile. "The girl merely wore it for a season. And that was two years ago."

The girl, Cordelia, was now a junior at Radcliffe and only came home for holidays, the off weekend, and of course, summers at the family's Martha's Vineyard oceanfront, eighteen-room, brown-shingled cottage.

In the parlor, Caroline picked up her favorite family photo from the top of a Colonial-style, drop-front mahogany desk. It was of Woodleigh, or "Wooley," as the family came to call the cottage because, as a little girl, Cordelia couldn't pronounce its proper name. The image captured, in her brother's words, "the four family" playing Monopoly at a charmingly worn wicker table on the sweeping front porch. Grammy Parker had snapped the picture when they weren't looking. "Those days were the best of times," Caroline wistfully said to Hilda, "when the children were young and my husband wasn't so tied to the family business. But of course, his father was living then."

As Caroline put the photo back in place, Hilda inquired, "Will Miss Cordelia be coming home for Easter?"

"Oh yes! She will, Hilda. You and Rolf had best prepare yourselves because she's asked to bring home some of the gang, as Cordelia insists on calling her friends. Most of her gang live out of town, and it seems that my daughter has become a mother hen. It's a good thing you thought ahead. I'd completely forgotten to tell you there will actually be twelve of us for Easter dinner, which includes you and Rolf, of course."

Caroline was insistent about Hilda and Rolf joining the family for holiday dinners. The thought of them eating their Easter meal all alone in the kitchen or in their small apartment over the garage was positively unacceptable.

"Mrs. Parker, that would make yourself, Mr. Parker, Pip, Cordelia and her gang." Hilda's full face grinned at using the word. "And I assume Mr. Parker's aunts will be joining us as well?"

"Oh, yes, they will. And you can plan on Aunt Martha walking right through the front door as she has every Easter, with a large egg-shaped box of Fannie Farmer chocolates and of course her sister will bring Easter baskets for the

The aunts looked forward to their traditional errand and a brisk walk across the Common to the Fannie Farmer Candy Shop at Charles and Boylston Streets. After fastidiously selecting everyone's favorites together—Pecan Dixies and Mint Meltaways, among others—one sister peeked over the pristine glass case to see how much room was left in the egg-fashioned box, while the other "saved time" and gleefully chose this year's Easter baskets on her own.

children. I tried to get Aunt Agatha to understand they're college students now, and it wasn't really necessary, but she wouldn't hear of it. You know the aunts, Hilda, no changing their stubborn Yankee minds once they're made up."

"So, Mrs. Parker, if my arithmetic is right, that means Miss Cordelia will be bringing four of her friends. Is it possible for us to get their names this week for Easter Sunday's place cards?"

"Yes, of course. But you'll need to make the phone call yourself, Hilda. And I suppose Cordelia will expect them to spend the night as well. Oh my, and just as we were finally getting the household in order." Caroline often longed for the days when her son and daughter were children and life was easier to manage. "Now we have young people coming and going at all times. It's very difficult to keep everything as orderly as Price prefers. But wasn't it wonderful of him to suggest we hire those two women from South Boston?"

"Yes, Mrs. Parker."

He was eager to actually. Mr. Parker was leaving the office late one night and overheard them speak so favorably of Parker Shipping he determined to offer them whatever work he could.

Hilda shifted her weight to the other foot.

Caroline adored her husband and delighted in telling anyone who asked about their courtship, "I set my cap for Price the minute we met. He's the first and only boy I ever kissed." Their young adult children, Price Irving Parker III (Pip) and Cordelia Anne Parker (Cappy), considered their parents' love story embarrassingly old fashioned.

Earlier that morning, as Caroline and Hilda were freshening the master bedroom, a piece of stationery slipped out of the small stack of books Hilda held under her arm while dusting Price Parker's nightstand.

"Mrs. Parker, I'm sorry but this fell from your husband's Bible, and I don't know exactly where he had it placed. Do you?"

Caroline Parker received the familiar, though not seen for years, whisper-pink vellum notepaper from her housekeeper's hand. She perused the correspondence, removed her chain-held glasses, let them fall gently on her chest, and said, "I gave this note to my husband before we were married, at our wedding rehearsal dinner to be exact, and asked him please not to read it until he got home. Shall I read it to you?"

Hilda knew this wasn't a question, so she stayed put but was not without surprise at being told something so personal. Holding the delicate notepaper in her right hand, Mrs. Parker read aloud.

Our Wedding Day

You in your home, me in mine, will begin that morn as two
Then you as Groom and me as Bride will sweetly say, "I do."
And at the close of our wedding day,
when the moon says goodnight to the sun
I'll be yours and you'll be mine and we'll end the day as one.
God bless you always my spouse to be with
love and peace and laughter.
And may He bless our days together with, "...happily ever after."

All my love,
Caroline
June 3, 1922

"And just for fun, Hilda, let's put it in the first chapter of the book of Ruth, and see if Mr. Parker notices," she continued. "You see, as part of our wedding vows, I recited Ruth 1:16. Truth be known, it was at his mother's secret request. 'Where you go I will go, and where you stay I will stay. Your people will be my people and your God my God.'"

Hilda panicked. *I've never heard of Saint Ruth. I don't know where the book of Ruth is. Mother of God, please help me.*

The housekeeper feared her ignorance of the Bible would reveal the Catholic faith she and her husband did such a good job of hiding, out of deep concern for their jobs. As far as Caroline Parker knew, the one and only church the couple attended was the German First Lutheran Church of Boston. Miraculously, a way out came to Hilda. She picked up the lamp from Mr. Parker's nightstand with her right hand; her left held a dust cloth and the books. Mrs. Parker retrieved the Bible and placed the pretty paper within the first pages of Ruth.

Relieved, Hilda turned toward her employer and gleamed. "In the old country, when Rolf told me it was time we marry, I said, 'Ya, but only if you promise we will go to America. Then I'll marry you. Otherwise, I stay here with Mama and Papa.' The next day he came back to my papa's house with two steamship tickets for Boston."

"Well, I'm delighted Rolf was that determined. How would we possibly manage without you two?" Mrs. Parker said.

⁐

Ever since the Parker children were in their adolescent years, Caroline's husband, Price Irving Parker II had been solely responsible for Parker Shipping with its fleet of cargo ships, employee base of one hundred, and the weekly administrative staff meetings that kept it all going. This required a great deal of time away from home, both around the country and abroad.

Price Parker owned most of the company, having bought out his brother years ago. However, two maiden aunts, his late father's younger sisters, and his late brother's three adult children's trusts still had small interests in Parker Shipping. His niece and nephews seldom asked about the state of the company, other than a polite inquiry at family gatherings, however, the two aunts frequently phoned their nephew to see if there had been any changes they needed to know about.

Price Parker knew their calls were made more out of loneliness than concern for profits, and after bringing them up to date, he would often extend a lunch invitation. "I know you ladies enjoy Italian food. We could go to the North End, or maybe you'd like to go to Chinatown? I'll come by and pick you up."

The aged but quite sprightly aunts, Agatha Camellia and Martha Hepatica—their middle names inspired by the language of flowers and their meanings, excellence and confidence—lived together and had a tendency to frequent the same establishments within a safe walking distance. Although both ladies were well traveled—with trips to the Orient, Europe, and most recently, India, with the assistance of a hired companion for such endeavors—they hesitated to venture into Boston's Chinatown or Italian North End. Neither sister drove, and both were much too thrifty to pay for a cab. They wouldn't consider taking the subway. "But we don't mind boarding the trolley once in a while," they would say.

The Parker household was abuzz with such busyness.

Caroline loved gathering the family together for the holidays, but especially for Easter. She truly enjoyed the tether of getting ready for company. *It's the perfect excuse for getting the house and garden in order and good repair.* Preparation was well underway with the many workers at their tasks and the Beacon Hill matron's focused supervision.

"Hilda, we need to continue sweeping through this house—" All of a sudden Caroline picked the red coat up from the entry settee. "I wonder if Cordelia has forgotten about this." Just as quickly, she put it down again, giving strict orders. "And Hilda, please see that none of these items go to Saint Vincent de Paul. I don't trust the Catholic Church. How do we know they don't sell our things and keep all the money for themselves?"

Hilda answered, "Frau Parker." Her domestic service had begun in Germany when she was a young girl and *Frau* came to her more naturally, but she corrected herself immediately. "Mrs. Parker, will the Salvation Army over on Berkeley Street be satisfactory, or shall I send everything to the Morgan Memorial in the South End?"

Hilda was almost out of the entry, but Caroline was merely taking a breath. "Have you seen where some priests of the Catholic Church are now residing?"

"Mrs. Parker, it's not my place to know where the priests live."

"Hilda, imagine this, if you will. As of last month, priests are now living in the Andrews mansion. It must cost a fortune to maintain it. William Andrews was out of his mind, giving that splendid home to the Catholics."

Believing "Catholics" was the last word, Hilda turned, took two steps, and was on her way out of the room with one foot on the threshold, when Caroline continued.

"His children, of course, contested the will. But it was ironclad. Fortunate for those papists, Cardinal O'Connell befriended Mr. Andrews in his later days. And it's a good thing his Protestant mother isn't alive to see priests are living in her home."

Hilda was saddened by Mrs. Parker's tone when she said "papists," and remained concerned her employer might one day discover Hilda herself had Catholic roots. Though she claimed the Lutheran church as her own these days, on occasion Hilda would make her way to Holy Trinity Catholic Church and pray the prayer she loved best. *Gegrüßet seist du, Maria, voll der Gnade. Hail Mary, full of grace.*

As they walked past the parlor, Caroline finally answered Hilda's question. "Let's send it all off to the Salvation Army this time."

Mary and Norah were moving the parlor furniture and rug to one side of the room so they could scrub the other side thoroughly, and overheard Mrs. Parker's instructions. "Norah," Mary said quietly. The two women spoke only when no one else was in the room, and even then, very softly. "What harm will it do you to ask Mrs. Parker for the coat? And wouldn't you be regrettin' it if you saw that lovely red coat goin' down the street on another young girl in Southie?"

Norah stopped scrubbing. "I'm thinkin' about it, Mary."

⁂

Hilda was standing in the kitchen gathering a white broadcloth café curtain onto a brass rod as Mrs. Parker perused her list of things to do. "There's so much to accomplish today. It's positively overwhelming." And then she whispered, but the Irish women, who seemed privy to everything said that day, still heard her. "When I see these two earnest women on their knees, washing my floors, well, heaven forgive me for complaining." Caroline's voice returned to normal. "How am I supposed to finish collecting all these unneeded garments and items, help you with the table setting for tonight, wrap the gifts, have my nap, and be decently dressed and ready to welcome guests for my uncle's birthday dinner—all in one afternoon?"

The floor washers were still listening. Mary caught Norah's attention by lightly touching her forearm, and they grinned and rolled their eyes at what the lady of the house considered "overwhelming."

Mrs. Parker declared, "I'll simply have to miss my nap."

Norah rose to her knees, put both hands at the small of her back, and thought of the only people in South Boston who took naps. *Babies, cranky children, the elderly, and husbands who work the night shift.*

Mary had her own thoughts about Mrs. Parker's dilemma. *God in heaven, and don't most of Southie's mothers work the three, four or more nights a week after a long day of carin' for their children, housecleanin', shoppin', cookin', sewin', and doin' all sorts of laundry?* Mary leaned over and whispered to Norah. "It's Saint Caroline, most blessed martyr, we're workin' for here."

"God Almighty, Mary, shhh. She'll hear ya, and we'll not see her kindness nor the inside of this grand house again."

They were hard at work when Norah said just above a whisper, "Sure and John wasn't one bit happy about the lot of 'em gettin' the new clothes and shoes as well." She scrubbed a stubborn scuffmark with both hands on the brush. "But I told himself if it meant we had to eat but two meals a day for the short while, so be it. I'll not have our children walkin' into the house of God on Easter Sunday lookin' like ragamuffins."

Mary put her wet hands on her apron–covered thighs and leaned forward as she softly answered, "And isn't it good for their souls, Norah, to be makin' such a sacrifice durin' Lent? For didn't God Almighty sacrifice His only begotten Son so they'd have a church to walk their brand new shoes into on that most Holy Day?"

The women returned to their work and their thoughts. Norah was eager to get back to Southie. *I need to make sure everything's in order for Palm Sunday.*

Timmy and Tommy are handin' out the palms after Mass, and Rita's helpin' too. If there's any laundry to be done, and I get home quickly, there'd still be enough time to get it washed, towel dry what needs it, and iron. Mother of God, I hope John didn't go to the pub today. There's no money for it, and the trouble. She scrubbed faster.

Mary was entertaining a detour to Brigham's Ice Cream Shoppe. *What would it hurt to spend a nickel, get a scoop of that delicious vanilla, sprinkled with the chocolate jimmies? I'll buy one for Norah too. All right then, it's the ten cents I'll be spendin', but I'll tell himself if it wasn't for Norah King gettin' me work, there wouldn't be any extra money. What am I thinkin'? God forgive me. It's Lent. Okay then, we'll have a cuppa instead, and share one of those delicious grilled cheese sandwiches. Oh, I'll have to be convincin', for isn't Norah forever in a hurry to get home?*

It seemed to Norah King that she had been standing before her would-be benefactor for an eternity, when in fact it only took Caroline Parker a moment's hesitation. She knew what her mother would have said when a "servant" stepped out of line, but Caroline had a gentler way than her mother, and the term "servant" no longer applied. Norah was a domestic worker employed for the day, and Caroline was greatly moved by the Irish woman's love for her daughter.

"Why, yes. Of course," she said, putting her head slightly to one side, and bringing her hands together, folding them palm to palm.

"I'll have Hilda put the coat in a bag for you."

CHAPTER 2

A postponement till morning,
a postponement forever.
Irish Proverb

Mrs. Parker's housekeeper put the prized red coat in a plain
brown bag, concerned if she packaged it in a fancier one, say R. H.
Stearns or Lord & Taylor, the parcel might be grabbed right out of
the scrubwoman's hands once she arrived in her own poor neighborhood.

Hilda was mistaken.

South Boston's residents may have been short of money, but as Norah told
her children many a time, "We're not poor by a long shot. God has richly blessed
us with the Church, a home by the sea, neighbors who care, parochial schools,
and enough Irish pride to carry on no matter what." Southie was holy ground
to those who called it home, and its citizens were a tight-knit clan that banded
together in work, celebration and sorrow.

Blessedly, in the monotony of her work Norah had a secret joy. She loved to
bring to mind her neighbors' triumphant stories.

The tale had been told many times. How Father Kenney was on his way to
Morris' Pharmacy & Fountain at H and Broadway to redeem the ice cream soda

As soon as it was within his power to do so, Boston's much loved and respected Cardinal Cushing, then Archbishop, changed the benevolent 788 Harrison Avenue institution's name to:

The Home for Catholic Children

pharmacist George McDonough urged him to enjoy on the house, when he saw Mr. and Mrs. O'Meara. James was still walking with a limp and Addie practically sang hello, her joy evident, as she held on to James' brawny right arm.

Father Kenney remarked, "You look more like a couple about to post their engagement banns than one who's had a bit of trouble. How's the leg, James?"

"Fine Father." James shook the priest's hand. "Addie and me wanted to express our gratitude for protectin' our family. What if Social Services had their pitiless intentions met? They'd never have let our five out of the Home for Destitute Catholic Children."

Father Kenney gently chided, "But aren't they a good lot we've got here at Gate of Heaven? It was Mrs. Connelly's announcement at the bazaar saved the day. 'James O'Meara broke his leg loadin' one of those cargo ships. But he's on the mend and will soon be workin' again. Social Services is comin' their way. We've got to do somethin' to keep 'em from takin' the children.'"

Addie said, "Rumor has it some busybody made a call. Who would do such a thing?"

Father Kenney knew the truth but kept it alongside the many confidences his heart was accustomed to holding and answered, "Nonetheless, those with some cash reached into their pockets and those without took from their cupboards and iceboxes so yours could be filled.

James said. "Father, did you know that our landlord is lettin' us stay—says we can make up the rent in time."

Norah had heard all about the landlord too, how he'd been at the bazaar, declaring, "Sure and we can look after each other without Social Services poking their trouble-makin' noses where they're not wanted." He took his hat off, put money in, and passed it along. His beloved wife had spent most of her child-hood in The Home for Destitute Catholic Children, a kindly institution but not home, and she would sometimes weep at the memory of being taken from her caring mother's one-room apartment, the only affordable place after her father died.

In Southie, Norah happily recalled, as she took a coarse cloth to a stubborn scuffmark, there was never a shortage of rich, "this is the honest-to-God's truth" recollections.

Last week at the church supper, aged but spry Aidan and Fiona Clancy had their turn.

Aidan's melodious speech held everyone's attention "Wasn't it a grand American wake the fine people of Roscommon gave Mrs. Clancy and me, with the Bishop himself showin' up with scapulars for the pair of us? And wasn't it those very scapulars saved our lives during the voyage over? It was a night without a ray of light, and a fierce storm about us. It's then that Mrs. Clancy and I threw the scapulars into the angry sea as a personal sacrifice. Fiona darlin', please tell these fine people the miracle of it all."

Scapulars are two small squares of cloth usually stamped or appliquéd with a picture of our Lord, the Blessed Mother, or a saint. They are suspended from sturdy strings, worn under cloth-ing, and thought to bring Divine intervention and protection to all who wear them.

Norah smiled at the thought of how quickly his wife had jumped up. "When those scapulars met the water, fast as a virgin runs from an old bachelor, the sea's anger disappeared. And wasn't she, for the rest of the voyage, just like a lovin' mother gently rockin' us to sleep that night and safely carryin' us into Boston Harbor the two days later."

It was picturing the multitude of God's houses in Southie that made Nora beam in the midst of changing out her scrub bucket water.

South Boston proudly possessed seven magnificent Catholic churches, and on Holy Thursday night, countless people crowded its streets as they made "the walk," a visit to each parish where they'd light a candle and say a prayer with the highest of hopes.

Norah went to Mass every morning and as a known woman of faith she was often approached to give a word of assurance, most recently by a young lady who feared the pending war would take her sweetheart's life.

"Now don't be cryin', darlin'," Norah comforted. "There's nothin' that happens that our Lord, his Father and the Holy Ghost don't know about. And wouldn't the Blessed Mother be after all three if she thought they were neglectin' your prayers?"

Though talking with Mary at any length was prohibited while they worked, it didn't prevent Norah from bringing to mind one of Mary's hilarious conversations from the past.

Mary had exaggerated, "This year's Saint Patrick's Day Parade is bringin' Una Mahoney's boastin' to a whole new bloody level. She's been tellin' the entire world, 'Now that my Jake is on the force, aren't we after callin' him Officer Mahoney and won't one and the same be marchin' at the very front, not bringin' up the back like every Tom, Dick and Harry? And won't his father be tellin' anyone who'll listen, see that handsome one? He's me own."

There was never a shortage of music either, as much a part of Southie as the pubs, churches, sports clubs and beaches. It was almost impossible to go down any street without hearing a whistle, song or fiddle, and from homes with a penny or two, the pleasure of a piano.

It was the sense of one for all and all for one that made Norah never want to live anywhere else, even Beacon Hill. In Southie, Catholic parents wholeheartedly supported parochial education, Mary being one of the most enthusiastic.

"And won't my twin girls be Irish dancin' together at Saint Augustine's minstrel show? And aren't we havin' a grand time sewin' their lovely costumes with Mother Superior herself takin' up a needle and embroiderin' J.M.J. (Jesus, Mary, and Joseph) where you'd see a label if there was one."

South Boston was not poor by a long shot.

∽

Mrs. Parker promptly walked up to her housekeeper. "No need for the brown bag now, Hilda, I've found something better. Can you imagine? Cordelia had this perfectly good garment bag lying on the floor at the back of her closet!

Honestly, how do girls without mothers manage?" She took the coat from her housekeeper, carefully hung it on a wooden hanger, buttoned it from top to bottom, and without revealing her secret gift, tucked a lace trimmed mono-grammed hankie in the right pocket.

Caroline's mother, Rebecca, had passed away only four months before, leav-ing the brand new R-embroidered Irish linen hankie behind. She then placed the coat in the recently discovered Jordan Marsh garment bag.

Norah and Mary had finished scrubbing the sizeable marble entryway floor and stone solarium floor, and moved on to the quarter-cut cherry hardwood floor of the butler's pantry, a long, well-appointed service room between the spacious kitchen and formal dining room.

The upper walls on both sides of the butler's pantry were lined with beveled-glass cupboards filled to capacity with china and crystal. Exquisite tureens and pitchers were artfully displayed on the ebony marble countertops while silver platters and trays leaned against the hand-painted, green Italian tiled walls between cupboard and counter. Below, deep drawers and cabinets held silverware, table linens, place cards and holders, salt cellars with tiny silver spoons, crystal knife rests, fingerbowls, and at Mr. Parker's request, toothpicks, which Mrs. Parker had placed in a small, cut-crystal pig standing on his hind legs. She hoped the elegance of the crystal and whimsy of the pig would soften what she considered vulgar. Two of the lower cabinets contained a bevy of select liquors.

They were at the very end of rinsing this last floor, making their work day over, when Mrs. Parker, whose delicate, French White Blossom Perfume pre-ceded her, appeared in the doorway of the butler's pantry with the garment bag over her arm. "I'm sorry. I don't know your names."

Both women, on their knees, looked up at the same time.

"Mary Callanan."

"Mrs. John Joseph King, Norah."

"Well, Mrs. King, here's a marvel for you. I found the very bag the coat came in."

Norah stood, and for the second time in Mrs. Parker's presence, dried her hands on the crisp folds of her apron.

"Mrs. King, if you wanted, you could tell your daughter you purchased it yourself."

"And wouldn't the tellin' of it be puttin' a curse on the very blessin' God has sent my way, to be lyin' about that beautiful red coat? With all due respect, Mrs. Parker, I won't be tellin' her any such thing. The blessin' will be twice as rich when Rosemary learns of your generous heart by bein' a fine lesson for her own. And wouldn't she want to be prayin' for you after doin' such a grand, kind thing? On the odd chance there's more than one Mrs. Parker our Lord's receivin' prayers for I'm sorry, but I don't know your proper name."

Being careful not to step on the wet floor, Mrs. Parker kept her feet on the threshold and leaned as far forward as she could manage, the garment bag held high, and handed it into Norah's expectant arms.

"Caroline," she answered.

CHAPTER 3

The longest road out is the shortest road home.
IRISH PROVERB

THE TWO WOMEN USUALLY WALKED with a matched pace, quick and purposeful, and only a little slower on the way home from work. Today was different. Norah was tired but her step was lively. She could hardly wait to give the coat to Rosemary.

"This isn't a day for strollin', now is it, Mary?" Norah held the garment bag even closer, patting it twice to her chest.

Mary and Norah were about the same age, late forties, their children all went to Gate of Heaven School, and both husbands worked as laborers, Norah's John at Brown-Wales Steel and Mary's Frank at the Gillette factory. All four were from the west of Ireland and enjoyed bantering about which county was the best, with John Joseph King forever getting the last word. "And if either of ya's or anyone you know or are related to or have heard about or those people I just mentioned have heard about, has ever caught forty fish in one net, all of them at the one time, speak now."

No one in the pubs where he regularly put forth the same challenge ever contested his claim to the abundance of fish in Galway waters.

Mary hooked her arm through Norah's as they hurried to the train station. "And don't I understand why you're actin' like a sixteen-year-old girl after her first kiss, scurryin' back, scared she'll miss the second. I'm sure Rosemary will be right where you left her, Norah."

"And aren't you the clever one with your sixteen-year-old comparisons?" Norah smiled. "Do you think you could find it in your heart to forgive a friend for bringin' you along so fast? But don't you know this coat is cryin' out for its rightful owner? We'll go to Brigham's another time, after Lent, and then you can have your ice cream with the chocolate jimmies."

With that Norah stopped and looked at her friend. "I can only imagine the look on me darlin' girl's face when she sees her own mother comin' through the door carryin' this grand bag over her arm. And that's only the beginnin'. Sure and she deserves every red fiber."

They picked up where they left off, Mary at her own insistence on the outside, closest to the street and Norah on the inside, because of the coat. "God forbid anything should happen to it now, Norah, like the splashin' up of mud, or you accidentally droppin' it and a car or bus runnin' right over that Jordan Marsh bag."

Mary usually did most of the talking, and Norah often told her husband John, "I get the occasional word in but that Mary, angel of a friend that she is, could talk the ears off a brass monkey."

Today, for the first time in their long friendship, Norah was the talker. "Didn't God and all His angels know I couldn't look after the eight children without Rosemary's help? That's why He sent her first, ahead of the others, and she never complains. As God is my judge, she never complains. Not like that cheeky Bridget O'Leary, complainin' about school, complainin' about havin' to look after her brother and sisters, complainin' about her poor mother's cookin,' and worst of all, complainin' about being Irish. If her Da ever heard the way she talks to her darlin' mother, don't you know he'd push a whole bar of Fels-Naptha soap in where kind words should be comin' out?"

The long, yellow, pungent bar of Fels-Naptha Soap was used for laundry, floor washing, and generally anything that required a strong solvent to remove soil and stains.

Mary Callanan had her own long-winded contribution to the going–over of Bridget Kathleen O'Leary. "And wasn't my Frank right there in Saint Augustine's, tryin' to say his penance when he overheard Bridget tell, not ask her poor mother, the two of them havin' this conversation right there in the pew, mind you." Mary put her hand to her chest. "Bridget told her that she was goin' downtown alone to meet some fella. And her poor mother, God bless her, tryin' to convince Bridget otherwise by bringin' the Blessed Mother into the whole mess. Didn't Mrs. O'Leary use her daughter's full christenin' name, sayin', 'Bridget Kathleen O'Leary, can you imagine Holy Mary doing such a thing? Meetin' a man all alone? Next you'll tell me he's meetin' you at Scollay Square, and won't that be a fine kettle of fish?'"

Norah made the sign of the cross. "Heaven forbid a Catholic girl would be in a place like Scollay Square with all those honkytonks and chippies. You don't think she'd go that far, do you, Mary? How in God's name did it come to this?"

"Well, Norah, according to Mrs. Nolan, who lives downstairs from the O'Learys, wasn't Bridget introduced to Mr. Louis Kolodynski through one of her classmates over there at South Boston High School? And didn't she, tell her poor, unfortunate mother, 'I'm goin' Ma,' who in all probability was cursin' the day she let Bridget go to that public school with all those independent thinkin' Protestants. And wasn't I tellin' my Frank, respectfully of course, Norah, for won't our children be disrespectin' their father if they see their mother doin'

Saint Augustine's Church
SOUTH BOSTON, MASS.

Scollay Square was the location of primarily risqué entertainment. Eager patrons ran the gamut from blue collar to Harvard boys, couples, and Beacon Hill gents. The Old Howard Theater was host to vaudeville acts and most famous for its beautiful burlesque queens. The Crawford House packed 'em in, for three shows a night, and everyone came with one thing in mind: "Seeing dancer, Sally Keith, make her tassels go in two different directions."

*Cast Your Vote for the Mayor with
a Heart James Michael Curley*

*The illustrious, four-term mayor of
Boston, governor, U.S. congressman,
and son of Irish immigrants, James
Michael Curley, was a passionate ad-
vocate for working classes, the poor,
and immigrants. Mayor Curley took
a risk when he gave an earnest but
fearfully uncertain man the help he
needed to pass a civil service exam.
The mayor stood in his stead and was
caught and imprisoned for five months.
Voters perceived Mayor Curley's illegal
act as benevolent and selfless. Already
popular, his favor skyrocketed, and he
was reelected while still serving time
in prison.*

the same? 'Well,' I said, the O'Learys have enough trouble without you, Frances Terrence Callanan adding to their misery by reportin' Bridget's every offence.' And didn't I remind him what Father Sweeney said about gossip last Sunday, 'If you're not a part of the problem or the solution, it's not yours to tell.'"

Norah shook her head and gently laughed. "And where would that put our conversation, Mary Margaret?"

Mary went right on to the next subject. "Did you hear of the kindness Mayor Curley did last week?" she inquired as they walked into the subway entrance. "Our most honorable mayor was on his way home from some posh affair when he decided to stop by the State House. And wasn't himself stunned to see the building full of Irish women, his very own, on their hands and knees, scrubbing the floors and stairs, every one, happy for the work? Well, Bridey Sullivan told me that when Mayor Curley appeared the women stopped, thrilled to see him up close, and every one got on her feet and offered a 'Good evening, and God bless you, Mayor Curley.' Then himself stood at the bottom of that grand staircase and said, 'Dear sisters of Erin, please know that this is the last time you will ever be scrubbing the floors of the State House of the Commonwealth of Massachusetts, as you are to-night.' God in heaven Norah, some of the women misunderstood, thinkin' it was the end of their jobs, which of course, distressed our mayor. 'My dear ladies,' he said, 'there's no need for alarm. You still have employment. I only mean to say that tomorrow your situations will be much improved. Good night, and God bless the work.' And didn't Mayor Curley make good on his word and order his staff to provide a mop, and one of those fancy buckets that wrings them out, to every last one of his 'splendid workers,' as he called them? I heard this from Moira O'Toole, who works days, dustin' and sweepin' about the place."

"Splendid, is it? Norah raised her brows and smiled.

Their mutual laughter rang soft as a tea table bell while they climbed down the steep subway stairs, went through the turnstiles, and stood waiting on the platform for the train home.

"You've got to watch yourself now, Norah," Mary said as she held on to her. "Have you not heard of the woman who was pushed down onto the tracks by a man gone mad? Sure and it's the God's truth. Here, step back a bit more, and we won't be givin' the devil a chance." Mary returned to their previous conversation. "To be quite honest Norah, I don't think I'd want to be usin' a mop. You're so far away from the work that way."

Norah lightheartedly replied, "Well it's done then. Parker Shipping has provided just what we need, scrub brushes, rags, and buckets. It's comin' now. The train is comin'. Can you hear it? Will you step up with me, Mary? Or is that devil of a mad man still runnin' about?" The two women linked arms and laughed again.

They left the train station and walked back home in good spirits—Norah's, at 567 E. 8th Street, was the middle floor flat of a three-family apartment house and would come first with Mary's single-family house farther past. The two women were only four blocks away and their neighborhood bustled with Saturday activity.

"Oh, will you look at that Robert Donnelly 'dimple on the chin, devil within' is what me mother said of fellas that handsome with the cleft and all," Norah observed as they approached a group of boys playing a rowdy game of kick the can in the middle of the street.

"But, Norah, he's such a good boy. Isn't his younger brother, the one with the cerebral palsy, almost always at his side, as he is right now?"

The Donnelly boys—thirteen-year-old Buddy in his wooden wheelchair, who'd been in the house all day and sixteen-year-old Robert, his hands gripped securely on the chair's handles, just home from his job at the shipyard—taunted their favorite players. "Come on, Sean! Ya grandmother could do better than that. Come on." Robert shouted at his best friend.

Buddy stammered, "L-lefty R-r-r-ryan, s-s-s-start 'em cr-cr-cryin'!" with a big smile as he involuntarily rocked back and forth, his palsied hands turned inward.

"Robert's not the one bit embarrassed about pushin' that poor crippled boy about. I've seen it with me own eyes. For those who stare, he makes introductions; for those who glare and make fun, God help 'em. With all respect for your dear mother's wisdom, I'd have to say 'dimple on the chin, saint within' for that one."

They passed Crowley's Corner Grocery, where Mrs. Crowley's elderly father sat outside on a wooden crate, grinning toothless from ear to ear, and tipped his hat as the two women walked by. "Fine afternoon we're havin', ladies."

"Yes, Mr. Gowan, spring's here at last," Mary said.

"And just in time for Holy Week," Norah added.

Once they were past the grocery store, Mary advised, "You've got to watch those Crowley's when they've got somethin' on the scale. Last week, I was buyin' cold cuts for the family. Frank likes the fried bologna with onions, havin' it sliced real thin–like, makes it go further. Anyway, didn't Alice Crowley try and hide her thumb with that waxed paper they use? And didn't I say, 'Oh Alice dear, your pretty thumb's pressin' on me bologna. Sure you'll be chargin' more for the beauty you're addin'?' And didn't she turn two shades of red quicker than the rent's due?" Mary tapped Norah's sleeve. "Just be watchful when you're tradin' there."

"I will, Mary, but we usually trade at Dwyer's. And this year, I'm surprisin' the family with a leg of lamb for their Easter dinner. I've been savin' and it's ordered now, with a deposit. I'm afraid there's no turnin' back. God help us, if himself gets angry about the cost." Norah's fingertips instinctively reached for the silver Celtic cross that hung from a chain around her neck and rested on her heart.

"And aren't we the grand lady, havin' lamb for your Easter dinner? Sure and the whole lot of ya's deserve it. John'll be fine, Norah. Don't worry."

Here and there, the smell of early dinners drifted toward them—roasted meat, boiled vegetables, and from the house where the Mister was out of work, the distinct aroma of poverty-stew: potatoes, onions and water. "I don't know about you," Mary said, taking a long sniff, "but my kids love the stuff. Frank won't let me make it unless I keep the windows closed. It's pride. Doesn't want the neighbors thinking—" Her lengthy explanation was cut short.

"Tenement to let, apply within, if I move out, let—Judith—move in," echoed from the other side of the street as girls jumped rope and several more sing-sang the familiar jingle. Norah longingly thought of her second-to-youngest daughter, and her hand briefly touched the cross again. *My angel, Noni, was so good at jumpin' rope.*

Her thoughts were interrupted by Mary's kidding. "Hand that coat over to me Norah King, and join the girls, why don't ya? For aren't you a woman who knows how to jump? Haven't I seen it with me own eyes, jumpin' only God knows how high when your Mister asks for his tea?"

"You're mistaken, Mary Callanan. It's not jumpin' to himself's request that you're seein'. It's me own way of doing the occasional callisthenic, and isn't that how I'm able to keep this girlish figure of mine?" Norah grinned. "Sure and you're just looking for an excuse to get your hands on this elegant coat I'm carryin'."

The two women were now approaching what was locally known as "widow's row." One after another, four houses in all, without a husband about the place.

A dog's yip pierced the din of children playing. "Ah, gone on with ya's," old widow McCormick chided her noisy brown mutt, which she preferred to call "a rare breed of Irish Setter."

His wet nose pressed through a space in the chain–link fence surrounding her house. She called him Mike after her late husband, Michael Frances McCormick, and chided him again, "Ah, gone on with ya's, Mike. It's just the children playin' and a couple of me friends comin' along. Good afternoon Norah, Mary."

"And to you too, Mrs. McCormick," they said in unison, never missing a step at Norah's insistence, when she said under her breath only a moment before, "Mary, we've got to keep movin'. If we stop to chat, we'll still be in front of the widow McCormick's house tomorrow mornin'."

When they were a safe distance away, Mary said, "God bless her, Norah. I don't think there's anyone home upstairs, if you know what I mean. Didn't I hear her one time askin' that aggravatin' animal what he wanted for his dinner?

'Is it the corned beef you want tonight, Mike, or a smoked shoulder? Just tell me darlin', and it's on the table."

The widow Sweeney and her new tenant, Mrs. Lonergan, were standing on the front porch of Mrs. Sweeney's three-family apartment house, commonly known as a three-decker. Both women held their arms folded, as women often do when they're standing still in conversation, leaning down to a car window with one more goodbye, or bending over a baby carriage cooing.

Agnes Sweeney glanced up and down at the Jordan Marsh bag. "And where would you two prosperous ladies be comin' from on this sun kissed afternoon?" To Norah's mind it sounded like an accusation.

Mary's heart, as close to Norah's as a friend's can be, had the same impression. She mischievously responded with one hand resting on her hip, the other helping to gloriously tell the story. "Haven't we spent the entire day on Beacon Hill? And isn't it grand this time of year with tulips pokin' their pretty heads out of window boxes and dancin' with daffodils 'round the trees and across borders in those beautiful uptown gardens? Sure and you would have loved the sight, Agnes Sweeney, and don't we want you to join us next time? Isn't that right, Norah? And wouldn't our new neighbor, Mrs. Lonergan, be welcome too?"

Nola Lonergan and her family had just moved up from a cold water flat. She found the Jordan Marsh bag a bit intimidating let alone Mary's account of where the two women had spent the afternoon, and only hoped she'd be able to fit in with these sophisticated ladies.

Norah adjusted the bag, an indication she'd be walking on, but courteously offered her own contribution. "And don't I regret departin' your good company, Mrs. Sweeney, and you too, of course, Mrs. Lonergan? Surely we'll be comin' to know each other better, but me family will be eagerly waitin' for their supper. We'd best be on our way."

As soon as Mary and Norah were out of Agnes' sight, they leaned against each other and giggled like two schoolgirls who had just pulled one over on Mother Superior.

Mary spoke first. "That one thinks she's so high and mighty, bein' landlady to the two families. If it wasn't for her late, dull, husband——" they both laughed again. "God in heaven, Norah. Jack Sweeney was the dullest man I ever met. Well, if it wasn't for his one moment of intelligence, buyin' life insurance, Agnes

Sweeney'd be livin' in Gate of Heaven rectory; cookin' and cleanin' for the priests instead of acting the grand lady and takin' them all out to Durgin Park Restaurant for their Sunday dinner."

Norah was ashamed to add to such talk, but found the opportunity irresistible. "And don't you find it amusin' she's constantly tellin' us what they ordered for their dinner, as if lettin' us in on some big Vatican secret, and implyin' we'd be closer to the Almighty if we did the same?"

Mary went on. "And isn't she ever so careful to state it isn't her alone with all those priests and Monsignor? That she never goes without the company of another widow."

Norah quipped, "Sure and we're all so concerned that those darlin' priests are just waitin' to get all two hundred pounds of her alone, so they can steal a kiss."

"God forgive us both," Mary petitioned. They laughed again.

Mary's daughter Marion stood up and called out, "Ma, I'm over here." She parted from a group of teenagers sitting right down the middle of Mrs. Riordan's front porch steps, taking great care not to bump one of the eight red geranium filled flowerpots on either side. Mary loved the sight. *There's the loveliness of youth and nature all in the one place.*

"Hello, Ma, Mrs. King."

Mary whispered to Norah, "And isn't this the first time in the three weeks since they discovered each other that I've seen my Marion in public without your John Michael at her side?"

Nora answered, "I know he was workin' at the pharmacy early this morning restockin' before hours. Maybe Mr. McDonough needed him to work the fountain too."

Morris's Pharmacy had three part-time soda jerks, but John Michael brought in the most business with his captivating smile, twinkling blue eyes, and quick wit.

Mary smiled at her daughter's joy, while the group tapped their feet to the big band music of Glenn Miller, "Chattanooga Choo Choo" coming from a radio plugged into an extension cord that wound its way into a downstairs window.

Mrs. Riordan had warned the young people when her son asked if they could listen to the radio. "I don't mind, as long as you keep the sound down and your fannies on the steps. Do you hear me? It's indecent for ya's to be dancin' anywhere but a hall."

Mary said, "Hello to you, Miss Marion Callanan. And I trust you've done your Saturday chores. For no daughter of mine would be carryin' on with the music and all if there was work to be done."

"Ma, it's all done. And I've even set the table."

"I'll see you in about an hour then?"

"Yes, Ma." Marion began to sit down again, holding the back of her plaid skirt close to her legs, but stopped herself. "Mrs. King, could you please tell Rita I missed her? We were supposed to meet in the church basement this afternoon. Sister Veronita asked if a few of us would help put the palms in order for Sunday Mass."

"You two are becomin' palm experts, for didn't you do the cleanin' and sortin' last year?"

"Yes," Marion answered, her easy smile as sweet as they come. "And this year Sister Veronita surprised us. She had a Devil Dog for everyone there. I went by your house afterwards but no one answered the door. Here's Rita's."

"Sure and you'll be friends for life sendin' this cream-filled chocolate cake her way."

Norah held the coat closer, with both hands now, and felt a lump in her throat at the thought of what her missing children might be enduring. She knew Mary understood, but Norah chose not to talk about it. She wanted a few more minutes of peace and to speak of Rosemary's goodness.

"You know, Mary, there's not a finer daughter, God love her. Were you aware Rosemary has a scar on her right arm? Will we never forget the day it happened, though it was fifteen years ago this coming November? Sure and it's a shame we're always rememberin' it on Rita's birthday. For wasn't she born at home, and wasn't Rosemary helpin' the doctor, gettin' the kettle of hot water off the stove when the burner flipped up and stuck to the underside of her delicate, bare, seven-year-old arm, brave little thing? She only let one cry be heard, and when I shouted from me bedroom in the midst of givin' birth, 'What is it darlin'?' she came to the door and without lookin' in said, 'Nothin', Mummy. I'm just excited about the baby comin' so close now.'"

CHAPTER 4

May the roof of your house never fall in and those beneath it never fall out.
IRISH BLESSING

A S WAS THEIR CUSTOM ONCE they arrived at Norah's home, no matter where the two women were in a good story, lament or complaint, the conversation stopped but their feet kept moving, with Norah taking a soft right and Mary continuing much further down to N Street. There would be no lingering.

But today, their conversation ended as soon as the Kings' apartment was within sight. Norah stopped walking, still looking in the distance and Mary stopped one step past her. The shades at 567 E. 8th Street, middle floor, were down. Drawn shades while it was still daylight meant one of two things: a night worker was getting rest, or there was trouble. John Joseph King didn't work nights.

Moments before nineteen-year-old Norah Catherine Foley boarded the ship for America, her tearful mother removed a small crucifix from around her neck and put it on her firstborn. "When times are hard darlin', press your hand to the cross, and God'll let me know I need to be prayin' for you."

Norah pressed her crucifix *Dear God, not again.* "Come on now, Mary" she said. The two women walked without a word between them until they reached Norah's address.

"Goodbye, and God bless you, Norah King."

"Goodbye, and God bless you too, Mary Callanan."

"And Norah," Mary called as she turned around, pocketbook dangling from the crook of her arm like the legs of a hip-held child, "God bless your family. God bless 'em all."

Three-deckers provided somewhat affordable housing for families of modest means. The sturdy buildings held three or six flats and a small back porch for each. This ingenious urban design was driven by the influx of immigrants during the late 19th and early 20th centuries.

Norah King's fingers had barely touched the front doorknob of the three-decker's common entrance when she pulled away. She was frightened the landlords, Marie and Gerard Flynn, might have their apartment door open as they often did, for the chance of a friendly hello or conversation.

The Flynns were childless, which by Southie's large-family standards made them poor and the Kings, their tenants with eight children, rich. Norah felt certain the landlords had once again heard sounds of beating, cursing, and crying coming from her family's apartment, and she didn't want to have to explain John's drunken violence with a lie, as she had many times before. "I'm sorry for any disruption we may be bringin' to this fine house with the boys tossin' each other about, and Mr. King's disciplinin' of our brood. Sure and he doesn't want the children growin' up to be hooligans. And it's their father's opinion the occasional corporal punishment helps them to remember their place. *But didn't Father Kenney say it wasn't lyin'?* She quietly returned to the sidewalk. *Goin' in the back way will be safer."*

Father Kenney had known the King family since they first moved to Southie. He baptized four of their nine children and gave First Holy Communion to the oldest three, though shortly after he saw the family through a tragedy no parent wants to bear, they moved from Saint Augustine's parish to Gate of Heaven on the other side of town. Rita Margaret, the Kings' seventh child and youngest girl, was his favorite. "They're all beautiful children," he said, "but that Rita, she's a shiny penny."

Just one month ago, on a blustery March afternoon, Norah returned to her old neighborhood and looked in on an elderly shut-in. Norah believed if she looked after that dear old woman, the angels would lead someone to look after her own dear mother in Ireland.

When she took an apron from the back of the kitchen door, Lillian Gallagher protested. "With a family the size of yours, Norah King haven't you enough to do? Put the kettle on, and we'll have a cuppa."

Norah smiled. "It'll only take a few minutes to scrub the bath and do a little sweepin'," she said, while laying a small blanket over Lillian's knees. "You've got to watch yourself, now. For isn't that demon pneumonia just waitin' round the corner of every cold room?"

Lillian gasped. "How'd you get those awful bruises on your arms?"

"Oh, aren't I forever bumpin' this way and that, maybe doin' the laundry or shovelin' coal in the furnace."

Lillian simply said, "Go to Father Kenney, Norah. He'll help ya out."

On her way home that day, Norah King walked right by Saint Augustine's rectory, turned back, made the sign of the cross, and while she still had the courage, went up and rang the doorbell. The housekeeper answered, opening the door only partway, with one hand folded around the door's edge. Warmth and the delicious smell of a pot roast dinner wafted out into the cold, damp afternoon air.

"Good afternoon, Norah King. What can I do for you?"

"Good afternoon, Jean Adair. If it's not too much trouble, would you ask Father Kenney if I could please have a moment of his time?"

The housekeeper, a middle-aged spinster and one of the best cooks in South Boston, prided herself on protecting the priests from what she considered unnecessary intrusions. "Aren't you over there at Gate of Heaven now, Norah? Do the priests of that parish not have time for their own people?"

"I was just passin' by—"

The housekeeper interrupted her. "Fine then, just come in." She led Norah to the parlor. "Have a seat. I'll inquire if the good Father can see you."

Jean Adair considered Norah's request as she walked across the hall. *Thinks she's pulling the wool over my eyes with that "just passin' by" nonsense.* She quickly rapped—one, two—on the large pocket doors of the priest's study. *A person knows a person goes to another parish when they don't want the neighbors seeing them walking into the rectory.* Not waiting for an answer, Jean Adair pushed the doors open. "Begging your pardon, Father."

Jean Adair's parents doubted they'd ever be asked for her hand and dreaded the thought of spending old age with such a bossy daughter under their roof. When she got the job of cook and housekeeper to the priests, which provided two rooms of her own in the rectory, Jean's parents fell to their knees and thanked God.

Norah, too anxious to sit, stood right where the housekeeper left her. *What a lovely room they've got here.* The gleaming hardwood floor and woodwork, jewel-toned area rug, Connemara marble fireplace, deep maroon divan, several overstuffed chairs, and a good-sized tea table in the middle of it all, provided a welcome distraction.

The housekeeper, so tall and thin that some parishioners secretly called her "Olive Oil," had a fairly light step and ten minutes later, she startled the former parishioner when she briskly said, "He'll see you. And please remember the Father's time is very limited."

Father Kenney wore well-pressed black slacks, scuffed black oxfords, a black shirt with a white Roman collar, and a brown cardigan sweater. Saint Augustine's most popular priest was in his early fifties, and was portly, with a shock of salt and pepper hair, expressive brown eyes, and a ready smile. His reputation for kindness made the lines at his confessional longest. People were always willing to wait for mercy and grace.

Father Kenney sprang from his desk chair. "And how's the mother of the eight best behaved children in South Boston?"

Norah stood tall, feet together, hands clasped. "Thank you for seein' me, Father. It's the church's advice I'm seekin'."

Father Kenney had only seen Norah King this grave once before. Extending his hands, palms up, looking very much like the statues throughout the church, he said, "God has been with us in times of joy and sorrow. He'll not leave us now. Please, Mrs. King, let me help you with your coat."

Norah, embarrassed because the lining of her ink-blue wool coat was so threadbare it had fallen apart under one arm, said, "Thanks just the same, Father, but I'm still a bit chilly."

"Would you like me to have Miss Adair prepare us some tea?"

"No, thank you, Father."

"Please, have a seat," he said.

Norah sat down on one of two well-worn upholstered chairs across from his desk, on which books and papers lay in scholarly disarray. The priest returned to his chair and pulled a small tray from the side of the desk toward him. "Can I pour you a glass of water then, Mrs. King?"

"Thank you, Father, yes." Norah silently thanked her benefactor too. *It's you, isn't it Blessed Mother, made him ask because you know how warm I really am.*

Father James Daniel Kenney prayed without a sound as he picked up the carafe and poured a glass of water for each of them. *Sacred Heart of Jesus, please give me the right words for this grieved, good woman who sits before me.*

"Now tell me what's on your mind?" Father Kenney leaned forward, resting his folded hands on the desk.

"Father." Norah hesitated. "It's my husband and the drink." She hesitated again. "I'm not even sure I should be tellin' you any of this."

"You're doing nothing wrong. Please, continue."

"Father, when he's drunk, John beats the children. Me too. And all the time he's yellin' horrible things at the top of his lungs for the neighbors to hear. I'm scared to death the landlords are goin' to throw us out. And aren't they forever askin', 'Mrs. King, is everything all right up there?'" Norah used an American accent when she quoted the landlords. Her own lyrical speech returned with the next sentence. "Father, I've been givin' them this excuse and that, but I can't go on with the lyin', knowin' it's an offence to God Himself, let alone the blight on me own soul."

"Excuse me please." Father Kenney took a sip of water. *God help me. How many women have sat in that very chair saying more or less those very words and guilelessly trusting me to come up with some kind of miraculous solution to their predicament?* "Has it always been this way, Norah?"

"No, Father. Just let me say, I've no trouble with Mr. King stoppin' at the pub after a hard day's work. Sure and it's the part of Ireland that none of the men left behind. And that was John's way, with the occasional drunkenness. But he's been comin' home drunk most of the time and bringin' more of the stuff into the house with him." Norah took a quick breath. "And don't the children and I pray to Saint Jude that their father will go straight to the bedroom when he walks in the door that way? And he does, some of the time." Norah took another breath. She wasn't accustomed to speaking so quickly but she was mindful of the housekeeper's warning. "Just this last Monday, Father, I had to lie to the landlords again with the two youngest, Timmy and Tommy, standin' right there beside me. What kind of example is that to be gettin' from their mother? What am I to do, Father?"

"Do you think your husband would meet with me?"

"No, Father. And he'd be furious if he knew I was here talkin' to you as I am."

"So tell me, does Mr. King still go to work every day for the good of your family? And do I understand that he is indeed coming home at night?"

"Yes, Father. No one could ever accuse John Joseph King of not bein' a hard worker. And he spends every night in his own bed."

Father Kenney got up from his desk, pulled a large volume from the bookcase behind him, thumbed through it, and said, "Have you ever heard of mental reservation?"

"No, Father. I can't say that I have."

"Here it is. Now listen closely, Norah. 'Mental reservation, adding certain modifications to solve the dilemma of keeping a secret without actually lying.' Do you understand, Norah? The secret of what goes on in your home must be kept for the benefit of your children and the pride of your husband. These family situations are common. You're not alone. And please be comforted in knowing that your days in heaven will make up for it. Now let's have a prayer." He crossed the room. "Will you kneel with me, Norah King?"

The forty-six-year-old wife and mother knelt a decent distance before the priest who was already on his knees. Together they made the sign of the cross. Father Kenney continued, "Our Father in heaven, please help this troubled woman with her wifely duties. Help her to keep her husband happy and children safe. And as she endeavors to keep the peace, help her to accept mental reservation in place of what she has so innocently misconstrued as lying. Let us not forget that Your own beloved Mother suffered for the greater good. Please, Almighty God, in your infinite mercy, give her landlords less curiosity and no thought of eviction." Father Kenney whispered, "We'll end now, Norah." They closed their prayer as they had begun it. "In the name of the Father, and of the Son, and of the Holy Ghost. Amen." After meeting with Father Kenney, Norah reluctantly practiced *mental reservation,* but only when there was no way around it.

∞

As Norah walked down the narrow passageway between her apartment building and the one next door she thought, *Mother of God, last night him comin' home so late, three sheets to the wind and angry 'cause dinner wasn't waitin' on the table at ten o'clock. I can take it for myself, but when he goes after the children I can't bear it.*

When her husband was what Norah called "out of sorts," she remained calm, stood between John and the children, and gently coaxed him, as she did last night, into the kitchen for a cup of tea and something to eat.

Norah could still hear his high-pitched mock. "'Can I fix you a cup of tay, John? Would you like a little somethin' to eat too? I've some cold meat and po-tatoes. Let me fix you a plate now.' Why don't you let me fix you a plate, Norah King, right over your once-pretty head." The "once pretty" was a drunken lie, and by God's grace Norah didn't take it to heart. It was the least of her troubles.

Unbeknownst to Norah, soon after she had left for Beacon Hill that morn-ing, accompanied by her son John Michael who had an early work call, her husband walked into the kitchen, where his two oldest sons were still eating breakfast. John Joseph King was of average height, had a strong lean build, fair skin, thick, coffee-colored curly hair, intense light blue eyes, and dimples. He still wore his clothes from the night before.

"Morning, Dad," Patrick and Joe said one after the other.

"Boys," he said, raising a half-full pint of whiskey in the air and swallowing a mouthful. "And where are you two takin' yourselves this fine spring day?" He took another swig. "Is there a pretty girl waitin' for either one of ya's?" He pulled a handkerchief from his pants pocket and wiped his mouth.

Rosemary entered the kitchen with her younger sisters, Kay and Rita. "Good morning, Dad," she said, while pulling an apron over her head.

Her father answered, "If it isn't the sweet Rose of Tralee." He had a stale smell of tobacco and alcohol, and it churned her stomach.

Taking a seat with his back to Rosemary, John Joseph put the bottle of whiskey on the table and said, "Make yourself useful, Patrick, and pour your father a glass. 'Bite the hair of the dog who bit you' is the best cure for a hangover."

Patrick, sitting across from his father, glanced at Rosemary, who closed her eyes and shook her head. Patrick sheepishly suggested, "Ah, Dad, maybe it would be better to wait until tonight?"

"Tell me I didn't hear what I think I did, Patrick? You pathetic, kinky-haired, skinny nothin', you, suggestin' to me, your father, when he should and shouldn't take a drink? Jesus!" He pounded his fist on the table. Milk and tea spilled, sugar seemed to be everywhere and the whiskey bottle fell, every last drop absorbed in the tablecloth.

John King jumped up, knocked over the chair he'd been sitting in, grabbed Patrick's shirt with one hand, and awkwardly tried to remove his belt with the other. Frustrated, he punched Patrick in the mouth, and blood spurted on both of them.

"Dad, please stop!" Joe shouted, while grabbing his brother out of his father's grip.

"Joe, let go of him, or you're next," his father demanded. Joe didn't.

Rosemary pulled her sisters out of the kitchen, but this time she urged Kay to sneak out of the house and get their brother John Michael from the pharmacy. "Joe and Pat will need all the help they can get, Kay. Hurry!" Rosemary said. Then she and Rita hid.

"I'd hit you with me bare hands again if I didn't need them to support this poor excuse of a family."

The boys ran out of the kitchen.

When John Joseph entered the hallway, they were nowhere to be seen. "You'll answer to me, mind my words, you'll answer to me," he shouted, running frantically from room to room. "Don't I work meself to the bone in that sweatin' hot foundry? And what thanks do I get? Me, John Joseph King, forced off me family's property because I'm the younger brother."

He ended up in the living room, stumbled over to the windows and pulled down the shades. His bitterness about not inheriting the family farm back in Ireland came out only when he was drunk. Sober, he never talked about it. Except to Norah. His rant continued. "Now I'm pourin' molten steel down at that feckin' foundry because I've got to feed the likes of you. I never asked for any of you. All I wanted was to lay with me wife who too soon became your mother. *Go hIfreann leat!* To hell with you!"

This was the first time John King had ever made an implication about sex during one of his tirades. Rosemary, out of concern he would go even further, stepped forward from her hiding place behind the couch. He saw her from the corner of his eye, lunged in her direction and slapped her hard across the face.

"You think you're so high and mighty, don't you?" His voice became shrill. "'My name is Rosemary Virginia King and I'm going to be a social worker. I'm almost finished with my classes. Oh Ma, can you imagine?'" He mockingly put his hand on his hip. "'Your daughter, a social worker?' Social worker, my arse, who in the hell do you think you are?"

He dragged Rosemary by her hair into the hallway, closing the living room door behind them. "Get out here now, ya demons. Now, I say." Fifteen-year-old Rita appeared in the hallway, scared of what might happen to Rosemary if she didn't.

Rita spoke first. "Dad, we didn't do anything wrong."

"Ah, don't play the innocent with me, yer trollops," he screamed. "If you wore skirts that short in Ireland, sure and they'd tar and feather you from head to toe. I've seen it done to better than the likes of you."

John Joseph King's hell-scripted words stuck to the sides of his children's hearts, made their way into his children's dreams, and birthed nightmares that, for some of them, lasted a lifetime and wormed their way into the next generation's slumber.

"I've not had me breakfast. And it's your entire goddammed fault." He spoke in a mocking tone again. "'The children need new shoes, John. And hasn't Mr. Parker asked Mary and me to do up the floors of his home? It's just the bit of cash we need.'" He tried to grab Rita and missed. She bolted, running as fast as she could, heart pounding. "Get back here for your due punishment now!

Thanks to you, your mother has to work on a Saturday, and I have to go without bein' properly fed."

Just then, two-at-a-time footsteps could be heard coming up the flight of stairs. Rosemary knew it was Johnny. The front door burst open. John Joseph grabbed Rosemary by the hair again. Johnny, quick on his feet, ran down the hall, pulled his father off Rosemary, and stepped back, gaining his balance when John Joseph put his hands around Johnny's throat. "You goddam blackguard. Did you really think you could take me on? I'm twice the man you'll ever be. Get ready to meet your Maker, boyo. 'Cause you're on your way."

Kay rushed through the open doorway, pushed the door closed behind her, and ran straight to Rosemary's side. John Joseph's grip on Johnny's neck grew tighter, and the sixteen-year-old began to turn blue. The other boys suddenly appeared.

Joe, the oldest, yelled "Dad, you don't know what you're doing. Stop!" He pulled on his father's right arm while Patrick pulled on the left. As the three girls clung to each other, Rosemary whispered, "Thank heaven Timmy and Tommy are still outside playing."

Kay answered, "Don't let him hit me, Ro. Please don't let him hit me."

John Joseph calmed down enough for the boys to let go. He glared at Johnny. "You'll pay for interferin'." Then he went to his bedroom and slammed the door with all his might. The children knew from experience there was a good possibility he'd sleep until the next morning. They didn't want to think about what would happen if he woke.

Johnny was sitting on the floor with bent knees, his back against the wall and head in his hands. Rosemary tapped his arm. "Hey, kiddo."

Johnny looked up. "Thanks for saving me." His hair was disheveled, and his shirttails were out. "Jesus, I gotta get out of here. I hate to say it, Ro, but you'll have to start looking for another knight in shining armor. I'm shipping out."

"What? Are you telling me you're going to join the Navy? Johnny, that'd break Mum's heart."

"Listen, Ro. I'd rather be killed by a Kraut than my own father."

"We'll talk about it later. Do you want me to run an iron over your shirt before you go back to work? It looks like you slept in it."

"No, I've got a fresh one. Thanks anyway." He slowly walked down the hallway to the room he shared with his brothers.

The Kings' apartment had three bedrooms, one for the parents, one for the girls, and another for the boys.

"We need to get this place picked up," Rosemary said. "Joe, Patrick, you can put the furniture back in place. Rita, why don't you clear the table. And Kay, if you could get the dishes started, I'll be back in a minute. I'm going to run to the corner and get Mum some milk for her tea. If the little boys come home, don't tell them anything other than they need to be very quiet. If they're hungry, you can make them a sandwich. Jam or peanut butter."

Joe, Patrick, Kay, and Rita did exactly as their older sister asked. Rosemary took the apron off, smoothed her hair, grabbed her brown tweed coat from a peg rack by the back door, and went out the front door, down the stairs, out of the building, and up the street to Crowley's Grocery & Fine Meats. *Shipping out. Oh God, he can't do that. He can't.*

The day had been a long one for Norah and cares aside, she was glad to be home. She stepped into the small back hallway. *Please let himself be sleepin'. I've no strength for a row. None.*

Norah spotted a small package resting on the first step of the stairway. It was waxed paper-wrapped and tied with a blue ribbon. Her name was written in their landlady's pretty hand, on a torn piece of brown paper tucked under the bow. She picked it up, and a delicious aroma revealed the contents: Marie Flynn's homemade seedcake. Norah softly sighed with relief, knowing it had been placed there as a gift of reassurance and understanding. *Sacred Heart of Jesus, please bless Marie with that baby we're always prayin' for. Forgive me for avoidin' the Flynns and thinkin' the worst. If they saw this Jordan Marsh bag, they'd believe John and I had more money than we let on to and raise the rent. God bless 'em. They have no way of knowin' how hard it is for us to keep our heads above water.*

CHAPTER 5

A good laugh and a long sleep are the best cures.
IRISH BLESSING

TRUTH WAS NORAH MISSED ENTERING through the front door, which brought with it a feeling of gratitude and wellbeing. Today, the back door was safer and would give her a chance to hide the red coat before facing her husband. *Sure and he'll see it as a castoff from "those that ran us out of Ireland" and demand it be returned with nothing less than a speech by me, admitting error of judgment.* Norah felt certain the Parker family of Beacon Hill wasn't directly responsible for the Irish famine, but John Joseph felt certain that anyone with an English surname was.

Every house has its recognizable sounds, and 567 E. 8th Street was no different. There were stair sounds, floor sounds, plumbing sounds, the rattling of brass mailboxes on the entry wall, the bump of a baby carriage, bike or wagon being pulled over a threshold, doors opening and closing, the tapping of a wet umbrella, or thud of snow boots dropping to the floor, and the sound of footsteps.

Kay, sitting quietly in the kitchen, heard those surefooted but almost dance-like steps, with rhythm so even-paced. *Mumma's home.* She ran to meet her halfway down the flight of stairs. "You'd best have a light foot, Mum. He's sleeping. We've had a horrible time of it."

Norah briefly touched the shoulder of her second born, Barbara Catherine, who everyone called Kay. "Stay here on the stairs with me for a minute darlin'. Let's pray and ask Saint Jude to help us, for isn't he the saint of all that's impossible, God forgive me."

Kay, only fourteen months younger than Rosemary, was the other half of what their father called "Rose Red and Snow White" with black hair, porcelain skin, and violet-blue eyes. "The two of you are beauties," he'd say. "Sure and I'll have to put your brothers guard by the doors day and night to keep all the young bucks away."

Kay had a head for numbers and a heart for getting ahead. She couldn't wait to tell her mother the good news. Placing her hands on Norah's forearms, Kay spoke quickly. "Mum, Rita, Ro, and I just got back from confession, and we saw Sister Josephine at church. She says I have a good chance for a scholarship to the Katharine Gibbs School. Isn't that swell? They award two of them for accounting."

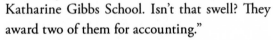

Katharine Gibbs School was a private for-profit institution of higher learning for the career education of young women "With high standards of dress and decorum, the secretarial schools cultivated an image of sophistication and efficiency. . . . Its legions of graduates, once known as "Katie Gibbs girls," were long considered the elite of the clerical field, renowned for their professionalism, poise, and polished appearance."

The Boston Globe

"That's grand, Barbara Catherine. We'll talk more about it later." Disappointed, Kay let go of her mother's arms.

Norah was delighted by Kay's news, but eager to give Rosemary her gift before John Joseph woke. *Now, we've an even blessin' for the sisters. Barbara Catherine with her scholarship hopes and Rosemary with her much needed coat.*

"I'll pray, Mum. Do you want to sit down?"

"No darlin'. I'm afraid I'd never get up."

They bowed their heads.

"Please, Saint Jude, help my father, John Joseph King, if you don't know him, to stop the drinking."

Norah interrupted. "Ask him darlin' to have your Da in a good mood when he wakes. And ask that he not wake until after we've all had a peaceful supper."

"God in heaven, Mum, I'm trying to say the prayer." Kay sighed. "And please, Saint Jude, if you don't think it's asking too much, let there be peace in our home tonight. Please protect our family. Thank you for standing by us in these hard times. And thank you for hearing our prayer."

Mother and daughter made the sign of the cross and then each brought her hands together, fingers up, pointed toward heaven, and thumbs crossed, as they'd both been taught by nuns, who admonished generations, "Don't be folding your hands intertwined in the lazy Protestant way." They opened their eyes on "Amen."

Norah wasn't necessarily affectionate, but tears came to her for the way Kay could say a prayer. She took her daughter's right hand in her own and kissed the back of it. "God bless you, Barbara Catherine. Now let's get up those stairs before himself wakes." They tiptoed. "How long has he been down?" Norah whispered.

"I'm not sure, a while now. It was pretty bad, Mum. Johnny says he's joining the Navy as soon as he can. He said he'd rather fight the Krauts than be killed by his own father. You've got to talk to him, Mum. I think he means it."

Norah stood on the landing at the top of the stairs and took a deep breath at the thought of making everything right for her children, cooking supper, and contending with John Joseph when he woke. As Kay opened the door for her mother, it squeaked. "It's okay, Mum. On second thought, I think the dead will wake before Dad does." She eyed the Jordan Marsh bag.

"Don't be askin' any questions, Barbara Catherine. But what I will say is what's in this bag is not meant for you but will perhaps, one day come to you."

Norah wanted to surprise Rosemary, so she folded the garment bag in half and half again, opened the pantry door, which was next to the back door, and placed the bag on the top shelf. Led by the aroma of onions and butter, she walked into the tidy kitchen.

A starched simple white curtain hung on the window over the sink, and could be pushed back on either side when there was a need for fresh air or for calling the younger children inside. An ironed red print cloth covered the table already set for supper with heavy, white dinnerware,

The modern tablecloth, not Norah's taste at all, was the first thing John Michael chose to buy with the money he earned as a soda jerk.

tumblers for the younger children; teacups and saucers for Norah, John and the older children; assorted silverware and a candle. There was always a candle, as there had been when Norah was a girl at her own parents' table. Last week, her husband questioned it. "Don't I pay the electric bill every month? We need a candle too?"

"It's nothin' to do with electricity, John. The glow of it calms the family and lights the way to good conversation."

"Fine then, have your candle."

Before Norah was married, she bought a silverware service for eight, piece by piece, when she got her wages. She never imagined there would be more than eight in her family. Subsequently, she'd bartered for more pieces at various rummage sales.

The stove was big, black, and iron, requiring coals and wood for heat. And the Sacred Heart's framed image had been placed on a wall closest to the table while palm fronds woven into a cross hung over the doorway that led to the rest of the good-sized apartment.

Rosemary, wearing an apron and standing at the sink, slowly turned around at the sound of her mother's footsteps. "Hi Mum, I've put the water on for tea."

"And you've got onions brownin'—" Norah gasped and brought both hands over her heart, horrified at what she saw.

Rosemary's eyes were tear-filled, and the right side of her face was red and slightly swollen. "He hit you didn't he? What set him off? Kay, go keep your sister Rita company. I need to talk with Rosemary. Go on, darlin'." Norah cupped her hand beneath Rosemary's wounded face.

"I don't want to talk about it, Mum. What's done is done." She tightened the apron bow. "I've no idea what you're planning on cooking for dinner tonight, but I knew you wouldn't object to beginning with onions and butter. It just seemed right to fill the house with a good smell."

Maybe because she couldn't hold them in any longer, but probably because the love of her mother was there, Rosemary's tears fell. And Norah's tears met them. Neither mother nor daughter acknowledged their sorrow verbally, but went about the task of pushing back some of the supper dishes to make room for tea.

Norah sat down and slipped her coat off, letting it fall back on the chair. "So tell me, Rosemary Virginia, where are your brothers keepin' themselves?"

"Joe and Pat went to Sully's to see if they could get some work, Mum."

Sullivan's Surplus was locally known as "Sully's Junkyard," and Francis Sullivan was a genius at turning scrap anything into profit. From time to time, he'd hire the King brothers to sort, always giving them the same warning. "I'm payin' ya by the job, not by the hour. Money's the same if ya sort fast or sort slow. But if ya want to work here again, I'd recommend ya's work hard and fast."

Rosemary poured boiling water into a floral porcelain teapot, a wedding gift to her parents from Norah's employer at the time. While the orange pekoe steeped, she brought down the matching gold-rimmed teacups and saucers from the highest shelf in the cupboard and put them on the table. "To what do we owe this grand place settin'?" Norah asked. "I don't know, Ma. It just sits up there on the shelf."

"Look what I've got here, darlin'." Norah took the wrapped seed cake from her lap and presented it with both hands. "Sure and we've a party in the makin'. Tonight we'll have dessert first." Rosemary reached up and brought down the rest of the tea set: dessert plates, a sugar bowl, and a pitcher for milk.

Norah used evaporated milk for her tea, as most of Southie's Irish did. Pet was the preferred brand because they honored saved labels with compensation to local schools.

"I understand that you, Barbara Catherine and Rita went to confession. I hope the others have too."

"Mum, no need to worry."

"Where are the little boys?"

"Timmy and Tommy should be home any minute now. They've been out playing most of the day and were here for a little while after lunch, but then Kay shooed them off to confession. Timmy wasn't too happy about having Tommy tag along again. He whispered, 'Geez, Kay, Tommy isn't even old enough to go to confession.'" Rosemary took a covered glass butter dish out of the icebox. "But he didn't want to hurt Tommy's feelings, so off they went. You know Timmy, Mum."

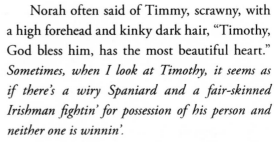

Black Irish refers to olive-skinned and/or dark-haired Irish men and women—a direct result of the Spanish Armada's 1588 landing in Ireland. Scrawny Timmy grew up to be a handsome, chiseled, lightweight boxing champ.

Norah often said of Timmy, scrawny, with a high forehead and kinky dark hair, "Timothy, God bless him, has the most beautiful heart." *Sometimes, when I look at Timothy, it seems as if there's a wiry Spaniard and a fair-skinned Irishman fightin' for possession of his person and neither one is winnin'.*

On the other hand, the neighbors often likened his siblings to movie stars, particularly Rosemary. Recently, two women spoke of Rosemary's potential while watching her cross the street. "And doesn't the beauty of Rosemary King bring Carol Lombard to mind or is it Veronica Lake I'm thinkin' of? Sure, she takes a person's breath away, that one, and speaks well too."

"Rosemary King could outdo any of those Hollywood types."

"Oh wouldn't it be grand to have another one of our own up there on the silver screen? Just think, 'Starring Rosemary King and Maureen O'Hara.' I don't think Miss O'Hara would mind the order of billin', seein' as it's alphabetically correct. Unless of course she considers the Hara part of her name as comin' first, in a technical sort of way. I mean the O isn't really much of anythin' by itself now, is it?"

Rosemary was putting additional plates on the table for her sisters when Norah said, "Let's just be the two of us for now darlin'. They can have their cake after supper."

Rosemary brought her hand to her face. "Mum, do you think the mark will be gone by tomorrow? I don't want to walk into church this way."

"When the boys come home, I'll send one of 'em to the market for a small piece of beefsteak. That'll reduce the swellin', and later I can make beef tea out of it for Rita. Didn't that rheumatic fever take the roses right out of your sister's cheeks? There's nothin' like beef tea to bring 'em back again." Beef tea, made from beef steak, water, and salt cooked for hours, was thought to build up health. To her siblings' shock, Rita loved it.

"How did it all start, darlin'? Did he strike anyone else?" Norah placed her hand on Rosemary's wrist but she pulled away.

"Let's just enjoy our cake, okay, Mum?"

"Yes, you're right. And you'll want to put a little butter on that cake. Sure and it's like gildin' a lily but I wouldn't want you missin' the delicious pleasure of it."

Rosemary smiled at her mother and reached for the butter dish. "Oh Mum, I almost forgot." She sat up straighter. "Steve Chalpin asked Kay to the prom a week ago now. Mum, she really wants to go. Do you think Dad will let her? What are we going to do for a dress?"

"Please don't worry your pretty head about a dress. Things have a way of workin' out. Enough about Kay, let's talk about you and the lovely surprise that's waitin' for you right outside this kitchen door."

Norah got up and left the room. She carefully pulled the Jordan Marsh bag from the pantry shelf, smoothed out the soft wrinkles, and returned to the kitchen holding it up in the air like a trophy.

"Mum, what in the world?"

"Take it, darlin'," Norah said, handing the bag to Rosemary. "It's yours."

"Mum, I can't believe this." Rosemary held the bag off the floor and carefully removed the coat.

"And aren't your eyes as big as saucers?" Norah said with a smile.

"Oh my God, Mum. It's so beautiful! How did you ever—?"

"The lady of that grand house on Beacon Hill gave you this coat. Sure and her own daughter has grown out of its beautiful threads, and she was delighted to send it your way. Her name is Mrs. Caroline Parker, and I'm sure you'll want to be askin' our Lord to give her a blessin' or two for the kindness of it all."

Rosemary took the coat in her hands, twirled, and placed it gently on a nearby chair, as if it were a child sitting alone for the first time. She removed her apron and walked toward the door.

"Where are you takin' yourself, Rosemary? Sure and I thought you'd have that coat on sooner than I could hang up me own."

"My hair is mussed, and I want to put on a little of that new Tangee lipstick you said Kay,

Tangee Lipstick

"Ideal for Women Who Want to Look Beautiful Without Looking Artificial The lipstick that goes on clear and gradually transforms into the perfect shade for you."

It was the only cosmetic, other than a powdered nose, Norah allowed her girls to wear.

Rita, and I could wear for special occasions. First impressions are lasting, Mum. I'll be right back."

Norah stepped into the hall, hung her own coat on the third peg of the rack John made, and let her mind wander to happier times.

"Norah, there's only room enough for the twelve pegs. Nine for the children, one for you, one for me, and the twelfth, no, make that the first, is for the Almighty."

"And isn't the Holy Trinity three in one, John Joseph, makin' the single peg enough for them all?"

Reentering the kitchen, Norah lowered her head and with both hands, pushed back several strands of hair that had escaped her neat-as-a-pin bun. As if choreographed, she raised her head in perfect synchronization when Rosemary pulled the red coat's double-notched lapel collar up around her neck and once again exclaimed to her Maker and mother, "Oh my God, Mum. It's as though it was made for me. What do you think?"

Norah brought her hands together and smiled "Ah darlin', of course it was made for you. Didn't God and His angels plan the whole thing and kindly let those Brahmins borrow it for just awhile?"

Rosemary twirled again. Her blonde shoulder-length hair flew from her shoulders, and the bottom flap of the coat came open, revealing her simple navy-blue print dress and slender legs, while the soft click of her T-strap shoes landed on the shiny linoleum floor.

"It's a sight for sore eyes, seein' you so happy. And doesn't the color of it look grand with your light locks?" Norah was beaming. But as Rosemary completed the turn, Norah noticed her daughter had powdered the bruise, and she got a knot in her stomach.

"Mum, I'm going to show my new coat to Kay and Rita."

"Careful now. Don't be raisin' your voices."

"I know." Rosemary walked toward the door and then turned around. "It's so nice and warm." She held the coat open and lifted an edge of the taupe satin lining, exposing a layer of wool felt. "Look. Oh I wish it wasn't for winter so I could wear it right now. Maybe I'll wear it anyway," she said with a fleeting grin. "But what do you think, Mum? Could I get away with wearing a red winter coat on Easter Sunday?"

"I don't think so, darlin'. It's not the sort of thing you wear in the spring, especially on Easter. It'll keep."

"I guess I already knew that. It'll look wonderful next Christmas though. I can't wait." Rosemary folded her arms and shrugged her shoulders. Norah good-naturedly waved her daughter out of the room. "Go on now, and show it to your sisters." Rosemary kissed her mother on top of her head, ran out of the kitchen and tiptoed down the hall.

Norah got up from the table. She poured the cold tea into the sink, sat down, and poured hot tea into the cup. Adding a little sugar, then milk, she picked up a teaspoon and stirred and stirred as she silently spoke to her closest confidante.

"Hail, Mary, full of grace, the Lord is with Thee."

Please help me do what's best for the children.

"Blessed art Thou amongst women and blessed is the fruit of Thy womb, Jesus."

Won't you talk to Your Son about my son John Michael, that He'd keep him from goin' off to war?

"Holy Mary, Mother of God,"

It's a comfort knowin' I've the help and wisdom of another mother comin' my way.

"Pray for us sinners,"

Please, Mother, if there's any way within me that's provokin' my husband's bad behavior, point it out so I can put a stop to this horror our children are havin' to endure.

"Now and at the hour of our death."

Sure and he's going to kill one of us someday if this drunkenness continues.

"Amen."

CHAPTER 6

But come ye back when summers in the meadow
Or when the valley's hushed and white with snow
'Til I'll be here in sunshine and in shadow
Danny boy, Oh Danny boy, I love you so.
"OH, DANNY BOY"
FREDERICK WEATHERLY

"IF IT ISN'T MR. AND Mrs. King and the royal family." Peg Hennessey, Marie Flynn's widowed mother, had been listening for footsteps all morning long. She didn't want to miss seeing the Kings on their way to Easter Sunday Mass. And now, here they were. "Well, some of them anyway."

Peg was ready for church except for the stockings rolled down around her ankles due to the painful press on her plump thighs once they were clipped to her girdle. She wore house slippers until the last minute too, before squeezing her feet into "me Sunday best, those torturous beauties." Peg was seldom seen without an apron. Today's was a cheery, yellow floral in honor of Easter.

Norah crossed the narrow entry hall and took one of Peg's frail hands into her own strong ones. "Happy Easter to you darlin' neighbor."

"Happy Easter to you too, darlin' neighbor," Peg said, patting Norah's hand.

"You two, darlin' this, darlin that!" John Joseph chided as he kept one eye on the stairway. "Happy Easter just the same."

Peg thought how lovely Norah looked in her steel-blue, beige pin dot dress, laced navy-blue pumps, straw hat with a miniature bird jauntily perched on the side, a few artificial sprigs of green tucked around him, and once fashionable, but still good enough butterscotch coat. The coat, purchased long before Norah married, was much too small, but she thought it a secret well kept when simply put over her shoulders. *The warmth's there all the same.*

Norah King beamed as she stood next to her husband and the three oldest children, Joe, who was pacing, Rosemary, and Kay.

"Mum," Joe said, "I thought you said everyone had to be dressed and downstairs by eight-thirty."

Norah looked at the modest locket watch pinned to her dress. *Eight thirty on the dot.* Just then, more of her family came running down the common front stairway, with Timmy and Tommy leading the way.

"We're comin', Mum," they called, giggling.

"Pat can't find his new socks and wants to know if he should wear his old brown ones," Timmy reported, glancing at his father, ready for trouble.

Norah smiled and sighed. "God in heaven, you don't mean to tell me he's lost the new pair already?"

John Joseph bounded halfway up the stairs, pushing past John Michael who was on his way down.

"Mornin', Dad." John Michael stepped aside, his uneasiness evident.

"Happy Easter, John," he replied, much to his son's relief. He stopped at the next step, grabbed the railing, and yelled, "Patrick! Patrick!"

The thirteen-year-old, barefoot boy appeared on the landing. "I'm sorry, Dad."

"Sorry's not goin' to find those socks. Find them, Patrick. Just ask yourself, where would I be if I were a brand new pair of socks? And be quick about it."

John Joseph came back down. "Well, we've got most of them then. Let's see. Where's Rita?"

Norah turned to Rosemary. "Do you have any idea what's keepin' your sister?"

"Mum, it's Rita. She's never on time," Rosemary blithely replied, and looked toward Kay, who snapped her brand new white gloves in Rosemary's direction and sing–sang, "Never, Ro, never."

"Found 'em! Found 'em!" Patrick slid down the railing hoping to gain time.

John Joseph caught him, tightly squeezed his upper arm, and said in a low tone, "It's a good thing you did, boyo." He dashed up the stairway again. "Rita Margaret King get yourself down these stairs now!" he bellowed.

Rita quietly closed the front door and descended the newly waxed stairway as if she had time to spare.

"Happy Easter, Dad," she said, pulling on one of her scallop-edged white gloves.

Petite, auburn-haired, green-eyed Rita was radiant in her pinkish-tan, long-sleeved dress with white cuffs, white embroidery on the pockets and matching Peter Pan collar. Her Easter bonnet was a simple band with petal-pink flowers, and her shoes, barely pumps. She'd begged for stockings instead of white anklets, but Norah wouldn't budge. "You'll have your first pair of hosiery in November, on your 16th birthday. No sooner." Rita held Rosemary's beige faille clutch purse under her arm, being careful not to crush the corsage pinned to it, a gift from an unknown beau. She was pulling on the second glove when she caught her father's too-long gaze at the bodice of her dress.

John Joseph's youngest daughter's budding beauty stopped him in his tracks, but not his anger. "Why are you the one we're always waitin' for?"

"I'm sorry, Dad. It's just—"

"Just nothin'. Pick up your step young woman."

"Yes, Dad." When he turned his back, she crossed her eyes. The little boys swallowed their giggles, and Peg Hennessey put her hand over her mouth for the same reason. Norah looked the other way.

"And aren't the whole lot of you a feather in God's cap? That is, if He's inclined to wear one," Peg said, helpfully removing a bit of lint from young Joe's suit sleeve.

"It's a kind word well taken Peg Hennessey. Sure and it's no easy task getttin' this bunch out the door." Norah turned to her family. "And out the door we're goin', right this minute."

John Joseph was waiting on the porch, but Norah still took the time to ask, "Did you want to walk to Mass with us then, Peg?" *Please dear God, let her say, no, seein' as she's not fully dressed yet.*

"Oh that's nice of you, Norah. But Marie and Gerard are takin' me to the ten o'clock in the car."

⁓

All the King children had new Easter clothing, with the exception of something borrowed or handed down and only then if it looked absolutely pristine. However, Norah made sure every one of her children had brand new underwear. "What good is it to have the outside lookin' new when the inside is old and tattered?"

John Joseph found it amusing to introduce his dark-haired oldest son as, "the black sheep of the family," a name Joe would eventually grow into.

For the first time in his life, young Joe—sinewy, with dark, ink-blue eyes, and curly hair black as coal—had a brand new suit. Thanks to Mr. Karp.

Norah King had stood proudly when the tailor pinned up the hem of Joe's new slacks. "You're a young man now, Joseph. And this suit is intended to send you in the right direction."

Mr. Karp was respectfully known in the neighborhood as "our Jew." To Norah he was an answer to prayer. Morrie Karp linked those with little cash to suppliers and funded their purchases with enough interest to make it all worthwhile. When Norah said her son needed a suit, Mr. Karp shuffled his assortment of business cards until he found, Sam Ruben's Superior Clothing for Gents. "Mrs. King, you and your son will show Sam his own card, say Morrie Karp sent you, and I'll take care of the rest."

Morrie Karp was a shrewd businessman, but he granted his customers their dignity. "One missed payment is allowed. One. We all get into a pickle, but I can only afford one pickle. You'll make the next payment on time, I'm sure of it."

A sullen John Michael wore his older brother's outgrown sports coat, formerly owned by the late Mr. Sweeney. "Ma, everyone will know its Joe's hand-me-down."

"First of all, John Michael, you'll not be callin' me Ma. Sure and it's hooligans who call their mother such a thing. Have you got it then? And about the jacket, your brother hardly wore it. And haven't you a brand new shirt, slacks, and shoes? Just like Mickey Rooney in one of those Andy Hardy movies. Only much better lookin'."

"Thanks, Mum." John Michael kissed his mother on the cheek.

Timmy and Tommy were dressed identically in gray knickers. All the boys proudly wore new shirts and ties. However, Patrick felt he should have a dress coat like his older brothers.

"Patrick, God put you in the middle, so it's middle clothes you'll be wearin'. I don't want to hear another word about it." Norah had spoken.

Kay's lavender Easter dress was borrowed from Patsy Sheehan, and Rosemary cleverly impersonated Kathryn Hepburn as she teased Kay about the "frilly *buttahfly* sleeves" and "*adorahhble* flounced skirt,"—an about-face from Kay's standard tailored style. "That's a *Gingah* Rogers dress if *evah* I saw one."

"*Somehow, by hook or by crook, and mostly with the help of our Jew, my brothers and I always had new clothes for Easter Sunday. Everyone in Southie did, can you imagine? Nobody had any money to speak of. My mother paid him a dollar a week for as long as I can remember. As a matter of fact, we bought my wedding dress with his help. How would we have possibly gotten by without our Jew?*"

Mrs. Jane McDonough Hayden

Rosemary bought her own Easter outfit with money she earned as a typist at the Carney Hospital. She found a discounted suit in Blessed-Mother-blue at Mrs. Rosengard's store on Broadway, put it on layaway, and made the last payment on Good Friday.

At her mother's request, the netted veil on Rosemary's small Juliet hat was pushed back. "It's my opinion that only married women should be wearin' the veil pulled over their eyes, and even then, I'm not sure I like the look of it. Too beguilin', if you ask me."

John Joseph wasn't flashy, but he was hard to please, and Norah indulged her husband with his very specific requests for Easter Sunday: a new white dress shirt, a new tie, and a proper soft hat this year, which, Norah didn't mind. Like many men in the parish, he wore a tweed cap, a scally, which she felt unsuitable for Easter Sunday. He'd also requested, "Have one of the boys polish up me oxfords, and I'll make due," and thought of himself as cutting corners. He never gave a second thought to how difficult it was for Norah and the children to earn and scrape together every cent that made him look like a good provider.

Church bells pealed, bare trees peeped green buds, and early garden flowers greeted the fresh, spring Easter morning.

Southie's streets were bustling with people on their way to Easter services: mothers, fathers, children, babies in carriages, grandparents, maiden aunts, bachelor uncles, and everybody in between, all dressed up in their finest clothes or someone else's and politely greeting one another with inquires and exclamations.

"Happy Easter to you and your family."

"Did the Easter Bunny stop at your house?"

"No, not yet. We've requested he make his visit while we're still at Mass. If that overrated rodent comes any earlier, it's too much of a distraction from all the gettin' ready."

Gate of Heaven Church
SOUTH BOSTON, MASS.

"I'd stop to chat, but Mass begins in ten minutes. And you know Father McNulty, he's no reservation about speakin' his mind to the tardy."

Irish-born Father McNulty, in regal white-and-gold vestments, forearms resting on his stomach, hands hidden within the folds of his cassock sleeves, stood at the church door welcoming one and all.

The quick-witted older priest was well loved but not without the reservation and strictness parishioners expected from a man in his position. At the stroke of five minutes to nine, Father Mychal Seamus McNulty loudly announced to stragglers, "This door is closing in two minutes. If you don't want a mortal sin on your soul for missing Mass on this holiest of days, run, or go to the ten o'clock with all the other Tardy Tillies."

Gate of Heaven's white marble altar shone, and beams of jewel-toned sunlight streamed from the magnificent, stained-glass windows. Gone were the purple mourning cloths of Lent. Once again, the Stations of the Cross, every crucifix and statue, were in full view. The entire church was filled with lilies: on the stairs leading up to the altar, on either side of the tabernacle, on both smaller side altars, before every statue, around the Baptismal font, and at intervals along the Communion rail.

There was just enough room in one pew for the ten Kings. It was crowded, but Norah whispered, "It's better this way, all of us in the one place."

John Joseph whispered back, "No, it's not," and ordered John Michael to sit in the pew behind the family. "Jesus, Mary, and Joseph! How's a man supposed to worship properly when his bum's crowded right and left? You should have offered to move, John. Now I'm tellin' you, get back there."

John Michael had no way of knowing why his father routinely singled him out whenever he had a complaint. He was, in fact, the spitting image of John Joseph's older brother, Ian, who inherited the family farm back in Ireland. John Joseph hated Ian, and every time he saw John Michael it was as if "the fair haired prince" was standing right in front of him.

All at once Rita got up. "Excuse me, excuse me, I need to get out," she said softly. She slid past her sisters and parents, managed to pull loose from her father's quick grip on her wrist, ignored Kay's questions, genuflected, took one step backwards, genuflected again, slipped into the next pew, and sat alongside John Michael, the closest to her in age among all her siblings.

"Rita," he murmured, "what are you doing? You'll get killed." Their father looked over his shoulder and scowled.

"He doesn't scare me, Johnny. Mum will be there. And besides, I don't think Dad'll act up today. The pubs are closed." She patted the corsage on her purse and smiled impishly.

"Guess who?"

Now Norah turned around. "Shhhh."

John Michael looked straight ahead and bumped his sister's knee with his own. "Thanks, sis."

The family worshipped—kneeling, sitting, and standing at the appropriate times—under Norah's watchful eye; only the three youngest needed prompting.

When it was time for Communion, organ music filled the great cathedral, and Norah closed her eyes to better hear the sacred composition, as the choir led parishioners in her best-loved hymn, sung in Latin. *"Tantum ergo Sacramentum."*

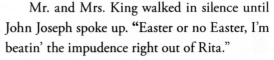

The walk home was swift. Norah's family was hungry and eager for the leg of lamb she put in the oven before they left. Much to her relief, John Joseph took no issue with the expense. His only comment was, "Tell me you've mint jelly to go with that supreme piece of meat."

"And what do you think I am, Mr. King, a wife who doesn't know her own husband's preference? Of course, we have the mint jelly. It's coolin' in the icebox right now. And haven't I butter for your potatoes too? There'll be no oleomargarine on Easter Sunday."

Inexpensive oleomargarine, made primarily from white beef fat, was mixed with yellow food coloring to look like butter.

Mr. and Mrs. King walked in silence until John Joseph spoke up. "Easter or no Easter, I'm beatin' the impudence right out of Rita."

"Come on now, John. The girl was only tryin' to be polite."

"I'll think about it. If not today, tomorrow then."

Norah returned to the joy of Easter. "Timothy, Thomas." She playfully ran up to them. "Please stay in the backyard until you're called upstairs. The Easter Bunny has some unfinished business and wants no interruption."

The little boys mockingly boxed each other, and Tommy chanted, "We're gettin' candy! We're gettin' candy!"

John Joseph egged the older boy on. "Come on now, Tim. Show your brother that quick left you've got. You're a champion, you are."

Norah turned around. "If I didn't know better, I'd say you're gettin' that boy ready for the ring." She returned to her husband's side and, for just a moment, put her hand in the crook of his arm.

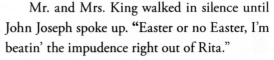

Once they reached home, most of the brood ran upstairs and straight to their bedrooms, removing hats, gloves, coats and sweaters. Others raced for the bathroom. When John Joseph showed up, they stepped aside, leaving the door wide open for him. Norah headed for the kitchen and got down to the business of putting dinner on the table. All three girls were soon by her side, taking up their usual tasks, Norah at the helm of it all.

With Kay's help, Rita set the long table, and cheerfully placed a large, pink, potted geranium right in the middle, with a lone blue-and-white willow saucer beneath it to protect Norah's cherished Irish linen cloth. Tall glass candlesticks were precisely placed on either side.

"Mum, do you want me to light the candles?" Rita asked, matches in hand.

"Not yet. I'll let you know. But for now, go look under my bed and you'll find two chocolate bunnies for the little boys. We'll make it a surprise and put them on the table as part of our decorations. Then you can call your brothers inside."

Rita, disappointed Norah didn't have candy for all of them, pouted.

"And don't be moonin' about. You'll also find a bag holdin' six of Fannie Farmer's best chocolate cream eggs for the rest of you. Put one by each place then."

Without warning, Norah gasped, and caught herself on the kitchen sink. For the first time in her life, she felt faint. Kay was getting milk from the icebox and ran to her, while Rita pulled a chair from the table. "Here, Mum."

"I don't know what came over me. One minute I'm strainin' the potatoes, and the next I thought I'd find meself on the floor."

"Do you think it has anything to do with your foot, Mum?" Rosemary asked, referring to the lump that had been on her mother's right foot for weeks.

"It has nothin' to do with that, just an odd moment, that's all."

"Mum, I'll take care of the potatoes." Rita went to the sink.

"You can strain them darlin', but better put an apron on first and get one of the boys to do the mashin'. It's too much for you, mashin' potatoes for ten people." Kay and Rosemary exchanged knowing glances. If either of them had been about to do the mashing Norah wouldn't have objected. Rita was, even at fifteen, her mother's baby girl.

Rosemary handed Norah a cup of tea. "This should pick you up, Mum."

"Thank you darlin'. Girls, we're havin' a nice Easter, and I don't want anything to spoil it. So please don't mention this to your father."

When they were all seated at the table, John Joseph called his family to order. "Pay attention to your mother now."

Norah paused and looked around. *What lovely children and they're all mine. God bless the whole lot of them.*

Her husband was curt. "Norah, the foods gettin' cold."

She nodded her head in his direction "We'll be thanking God for this fine meal and make the sign of the cross together now." And so they all did, including the head of the household who most of the time seemed godless. "Bless us, O Lord, and these Thy gifts, which we are about to receive from Thy bounty through Christ, our Lord. Amen."

After dinner, everyone picked up their place setting, and walked toward the sink, except for John Joseph, who headed for the living room calling back over his shoulder, "Joe, I want a word with you."

Norah was putting away the only leftover when she heard her husband yell. "What? What? Norah, come in here right now!" She laid the half-full bowl of cauliflower on the kitchen table, and rushed to the living room with Rosemary, Kay, and Rita following close behind. The other children peeked out of doorways, looking at their mother for answers. Norah indicated with a whisk of her left hand they should remain where they were. The girls stayed in the hallway.

"It took you long enough to get here, Norah. It's a good thing I wasn't yellin' fire. The house'd burn down before you'd be of any help." John Joseph sat on the edge of the couch. "Well, guess what your firstborn son has up and done? He's joined the United States Navy."

"Joseph Frances, is this true?" Norah, still standing, folded her arms.

John Joseph spoke before Joe could answer. "I was tellin' him there's a job openin' at the foundry, and this is what he comes back with. 'Well, Dad,' he says, 'I'm afraid I won't be able to go after that job right now.'"

John Joseph jumped to his feet. "'I'm shippin' out in two days,' he says." He grabbed Joe by the collar and pulled him out of the chair he was sitting in. "And when were you goin' to tell us, Joe? Or were you going to sneak away in the middle of the night like a bloody coward?" He let go, and his son fell into the chair with a thump, gripped the chair's arms, and clenched his teeth. For an instant, Norah thought he might go after his father, but he didn't.

Norah crossed the room. "Joe, why would you do such a thing? Goin' behind our backs like that?"

"Mum, I didn't do it to go behind your back." Young Joe leaned forward, forearms on his knees. "It's just that some of the fellas were signin' up, and it seemed like a good idea. The Navy's a first-rate place to learn a trade. Say, electronics. And then, I could get into the union and--"

"The fact remains you joined the U. S. Navy and never said a word about it. And now, you're shippin' out in the two days!" Norah brought her hands to her lips as if in prayer, closed her eyes, opened them, and put a hand to her heart. "Are you aware, Joseph Frances, there's a war goin' on in Europe? If the Germans take your life, you'll have no need for electronics. For I've never seen a dead man do a day's work yet. Have you?"

John Joseph shot up from the couch. "You've dug your own grave, Joe. And I'm puttin' you in it meself before some goddam German has the pleasure."

Norah stood between them. "John, for the love of God, please stop."

John Joseph pretended to strike her with the back of his hand and smirked. "You're not worth the trouble." He walked over to Joe and said, "*Imeacht gan teacht ort.*" May you leave without returning. He went to his bedroom, and slammed the door with one last complaint. "What kind of goddam holiday is this anyway, when a man can't even raise a glass to the occasion?" He immediately opened the door, yelling at the top of his lungs, "But you managed to have enough money for the lamb! Didn't you, Norah?"

Rosemary, Kay, and Rita returned to the kitchen. The others went outside.

Norah sat on the couch, hands folded on her lap. Joe was still sitting in the chair. Neither mother nor son spoke. The apartment smelled of Easter dinner, children could be heard playing in the street below, and shadows from Norah and Joe's images fell on the slightly frayed area rug. "Mum, I. . ."

"Let's sit here quietly for a few minutes, Joseph. I need to think this over, and you do too. Be still now."

Norah contemplated her son's decision. *On the one hand, he's been spendin' time with the wrong crowd, congregatin' on the corner and smokin', lookin' for easy money in the pool halls when he's got a nickel or two. Workin' here and there, nothing steady, although every place has called him back. The lad isn't afraid to get his hands dirty, and God knows he gives me every cent he can spare before it's all spent or his father takes it. Mary, Mother of God, I can't believe this is happenin'.*

Norah worried about Joe. Of all the children, his temper was the most like her husband's. And his discovery of liquor frightened her. *Last week, him comin' home three sheets to the wind. I'll have to warn Joe how liquor can change a person, impairin' judgment and tearin' down all those about them.* Norah reconsidered her son's enlistment.

Norah Catherine Foley King knew what it was to leave home. *Didn't I leave me own parents at about the same age?* She wistfully recalled her mother's parting words. *God bless your way, you darlin' brave girl.* And her dearly departed father, as he handed her a sealed envelope shortly before she boarded the ship for America. *"Norah, put this in a safe place now. I'll not have one of me own goin' to an unknown land without a few extra coins 'til there's work.*

Years later, when the time came, mother and son were buried in the same grave. But Joe's name, Joseph Frances King, at his brothers' firm decision, would not be on the headstone with those of his parents and sister.

Norah rose from the couch, walked across the room, and put her hands on Joe's broad shoulders. "Well, what's done is done, and I can't say it's an altogether bad thing. But Jesus, Mary, and Joseph, Joseph. You might have told me before I bought you that fine-lookin' new suit. Now I'll be payin' Mr. Karp for God knows how long, only to have it hangin' in the closet."

Joe had tears in his eyes but a smile nonetheless. "Maybe John Michael will grow into it soon, Mum."

Norah took her eldest son into her arms, kissed him on the cheek, stood back, and adjusted her apron. "We'll have a send-off for you then, though heaven only knows where we'll get the money. I've spent every dime on Easter and your new suit." She smiled.

"I don't want that, Mum. I just want to go. All I ask is that you, and maybe some of the kids, see me off at South Station. I don't want the other fellas thinkin' I'm an orphan or somethin'."

"We'll all be there, Joseph. Though I can't speak for your father."

"Mum, I don't really care if he--" Joe angrily held his hands out.

Norah shook her right index finger. "Joseph Frances King, I don't want to hear it." She brought her hands together and said, "Know that I understand and let that be enough. Please."

South Station
BOSTON, MASS.

CHAPTER 7

"Nobody who has not been in the interior of a family can say
what the difficulties of any individual of that family may be.
PRIDE AND PREJUDICE
JANE AUSTEN

AFTER A BEVY OF DESSERTS—COCONUT cream pie, pineapple upside-down cake, individual butterscotch puddings with whipped cream—and before the requisite game of charades, Cordelia and her college friends lingered at the table nibbling candy from the miniature glass baskets at each place setting. The aunties picked theirs up and retired to the parlor for catnaps. Caroline and Price Parker walked Eleanor Brewster, her husband Sinclair, and their baby boy to the front gate. Young Jonathan needed his nap too.

"Thank you so much," Eleanor said as Price lifted the black, cast-iron latch. "This was a perfect Easter Sunday."

"Well, Eleanor, it was Providence, meeting as we did last week." Caroline stroked the baby's hair. "Oh, to have a son." She extended an open invitation to his doting parents. "What a delight to have your family at our Easter table. We'll have to make it a tradition."

Price Parker II was six foot two with boyishly mussed gray-brown hair; two cowlicks prevented every strand from staying in place. He had a tendency to hold his chin up, and a generally reserved manner. Dressed in Brooks Brothers clothing—white dress shirt, bow tie, suspenders and pinstriped navy suit—he tenderly patted baby Jonathan's back and heartily agreed. "Absolutely."

The young people were still seated at the dining table and making plans.

"Who's in for a walk on the Common after charades?" one of the boys asked, tipping his chair back, precariously balancing on the legs. Another did the same, although their rocking was at odds; when one came to, the other went fro. Cordelia's older brother, Pip, sat forward, both hands on the edge of the table, looking as if he was ready to push off at any moment.

The Buddies' Club

"That's a terrific idea. Bet they've got music at the Buddies' Club tonight. Probably the only place in town that does."

Located on Boston Common, the Buddies' Club provided hospitality to the armed services. Young women volunteers served coffee and donuts, and in many instances, met their future spouses at the club.

Price Irving Parker III, "Pip," was the image of his good-looking father, but the similarity ended there. Pip was interested in all things glamorous and fast—nightclubs, cars, and cocktails—and according to his Harvard roommate, he was quite experienced with the ladies.

Pip had been nicknamed after his mother's imaginary first love, Pip, from Charles Dickens's "Great Expectations," and the summary of his own initials. Caroline had great expectations, indeed, for her only son and favorite child, "My Pip."

Cordelia's good-natured, closest male friend, George Leland, the only young man at the table still wearing a jacket, beamed his best smile and knocked on the white damask-covered table for emphasis. "You need to be a serviceman to get into the Buddies' Club, remember?"

George, tall and reed thin, his receding ash-blond hair combed straight back, was a divinity student at Harvard. And the gang could always, if not reluctantly, depend on him to be their moral compass.

"That doesn't mean we can't stand outside and listen, does it, George?" chic Abigail Dubois asked. Her dark hair coiffed in a Buster Brown cut, and flirty brown eyes mischievously looking here and there, she rhythmically clinked a silver teaspoon on the crystal goblet before her. The others gaily followed suit. Clink, clink, clink, sounding like a would-be Lilliputian band.

Pip turned to Abby. "Maybe you'll meet a good-looking sailor boy?"

Abigail continued to play her silver spoon tune. "Knowing my luck, he'll probably be Irish and from South Boston."

Cordelia, dallying with her pudding, was sitting right next to Abby. "Well, Abigail, he could look like the movie star Tyrone Power. That wouldn't be half-bad now, would it?"

They all laughed.

Brawny Spencer Clark—better known as Skip—member of the Harvard rowing team, heir to his family's banking business, and designated mascot of their gang because he was the youngest, chimed in, "Careful there, Miss So-and-So. My father says some of his best workers are from Southie. It could happen, Abby. You'd fall in love with his Irish eyes, marry, and establish your own "Blue Heaven" on the first floor of a charming three-decker."

The entire table broke into the popular song, following George's lead.

Abigail and her three sisters were all named for American first ladies. While studying at the Sorbonne, her mother fell in love with and married a French architectural student. Mindful of her Yankee lineage, Mrs. Dubois chose to give her daughters names that would leave no doubt they were all American girls:

Dolley Madison Dubois,
Abigail Adams Dubois,
Martha Washington Dubois,
and Grace Coolidge Dubois.

Sarah Armstrong, Cordelia's college roommate, threw a jellybean at George and giggled. "George Leland, you're positively appalling." Sarah was pleasingly plump, and her flaxen hair was arranged in curls that were drooping more by the minute. She had a flawless but pale complexion and a nondescript style, other than to say it was extraordinarily plain. Always proper, Sarah had an ability to giggle, as Cordelia would say, "like nobody's business." An Ohio native, she attended Radcliffe through the generous inheritance of a deceased maiden aunt, majored in journalism, and dreamt of writing the great American novel. Her friends said she was destined to be a clergyman's wife because Sarah blushed whenever George Leland was around, and because it was absolutely reciprocal.

Pip was brilliant at staying in his parents' good graces, despite their disapproval of his social choices. When he saw his father walking past the dining room, Pip asked the others, just loud enough to resonate into the hall, "How about a game of charades? Our parents would be disappointed if we didn't play at least one round."

Only family and close friends called Cordelia, "Cap," or "Cappy," her mother's clever blend of Cordelia Anne Parker's initials and a whimsical reference to Shakespeare's Juliet Capulet, the lovely young maiden who knew true love but never married.

Abby proposed a plan. "Let's play right now, so we can take that walk before it gets too late." She stood—Spencer helped with her chair—and she turned to Cordelia. "Cappy, may I borrow a coat? Looks like it's getting cold out there, and I merely have that light spring dress jacket I wore to church this morning."

"Of course. I have just the one! And it's in your best colors." Cordelia paused and smiled. "Red, red, red. No one wears red as well as you do, Abby. I'll go upstairs and get it right now. Excuse me, all."

Caroline Parker was on her way to the parlor, carrying an open, egg-shaped box of Fannie Farmer chocolates, when Hilda approached her.

"Mrs. Parker, your presence is needed upstairs. Miss Cordelia is all in a dither."

"Why, Hilda, what could she possibly be upset about after such a lovely Easter dinner?"

"I think it's best if you ask her, Mrs. Parker." Hilda walked toward the kitchen.

"You and Cook certainly outdid yourselves this year."

Hilda turned around. "Thank you, Mrs. Parker."

"The pineapple-raisin sauce was perfect. And I so enjoyed that new turnip-potato dish. Oh my, I'm afraid I'm doing it again, circumventing the subject at hand. I'll go upstairs right now. Please tell Mr. Parker I'll only be a minute, will you? Oh, and if my turn at charades comes up while I'm gone, tell them you'll be filling in for me. My Price is such a stickler for order."

Hilda was unnerved at the thought of pantomiming. *I'll make a fool of myself. What do I know about the kind of books they read? And moving pictures?*

"Mrs. Parker, wouldn't you prefer I set the sideboard for a light supper? I'm sure everyone will be hungry before bedtime."

"Very well, Hilda, but deliver my message nonetheless. I don't want our guests to feel I've abandoned them. Oh, and Hilda, you needn't have been so skittish about charades." Caroline smiled and adjusted the cuffs of her new white silk blouse beneath the sleeves of last year's light, jade boucle suit.

"Thank you, Mrs. Parker." Hilda inclined her head in a bow and entered the parlor as her employer ascended the spiral staircase. Price Parker's ancestors peered out from exquisitely framed oil portraits on Caroline's left, and she nodded to each. *How pleased you must be to see the family home filled with such happiness and good fellowship. Your efforts are rewarded.*

Caroline knocked softly on the open door before entering her daughter's spacious bedroom, its walls covered in a petite, green-rose-and-buttercream, floral-striped wallpaper, the twin, four-poster beds skirted in natural linen, and made-up with pristine white sheets, ivory blankets, and butter cream coverlets turned back, revealing Cordelia's monogram on the top sheet, $\mathcal{CPA}$. Quilted linen spreads, piped in rose, were tiered like layer cakes at the foot of each bed and coordinating pillows were neatly tossed on a sizable window seat.

When Sarah and Abby saw Cordelia's bedroom, they swooned. Sarah said, "Jeepers, Cappy, this is gorgeous." And Abby quipped, "My mother would never trust me or my sisters with such elegance."

Caroline was stunned to see clothing and hangers all askew on one of the beds, with more thrown on a dressing table chair and across the window seat. Her daughter appeared to be frantically looking for something in the closet when Caroline inquired, "Cordelia, what's the meaning of this?"

Cordelia Anne Parker—tall like her mother, and nice-looking, though not quite as pretty, with the pear-shaped build of the women in her father's family, dressed in a new, mauve, Scottish-tweed suit—abruptly turned on the right heel of her black kid pump. "Mother, I'm trying to find my red coat. And I distinctly remember hanging it at the back of this closet. Hilda mentioned spring cleaning before running from the room saying something about you possibly giving it away. Is that correct, Mother? Did you give my coat away? Why would you do such a thing without asking me first?" Cordelia folded her arms, and slightly tipped her dishwater-blonde head. "Mother?"

Caroline sat on the edge of the bed closest to her. "First of all Cordelia, I don't care for your tone. And before answering any questions, I have one of my own. Why are you suddenly interested in a coat that hasn't been worn for two years?" Caroline Parker had no way of knowing Cordelia intentionally put it out of immediate reach because of who had his arm around the shoulder of the red coat the last time she wore it.

Ever since childhood, Cordelia had loved Norman Alden Prescott—tall, sandy-haired, good-looking and genial, in the most masculine sense—but he preferred being friends. She truly believed it was just a matter of time before he'd see her as someone to build a suitable and pleasant life with. *After all we have everything in common, growing up two streets apart here on the hill, our families spending summers together on the Cape, not to mention Shaw Prep, cotillion, church and our parents' long-standing friendship. Someday he'll see me differently.*

It was two years ago, Cordelia's freshman year at Radcliffe, during winter break and three days after Christmas, when she, Pip, Norman, and his two visiting girl cousins decided to go ice-skating on Boston Common's Frog Pond.

The red coat was new, and Cordelia wanted to look her best so she chose it over a more suitable, shorter one. On the way home, after hours of skating and happiness, it snowed. In the joy of the moment, and in an effort to keep warm, Norman threw one arm around Cordelia's shoulder and the other around his cousin Amy's. Pip had already made his move on Amy's older sister, Alice, and they walked ahead of the others, hand in gloved hand. Cordelia was certainly warm enough—the red coat had a double lining—but she had goose bumps from head to toe. *Norman is actually embracing me.*

After a somewhat stretched out goodbye, Cordelia went straight to her room and lovingly laid the red coat across one of the twin beds, where she could dreamily stare at it. A couple of days later, she hung the cherished garment at the back of her closet for the safest of keeping.

Offering to loan the red coat to Abby was easy, because Abigail Adams Dubois was the one and only person in the world who knew of her unrequited love. And she had promised time and again, "Cappy, I'm keeping my fingers crossed for you and Norman." The hopeful memory would be safe on Abby.

"I'm sorry if I was snippy, Mother." Cordelia pulled a moss-green skirted chair away from her dressing table, retrieved the two pieces of clothing laying over it, and put them on her lap as she sat down. "The boys suggested we take a walk around the Common and Abigail asked if she could borrow a coat. She's such a little bird, not an ounce of fat on her. Did I tell you, Mother? "Bye, Bye Blackbird" has become our nickname for Abby? Well, actually, Birdie. It so suits her pretty little raven-haired being." Cordelia had her mother's penchant for "circumventing the subject at hand," and Pip constantly teased her about it. Cordelia let a smile escape her otherwise serious expression. "Mother, I assured Abby I had one in her best color, 'red, red, red.'"

"Red, red, red?" Caroline smiled too, and sighed. "Cordelia, I'm so sorry about your red coat. But I was under the impression you were through with it. Last Saturday, we were gathering every piece of unused clothing, and Hilda piled it all on the settee in the entry. Your red coat was on top. Two women were here scrubbing our floors, and one very politely asked if she could please have it. That Irish woman didn't ask for herself—simply wanted the coat for her daughter, Rosemary. Isn't that a lovely name, Rosemary?" Cordelia's eyes narrowed as her mother continued. "If I thought for a minute . . . I never would have given it away. Meanwhile, I'm sure we can find something suitable for Abby to wear. How about my three-quarter-length camel hair coat? That should keep her warm enough."

"Mother, I'd like to get my red coat back. Is that at all possible?"

"It's only one coat, Cordelia, and you have many."

"Lovely, Mother. My gorgeous Jordan Marsh coat now belongs to a scrub-woman's daughter."

Caroline was losing her patience. "Oh, for goodness sake. What's done is done Cordelia." She added a comment far more upsetting to her daughter than the issue at hand. "Your brother would never behave in this manner." Caroline began putting clothes back in the closet. "I'll come up here later and get things in order, after you've all left for your walk. For now, let's return to our guests."

Cordelia preceded her mother out of the room in absolute silence but not without thought. *All this upset because some Irish woman had the nerve to ask for my coat. And once again, my brother comes out smelling like a rose.*

Cordelia Anne Parker had lived in the seemingly perfect shadow of her handsome older brother since the day she was born. And her edge, in an otherwise pleasant personality, came from the fruitless pursuit of trying to gain the same kind of love her mother had for Pip, unconditional, preferential, and adoring.

Price and Caroline Parker's second born stopped by the grandfather clock and held her arms, like people do when they are very cold. "I'm sorry, Mother. It's just so upsetting when something you assumed would be in place is missing."

CHAPTER 8

May God be with you and bless you.
May you see your children's children.
May you be poor in misfortune, rich in blessings.
May you know nothing but happiness from this day forward.
IRISH BLESSING

"MA, PLEASE. JUST SIGN HERE."

It was late, eleven thirty. Norah took the paper from John Michael, who'd just returned home from work, and held it beneath the only light on in the kitchen, a small, shaded wall lamp by the stove. She looked back at him and scowled. "And what made you think I'd do such a thing, sign me own boy over to the U.S. Navy when the whole world's threatenin' to go to war?"

"Dad signed this morning, Ma."

"God in heaven. How many times do I have to tell you and your brothers and sisters, don't be callin' me, 'Ma!'"

"Mum, I have to leave. And I think you know that."

"Did you have somethin' to eat at the drugstore? I'm sure Mr. Mac watches out for you."

"Yes, Mum. About five o'clock I had a cheese sandwich and vanilla frappe."

"That was over six hours ago. Here let me scramble you a couple of eggs."

"Mum, it's not workin' out for me around here. And it'll be better for you and the kids too . . . less commotion."

John Michael pulled a chair away from the table. He sat down, slouched, and stretched his legs out in front of him. "It's been a long day's work, Mum." He clasped his hands behind his neck. "I think I'll take you up on those eggs. Can you spare a glass of milk, and maybe some toast too?"

"It'll only take me a few minutes to put it all together. Meanwhile, it'd do you good to close your eyes."

"Not when I'm with the most beautiful girl in Southie."

Norah removed her rosary from the kitchen table, kissed the crucifix, and tucked it in her robe pocket.

"Sorry if I interrupted your prayin', Mum."

"And wouldn't the Mother of God rather I do what needs doin', takin' care of you, than sit at the kitchen table finishin' me prayers with her? She knows I'll be back."

John Michael closed his eyes.

He was doing okay at Gate of Heaven School, liked his summer job at the drugstore, and had eyes for no other girl but Marion Callanan. But Johnny, as most called him, knew he had to leave home before the fights with his father killed him. *Or God forbid, that one of these days I kill my own father.* The prospect of joining the Navy lured him into a different kind of battle, one with honor and the promise of learning a trade. His seventeenth birthday was next Saturday, July 14th, one week away.

The only sound was the sizzling of butter in a small, black iron skillet, then crack, plop, crack, plop. Two eggs went into a bowl, and the distressed mother quickly beat them with a fork. *Holy Mary, Mother of God.* She added a little milk. *Please help me to do the right thing by my Johnny.* She briskly beat the eggs again.

Norah put the plate of steaming-hot food before her son. Straightaway, he slid the Navy document across the table in her direction and laid a pocket pen beside it. "Mum, please."

She picked up the pen, leaned down, reluctantly put her signature on the paper, and silently made the sign of the cross: *In ainm an Athar agus an Mhic agus an sporaid Naoimh. Áméin.* She walked away. "Your toast is comin'."

"Thanks, Mum." John Michael took a bite of eggs, slid the paper back toward him, looked at Norah's signature, and got a lump in his throat. The Navy document was stained with his mother's tears.

It all began when John Michael heard from his friend Lefty Roach that you could enlist in the U. S. Navy at age seventeen if you had your parents' signed permission. Lefty's good news was practically up there with slugger Ted Williams leading the Boston Red Sox with a batting average over .400. Ted made the home team look good, and Johnny had found an honorable escape from his father's wrath.

It seemed easy enough to get approval from his father, who straightaway saw his son's pending enlistment as one less mouth to feed. That is, until he just as quickly realized John's absence would also mean a loss of income for the family. "And what do you think we're supposed to do while you're off enjoyin' yourself? Don't your earnings, meager as they are, help put food on the table? I'm not signin' anythin', and you're not goin' anywhere."

John's father threw the Navy consent form on the living room floor, returned to his newspaper, and searched *The Boston Globe's* obituary column for familiar names.

Rosemary sat on the sofa across from their father hemming a pair of hand-me-down trousers. Norah's mending basket was at her feet, with only one more item that needed attention. She caught John Michael's eye and mouthed, "Sorry." He nodded, walked over to the bowed front window, looked out, and wondered what would come next. The apartment was empty except for the three of them. You could have heard a pin drop, and the silence in the room practically strangled John Michael with its hopelessness.

Suddenly, Rosemary sprang from the sofa and said, "Please, Dad, John, stay where you are. I'll be right back." She picked up the Navy document from the floor on her way. *Dear God in heaven, please keep everything calm in there until I get back.*

Norah left early that morning to go grocery shopping, and brought Timmy and Tommy with her to help carry the treasured bundles home. Sullivan's Surplus had sent word to thirteen-year-old Pat they needed help sorting items salvaged from the Old Colony building site, beginning Saturday morning. Sully's cousin's wife's brother-in-law, a foreman on the site, arranged for Sully's crew to pick up "surplus" at the end of every work week "after midnight, when it's not so busy."

"Old Colony Housing Project, a complex of three-story brick buildings, 843 units in all, built for low and moderate-income individuals and families, sits on 15 acres of land across the street from Carson Beach."

South Boston: My Home Town
Thomas H. O'Connor

And Rita left bright and early for her Saturday job in the lingerie department at Grants where she learned all the neighborhood ladies' secrets. "Mum, did you know Mrs. Curran wears two girdles at a time? Says it makes her look a lot slimmer. Mum, she doesn't look slim at all. She's built like a battleship."

"I wonder if Mr. Grant would want you workin' in his store knowin' you're comparin' one of his best customers to a war vessel. Mind your tongue now, Rita Margaret, or God will punish you."

"I'm sorry, Mum." Rita tucked her soft auburn curls behind each ear. "But can I just tell you about Mrs. Day?"

"Absolutely not." Norah smiled at the daughter who never ceased to make her laugh.

Kay, Rosemary and Johnny were all home on Saturday mornings, and Norah expected them to help around the house. "You're the oldest now and need to be settin' a good example for the others."

Kay and Rosemary had nine-to-five, Monday-through-Friday clerical jobs, Rosemary worked for the Carney Hospital and Kay assisted the bookkeeper at O'Toole Bros. Furnace Sales, Installation & Repair – Family Owned Since 1918. To Norah's absolute pride, both girls had high school diplomas and took advanced education classes at night.

John Michael worked all day Monday, Wednesday, and Friday, and on Saturdays from noon to eleven o'clock closing, at Morris's Pharmacy and Fountain on the corner of Broadway and H, where he did a little bit of everything—stocking, sweeping, prescription delivery—but mostly worked the fountain. Johnny King made ice-cream sodas, sundaes, and frappes with such flair that people who came in for medication, cosmetics or sundries made it a point to stop by the fountain because of the young man pharmacist George McDonough had come to call, "my cracker-jack soda jerk."

When concocting ice cream sodas, Johnny would throw a glass in the air with one hand, turn around, catch it with the other, twirl the ice cream scooper, and ask, "What'll you have, strawberry, chocolate, vanilla, or coffee?" Then he'd raise the soda water hose as high as it would go and squirt "bubbly" into each glass with an exaggerated up and down motion. He did the same with milk and whipped cream too. When it was time to put a maraschino cherry on top, Johnny'd wink and say, "Cherry for your thoughts." The girls loved him.

Although Kay said she was going on a walk that day with her friends, Rosemary and Norah knew better. Kay would be "steppin' out" with Steve Chalpin, a Polish young man her father had forbidden her to see. She'd secretly talked marriage to her sisters. "Why should we wait? Steve's twenty-three and has a good job, and I'll be through with my accounting courses at Katherine Gibb's before you know it. I don't care if he isn't Irish. He's the kindest man I've ever known and I want to become his wife before he finds another." But she wouldn't leave before completing her part of the housework as requested.

"Barbara Catherine, there are a few things that need doin' before you go anywhere. Please run a dust mop throughout the place, and don't forget under the beds. Take the sheets and towels off the clothesline, fold them, and put everything away. I don't want laundry lyin' about. That's a good girl. And John Michael, I need you to put a bit of polish to the stove. It's lookin' rather neglected. You'll find the stove black under the sink. Thank you. I'll see you later then." The high heat of cooking left Norah's cast-iron stove ashen, and spills rusted it. The waxy stove black was liberally applied, left to dry, and polished. A well-blackened stove was considered a sure sign of good housekeeping.

Norah left Rosemary with a small basket of mending, and instructions to help Kay. "If you could iron the little boys' Sunday shirts, and please tip the chairs to make the dust moppin' easier for your sister. Many hands make light work. Oh and girls, be sure to ask your father if he needs you to fix him somethin' to eat. Please don't forget. I'll leave it at that."

83

Rosemary went as fast as she could to the room she and her sisters shared, put the Navy document on top of the dresser, opened the closet door, and pushed wire hangers aside one by one until she found what she was looking for, the Jordan Marsh garment bag that held her red coat. *I hope I'm doing the right thing. If Johnny doesn't leave this house it's just a matter of time before our father—He has a better chance of surviving the war, and if he doesn't—Blessed Mother, please send me a sign that I'm doing the right thing.* Rosemary blessed herself before reaching into one of the red coat's pockets.

Her sister Kay walked in, having just returned from a stroll on Castle Island with her "friends." The delicious aroma of fried clams and French fries came in with her.

Kelly's Landing
South Boston, Mass.

Kelly's Landing was the place for "South Boston caviar" (fried clams) and French fried potatoes (best with a sprinkling of vinegar) and was extremely popular with young people. If money was scarce you could always manage to find enough change for a cup of clam chowder. And if you had a regular job like Steve Chalpin, you could order anything you or your sweetheart wanted. Kay and Steve called Kelly's "our place."

"Hi, Ro. What in the world are you doing?"

"I'm trying to save Johnny's life by giving Dad cash to make up for the money that won't be coming in."

"Okey-dokey. Um, would you like to fill me in on the details?"

Kay sat with a bounce on the double bed she and Rosemary shared, kicked both shoes off, and began rubbing her feet. "My dogs are barking. I really should wear socks on these long walks, but they make my legs look stumpy."

After hurriedly telling her sister about Johnny's request and their father's ultimatum, Rosemary explained, "I'll be bringing in more money after I start that new job next week." She'd completed her night school studies and secured, as her mother told anyone who'd listen, "one of those grand civil service situations with the benefits and all." In her new job, Rosemary Virginia King would report downtown each morning before returning to Southie and making her rounds as a social worker.

Rosemary held a handful of cash neatly secured with a rubber band. "This money should keep Dad happy until my first paycheck."

Kay, shocked by Rosemary's proposal, spoke from the top of her heart. "Do you mean to say that you're paying our father to send our brother away, possibly off to war?" But Kay knew it was the only thing to do and went to the dresser the sisters had shared since childhood, opened one of the two bottom drawers that were hers, and reached for a pair of little, brown, buckled shoes tucked in the back corner beneath a small stack of undies.

"I always forget which shoe I hide my money in."

"It's the right one, Kay."

"Ro!"

"Your secret's safe with me. I was looking for my sweater clip and thought you may have borrowed it. That's the only reason I opened your drawer. When I did, the change jingled, and I was curious. Kay, I didn't' realize you kept Nonie's shoes. Does Mum know?"

"She doesn't. Ro, I just couldn't part with them. Noni's our angel, we've said that all along, and I knew she'd watch over the money.

"I miss her, Kay."

"Me too, Ro."

⋙

Noni was the second youngest of the four King girls and smallest in stature, with an uncanny ability to jump high and long, earning her the reputation of being the "best jump roper in Southie," as her girlfriends bragged when they split into competing teams. Noni's light step and endurance didn't go unnoticed by adults either.

Mrs. Moira Brennan, who taught Irish dancing in the basement of her home, which she preferred to call "a small studio of me own," saw the tiny girl's potential to be a champion Irish dancer, and she asked Norah time and again, "Won't you please let your daughter give it a try?" Finally, she realized the modest fee was beyond

In Southie they had a saying, "In this neighborhood a fella's got four choices: He can go into the service, be a cop, a priest, or a criminal." None of the King brothers became priests.

the family's reach. "Norah King, wouldn't you be doin' me the best of favors if you'd let your Noni be my first, I believe it's called, protégé? Sure and she's the ability to put South Boston on the map with her gift of movin' like a fairy."

"All right then, Moira. We'll give it a go. My Noni dancin' to your own tune."

The elated patron thought of everything. "Norah King, would you do me the additional favor of allowin' your Noni to wear my Kathleen's green velvet dress for the competition? Sure and it's full of good luck, for didn't Kathleen place first in her division wearin' one and the same?"

Moira Brennan grinned from ear to ear whenever Noni was in the studio. It was as if the girl had been taking lessons on the sly. That's how good she was. "You're a born dancer, Noni King. And won't you be the showstopper of all time with leaps as high as your own?"

"Thank you, Mrs. Brennan," Noni said. She pulled up her socks and ran and hugged her benefactor's legs. "Thank you for letting me come here." This little girl was going to make everyone look good. Her first competition was only a week away when the dreadful accident occurred. Noni King was run over by a delivery truck. She was eight years, six months, and nineteen days old.

Norah King baked her own bread, saving some of the dough to roll into little knots she deep fried and dipped in sugar as a special treat for her children. John Joseph favored rye bread, which Norah didn't bake. Buying it was a luxury, but she liked to please her husband. And so, from time to time, she would send one of the children to the grocery store for "a loaf of that good Jewish corn rye for your father." That day, it was Noni's turn, and she was excited to be entrusted with the one errand that would make her father happy.

The little girl with the curly, strawberry-blonde bob, an oversized yellow bow holding some of her locks in place, lay in the street on her stomach, her pastel plaid dress embossed with tire marks. When police arrived on the scene, they gently turned her over and saw a cherub face with a sprinkling of freckles and eyes still wide open in terror.

Officer McCarthy pulled out his handkerchief and wept, while Officer Palma removed his coat and covered the dead child. Coincidentally, they'd been only a half block away when an alarmingly loud screech of brakes caused them to run and see if anything of consequence had taken place. Although this was their regular beat, the policemen had no way of knowing who the girl was.

There were so many children, who could keep track of them all? It was early morning with very few people around, and those that were didn't know who she was either.

The policemen moved Noni King to the sidewalk, and left her in the care of an elderly couple who'd been out for a morning stroll. They asked another witness to telephone the police department, and demanded the driver of the delivery truck stay put until the other officers arrived. "Jesus, pal. How fast were ya goin'? What ya got in the truck that's worth the life of this innocent little girl?"

They tenderly removed her small shoes and went door to door asking, "Do these belong to anyone in your house?"

The two policemen heard fiddle music as they climbed the stairs to the Kings' apartment, and they knocked on the door with a heavy rap. Kay, age eleven at the time, ran and opened it, only to see her younger sister's shoes in the hand of Officer McCarthy. "Do you recognize these, young lady?" he asked.

"I think they belong to my sister," Kay answered, frowning with bewilderment. "She just went to the store for my mother. She'll be right back."

Norah came up behind Kay, saw the shoes and gasped. "Officers, where is she? Where's my daughter? What's happened?"

Once again Officer McCarthy pulled out his handkerchief and Officer Palma delivered the painful news. "I'm afraid there's been an accident Mrs. . . ."

By the look on the officers' faces, she knew that her small daughter's life had been taken. Norah bent down and whispered into Kay's ear, "Go get your father." As she stood, she pushed her and hysterically cried, shaking her hands as if reaching for something, "Get your father! And tell the others to stay where they are."

Norah King took the shoes from Officer McCarthy, held them to her chest, closed her eyes, opened them again and began swaying, the way mothers do when they want to keep their babies from crying. "Noni. Her name is Noni, short for Norah, like meself. Norah Virginia King and she's eight years old. Where is she, Officer? Where's my—"

Just then John Joseph appeared with a smile, the fiddle and bow held together in his left hand as he amiably extended his right. "Mornin', Officers. What's goin' on here? Have me boys been up to some kind of mischief?"

Trembling, Norah held out the shoes. "John . . ."

He took them from her and laid his fiddle and bow on a small table by the door. Confused, he asked, "What's the meaning of this? Aren't these Noni's shoes? Or are they Rita's? But wait, Rita's in the . . ." He looked over his shoulder. "Kitchen." He looked back at the police officers. And as if someone held up a sign with the answer, he knew. He bowed his head and ran his hand over his thick hair. "God Almighty." The panic-stricken father practically threw the shoes at Kay. "Hold onto these." John Joseph ran after Norah who'd already pushed past the policeman, crying, "Noni, Noni darlin, I'm comin'," as she ran down the stairs.

Norah and John's footsteps sounded like thunder on the bare wood stairs, and her cries pierced the air with alarm. Other apartment doors opened, and the landlord shouted as the couple ran past him, "What is it? What's happened?"

Norah kept crying out Noni's name, and John demanded, "Where is she Nor'?" following her lead down the dewy, early morning streets.

"I sent her to the store for a loaf of that rye bread."

Neither one was prepared for what they saw next. A paddy wagon, ambulance, and countless men, women, and children were crowded on the street in front of Mulkerrin's Grocery Store with several policemen saying, "Break it up now. Move along folks. Let's show some respect here." Officers Palma and McCarthy were running close behind the distraught couple, and one yelled, "Make way for the girl's parents."

The curious crowd parted, creating a path no parent wants to take and sight no mother or father should ever have to endure. Norah reached Noni first, fell to her knees, and pulled back the officer's jacket. She took her second youngest daughter into her arms and rocked back and forth, keening, "*Éirigh agus seas suas. Éirigh agus seas suas.*" Rise and stand up. Rise and stand up.

John stood straight as a rod before his wife and daughter, arms folded across his chest and legs apart. Turning toward the crowd, and sheltering Norah and Noni as best he could, his

GIRL FATALLY HURT BY TRUCK IN SOUTH BOSTON

Norah V. King, 8, of 2 E Street, South Boston was fatally injured by a truck while crossing the street. The operator, Harold Geisler of South Boston, was booked at the Athens St. Police Station on the technical charge of manslaughter and released on bail for appearance in the South Boston District Court.

The Boston Globe
Saturday, July 20, 1929

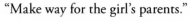

arms sprang from their locked position and his hands, knotted in fists, shook as he furiously shouted, "Have you no decency? The child is gone. Haven't you seen enough? Go home!"

It's said that God doesn't give us more than we can bear, but "the tragedy," as it came to be known, met John Joseph's family predisposition for the drink outside a pint or two after work. It marked the end of family joy, and beginning of drunkenness, violence, and financial strife beyond Norah's ability to stretch a dollar. Eventually, John only paid the rent, and more times than not, the electricity. The rest: coal, food, clothing, school supplies, medicine, and everything else, was up to Norah and the children.

∞

"Here, Ro, add this too. Now all we have to do is pray the old man doesn't drink every penny of it."

"Of course he'll drink every penny, Kay. I'm only giving half to him and the other half to Mum later on." Rosemary had two five-dollar bills, seven singles, and now with Kay's three dollars, twenty in all. She chose to give her father the ten singles hoping the sheer volume would please him and sway his thinking.

"Thank you, Kay. With all my heart, thank you." Rosemary tucked the rest of the money in the sleeve of her cardigan sweater and reached for her sister. They held hands and exchanged a look of surety as Rosemary said, "John Michael will come back to us, Kay. He'll come back," while the roar of their father's shouting echoed down the hall.

"Rosemary, where the hell are you?"

∞

John Michael King walked to church on Sunday morning a new man. He slipped out of the apartment early to avoid going with his family, and so he could meet Marion Callanan without his siblings jibing, "John, whose yer girlfriend?" Or as Timmy had teased last week when he saw Marion wave to Johnny from a distance, "Oh, Johnny boy, I've been waiting for so long." This way there wouldn't be anything to be concerned about other than the preferred company of "the one."

89

John pulled the Navy paper out of his shirt pocket. *Will ya look at that. They both signed.*

Mr. John J. King - July 5, 1941

Mrs. Norah C. King - July 5, 1941

One week, and I ship out. Now all I have to do is convince Marion it's for the best, and ask if she'll wait for me. Oh God, what if she says no? His heart wandered back to the beginning.

Rita and Marion were the best of friends and each was the sixth child in a large family. The Kings had nine children, and the Callanans beat them with twelve. One day, after the teen girls got ice cream cones at Morris's Drugstore, pharmacist George McDonough teased the soda jerk, "Ah, John, it's a wonder how you can get a double dip in the single scoop. I don't mind, but you'll want to keep an eye out for Mr. Morris. You never know when he'll walk in."

George Mac, as most called him, chucked Johnny on the shoulder. "You wouldn't be tryin' to impress that cute blonde now would you?"

What Johnny didn't know was that, on the way home, Marion had asked Rita, "Does your brother have a girlfriend?"

"No. But the way you two were making eyes at each other, I think it's pretty safe to say he'll have one pretty soon."

⁓

Marion Callanan was standing right where she said she'd be, by the main doors. "And I'll be there early, so we have plenty of time to say hello, go in, and find a good seat," she'd promised.

That statement surmises just what attracted John Michael King to Marion Louise Callanan, well thought-out planning, dependability and a desire for good. Well, that and a great pair of legs. Lithe Marion was tall, fair-haired, blue-eyed, and according to Johnny, "sharp as a tack, always ahead of the game."

Marion waved. He waved back, began jogging and ran up the church stairs. "Hi doll. You look great." He kissed her on the cheek.

"John, not in front of the church and all these people." She took his hand. "I'm glad you're here though. Come on, let's go in."

"Mar, I have something to show you."

"Can't it wait?"

"No, please, Mar. We still have time." He handed his sweetheart the Navy document. "Read this."

Marion read only as far as she needed to. "Why?"

"I've got to, Marion. You know how it is with the old man." Johnny held the valued paper up in the air, at eye level between the two of them. "Consider this an investment in our future. I'll be able to save some money, and they teach you something, Mar. I can get a real job when I get out. The big question is, are you willing to wait for me?"

Marion began to cry, threw her arms around John Michael, and kissed him right on the lips. "Of course I'll wait for you. No one else could fill your shoes, no one."

CHAPTER 9

On New Year's Eve in days of old, single young Irish girls went to bed
with sprigs of mistletoe, or holly and ivy leaves under their pillows.
According to legend, this hopeful act would bring
a dream of their future husband.
Moments before going to sleep, some might say,
"Oh, ivy green and holly red,
Tell me, tell me, whom I shall wed?"

IRISH LEGEND

"SO, I TOLD THE FELLA next to me, 'See that girl, the one in the red coat? I'm going to marry her one day.'" Tony Williamson loved to tell his "the first time I saw Rosemary" story. "That fella thought I was dreaming. Rosemary far outclassed me when it came to looks, and besides that her friends thought I was a stick in the mud. She enjoyed a good time and was always laughing. They simply couldn't imagine the two of us together. And for a while, neither could she but I finally brought her over to my side. Must have been my Italian charm."

The reference to being Italian was made tongue in cheek. Tony's name was misleading, and when it went before him, most people thought they would be meeting an Italian, including Rosemary's father, John Joseph King who'd roared, "No daughter of mine is steppin' out with a goddam guinea."

Scotch Irish, Tony Williamson was an only child, whose parents married late and, against all odds, miraculously conceived. They gave Saint Anthony, to whom they prayed night and day, fearing Mrs. Williamson's fertility had been lost to an advanced age, all the credit. And when it came to naming their son, they paired the patron saint of things lost, Anthony, with Ignatius, the patron saint of generosity, believing God exceedingly generous in giving them such a healthy baby boy. There wasn't an ounce of Italian blood in Anthony Ignatius Williamson, but you couldn't convince John Joseph King that someone named Tony wasn't a "wop."

At the time, the Jesuit-founded Boston College was primarily a commuter school and almost exclusively for male students.

Tony was tall and lean with a long neck, observant hazel eyes, and straight brown hair save the slight wave where he combed it back, and though he and his widowed mother were of modest means, he had the carriage of an aristocrat. His keen intelligence and clever way with words won him a scholarship to Boston College where he majored in business. One night, as the story goes, after a Christmas concert, there was a party in Milton, at his friend Don Campbell's family home. And when one of the other BC "fellas," James Sheehan, walked in the door with his sister, Patricia, and her best friend, Rosemary King, for Tony, it was love at first sight.

The Campbell home looked like houses Rosemary had only seen in Christmas cards. Visible from the main road, the thirty-eight-room Victorian mansion, with glowing candles in every window, sat atop a long, sloping hill—the surrounding snow undisturbed, as if in preparation for the perfect Christmas party. At first, Rosemary thought the meandering, freshly plowed driveway was a street. James Sheehan slowly drove up to the porte cochere in a Ford coupe his uncle had loaned him for the night, and his sister, Patricia, spoke first. "James, you actually know these people?"

"Just the son," her brother answered.

Rosemary was astonished by the mansion's size. "Can you imagine living in such a place, Patricia? Oh, I can't wait to see what it looks like inside." She thought of her mother, and how they'd sit at the kitchen table later that night, and she'd share every detail about the party.

"Are they snobby, James?" Patricia asked, peeking over the front seat. "If they're snobby, I'm not going in."

"Come on, Patsy. We're going to have a great time. Don Campbell's a real, regular guy. One of the few I know who isn't working his way through BC, but I never would have guessed he came from this kind of money." James put the stick shift in neutral.

"Pop says that when the money's old, there's nothing to prove. Bet we're looking at an ancient fortune here. All right, I'm freezing. Let's go in." Patsy tilted the rear view mirror in her direction, pushed a few curls back in place and bit her lips to a fresh-faced pink.

They climbed a broad stone stairway to a deep terrace overlooking the property and went up more steps to the enormous, wreath-adorned front door, which was wide open, letting in the cold. Others had walked in only a moment before them. James turned to make sure no one else was coming, and tentatively closed the door, sealing in peals of merriment that had called all the way from the drive.

There was an air of gaiety and an abundance of guests, laughter, music, and holiday joy as people greeted each other with pats on the back, handshakes, hugs and air kisses. All the while, heads turned this way and that, looking beyond the person in front of them, and taking note.

Straight ahead was a grand, carved, dark wood staircase. Evergreen garlands tied with red satin ribbons festooned the railings, and midway up was a stained-glass window as large as any Rosemary had ever seen in a church. Except this one had an elaborate floral design. *What a shame to have something that special without a saint, our Blessed Mother, or the Holy Family gracing it.*

Arty Feeney and Tony Williamson were sitting on that very staircase, discussing Boston College's amazing victory over Tennessee in the last Sugar Bowl. It had been almost a year since the traditional New Year's Day game but as loyal Eagles, they relished going over the 19-13 victory, play by play, time and again. Then Rosemary arrived.

Later Tony would say that once he saw her "Arty's words sounded like they were coming from the bottom of a barrel." Everything was secondary to the radiant blonde in the exquisite red coat.

"Williamson, I don't think you heard a word I said." Arty waved his hand in front of Tony's eyes. "Williamson?"

"You see that girl over there, the one in the red coat? I'm going to marry her one day," Tony declared.

"Whoa! Who's that? Little Red Riding Hood, come to Papa. And look at those gams."

"Knock it off, Arty." Tony smiled, and stood up. "Come on, Mr. Feeney. Introductions are in order."

Rosemary went through the motions of removing her coat with James's assistance. "Here let me help you with that, Ro," he said as he lifted the coat off her shoulders and thought of how very good she smelled. Her fragrance was nothing more than soap, water, and Castile shampoo.

Girls in Southie called James a real catch because of his striking black Irish looks, athletic build, and promising future. "Jimmy Sheehan's going places. He's a college man," they'd swoon.

To Rosemary, he was simply Patsy's older brother, who always seemed to have a five o'clock shadow. James, who his family called "Plan man," because he was so good at reaching his goals, had big dreams: a college degree, law career, and life beyond Southie with Rosemary as his wife.

If Betty Boop had a less cute but prettier sister, it would have been petite Patsy Sheehan with her doll-like face, dark hair, and cerulean-blue eyes. James was the first in his family to go to college, and Patricia had established the small flower concession in their father's grocery store with the as yet undisclosed intent of opening her own "high-class floral shop" downtown one day.

Although James and Patsy's family owned a successful corner market in South Boston, it wasn't quite profitable enough to put their only son through Boston College. Breaking one of Boston's Blue Laws, which forbade the selling of alcoholic beverages on Sunday, paid for most of James's tuition. During the week, groceries went out the front door, but on Sundays, Mr. Sheehan's brother-in-law ran the illegal liquor business out the back door. The only stipulation made for purchase was that customers request it for "medicinal purposes," thus easing their consciences of any wrongdoing and avoiding "God forbid, bringing the place down with a curse for doin' regular business on a Holy Day of Obligation."

Sheehan's Grocery, Fresh Produce, and Meats was a perfect front for such goings-on, and was fiercely protected from the authorities by Southie's close knit community, including native son Police Officer Regan, who often enjoyed "a little pop" at the end of his beat, which happened to pass right by Sheehan's.

"And how are you doin' this fine day, Officer?" Colin Sheehan would inquire of his friend, Daniel Regan. The two men who had known each other their whole lives; made their First Communion and Confirmation together; played kickball in the same vacant lot; pilfered penny candy from that very store when it was owned by the Muldoon family; chased waves at Carson beach every summer and shoveled snow in front of Saint Peter and Paul's every winter, as all altar boys were required to do; danced at each other's weddings; and mourned parents now gone, would take the time to enjoy a bit of refreshment.

Around five o'clock, they'd sit out back on wooden crates pushed against the grocery store's brick wall. In the winter, they retreated to the shelter of Colin's cramped office, where they clinked teacups that never saw a cuppa with a familiar "*Slainte*," and more often than not, jumped at the chance to bless and amuse each other with a variety of Irish toasts.

Colin Sheehan took his "tea" leaning forward, hunched over. "Dan, just remember, God is good, but never dance in a small boat."

Officer Regan preferred to lean back and hold the cup and saucer close to his face. Sip. Clink back in the saucer. Sip. Clink. "I'll keep that in mind." Daniel Regan put his cup down, stood up, took his hat off, and held it respectfully across his chest. "Here's to Clare O'Hara, for her life it held no terror. Born a virgin. Died a virgin. No runs. No hits. No errors."

Saints Peter and Paul's Catholic Church & Rectory
SOUTH BOSTON, MASS.

James was duly impressed by the grandeur of the Campbells' home. He'd never been anywhere like this in his life. Impressed but not overawed. James liked who he was and where he came from. *But what a perfect place to bring Rosemary.*

In the middle of the mansion's grand entry, a round, marble-topped table held a huge floral arrangement of white roses, holly, and pine. Evening bags surrounded the sizable cut-crystal vase like clockwork, and Patricia tried to look nonchalant as she circled the table admiring each one, and finally placed her own simple, black, embossed-satin drawstring next to a golden-chained, plum needlepoint.

Rosemary peeked around the other guests into the expansive but still-crowded parlor, where a massive Christmas tree gave the room a warm, welcoming atmosphere, and the glow of its lights made everyone look, "just dreamy," as she later told her sisters.

All at once, Rosemary, Patsy, and James heard the most melodious voice, "Hello. I'm so sorry I wasn't here to greet you when you arrived." They turned to see the lady of the house, dressed in a dark green, brocade coat dress, its small rhinestone buttons catching glints of light from nearby candles.

"I was making sure things were coming along in the kitchen. Welcome. I'm Mrs. Campbell, and you, I assume, are friends of one of my sons."

"Why, yes, I am," James answered. "Don and I have a couple of classes together at Boston College. I'm James Sheehan. This is my sister Patricia, and my date, Rosemary King."

It caught Rosemary off guard to be called James's date.

"Nice to meet you," was exchanged by all, with James adding, "Thank you for opening your home," just as Mr. Campbell walked up to them and handed his wife a cocktail.

"You're a dear," Mrs. Campbell said as she received the exquisite short glass bearing an etched C monogram. Rosemary noticed she was wearing red nail polish, which in her neighborhood, because of the nun's strictly imposed standards, was considered cheap. However, here in this setting, it looked lovely. And she noted Mrs. Campbell's hands were without chafing or scratches, as if they were taken out of gloves only for special occasions.

"An old fashioned for my old-fashioned girl," Mr. Campbell replied with a wink and toasted his wife with his own glass, and another round of introductions were made.

"Here young man, let me hang up that coat." Mr. Campbell offered. He leaned toward the parlor with a long-armed stretch and was about to put his drink on the baby grand piano.

Mrs. Campbell rushed to his side. "Darling, allow me." She took his glass and placed her cocktail napkin beneath it. Rosemary had never seen a man drink like this, so casually and so slowly. Once her father had a bottle in front of him, most times it stayed there until it was empty.

"Cordelia. Cordelia Parker," Mr. Campbell called, just as he was putting Rosemary's coat in the guest closet. "Give me a minute."

The open door blocked the red coat from view as Mr. Campbell greeted its original owner, Miss Cordelia Parker of Beacon Hill. It was as if heaven had choreographed every move and protected Miss Rosemary King of South Boston from what could have been the most embarrassing moment of her life. Norman Prescott was a close friend of the Campbells' other son, Richard—Harvard man like himself—and he'd invited Cordelia to accompany him to the party.

"Cappy, it's been much too long," Mrs. Campbell said, taking Cordelia's hand. She was delighted to see the daughter of her old friend, Caroline Parker. "Tell me, dear, how are your parents?" Mr. Campbell inquired.

"Doing very well, thank you. They're at Symphony Hall tonight. Daddy and Mother have made *The Messiah* an annual tradition with his aunties."

Cordelia looked toward the others. *Obviously BC people.* Neither girl showed any sign of fine jewelry—no locket, signet ring, or charm bracelet. *Although the pretty blonde's fake pearls are quite attractive.* Cordelia prided herself on knowing who was who and what was what, and her friends found it quite amusing.

Rosemary was nobody's fool, and knew exactly what Cordelia was up to. "I don't believe we've met," she said with all the confidence of a Brahmin, and grace of a girl brought up by a mother such as her own.

Cordelia Anne Parker and Rosemary Virginia King had already engaged in a wordless

"Boston Brahmin" refers to Boston's WASP upper crust. Coined in the article, "The Brahmin Caste of New England," written by Dr. Oliver Wendell Holmes Sr. for the Atlantic Monthly, the term was inspired by India's caste system, in which Brahmin individuals are the highest ranking among Hindus. According to Holmes, Boston's privileged Brahmin society was "harmless, inoffensive, untitled aristocracy."

debate. *Mirror, mirror on the wall, who's the fairest of them all?* Rosemary knew her beauty had the power to please or provoke, and she'd learned how to manage both situations amiably. Cordelia's looks were classically English with a cameo complexion, flaxen hair, full smile and the faintest hint of what some called a "horse face," and others called "patrician." She stood a svelte five feet seven inches and was small bosomed, consequently the darts on her party dress almost looked like vertical seams. Rosemary couldn't help but notice and remembered how one of her friends used to cleverly stuff socks into her brassiere. "Just so I'll have a bump where there needs to be one," her friend would explain..

Rosemary King wasn't the least bit threatened by Cordelia Parker, and Cordelia Parker knew it. *Just look at that self-assured grin. Who does she think she is? Beautiful, I'll give her that. But she's definitely not one of us.* Cordelia was annoyed when Norman was particularly attentive to the unknown trio.

"I don't recall seeing you at any of the other parties," Norman told them. "Say, our whole crowd is going ice skating on the Common tomorrow. Would you like to join us?"

Before they could answer, Mrs. Campbell exclaimed, "My goodness, forgive me," and introduced one and all with Cordelia and Rosemary greeting one another in turn.

"It's a pleasure to meet you."

"I've been admiring your headband." Rosemary sincerely meant what she said about the headband.

Cordelia's pageboy was held off her forehead with a dove-gray faille, silver-dot-studded band. "Oh." She put her hand to it. "My mother gave this to me, and I'm afraid I've worn it tonight only because I thought there was a possibility of her being here later. It's not my taste at all. But thank you just the same. Your name again, please?" Cordelia had made her point.

Norman Prescott found Patricia Sheehan adorable and was pleased when she met his "Nice to meet you," with a sweet smile and "Nice to meet you too." He attempted to resume his earlier invitation. "As I was saying—"

Cordelia put her arm through his. "Norman Prescott, you told Jeff Atwater we'd join him ages ago," she said, pulling him away. "Merry Christmas," she said to the others, waving goodbye with her free hand.

Mrs. Campbell trilled, "We don't want to keep you young people from the festivities one more minute. There's lots of food and drink inside. Please, enjoy yourselves. Merry Christmas."

"Merry Christmas," they all chimed back.

Mr. Campbell offered Mrs. Campbell his arm, and they exited the entry hall chatting as if for the very first time. Rosemary was glad to see people her parents' age living so happily and was stunned to see Mr. Campbell walk past the piano without picking up his drink.

"Well, shall we?" she said to James with a smile and a slightly open hand indicating the parlor. Patricia had already disappeared into the sea of festive holiday attire before them. Velvet, taffeta, fine wool, satin, silk, and cashmere-clad young men and women bobbed amidst waves of laughter, dancing and conversation. Rosemary wished the evening would never end.

The phonograph was turned up to nearly full volume with a lively recording of crooner Bing Crosby and the gleeful Andrews Sisters singing *Jingle Bells*. A quartet of cheery coeds sang along to everyone's enjoyment. Mistletoe hung over several doorways, and eager boys volleyed unsuspecting girls in that very direction. The house smelled of pine, candle wax, a pleasant "something's in the oven," and beneath it all, a subtle floral fragrance. Rosemary thought everyone at the party looked so happy-go-lucky, and she longed for what they all appeared to have, the perfect life.

"Ro, can I get you something to drink?" James inquired as they entered the fray. "There's a punchbowl right over there," he said, pointing the way. "Please, come with me." James Sheehan knew if he left Rosemary alone he'd lose her to one of his friends. In fact, two were walking toward them right now. The tall one caught Rosemary's attention. She liked the way he was dressed. Even though his dark suit was a bit rumpled, his white shirt and red print tie looked good, and the small candy canes he and his friend had hanging from the button holes in their lapels told her he had a sense of humor.

"Merry Christmas, James," they said in unison.

"Tony, Arty, let me present Miss Rosemary King, and my sister, Patricia. Ladies, meet Tony Williamson, the brightest guy at BC, and Arty Feeney, our resident thespian and best Puck this side of the Charles River."

"It's a pleasure to meet you Miss King, Miss Sheehan," they said, one at a time.

"Nice to meet you too, Mr. Feeney, Mr. Williamson." Rosemary said, but she didn't extend her hand, much to their disappointment. Patsy pleasantly nodded in agreement while Tony and Rosemary gave each other coy smiles at the formality of their introductions.

Tony Williamson couldn't keep his eyes off Rosemary and asked himself why he would want to, noting that although slender, she wasn't without curves.

Rosemary King wore a black velvet, princess-styled dress, made by her mother only last week, accessorized with a string of imitation pearls, matching earrings and bracelet, black, mid-high heels, and she preferred to carry the black velvet clutch purse trimmed in tiny pearl accented braid that Patsy's mother had given her, saying, "I don't know why I bought this, Rosy. It's not like Mr. Sheehan and I ever go anyplace that fancy. But it was on markdown at Filene's Basement, and I couldn't resist. Here, you can borrow it, honey. What am I thinking? It's yours."

The contrast of Rosemary's golden hair against the silhouette of her dark dress was striking. She was one of two blondes in her family, with softly waved, shoulder-length hair that was tucked behind one ear and fell just far enough in front of the other. And because Norah had once overheard a Beacon Hill matron caution her own daughter, "Bangs are common. No bangs," Rosemary didn't have any either. "Darlin', you don't know where God will lead your feet once they touch the floor in the mornin', and we certainly don't want you showin' up common- lookin'," Norah had imparted to her beloved daughter.

Patricia wore a brand new, pale blue wool, swing-skirted dress borrowed from her sister; she'd shortened the hem a tad, and managed to get out the door before their mother saw what she'd done. Presently, she waved from across the room, indicating she'd saved seats on one of three sofas. Thrilled, Arty thought she was waving to him, waved back, turned to the others, and said, "Hey, I'll catch you later. I don't want to keep Miss 'five foot two, eyes of blue,' waiting. Nice meeting you, Miss King."

"Merry Christmas," she replied.

James Sheehan lightly put his hand on her back, indicating they'd be moving on, and said, "Tony, Rosemary and I were just about to get some punch." He'd seen the look in Tony's eyes and wasn't about to leave Rosemary with him for a minute. Rosemary, on the other hand, was annoyed by James's presumption because she wasn't his date.

Tony had his own agenda. "James, it's a zoo over there by the punchbowl. With Miss King's permission, I'd be honored to keep her company until you return."

Rosemary glanced toward the crowded refreshment table and saw a young man quickly open a hip flask and liberally pour what looked like whiskey into a punch cup, spilling it in his haste. She was concerned if she went over there, her new dress would be ruined.

Just getting Rosemary to the party had taken every penny she and her mother had between them, and fortunately, the black velvet had been on sale at Grants. Kay had a pair of real silk stockings she was willing to loan her sister, and Rita had put the costume pearl jewelry set on layaway months ago, with all three sisters making payments until it was theirs. Rosemary thanked God for the coat. *And for Mum getting it past Dad by stretching the truth. "Didn't I pick it up in town where they were practically givin' it away?"*

"That's perfectly fine with me, James," she said and glanced at Tony as if to say, "What's next?"

"We'll be sitting right over there." Tony looked toward a window seat.

"Can I get you some punch too, Williamson?" James was trapped, and he knew it.

"No, thanks. I'm all set," Tony said, and raised his cup. "But I'd sure appreciate it if you could bring back a few of those little sandwiches." Turning to Rosemary he asked, "Are you hungry, Miss King?"

"No. Thank you." She opened her purse, tucked her gloves inside, and gazed again toward the parlor. Conversation flowed easily between them. Tony couldn't believe he was actually talking with the girl of his dreams. He sat with his arms folded and legs straight out in front of him, crossed at the ankles. Rosemary caught sight of his well-polished shoes, found his long narrow feet elegant, and admired the genteel ease of his manner.

"So tell me, Rosemary—may I call you Rosemary?"

"Of course. Your formality is unnecessary, Mr. Williamson." They both laughed. She was sitting quite straight—but not stiffly—with her legs tucked close and crossed at the ankles, because her mother and the nuns insisted, "It isn't at all ladylike to cross your legs at the knees." Her hands rested on her lap, to the side.

"If you'll pardon my question, Rosemary, are you and Sheehan an item? I mean are you . . ." Tony nervously tapped his right heel, a habit he would have for the rest of his life.

"Tony, you don't mind if I call you Tony, do you?" Rosemary was still smiling although she was nervous too, and opened and closed her pocketbook. "James Sheehan's like a brother to me. His sister, Patricia, is my closest friend, and he invited both of us to this party. To answer your question, no, we're not an item." She was still smiling.

"Well, I'm delighted to hear it, Rosemary King. And if you don't think it too forward of this fella who's sitting before you, may I have your phone number?"

Rosemary put her pocketbook down on the window seat and turned toward Tony.

"I'm sorry to say—"

"Oh, oh. There's someone . . . else." Tony, captain of the debate team, could barely get the words out.

"My family doesn't have a telephone but you could leave a message with our downstairs neighbors, Mr. and Mrs. Flynn. They have one. And I'll get back to you as soon as I can. Or, you could call Patricia at her father's store, and she'll get word to me. We see each other almost every day."

It wasn't uncommon for a family not to have a telephone in their home. Many relied on the kindness of neighbors who had one to pass along important messages, or allow them to take and make calls of the same nature.

"That'll work out fine." Tony reached in his pocket for a pen. "I'll write the numbers right here on my cuff, that way I won't lose them." He pushed his coat sleeve back.

"What if the ink doesn't come out in the laundry?" Rosemary asked with the familiarity of an old friend.

"I don't consider that a problem," he assured her. "As a matter of fact, I'd regard it as Providence if it never came out."

Tony was on cloud nine and decided to go for broke and ask her for a date right then and there.

"Rosemary, a group of us are going to Blinstrub's on New Year's Eve for dinner and a show. It promises to be quite an evening. Would you consider being my date? I'm sure you'd like some time to think about your answer. May I phone you on Tuesday night?"

"No and yes. No, I don't need time to think about my answer, and yes, I'd enjoy going to Blinstrub's with you on New Year's Eve."

When Tony's friends invited him to come with them on New Year's Eve, he decided to go stag, because New Year's Eve was pretty special, and he didn't want to take just anyone. His friends were merciless. "Hey Williamson, you're not planning on being a priest now, are you?" He could hardly wait to see the looks on their faces when he walked into Blinnie's with Miss Rosemary King on his arm.

Rosemary liked Tony Williamson very much. It wasn't his charm, intelligence, or eagerness that won her over. It was the kindness she saw in his eyes and the way he looked at her.

~ Blinstrub's ~
The Showplace of New England
Delightful Dinners ~ Dancing
Two Shows ~ 8:15 & 11 PM
New Year's Eve
Reservations Include
Show, Dancing, Fun Favors,
Taxes and Tips
Reservations AN 8-7000
300 Broadway, South
Boston, Mass

Blinstrub's held over 850 people and drew the biggest names in entertainment.

Much like Mr. Campbell looked at his wife when she took his arm only a short while ago.

"That's swell, Rosemary. May I still phone you on Tuesday night?"

James Sheehan's hands were full. He balanced two punch cups in one and a plateful of finger sandwiches in the other. "I return with treasures from the table. Hope I didn't keep you waiting too long? Hey Williamson, some people over there were asking for you. Something about New Year's Eve plans. Said I'd send you right their way."

James thought he couldn't have planned his next move better if he'd tried. Tony Williamson was pretty cagey, but now he'd unknowingly provided a perfect segue to James's carefully rehearsed request. Asking Miss Rosemary King to be his date for New Year's Eve.

CHAPTER 10

*That I should love a bright particular star
And think to wed it is so above me.*
WILLIAM SHAKESPEARE

WHEN TONY PICKED ROSEMARY UP at her parents' apartment for their New Year's Eve date, there was, as later described by one of her sisters, "hell to pay."

"Mum, Dad, I'd like you to meet Tony Williamson."

Norah was pleased—*I like the look of him; there's depth in his eyes*—and tickled that her poised daughter was actually blushing. *Now that's a first.*

"Nice to meet you, Mrs. King." Norah's sturdy build and sense of propriety reminded Tony of his own mother.

"And you as well, young man. My daughters been speakin' of nothin' else but your good character."

Rosemary blushed again. "Mum."

Tony put the corsage box in his left hand and extended his right. "Mr. King, how do you do, sir?"

John Joseph looked Tony up and down. "I'm not shakin' the hand of a goddam I-talian. Tony?" He turned to Rosemary and back again to face the young man in question. "Who the hell do you guineas think you are comin' over here to South Boston for our daughters?"

Tony kept cool in the heat of John Joseph's tirade. "Sir, I have—"

Norah reached between them and lightly touched her husband's forearm. "John, they're only goin' out for a nice evenin' now."

John Joseph pulled away and continued to glare.

"Dad, his parents had a special fondness for Saint Anthony." Rosemary began to explain, and then Tony stepped in. "Excuse me, Rosemary."

Tony chose to state his respect for Rosemary, rather than ridiculously deny he had any Italian blood, and looked her father right in the eye. "Mr. King, I have nothing but the best intentions toward your daughter, and you can trust me to be a complete gentleman when we're together."

"Oh, and you're a smooth talker too."

"Dad, please! We have reservations at Blinstrub's, and the others are waiting for us."

John Joseph shooed Rosemary toward the open door. "Go, go on! Go out with him but don't come cryin' to your mother and me, when you're sorry for the day you met this Dago."

He opened the door wider. "Goddam smooth talkin', guinea." The cantankerous father walked toward the kitchen. "Norah, let's have a cup of tea."

Rosemary threw her mother a kiss on the way out, and Norah returned it.

Kay, Rita, Pat, Timmy, and Tommy waited until their father and mother were out of sight and then ran out the door and called down the stairwell.

"Happy New Year!"

"Love birds."

"No kissin' at midnight."

Kay and Rita returned to the couch and nervously waited for their own dates. "I sure hope dad doesn't make a scene again," Rita said.

"Plan on it, kiddo." Kay answered while looking in a compact mirror, freshening her lipstick. "Plan on it."

Kay would be spending New Year's Eve with sweetheart, Steve Chalpin. But his friend, Dan McCole, would be picking her up just to keep the peace.

Norah knew her girls would be concerned, and she soon returned to the living room. "The coast is clear. Your father's gone down the back stairs and to the pub. Your young men will only have me to contend with now." Norah smiled, pulled the lace curtain back, and looked out the window.

When Rosemary and Tony got outside, Arty Feeny and his date were parked at the curb waiting for them. Tony tapped on the windshield "Give us another minute?"

Arty wrote his answer, "OK," backwards on the foggy glass.

"Tony, I'm sorry about everything that happened upstairs." Rosemary had her arms folded against the cold. "I really don't know what to say, other than my father's opinions are not my own, and I'm sorry you had to go through that." Tony watched the breath of her concern fade into the freezing night air.

"Rosemary, it's fine. All that matters is you and me and the fabulous evening we have before us."

Tony presented the ribbon-tied box he'd been holding and gingerly removed a triple-rose corsage. "These are for you, but I'm afraid they pale next to the real thing."

Rosemary took the flowers in her hands and held them up to her face. "Tony they're so beautiful and they smell wonderful"

"May I pin it on?"

"Please."

"I'll try not to stick you."

"I think it would be easier if you let me hold the box." Tony possessed an awkwardness that Rosemary found endearing.

"By the way, I'm glad you're wearing your red coat tonight." Tony stood closer, put one hand beneath her lapel and fumbled with the corsage pin. "I had it in mind when I asked for white roses."

She could hear his steady breathing and got butterflies from the masculine scent of his aftershave. "Roses and Old Spice too, Mr. Williamson. Are all I-talians this suave?"

After several days of persuasion, John Joseph finally believed Rosemary's new boyfriend was indeed Scotch-Irish. But that didn't mean he would be civil to Tony, and he wasn't, ever. John Joseph's rudeness, by and large, escalated with each date.

"So, what are you doin' with my daughter this evenin'?"

"Tell me An-tony, do you know what it is to get your hands dirty? I've a cousin like you, learned, and he's nothin' outside the classroom. Hope you're not like Seamus. You're not now, are you?"

"How much money are they payin' ya at that cushy night job, down there at the *Globe*?"

Tony frequently repeated questions asked of him so he'd have more time to think about his answers, a strategy learned from one of his professors at Boston College.

Rosemary was concerned Tony's suitable, but what her father called "goddammed smart," answers, such as "What do I earn at the *Globe*, Mr. King? Enough to make it worthwhile, sir," would one day be met with a violent outburst.

Soon she suggested they meet somewhere other than her parents' home.

"That'll work out fine during the week, Ro, because of work and school. But I'm not running away from your father."

"You don't know what he's capable of."

"Ro, you don't know what I'm capable of when it comes to you." And neither did Tony, but he thought it sounded good, and refused to be intimidated by a man who'd obviously lost his way to decent behavior.

"Tony Williamson." Rosemary shook her head and gave him the smile that made his knees go weak. "What am I going to do with you?"

"Accompany me to Symphony Hall next Saturday. I'll pick you up at six o'clock, okay?

Boston Symphony Hall

Rosemary Virginia King and Tony Ignatious Williamson stole every moment they could get together. With her night classes and her job at the Carney Hospital, which everyone called "the Carney," and his full-time studies at Boston College and night desk job at *the Globe,* it was challenging. But love forever finds a way, and they frequently met downtown, away from their respective worlds and into one of their own.

Tony seldom had trouble spotting Rosemary, her red coat easy to find among the usual navy-blue, brown, black, khaki, gray, and sometimes green, jackets, coats and hats. More than once, when she walked toward him with that sprightly step of hers, Tony knew that God had sent him someone special and he couldn't decide what shone more, Rosemary's radiant smile, golden hair, or scintillating personality. Time and again a popular tune came to mind: "Got a Date With An Angel."

When Rosemary saw Tony first—which she often did because he stood above the crowd—and waved to catch his attention, he was the proudest man in Boston. *Yes, that beautiful blonde is my girl. Can you believe it?*

Rosemary was elated to have a man of Tony's distinction coming toward her. He was good looking in his own way, carried himself with all the self-assurance in the world, and possessed a calmness that made her feel safe.

Most often, they met at the corner of Park and Tremont, close to the subway exit.

Once the love-struck couple came together,

Boston Public Library

they took each other's hands and squeezed tight. Tony swiftly kissed Rosemary's cheek, she linked her arm through his, and they were on their way. Before long, Rosemary told Tony she felt more like his sister when they met. "There's nothing wrong with sweethearts giving each other a peck on the lips."

True to his gentlemanly reserve, Tony responded, "Let's keep kisses on the mouth private, Ro. And about that 'quick peck,' it'd be torture, torture I tell you. I presume you understand?" He was smiling now and kissed her on the cheek again.

Rosemary brushed it away. "Oh, brother." And she grinned at him. "Well, it's torturous for me too, Mr. Williamson."

The compromised, crazy-in-love couple patiently settled for long arm-in-arm strolls through Boston Common. They kissed each other's cheeks between sentences and grabbed a bite to eat if there was money for it. More often, Rosemary packed a couple of sandwiches, a thermos of hot tea or coffee, Oreo cookies, because they were Tony's favorite, and a package of pink coconut Snowballs, which were hers.

They sat on a public bench, weather permitting, or slipped into the Boston Public Library and found an out-of-the-way corner far from the librarians' watchful eyes, where they surreptitiously enjoyed what Tony called "the best food in the world, Ro" and deep languorous kisses.

CHAPTER II

Two features distinguished Irish immigration:
It was largely female, and most Irish who came to the
United States between 1850 and 1925 intended to stay.
Irish America: Coming Into Clover
MAUREEN DEZELL

"**N**EITHER HELL NOR HIGH WATER could make me give you away to a Polack. You're on your own young woman, weddin' dress, flowers, the works. I'll be providin' none of it." John Joseph stormed out of the kitchen, and shut the back door so forcefully a surge of holy water splashed from a small alabaster font next to the sash.

Kay, Rosemary, and Rita stood silently in the wake of their father's edict. There was only the sound of a dripping faucet and neighbor ladies talking across back porches while hanging up wet laundry. The girls would know Mrs. Ryan's booming lilt anywhere.

"So, did you make a big to-do about Valentine's yesterday?"

"Are you kiddin'?" Mrs. Farrell hollered back. "I just tell 'em the best way to celebrate Valentine's is by honorin' the Sacred Heart of Jesus and offerin' up a personal sacrifice, like not scratchin' when they need to or holdin' a sneeze close so as not to call attention."

Rita closed the kitchen window, dabbed the consecrated water off the wall with a hankie retrieved from under her sweater cuff and turned to her sisters with a dimpled grin. "Oh, poor Dad, now he'll have to cancel that ballroom reservation at the Copley Plaza."

Rosemary could impersonate anyone and was brilliant at her father's brogue. She sat in a kitchen chair and jauntily leaned forward the way he frequently did when making a point, right index finger puncturing the air. "Ah, it's a sorrowful day when a once-proud father can't give his own daughter the grand weddin' he's been savin' for all these years."

Kay smiled at her sister's attempt to lighten the moment. "You sound just like him." But she was angry. "What's Dad talking about? 'I'll be providin' none of it.' He doesn't even provide for us from day to day." She put a pile of clean plates in an open cupboard with a bang. "All I wanted was for my father to walk me down the aisle." And then she had second thoughts. *Maybe it's a blessing in disguise. He'd come to the wedding three sheets to the wind anyway. I'll tell Steve's family he's under the weather. One of my brothers will have to do the honors. I need to find a wedding dress. They're so expensive . . . maybe Mr. Karp . . . No, I don't want to start our marriage out in debt.*

Rita practically read her sister's mind. "Don't worry, Kay. Mum won't let you go without."

Rosemary folded laundry, adding to the piles of underwear, socks, towels, facecloths, and more, stacked on the kitchen table. She caught Rita's eye before saying to Kay, "I have something to tell the future Mrs. Chalpin."

Her lighthearted delivery told Kay it was something good. "What are you up to, Ro?"

Rita filled the kettle with water for tea, while Rosemary gaily continued. "Patsy Sheehan's New York cousin recently got married, and when I told Mrs. Sheehan about you and Steve, she wrote to her niece and asked could she find it in her heart to let you borrow her wedding gown and veil. Seems they're coming to Boston anyway for some kind of anniversary Mass. Oh, and her answer was, yes!"

"You're kidding me?"

"It gets better, Kay. But you'll have to wait 'til Mum gets home."

"Ro, come on! Out with it."

"I can't. Mum needs to tell you."

"Ro!"

"Okay, a hint. You'll have your pick of wedding gowns. That's all I'm going to say." The
sisters had formed a circle with their arms around
each other hugging, laughing, and crying all at
the same time, when Norah walked in.

"God in heaven, what's goin' on here? You
look like a bunch of footballers gettin' ready for
the challenge."

"We are, Mum," Rita said. "We're planning
Kay's wedding."

*It blessed Norah to say her firstborn's
full name though it was not the one
she'd given her at birth. Within
months of little Noni Virginia King's
tragic death, Mary Rose King made
her Confirmation. Catholic tradition
called for the selection of a middle
name if one wasn't already in place.
She adopted Noni's and adapted her
own, Rosemary Virginia King.*

Kay ran to her mother and gave her a kiss.
"Mum, I understand you have something to tell me."

Norah looked sternly in Rosemary's direction. "Rosemary Virginia King."

"Mum, I didn't say another word, only that she'd—"

"Where's your father then?" Norah put her worn canvas grocery bag on the
metal sideboard by the sink, opened the pantry, stood on tiptoe, pushed a loose
board above the top shelf, slid her purse into the space behind it and quietly let
the board down. Previous tenants had created "me own safe deposit box," which
she'd discovered while washing the pantry when they first moved in. Here her
pocketbook was safe from John Joseph slyly "borrowin' a coin or two."

"He's out, Mum," Rosemary answered. As she helped Norah take her long,
heavy cardigan sweater off, she relished her mother being so near. Everything
looked better, felt better, seemed better when Norah was home.

"Aren't I dyin' for a cuppa?" Norah looked toward the stove. "Which one of
you darlins put the kettle on?" Rita was quick to take credit and curtsied. "Me,
Mum, your favorite daughter."

Kay curtsied too. "Mum, please?" Her sisters laughed.

The mother of nine remained her usual calm, orderly self. "Come on now,
girls. First you'll need to run that laundry back to the bedrooms, so we can put

some cups and saucers on the table. And we'll put the groceries away too. Then I'll tell Miss Barbara Catherine King all about it."

Norah loved these times with her daughters, sitting in the kitchen sipping tea together. Rita took two teaspoons full of sugar and plenty of fresh milk in hers. Rosemary took hers black. She didn't prefer it that way, but was watchful of her slim figure; and because she drank at least five cups of tea a day, decided to forego the calories. Kay liked hers strong, with milk only. And you never knew how Norah would take hers. She simply drank a lot of it, morning, noon and night. Today, she stirred in a scant teaspoonful of sugar and smidgen of evaporated milk while peering over the top of her wire-rimmed glasses.

"Mrs. Connors, next door, doesn't miss a thing. And isn't she aware of you gettin' ready to marry now? Well, God bless her, she ran into Evelyn Barry this week, who was all worked up about her new daughter-in-law. Evidently, she's an only child. Who ever heard of havin' only the one? All that aside, Mrs. Barry boldly said she didn't think the bride was at all blushin'. 'How else would she have trapped her handsome son with 'that puddin' face of hers?' It's my opinion that kind of talk, said aloud or thought, just hangs there rottin' heart and soul."

Norah went to the icebox and brought a box of Velveeta cheese back to the table with a knife and plate. "Where was I? Oh, it seems the new bride rolled her beautiful weddin' dress and veil up in a ball, before leavin' the hall for their two-day honeymoon in Hull, and handed it to her mother-in-law sayin', 'Could you please do somethin' with this? I won't be needin' it anymore.'"

Norah got up from the table again. "If me head wasn't attached, I think I'd go the whole day without it. I bought saltines to go with that cheese." She got another plate and arranged the crackers in rows before returning. "And didn't Mrs. Barry tell Mrs. Connors, 'She'll be needin' it all right, for a second go 'round with another husband if she doesn't change her spoiled ways.' Well, Mrs. Connors, bein' the saint that she is, took Mrs. Barry aside, put her straight, and—"

Rosemary interrupted. "Mum, please, tell Kay about the wedding gown."

The sisters were astonished at the length of Norah's story. Their mother was ordinarily a woman of few words—not quiet, but choosy. "God help us, I'm becomin' like Mary Callanan, goin' on and on with everythin' this one and that one had to say." Norah sat back. "Well darlin' girl, the dress and veil are yours for the askin'." Her sea-blue eyes were glistening. "It's so pretty, Kay, so pretty. But I understand there's also the chance of a borrowed dress from New York."

Kay glowed with hope. "Mum, when you say the dress is mine for the asking, does that mean it would really be mine?" Kay reached for a slice of Velveeta and made a saltine sandwich.

"That's exactly what it means, yours to keep. Mrs. Connors offered to take it off Mrs. Barry's hands makin' it seem like a great favor and it's in her possession now. She was lookin' out for your interest alone, Kay. With seven sons, Fiona Connors's no need of a weddin' dress."

Kay loved the idea of the dress being her own. *A bird in the hand is worth two in the bush.* "Mum, when can I see it?" Norah took one more sip of tea and stood up. "We've only to go next door. Mrs. Connors's waitin' for you.'"

When Kay walked out of Mac and Fiona Connor's bedroom, her sisters right behind her, Norah clasped her hands beneath her chin and said, "If you don't look like an angel." The future bride didn't say a word.

Earlier the girls had asked Norah if she'd mind waiting in the hall; they wanted to surprise her. Now the overjoyed mother took the dark-haired daughter her husband called Snow White by the hand and led her into the living room. "The light's better, and Mrs. Connors is dyin' to see you."

Fiona Connors had been listening for Kay's response and spoke up from her favorite roost, the worn to an indented comfort corner of a maroon sofa. "Kay, you're not to feel obligated now."

Three of the Connors boys were standing nearby, and the oldest one, who they called young Mac after his father, said, "It's a white dress. That's all ya's need to get hitched."

His brother chimed in. "Yeah, it's white, ain't it?

While the youngest of the lively bunch told Kay, "I'd marry ya."

Fiona shooed them away "And who asked for your pitiful opinions? Go on, get out of here."

The King girls gave the Connors boys drop-dead looks, and one wisecracking brother got the last word. "Stuck up."

Kay held each side of the organza-wedding gown out the way little girls do. "Mrs. Connors, thank you for thinking of me. And please, be completely honest. Would you be insulted if I took the ruffles off the sleeves?"

"Kay King, you do whatever you want with that dress, and if you ask me, I'd do the same. It'll look much classier that way." Fiona Connors adjusted the colorful scarf wrapped around her pin curls and smoothed her apron-covered lap.

"Thank you. I'll take it!" Kay confirmed, as if she were in a bridal shop.

Rosemary quipped, in her stiffest imitation of a would-be Brahmin sales clerk, "Would madam prefer cash and carry, or shall we put it on account and have the gown delivered to your home?"

The room filled with glee.

"You're gorgeous."

"She's a princess."

"It's perfectly perfect."

As Kay slowly turned, she treasured what her Steve kept saying all along. *Everything's going to be okay. Mark my words, sweetheart. A-Okay.*

"Will you try the veil on too, Kay?" Norah held the cathedral length tulle in her hands and recalled what she'd heard as a girl. *The longer the veil, the purer the bride.*

"No, thank you, Mum. I want to save that part for the big day."

"You're right. We'll put it aside for the weddin'." Norah got a knot in her stomach at the thought of how she'd manage to be there.

John Joseph had forbidden Norah to attend, and for the first time in their married life she was going to defy him. *Didn't I get married without the presence of me parents? It's not right, goin' through the Sacrament of Holy Matrimony and your own mother not bein' there to see it take place. I'll not let it happen to any of my children, let alone a daughter.* Norah still felt a twinge of sadness at the memory, but took comfort that her parents had at least met John Joseph in the old country. *For that I'll always be grateful.*

∞

John Joseph King and Norah Catherine Foley were an unlikely match. He chased after skirts and pints, and his good looks and wily ways brought an abundance of both. Norah knitted caps and sweaters to bring in a few extra coins as a side to her family's farming and fishing dealings, never missed Mass or Holy Days of Obligation, taught young girls the art of knitting and the only lace pattern she knew. Móraí Audley, her mother's mother fondly bragged, "With her sprightly step and graceful carriage, our Norah's the finest dancer of all."

They met on market day, in Clifden, County Galway, on the west coast of Ireland, at his family's lean-to vegetable and fish stall. Both were reaching for the same cabbage—John, to fetch it for another buyer; Norah, helping herself. The youngest King boy was instantly attracted to the dark auburn-haired, bright-eyed girl, and he pre-

Known for the beauty of its moss green-gray bogs and rocky shores, Inisherk is a small island among several others in Galway Bay.

tended to accidentally brush her hand, which she instantly pulled back. "So tell me, are you sellin' this cabbage or keepin' it for yourself?"

"It's yours if you'll do me the honor of sayin' your name," he said with a smirk.

"I'll take this one." Norah picked up another and blushed. *Sure and he's the deepest dimples, and with that devil of a smile, he'll steal me heart before I know it.*

The old woman waiting for the cabbage in question scolded, "I've no time for your dilly-dallying or silly flirtations." And she walked away.

John Joseph crossed his sinewy arms. "Now look what you've done, and all because of your pretty face distractin' me from the work. So is it the two cabbages you'll be buyin' then?"

"I only need the one, and this is taking too long. My father will be lookin' for me."

"You'll get two just the same. One is a gift from the owners of this establishment, who are pleased you happened by."

Norah handed him a coin. "Sure and this is what you do with all the girls." She took one cabbage only, walked away, looked back over her shoulder, and said to his lingering gaze, "Norah Foley from Inisherk."

Two days later, John Joseph rowed out to the tiny island in his father's canoe-like curragh, built light to glide over rough seas and sturdy to hold a day's catch, and asked her father's permission to begin courting. He caught an abundance of fish on the way home and saw the catch as a good omen and second best luck of the day, the first being Mr. Foley's yes.

Love landed hard on Norah's tender heart, and John Joseph was determined to make a life with this decent, sensible, lovely young woman who caught his attention and—unlike all the others—kept it, despite her commitment to chastity.

Allan Line Royal Mail Steamer
"Numidian"

"You're worth the wait and then some, Norah Foley," he'd say. "But it'll be a while 'til we can wed. The farm goes to me older brother Ian, the fair-haired one, and there's no fairness in it. Da says I'll always have a place to lay me head and the work, but there's not enough land to support another family. So I'm left to figure it all out now, aren't I, a way of makin' a livin' apart from Ian's promised land. There's always America, but I'm fiercely opposed to livin' in a foreign country. We'll just wait a while now. Somethin' will come up."

The courtship went too long, and problems that could be contained in a marriage, but not in a "someday" promise began to tear them apart. Norah wanted to immigrate to America; John resisted. She spent two years of trying to convince her sweetheart. "There's nothing for us here but struggle, persecution, and the horrific British rule."

He stalled over and again. "If we go to America, we can't be sure of what we're gettin' ourselves into. And what if we can't find work right away? What'll

Parker House Hotel
60 School Street
BOSTON, MASS.

we do then, Norah Foley? Regret ever leavin' Ireland! That's what we'd do!"

She gave the same response every time. "We're young and strong John, I'm not afraid to go." And so did he, one time too many. "We'll wait a while now and see what happens."

Nineteen-year-old Norah Catherine Foley sailed for America alone on the, Allan Line Royal Mail Steamer, Numidian in the spring of 1910, with one valise, a large satchel, and a few favorite books. Safely tucked away in two hidden pockets her mother had skillfully sewn in Norah's camisole, were five American dollars, the equivalent of one-hundred-ten dollars today, a passport, and other important papers, including her sponsor's name and address: Miss Maggie Flaherty, Parker House Hotel, Boston,

Massachusetts. Maggie was a girl from home who'd secured a steady chamber-maid job "for a good wage in one of the finer establishments in the city."

After nine days at sea, the ship docked in Charlestown, and upon disembarking—all her worldly goods in tow—Norah was blessedly relieved to see a jubilant Mary Flaherty waiting by the gangplank, flowers in hand. "Welcome to America, Norah Foley."

One week after arriving in Boston, Norah found work as a live-in domestic for a wealthy Irish American couple, Mr. and Mrs. Alexander Collins of Brookline, an affluent town just outside of Boston. She enjoyed a kind, but as was to be expected, stringent, formal relationship with the family.

"If you please, Missus."

"Today's mail, sir."

"Young Master Collins, you'd best . . ."

And she endured an ache for her own family.

In the beginning, overwhelming homesickness would sometimes cause Norah to cry into a pillow at night, especially when she thought of her mother.

Norah was grateful to have every Sunday afternoon off. However, Sunday mornings held continued responsibilities: helping their cook to prepare a full breakfast for the family, the serving and clearing, assisting with "getting the whole lot out the door in good time for Mass" (Norah herself having already worshipped at the earliest), making beds and putting their things in order, setting the table for a midday meal, helping the cook to prepare it, serving, clearing, a last look around, and a respectful "Is there anything else, Mrs. Collins?" to which there was an equally respectful "No, thank you, Norah. That will be all for today." And up, up two flights Norah would quietly rush to her dormer room, quickly change into her Sunday best, including a recently purchased good-sized hat "with a grand ribbon bow and band," and take the trolley to South Boston, where she would visit with friends from home and stroll by the ocean—two of her favorite, life-long pastimes.

Beach and Boulevard, City Point
SOUTH BOSTON, MASS.

Norah Catherine still loved John Joseph but she wasn't averse to meeting someone who could take his place. Time was moving on. Norah was a country girl, and the practical lessons of her rural youth met the hard-earned dollars she saved week by week, building a modest nest egg for her fondest dream: marriage and a family of her own.

CHAPTER 12

The water is wide—I can't cross o'er
And neither have I wings to fly
Give me a boat that can carry two
And we shall row, my love and I.
"THE WATER IS WIDE"
TRADITIONAL IRISH SONG

KAY AND STEVE'S WEDDING PLANS were progressing nicely, despite John Joseph's objection. Norah altered the sleeves on "that beautiful dress," and she saved the leftover ruffled fabric, just in case. The family was ecstatic that both Joe and John Michael would be home on leave in time for the wedding. Norah and Kay's prayers had been answered.

As the oldest son, Joe was asked to walk Kay down the aisle, and Rita would be a bridesmaid. Rosemary's pride was slightly stung when Kay got engaged first, but she was truly happy for her sister. Besides, she knew Tony was the one and he'd said the same of her, but it was too soon for an engagement ring. Nonetheless, she was the older sister and would be standing next to Kay as maid of honor for all the world to see.

Timmy and Tommy were too young to be groomsmen, but glad to know they'd be sitting in the first pew. The mother of the bride would be seated right next to them but for now Norah had to keep it a secret, and she reassured Kay countless times. "You're not to worry, darlin'. I'll be there, but keep it under your hat. That way I'll only have to deal with himself after the fact."

"Himself," John Joseph, ignored anything said about the wedding and gave Kay the silent treatment except for an occasional dig. "Who needs ya?" he said. "You'd better prepare yourself. Those Polskis expect a lot of the bed, and I don't mean clean sheets."

Out of the blue, and for the first time anyone could remember the steel mill doing such a thing, John Joseph and five other laborers, described by the foreman as "the best damned workers you'll ever see," were going to be sent to Rhode Island "for a G job we gotta get out yesterday."

John Joseph's crew was scheduled to be gone the week of the wedding, and he smugly told Norah, "If ever there were a sign Kay's doin' the wrong thing, this is it. Don't you think the Almighty would have me here if I was supposed to stand up for her?"

The men took the train and were then transported in a company truck to an old lodge where half the rooms were closed due to disrepair. They doubled up, and when handed keys one man was heard to say, "First time I ever stayed in a hotel. How about you blokes?"

Breakfast was in a back corner of the slightly shabby dining room where other guests stared at the men's work clothes with disdain. A bag lunch was provided on the work site, and each man was given a small allowance for supper, with the fear of God put in him by the project foreman. "If I catch any one of you spending your stipend at a, and just so it's perfectly clear, bar-pub-saloon-lounge-tavern, you're fired, and you'll have to walk back to Boston."

At night, the laborers, who'd never experienced a vacation and thought this must be close to the real thing, played cards in one of the bedrooms and pooled their money for refreshments, purchased at a close-by package goods store. A venue the foreman had failed to mention.

∽

Everything for the wedding was going as intended except for Norah's health. Rita was the first one to be aware all was not well. The King girls' personal items for "that time of the month" were stored beneath a skirted table in the back hall, and for weeks now Rita had seen her mother go to it often.

One afternoon Norah was hanging laundry on the back porch and a puddle of blood suddenly appeared at her feet. "Oh my God," she said to Rita who'd been handing her the wet clothes one by one. "I'm sorry you had to see this. Finish up here will you please? I'll be right back to clean up." Norah grabbed a damp towel from the laundry basket and modestly pressed it against her housedress.

"That's all right, Mum. I can do it."

"Don't touch it," Norah said closing the screen door gently behind her. When she didn't return to the porch in good time, Rita went to find her and did, passed out in a pool of blood on the bathroom floor. Apparently the hemorrhaging had been ongoing for weeks, and Norah's body couldn't sustain her any longer. The wedding was only three days away.

◌≫

Norah King lay in her bed at City Hospital thinking there was something "unnatural about havin' your insides taken out," but Doctor Petrukonis said she had no other choice. "Hysterectomy or bleed to death."

The recovery pain was almost more than she could bear, but Norah wanted nothing to do with the morphine nurses brought to her. She didn't drink alcohol, never had, and was not going to let "that kind of medicine" come anywhere near her. "The ether was bad enough."

◌≫

On the morning of the wedding, Norah was still in the hospital but she woke up in high spirits knowing this is what Kay wanted, to marry Steve Chalpin. At the same time, she was sad she would not be there for her daughter. The mother of the bride chased her doldrums away with the solace of prayer. Her cherished rosary beads brought a familiar comfort as each one passed through her fingertips. She was on the Fourth Sorrowful Mystery: Jesus Carries His Cross—praying for the undaunted courage of Jesus in carrying her own—when she and the women in her ward looked up and at each other, curious about all the commotion they heard coming from the hallway: raised voices, clapping, and scurrying steps. Mrs. Angelina Mirabella, who occupied the next bed over was concerned. "Oh my God! Whatta ya think is goin' on outta there?"

When Kay woke on her wedding day, she made a last-minute decision to go to City Hospital so Norah could see her in her wedding gown. And she would go before the ceremony. Rosemary and Rita tried to talk her out of it, but the brothers offered to pay for a taxi and go along.

Joe, John Michael, and Patrick all looked dapper in the black tuxedos Steve Chalpin had rented for them, and fifteen-year-old Patrick was grateful to be included with his older brothers, rather than lumped in with the little boys.

Rita and Rosemary stood before Kay in stocking feet and identical pale green bridesmaids' dresses with matching floral headbands that crowned their heads like halos. The bride gazed at her sisters from head to toe. "You two look like movie stars. Kathryn Hepburn and Judy Garland, how do you do?"

Rita took both of Kay's hands. "You're absolutely, positively dazzling, Kay! Steve won't believe his eyes when he sees you walking down that aisle."

Rosemary agreed. "I'll say!" She added, "Rita and I aren't quite ready yet. We'll meet you at the church."

Boston City Hospital
818 HARRISON AVENUE

Rita handed Joe an umbrella and looked toward Kay. "April showers bring May flowers. Just in case."

A car horn sounded. "Oh, there's the taxi now," Kay said. "Don't be late," she told her sisters, "and put your shoes on or you'll run those stockings." She rushed toward the door where her brothers were lined up, eager to escort "the queen of Southie."

Rosemary suddenly remembered something. "Kay, wait just one sec." She dashed down the hall and came back with her red coat. "Wear this or you'll catch your death. It's chilly out there."

∽

When the yellow cab stopped in front of City Hospital, Joe asked the driver if he'd wait for them. "We've got to follow orders and get our sister back to the church on time."

The cabbie barked, "Don't worry. I'll be here." And following a hunch he looked over his shoulder. "Hey, any of you fellas in the service?"

"Yes, sir," John Michael answered. "We're both home on short leave from the Navy. I've been in the Pacific, and my brother's been stateside in New York but he's headed overseas. This one's too young." John Michael reached over the front seat where Pat was sitting and mussed his hair.

"Well just so ya's know, your money's no good with me." The taxi driver turned off his meter. "Service men don't pay when they're ridin' with Nick Madeiros. Take your time."

All three brothers hopped out, tenderly helped the bride exit, and tried to protect her wedding gown from being soiled. Joe told Pat to carry Kay's train and Pat balked. "How come I always have to do the dumb stuff?"

But he picked it up anyway and did a good job, which was no easy task because Kay moved quickly once she put her white-satin-shoed foot on the curb, her brothers practically running behind her to keep up. John Michael took the red coat from her shoulders as soon as they entered the building. He was proud of his sister and didn't want her bridal beauty covered up.

The hospital receptionist recognized Norah King's children because they'd visited every day, and she gladly waved them back to the women's ward. "Wait'll ya ma sees ya's!"

Patients and personnel applauded and called out as the striking foursome rushed by.

"Look at the beautiful bride!"

"Thank you."

"Congratulations to you and the three grooms."

"We're her brothers."

"What in the world's going on?"

"Our mother's a patient here."

When Norah heard what sounded like her own children's voices, she was puzzled—and then Kay appeared in the ward's wide doorway, brothers John and Joe on either side of her, Pat trailing behind with the train and veil.

Kay's fresh Lilly of the Valley fragrance wafted through the stuffy room as she rushed to her mother's bedside accompanied by the sighs and best wishes of the other women in the ward. "Hi, Mum. How do you like my wedding dress?"

Norah beamed with pride. *These gorgeous young people are me own.* Her hands reached for Kay's face. "Oh my darlin' girl, if you aren't the most beautiful bride I've ever laid eyes on."

After the gorgeous foursome left, Norah lay back on her pillow with every intention of finishing the Rosary, but, for the moment, she closed her eyes and blissfully recalled her own love story and wedding day.

༄

John Joseph King promised Norah Catherine Foley that he would one day come to America "when the time is right," but her hope waned. It had been too long.

Like Norah's family, John Joseph's owned their farmland outright, along with a couple of cows, several pigs, lambs and chickens, one rooster, and that small fishing boat. No matter how hard times got, with English occupation and merciless discrimination toward Roman Catholics, the Kings always had the ability to put food on the table. And in Norah's mind that was the problem. John Joseph King was much too comfortable. Though he'd never own the farm—it would go to his eldest brother Ian upon the passing of their father—John Joseph did have the promise of always being provided for, but he alone. The farm wasn't big enough to support another family.

Then, in Ireland's desperate move for self-government away from English rule, came the Easter Rising of 1916. It began in Dublin's General Post Office, where a Proclamation of Independence was read, and the grand Greek Revival building, burned and gutted in the ensuing battle. All of Ireland suffered as patriots were hanged, shot or imprisoned. Many young men were wrongly targeted as I.R.A., and none were free of suspicion—even in the small village of Carna, on the west coast of Ireland, that John Joseph called home.

Norah Catherine Foley never lacked for suitors in America but she didn't like "steppin' out" with a lot of fellas. *It's not respectable. I'll know the one when he comes along. I did once and I'm confident God will be right there helpin' me as before.* To date, no one had taken her first love's place. From time to time, John Joseph would write to her with news and a hint of affection. "Though I'm lonely for your company, I'm getting on fine." "How's Boston?" "Me mother met her Maker."

At last, the kind of letter Norah hoped and prayed and looked for every day for five years finally arrived.

To Norah Foley,

This is to let you know that I'm coming to America on the Allan Line Steamship Laurentian, the first of August 1917. I can only assume you'll know where we berth and will be there to meet me. I want to marry you Norah Foley and would like to do so as soon as the United States of America deems our union legal. My father and brother are sending me off with some money so as soon as we can I'd like to set up housekeeping and get on with it. This is of course unless you've met someone else. In that case, I'll still be coming to America and trust you'll tell me where I can find work and board. I await your answer to both situations and send you my love. I hope it's not too late.

John Joseph King
Ard East, Carna, County Galway, Ireland

According to an old Irish saying,
"November is the time to wed, the har-
vest's in and it's cold in bed."
The Traditional Irish Wedding by
Bridget Haggerty

John did indeed arrive in Boston on August first, the engagement was short, and the long-separated couple selected a November date for their nuptials.

Mr. and Mrs. Collins were delighted by Norah's news, and so fond of the maid they came to call "practically a member of the family," they offered to give Norah and her young man a small wedding.

The Collinses sat where Norah's parents would have, front pew, left side of the middle aisle, Saint Aidan's Church, Brookline, Massachusetts, November 21, 1917. When Monsignor John T. Creagh asked, "Who gives this woman to this man?" Mr. Collins stood dutifully at Norah's side and answered, "I do, in proxy of her father, Mr. John Patrick Foley, who lives in Ireland." Mrs. Collins nodded in agreement, and the feathers on her full-brimmed, aubergine hat nodded with her.

Saint Aidan's Church
BROOKLINE, MASS.

That Norah and John had a formal wedding at that particular church was extraordinary for the time and place. They were, respectfully, a domestic and a laborer. Saint Aidan's was one of the most prosperous and beautiful parishes in the archdiocese, and his Eminence, Cardinal O'Connell, Archbishop of Boston, moved to Brookline with the express purpose of making it his own church home.

When Mrs. and Mrs. John Joseph King stepped out of Saint Aidan's into the crisp autumn air, Norah glowed, *Husband and wife . . .* Her long veil blew in the wind and danced around them both while brilliantly colored leaves fell from surrounding trees and swirled on the ground, as if in merry celebration. John Joseph impetuously lifted his bride, and she held on to her headpiece with the same hand that held her bouquet; the other clung to his shoulder. The elated groom gave his bride two short kisses while church bells tolled and guests threw rice. Norah had never been happier than at this moment. *And now we're at the beginnin' of our life together.*

The reception took place at the Collins home on tree-lined Fuller Street, with a celebratory lunch of amber consommé; Waldorf salad,; crown roast beef; mashed potatoes; gravy; a relish tray of celery, olives, gherkin pickles and radishes; green peas with pearl onions; fresh horseradish; and Parker House rolls—compliments of Norah's dear friend Mary Flaherty.

When the meal was over, Mr. Collins extended an invitation to the twenty guests. "Please come into the parlor." The formal room was festooned with white tulle, chrysanthemums, and ferns.

The wedding cake, displayed on a small table, was topped with two small china bells, each hand-painted with tiny shamrocks and tied together with a white satin ribbon bow, its long streamers cascading over the three layers of white cake and butter cream frosting. More ferns encircled the traditional con-fection, and the table's edge was scalloped with additional tulle.

Norah took a silver cake knife into her gloved hand and whispered, "Will you join me now, John, and we'll cut the first piece together?"

John Joseph put his huge hands over her one, pushed down on the cake without announcement, and looked up with a smile. "There. It's done now, Mrs. King."

Norah beamed, and everyone in the room lightly applauded. Next, Mrs. Collins and her friend Mrs. Rose Kennedy, who lived only two streets over on Beal, walked to the piano, stood side by side, and sang "Oh Promise Me" to the accompaniment of teenage Elizabeth Collins's skillful playing. "Oh promise me that you will take my hand."

Last May, the Kennedy children's nanny had taken ill at a most inopportune time—the christening day of their second child. Norah volunteered her Sunday afternoon off to fill in and accompany the prominent family (Mrs. Kennedy's father, "Honey Fitz," was a former mayor of Boston) to Saint Aidan's Church, where she looked after active two-year-old Joseph while his baby brother, John Fitzgerald Kennedy, was being duly christened by, Monsignor Creagh.

City Hall and
Kings Chapel (Rear View)
School Street, Boston, Mass.

Rose Kennedy never forgot a kindness and offered to assist Madeline Collins however she could with "dear Norah's wedding lunch." "Oh Promise Me" and the exquisite wedding cake bells did very nicely.

Remembering those bright, hope-filled days brought Norah Catherine Foley King such joy, and she prayed that Kay and Steve would have a long, happy, peaceful life together. *"Glory be to the Father, and to the Son and to the Holy Ghost. As it was in the beginning, is now, and ever shall be, world without end. Amen.*

CHAPTER 13

Oh Mary! We crown thee with blossoms today
Queen of the Angels, Queen of the May.
"BRING FLOWERS OF THE RAREST"
MARY E. WALSH

MARRIED LIFE AGREED WITH KAY King Chalpin, all four weeks of it. She appreciated the well-being of living "close enough and far enough" in nearby Quincy. Should her disgruntled father decide to drop by, it would take some effort and that's exactly the way Steve wanted it for his bride's peace of mind.

The newlyweds lived on the top floor of a large Victorian home long ago converted into apartments. Theirs was the smallest, and according to the neighbors, who'd all had a look, also the coziest, with cute curtains Kay had sewn herself, and a few pieces of fairly decent hand-me-down furniture from here and there: bed, dresser, rocking chair and hassock.

Steve's parents gave them a brand-new brocade sofa, a bit blue for Kay's taste but she was too appreciative to say a word. And the small mahogany coffee table in front of it was a gift from their entire wedding party who pooled their money in order to get the couple "something solid." Rosemary suggested the table and they all jumped at the idea.

Prior to the wedding, Kay had been particularly excited when they found a kitchen table and chairs at a wholesale furniture store. "This is exactly what I had in mind. I love it!"

Steve said it was too pricey. "We can use the coffee table for the time being." But he surprised his bride, and the maple set was in place when they returned home from their honeymoon in Plymouth.

The new Mrs. Chalpin quickly made two tablecloths, "one in use, and one in reserve." Everything was falling into place nicely, and now Kay was looking forward to completing her classes at The Katherine Gibbs School and getting a better job.

⁕

The personnel manager of The Commonwealth Bank of New England was seeking to hire a couple of upcoming graduates who, "are really on the ball" and went to The Katherine Gibbs School to find them, with the request that they should be of Irish descent, if at all possible. The bank's founders had established this policy from the beginning. "Not to the exclusion of others," they explained, "but simply to give our own a running start."

Miss Olive Gilmore, one of the school's foremost teachers, was intrigued by Kay King, now Chalpin, impressed by the working-class student's ability to catch on quickly and equally impressed when she reviewed her student's written work. However, it would be remiss to omit what Miss Gilmore said to one of her colleagues when she learned Miss King was to be married. "What a waste of that young lady's abilities. Now she'll be keeping track of diapers instead of ledgers."

Shortly before graduation, and out of common courtesy, Miss Gilmore asked Kay what she'd already asked several other students in her advanced accounting class. "So, Miss King, I mean Mrs. Chalpin, what do you intend to do after graduation?"

Kay knew people like Olive Gilmore had pat assumptions about South Boston's Irish because of what the teacher had said in the past. "Miss King, you've enlightened me. I was under the impression parochial schools emphasized creed over the three R's. Your math skills tell me otherwise."

Kay gladly stated what she and her husband had planned. "First of all, Miss Gilmore, I'll begin looking for a better paying job. My education here has made that possible. Thank you. Then my husband and I plan to save for a down payment on a house, and I'll keep working, so we can build our savings up again. After that, God willing, we'll begin a family."

"Wonderful. Tell me now, is your husband in the service? *How in the world is this Southie couple going to buy a house? No doubt her husband's an enlisted man.*

Kay caught Miss Gilmore's drift. "My husband's a packaging engineer, and Uncle Sam says he's more valuable to the war effort stateside because of his job." The new wife was ready to pop her buttons because of her husband's professional status. "The Company he works for provides food to the military."

"Excellent, excellent. A home-front soldier." *Got herself a college man. Beauty can do that.*

"Thank you for asking, Miss Gilmore" *Bet she thought I was headed for barefoot and pregnant.*

⁊⁊

Young Mrs. Chalpin and her older sister boarded a train for downtown Boston, and there wasn't a seat to be found, until Kay spotted one. "Over here, Ro. Age before beauty, you take it."

"Oh, I couldn't possibly. You're the old married woman, you take it." Kay did.

Rosemary put her hand through an overhead loop, and their knees kept bumping against each other as they discussed the day's activities, primarily shopping at department stores. They'd search the racks at R.H. White (and buy some hand-dipped chocolates); Gilchrist's, Jordan Marsh, and Filene's upstairs, and then hunt Filene's Basement. "Our usual route, right, Ro?"

"Don't forget the Public Garden. I still want to see the flowers. Patsy said they're like something out of a storybook, crocuses, tulips and daffodils everywhere."

"This spring's so late. It's a miracle they even showed up."

"So, you're game, Mrs. Chalpin?"

135

The Boston Public Garden

There's no place quite like the beautiful city of Boston in the spring. "And it happened that the tulips in Copley Square opened that day, and shone in the sun like lighted lamps."

The Promised Land by Mary Antin

"Fine with me. But let's take the scenic route instead of Tremont. Okay? And then back to Jordan's for those delicious muffins." Kay had been looking forward to the delectable blueberry baked goods all week.

"Perfect. And let's buy something for Rita. She was so sad not to join us."

"I don't know who felt worse, Rita or Mum feeling bad for Rita. But work is work, and she has to be there or else it's out the door, no more job at Grants."

"It still feels empty without her."

This was a shopping ritual for the King sisters: get dressed up; go downtown. The Public Garden was an unusual detour.

The two eye-catching young ladies were oblivious to turning heads as they walked up Park Street, past the State House and along Beacon Street in the sunny, unseasonably cold weather, both without hats. Kay was freezing to death in her khaki all-weather coat, so wrongly named, but wore the stylish balmacaan because it was new and complemented her dark curls. Rosemary was snug as a bug in the red coat, and slipped her arm through Kay's. "I'll keep you warm, kiddo." Her golden hair bounced with every step.

"Can you believe we both found something today?" Rosemary was jubilant. They'd had great luck at Filene's Basement and carried the department store bags two in hand so they could remain walking arm in arm.

"Rita's going to love those slippers," Kay happily declared.

With straight-backed strides and vibrant smiles they appeared, as they were, confident and delighted in each other's company, and every so often, they stopped to admire a Beacon Hill mansion along the way.

"Ro, can you imagine how wonderful it would be to live in one of those swanky houses?"

Rosemary stepped back. "At one time this coat did." She made a quarter-turn and tucked her arm through Kay's again. Rose Red and Snow White ended the afternoon with a much-anticipated treat.

Jordan Marsh's Tearoom was alive with the sounds of Saturday shoppers: the hum of conversations, clink of silverware, cups returning to saucers, bustling steps of waitresses, whoosh of the swinging in and out kitchen doors, and the rustle of shopping bags being placed by or picked up from beside their owners feet like cherished pets. The room smelled of coffee, tea, baked goods, hot dishes, cigarette smoke, and a plethora of perfumes.

The King sisters drank pots of hot tea and ate "too many of those scrumptious muffins," and Kay announced her good news. "Ro, I have an interview with The Commonwealth Bank of New England. Can you believe it?"

"Fantastic. How did that come about?"

"I'll tell you in a minute. You've seen their building, haven't you? It's by the old State House."

"Of course, but I never thought my sister would be working there."

"I'm not there yet. They're looking for someone to work side by side with the controller's secretary. Miss Gilmore recommended me, just me, Ro, she says I have what it takes, but asked the most peculiar question beforehand." The two sisters made a classic silhouette leaning across the table confiding what they didn't want others to hear. "She asked, 'Are you sure you're Irish? King doesn't sound like an Irish name.'"

Jordan Marsh
Blueberry Muffins

Preheat oven to 450 degrees. Grease and flour a 12 cup muffin tin, and also the top of the pan (batter may spill over).

½ cup butter (Jordan's used Crisco)
1 cup granulated sugar
1/2 teaspoon salt
2 teaspoons baking powder
2 eggs
2 cups all purpose flour
½ cup milk
1 teaspoon vanilla
1-½ cups of blueberries, cleaned
   and rinsed
Sugar for sprinkling on top

Cream together butter, sugar, and salt for 3 minutes. Add baking powder and eggs and mix well. Add flour, milk, and vanilla, and mix again. Gently fold in blueberries.

Fill cups to the top. Sprinkle sugar on each muffin.

Bake at 450 for 5 minutes and drop temperature to 375. Bake 25 to 30 minutes more and watch closely at this point. Check doneness by poking a knife in the center of one muffin. When it comes out clean, the muffins are ready. Cool slightly and remove from pans.

"You're as Irish as Saint Pat. Honestly!"

"I told her that." They sat back again. "Ro, is there any chance I could borrow your red coat?" The object in question lay between them in the booth, and Kay put her hand on it. "The interview is next week, and I'd feel like a million dollars walking into that bank wearing your red coat."

"Of course you can borrow it." Rosemary motioned for the waitress. "But just for the interview, all right? There's a hankie in the right pocket. Please don't use it."

The middle-aged waitress whose nametag said she was "Trudy," arrived at the table and grinned. "You young women need hot water again? Say yes, and you're gonna float outta here."

"No, thank you. Just the check please," Rosemary said, and she offered a kind word. "Your handkerchief looks so pretty," referring to the pink, crochet-edged hankie artfully ruffled and pinned to Trudy's uniform.

"Edith over there did it for me. I couldn't make a handkerchief look like this if my life depended on it." She collected their dishes. "Thanks, doll. I'll be right back." Trudy returned with a box of muffins, told the girls, "No charge. They'll never miss 'em," winked, and put the check on the table.

Kay reached for the check. "I've got it, Ro. Thanks again for letting me borrow your coat. Oh, can I borrow your dress gloves too? Mine have seen better days."

⚬≫⚬

It took Norah a long time to recover from her hysterectomy, and the family had to tighten their belts with three wage earners out of the house now and Norah too weak to work.

Rosemary helped, but it wasn't enough to make up for the others, let alone cover her mother's medical expenses and supplement her father's daily drinking, card playing and "hale fellow" need to many times pick up the pub tab for others. Something had to give.

Norah and John Joseph slowly walked the strand along Carson Beach, side by side, no physical contact, looking straight ahead as they discussed how to keep hearth and home together, and Norah told her husband she was ready to go back to work. "Maybe two nights to begin with, and when I'm stronger, I can easily pick up more. There's always cleanin' to be done in the city of Boston."

John Joseph said, "I've no doubt the two nights will be too much, considerin' the shape you're in, Norah King, and then what? Back to City Hospital? No. You need more time. There's only one solution. Rita has to quit school. We need the money."

Norah would have nothing to do with it. "And what kind of future would she have then, John, without a high school diploma to her name? We'll manage. Haven't we always? I'm good enough for the work." Norah was still looking straight ahead.

"Listen to me now. The decision's not yours to make. Rita workin' only the few hours on a Saturday won't do." John Joseph was adamant. "I'm the head of this household, and I say she quits school." He turned to Norah, removed his tweed cap and ran his hand over his hair. "Besides, Rita's got a pretty face and comely shape. She'll have no trouble marryin'." He put his cap on again with a decisive tug. "That's her future."

Norah was silent.

"You know, Norah, none of this of this would be happenin' if Kay was still livin' at home. She's got that fancy bank job now, makin' good money, and none of it comin' to this family." He thought it very peculiar that Norah smiled.

But it is, John. How in the world do you suppose I've been keepin' food on the table? Every payday, Kay secretly got cash to her mother with the understanding that it was from Steve too.

"God only knows why you're smilin', Norah King. Did they take your sense out in that operatin' room as well?" John Joseph said it with a seldom-seen lightness.

Against her best effort, Norah's step faltered, and she reached for John's arm but he caught her first. "Lean on me." He circled her waist in the most supportive way possible, his ghost of an Irish whisper caught midst wind and sea. *"Mo ghrá."* My love.

⚭

Sister Veronita was shocked and saddened when Rita King told her, "Don't look for me on Monday, Sister. I won't be here."

All three King girls had been her students. And Rita, not unlike her older sisters, was a pleasure, even though she was tardy almost every time she entered the classroom, whether at the beginning of a new school day or after lunch. Sister Veronita only remembered having one other student who was constantly late. Her name was Diane Early but when the patience-worn nun began calling her "Diane Late" in front of the entire class, "Miss Late" became decidedly more punctual.

However, the good Sister couldn't bring herself to shame Rita to do the same, though the thought had crossed her mind. *Ah, royalty has at last arrived. Make way for Miss King, who enters my classroom whenever her majesty deems it convenient.* Truth be known, Sister favored Rita King, hoped she'd consider going into the convent, and even prayed about it. She loved the girl's kind heart.

Rita's classmates forever shunned Mary Ellen Dugan. With her pigeon-toed walk, eyeglasses thick as Coke-bottle bottoms, and manner of speaking that brought saliva to the corners of her mouth every time she opened it, Mary Ellen Dugan was not at the top of anyone's list. More than once, Sister Superior had lamented, "God love her. The poor girl can't help herself."

There was a good chance of being outcast by other students if you were seen with such an unpopular, unfortunate creature as Mary Ellen. But that didn't scare Rita, who was popular, and she befriended her awkward classmate without hesitation. She liked Mary Ellen's sense of humor, and despite outward appearances, Mary Ellen had an extraordinarily high IQ, was really good at math, and never hesitated to help Rita or anyone else who struggled with their sums. When the other girls saw them together, they'd whisper, "Why's Rita King walking with Doggie Dugan?" and "My mother says, you become like the friends you spend time with. It'd be a shame if Rita started spittin' when she talks, like her new best friend does."

Now, in the midst of tremendous disappointment and pending embarrassment at having to quit school, Rita was completely unaware she'd been recommended for an unlikely honor.

Sister Veronita petitioned the other nuns at Gate of Heaven to please make an exception for this year's upcoming May Procession. She nominated high school junior Rita Margaret King to be the girl who would place a crown of roses on the church's lifelike statue of Mary, the Mother of God and Queen of the May.

"Rita can't even finish out the year. The mother's sick, and the father insists she has to get a full-time job." The Sisters of Saint Joseph were more than sympathetic.

Traditionally, girls and boys dress in white for the May Procession. An outstanding high school senior girl is prayerfully selected to crown a statue of the Blessed Mother, and beloved hymns are sung, particularly "Bring Flowers of the Rarest," affectionately known as "Oh Mary! We Crown Thee"

"Tsk-tsk."

"It's not right."

"School's almost over."

"We've seen this type of situation one too many times, haven't we, Sisters?"

But they would need more convincing.

Sobriety was John Joseph's public face, and he was a charmer with a compliment for whoever came his way. Drunkenness and bad behavior were reserved for the pub and family, behind closed doors.

The Kings' apartment was close to Gate of Heaven, and it wasn't out of the ordinary for him to enter into passing conversation with one of the Sisters.

"Ah, if it isn't me children's favorite nun. And aren't Mrs. King and I grateful for the fine teachin' you're puttin' into their heads, not to overlook the good Catholic morals you're givin' 'em too? God bless you, Sister, God bless you and your kind." John Joseph King and his kind didn't fool one of them for a minute.

No matter the trouble at home, those Kings came to school spic and span, homework done, and ready to learn. This included Joe, off to war now, who had a hair-trigger temper, was forever fist-fighting with one boy or another, and spent so much time in Sister Superior's office he noticed when she moved the Infant of Prague statue from the narrow table behind her desk to a corner bookshelf. "Excuse me, Sister, but why'd ya do that? I liked the little guy where he was."

For days, Sister Veronita continued to plead her case. "You see how Rita is with poor Mary Ellen, let alone the way she looks after looney Miss Rooney."

The other nuns softly laughed while Mother Superior scolded from the doorway. "Sister Veronita!"

Sister Louise put her darning down, and came to Sister Veronita's defense. "Reverend Mother, with all due respect, have you ever heard anyone refer to Miss Rooney as of late without using the word looney in the same sentence?" The nuns laughed again, including Mother Superior who said, "God forgive us."

Looney Miss Rooney, a spry elfin elderly woman, spent her days helping the good Sisters with baking, dusting and running errands. It was her pleasure and pride, until she quietly slipped into senility.

One Sunday, Rita and her girlfriends were walking home after Mass, when they found Miss Rooney wandering with no idea where she had come from or where she was going. The teenage trio got her home.

Later that week, Rita arranged a "Miss Rooney rotation." In turn each girl committed to escort the bewildered woman to Sunday Mass and back. Often their mothers would provide her dinner. "Run this plate over to Miss Rooney like a good girl."

Before long, the girls established a service club Sister Veronita heartily sponsored and named the Daughters of Saint Christopher: "Young women who find time for the benefit of our dear ones who are lost in one way or another."

Cool spring rain pattered against windows in the convent parlor that evening, while the fireplace provided warmth and Sister Estelle played old-fashioned favorites on the piano. It was good to be home.

The sisters were their usual productive selves, correcting papers, sorting teaching materials. One was mapping out plans for this year's May Procession and asked, "If each of you could please provide me with the number of boys and girls in your classes." Another suggested, "This would be a good a time to decide who'll have the honor of crowning."

They were discussing devout young ladies of merit and grace, and Sister Veronita made one final appeal to the women she respected most in the world, these Sisters of Saint Joseph who were her family. "Rita has a heart of gold, and I say we give this tribute to the girl who so closely follows our Blessed Mother's loving example of comfort and mercy."

The sisters were unanimous in their decision. Rita King would place the crown. "In honor of our Blessed Mother, for whom this holy church is named, Mary, Mother of God, Gate of Heaven."

CHAPTER 14

Christ be with me, Christ be within me,
Christ behind me, Christ before me
Christ beside me, Christ to win me
Christ to comfort me, Christ above me,
Christ in quiet, Christ in danger,
Christ in hearts of all that love me,
Christ in mouth of friend and stranger
SAINT PATRICK'S BREASTPLATE
SAINT PATRICK, FIFTH-CENTURY CENTURY IRISH CLERIC

S TRAIGHT HAIR FELL LIMP AND curly hair kinked up.
That summer was brutally hot and clammy, with temperatures well over ninety and humidity almost as high. Talcum powder mercifully saved the day, and children looked like little ghosts with Johnson's Baby Powder lightly applied to their tummies, backs and anywhere there was a crease: elbows, ankles, knees and neck. Women dusted Cashmere Bouquet on places too private to mention in an effort to stay fresh, while Mennen's Talc tended to masculine needs. At night, bed sheets were liberally sprinkled with the soothing powders, so sticky bodies could glide comfortably into sleep.

Castle Island

*With its magnificent views of Boston
Harbor, its welcoming grassy hill,
sandy beach and circular walkway that
extends out over the water—has always
been one of South Boston's most popular
places to stroll, play, picnic and relax.
Also known as Fort Independence, the
strategic locale and ancient stronghold
played a key defense role in the turbu-
lent times of early America*

It was Norah's best effort to get some relief from the stifling heat of their apartment by taking her children to Castle Island as often as she could for a picnic supper. "It'll be cooler down by the water," she told them.

There, they all—Rita, Pat, Timmy, Tommy, and Rosemary when she could make it—enjoyed sandwiches, macaroni or potato salad, strawberry-flavored Zarex to drink, watermelon, and quartered "it goes further that way" slices of marble, raisin, or banana loaf cake.

In the early years, before the tragic loss of their little girl, John Joseph gladly went along as well, and when there was extra money, he'd offer to buy ice cream cones on the way home. "If any of ya's are interested I've a few coins here."

The children would screech, "Really, Dad?" "Honest?" and practically tumble over each other as they ran up to the window of a seasonal snack shack by the Sugar Bowl walkway.

After Noni's death, he preferred pub grub to picnics at the beach, the place his "little water baby" loved the best.

These simple times became cherished memories, and years later when Rita had children of her own who never knew their grandmother Norah, she spoke of eternity's shore. "In heaven we'll all go on Castle Island picnics with Grammy King."

⁓

Rosemary loved her new job as a social worker for the City of Boston and her second one of getting Patsy Sheehan down the aisle. Her best friend was getting married.

"Always a bridesmaid, never a bride." Rosemary was able to put any budding thought of jealousy aside, because she knew beyond the shadow of a doubt that her bridal day was coming. Tony Williamson was definitely "the one."

Patsy's parents didn't know whether to be happy or distressed with their daughter's choice, a Boston Brahmin boy, Beacon Hill born and bred.

Mrs. Sheehan chirpily encouraged, "At least she'll be well provided for."

But Mr. Sheehan was concerned, "Just so his people treat our Patsy right."

The couple met the same night Rosemary and Tony did, at the Christmas party in Milton.

Once Norman Alden Prescott met Patricia Ann Sheehan, he knew he had to see her again and immediately invited the petite beauty and her friends to go ice skating with his crowd the very next day. But before he could get an answer, Cordelia Parker strategically pulled him away. The moment of opportunity had passed, that is, until he spotted Patsy admiring the Christmas tree with other party guests, happily oohing and ahing as they pointed to exquisite ornaments.

Norman instantly left a lively group discussion on the war in Europe and completing one's education versus enlisting in the Armed Services with a simple "Excuse me." He rushed to Patsy's side, and once again extended the invitation.

Patsy accepted, they connected, and now, six months later with the country at war and his military duty just round the corner, the unlikely couple—six-foot-one, WASP Norman and five-foot-two, Irish Catholic Patricia, who friends fondly called "Mutt and Jeff"—were to be married in record time like so many other wartime couples.

∞

Norman's Mayflower-descendent parents had their own misgivings. "Do you think she'll fit in dear?" his mother had asked his father, "I mean she is from South Boston, and things are so very different over there. *Her people are grocers for goodness sake, not exactly what we had in mind for our son, let alone his progeny.*

Mr. Prescott misleadingly appeared to be without apprehension. "Don't you remember, Charlotte? My parents thought you and I were mismatched because your family hadn't lived on the Hill that long. As twenty-year residents, you were upstarts according to their standards."

Mr. Prescott thought it best to keep his true feelings to himself. *And now our grandchildren will have Irish blood in their veins. Fortunately my parents aren't alive to witness their grandson's interracial marriage.* "Not to worry dear. Norman has a level head. He'd never make a foolish match." *Unconventional perhaps, but never foolish or so I hope.*

"Of course you're right," Mrs. Prescott said somewhat unenthusiastically. "Now, if I can only get his betrothed to drop that dreadful Patsy and go by her middle name. Ann sounds so much better with Prescott, don't you agree, dear?"

♋

Patricia Ann Sheehan and Norman Alden Prescott were married in Gate of Heaven Church only two months after Steve and Kay. The flowers at their wedding were amongst the prettiest anyone remembered seeing. This was Patsy's time to shine both as bride and talented florist. However small her concession, Patsy still considered herself a florist, but after "I do," never practiced her trade again other than arrangements for her home, another Gate of Heaven wedding, and three South Boston funerals.

Father Norris presided but only because the groom had agreed to and signed a document stating they'd raise their children as Roman Catholics.

Norman Prescott possessed a peaceful nature and didn't tell his parents about the church's requirement. *At least for now, what they don't know won't hurt them or Patsy.* And he chose his words carefully when they'd asked prior to the slated wedding date, "How are things coming along with the Catholics?"

"Fortunately Mother and Dad, there's no objection to marrying us in the church."

Norman's parents, however, had their own objections.

The second wedding, or the "mock wedding," as Patsy called it, took place with a judge officiating in Mr. and Mrs. Prescott's garden.

Two weddings, two guest lists, two invitations, two receptions, one bride, one groom and a tremendous amount of planning.

Norman's parents made complete provision for the Beacon Hill ceremony and their invitation read:

Mr. and Mrs. Jeffrey Andrew Prescott
request the honour of your presence
at the marriage of

Ann Sheehan

to their son

Norman Alden Prescott

Saturday, the twenty-sixth of July
One thousand nine hundred and forty-two
at half-after three o'clock
24 Louisberg Square
Boston, Massachusetts

Dinner reception to follow

Mr. and Mrs. Prescott felt a civil ceremony would be best in light of Patsy's Catholicism and told her so. Actually, Mrs. Prescott told her so. "I'm afraid our people would embarrass you dear. There's not one who would have any idea when to stand, kneel, or sit in your church, or do you call it a cathedral? It doesn't matter," she added with the wave of a hand. "This way you'll have an unspoiled memory of the most important day of your life right here, in your future home's garden."

Patsy loved Norman too much to object, but didn't take the slight lying down and insisted a Gate of Heaven wedding should take place first. "I'm afraid my people would consider us adulterous without the blessing of the church."

⚮

It was later in the evening, after the "mock wedding," while Tony and Rosemary were sitting together on a Romanesque stone bench in the Prescott's verdant, walled garden that he proposed marriage, and eagerly slipped a diamond ring on her finger.

She promptly handed it back. "Tony Williamson. Please, not until I give you my answer."

"I'm sorry, Ro. I've never proposed marriage to anyone before." Tony smiled, got down on one knee, and this time held the ring before his intended. "Rosemary King, will you please do me the honor of becoming my wife?"

Steady splashing sounded from a nearby fountain that gently misted on all within its range, and Rosemary's eyes glistened as she answered. "Yes, Tony. Of course I will."

He stood and swept Rosemary into his arms. Her pastel handbag fell onto the damp, moss-encrusted brick walk, but neither of them seemed to care. It was the kind of kiss you remember until the day you die, the kiss that takes your breath away, the kiss that seals your love-filled heart to another 'til death do us part.

Music drifted out to the garden from the reception inside and the small band's crooner smoothly sang what became their song forever. "Our Love is Here to Stay."

The stars were out in great force that crystal-clear June night, and the newly engaged couple tried to locate constellations. "How about this one, Tony? What's the name of this one?" Rosemary said as she held her left hand out and the diamond ring sparkled.

"That's what they call a rose, a rose-cut diamond."

❧

Rita and Rosemary were making so much noise Norah got out of bed, knocked on the girl's bedroom door, softly coughed, and loudly whispered, "What in God's name is goin' on in there?" She coughed again.

Rita opened up to her mother's disapproving frown. "Sorry, Mum." She smiled and couldn't help but giggle.

"There are people tryin' to sleep, and I'm assumin' you've forgotten what your father's like if he's been unduly wakened?" Norah tied the sash on her chenille robe, looked at Rosemary, and broke into her own smile. "Show it to me. Show me the ring."

"How did you know, Mum?" Rosemary coyly held her left hand behind her back.

148

"There's no mistakin' a girl in love, and a girl in love with a diamond ring on her finger glows all the more. Now let me have a look!"

Rosemary supported her left wrist with her right hand. "Can you believe it, Mum? I'm going to be a wife?"

"And when exactly are you plannin' on becoming a wife, Rosemary Virginia?" Norah asked with a grin, and then the cough that had been so persistent these last few months came again.

Rita kept interrupting with "Ro!" and "Congratulations!" and "Here comes the bride."

"Tony wants to finish college first. He's so close. And then there's the Service."

"Well, it's certainly sensible to wait, but it's not goin' to be easy, now is it? I'm speakin' to you as a mother ought to, Rosemary. And it'll do you no harm to pay attention too, Rita Margaret. No doin' things you shouldn't before the weddin'. Wait, darlin'. You'll not regret it."

"I know, Mum. Don't worry." Rosemary was embarrassed, and Rita had no response other than her face turning pink in complete contrast to her mother's paleness.

"And Rosemary, you're not to be discouraged by anythin' your father may say. This is a happy time. You'll need to let his words run off your back like water off a duck. Promise me you'll do that."

"Mum, nothing could color my happiness." She took her mother's hand and squeezed it.

"He's a good boy, and you're goin' to have a good life together." Norah kissed Rosemary on the cheek.

Just then, John Joseph appeared in the bedroom doorway, both hands slightly above his head, pressing against the jamb on either side. "You can stop your whisperin'. I know all about it."

He blinked his eyes against the light and faced Rita. "I heard you screechin'. 'Oh, that's so wonderful Ro,' and you." He turned to Rosemary. "'Look at my diamond,' and all the rest of your blatherin'. Marry 'em, see if I care, but the same goes for you as Kay. I'm not payin' for a weddin'. Especially with your mother not workin' again and the doctor bills. What am I sayin'? If we didn't owe a penny, I'd still not spend one on your Dago weddin'."

"That's fine with me, Dad," Rosemary said. Norah tried to muffle her cough but wasn't very successful. Her hand dropped to her chest, and she coughed again.

Rosemary asked, "Mum, what can I do to help you?"

Before Norah could get the words out of her mouth, John Joseph still squinting, had more to say. "Don't get cheeky with me, young woman. 'That's fine with me, Dad.' Like how it's goin' to be is up to you. I'm not payin', and I'm the one to say whether it's goin' to be fine or not."

He grabbed Rosemary's arm. "Do you understand?"

She answered respectfully only for the benefit of her mother. "Yes, Dad, I understand"

"Now who's goin' to make me somethin' to eat?"

It came about so quickly, or so it seemed. Norah had been living with a bump on her right foot for some time, not giving much thought to the sporadic throbbing or slow-but-sure increase in size.

All three girls knew about it, but when they expressed their collective concern, their mother would answer, "It's nothin'. Sure and we've better things to be thinkin' about."

Shortly after Norah returned to work, the pain became so severe she took aspirin constantly and regularly put her foot in a pan of warm water for relief. It was sixteen-year-old Patrick who took notice this time. "Mum, you're sure soakin' your foot a lot. What's the matter with it?"

"I'm not sure, darlin', but I think it's time to see the doctor."

"I'll go with you, Mum." Patrick stepped closer. "Do you need more hot water?"

"You're a good son, Patrick Henry. But no, thank you. What I need to do is go downstairs and ask Mrs. Flynn if I can use her telephone to make a doctor's appointment."

Norah wearily reached for the skinny sixteen-year-old, her seventh child, the one who so easily slipped between the cracks of her attentions. "We'll stop by Joe's Spa on the way home and get you one of those chocolate frappes you're so fond of. Would you like that, Patrick?"

Joe's Spa was a specialty sandwich luncheonette and soda fountain popular with people of all ages but above all, teenagers and young adults. Truth be known, Patrick was mortified by the thought of walking in with his mother, but couldn't pass up the chance to gulp down one of those delicious frappes. "You bet, Mum."

∞

Doctor Petrukonis was puzzled as to why Norah hadn't brought the walnut-sized lump to his attention sooner. "Mrs. King, we've lost some precious time here."

"To tell you the truth, Doctor, I just thought it was from bein' on me feet so much. But after a long soakin' in Epsom salts, I'm good as new. It's nothin' really just a little painful is all. Can't you take care of it here in the office?"

Much to Norah's protest, and for the second time that year, Doctor Petrukonis needed to admit her to City Hospital for another surgery.

Rosemary, Rita, and Pat sat side by side on hard, wooden chairs in the hospital's crowded, noisy waiting room where families gathered like nesting birds, their necks craned in anticipation of news about loved ones. Finally the anxious trio heard someone call, "King, is the King family here?"

They jumped to their feet and stood like soldiers at attention. Doctor Petrukonis recognized them and saw that the father wasn't here this time. Pat felt he needed to be the man of the family and spoke first. "How's our mother doing, Doctor?"

"Mrs. King came through the surgery just fine. She's already awake, but you won't be able to see her until she's out of recovery."

According to Lorayne Joyce Carberry, Southie native, "Joe's Spa was the place to go. You could meet all your friends there and I could hardly wait to get my Ken (Carberry) in the the door when we first started dating so all the girls could see what a handsome guy my guy was."

**Joe's Spa
481 Broadway
South Boston, Mass.**

"Thank you, Doctor," they said.

And Rosemary asked, "Can we visit our mother tonight?"

"She can see you sooner than that. Say an hour or so."

Rosemary turned to her siblings. "I'm sorry to rush off, but I've got to get back to work or I'll lose my job."

The fatigued doctor—this had been his third surgery today—suggested, "Let me walk out with you." He lightly touched Rosemary's elbow and discreetly said, "There's more Miss King, but I think it would be better to discuss it in my office."

I knew it. Blessed Mother of God, please help us. Rosemary had certainly seen her mother under the weather before, however this time was different.

Norah had been meeting every worried inquiry with a plausible explanation. Her constant cough was "a tickle in me throat," and her pale yellow-gray pallor was "I'm at the tail end of recuperation. Come fall I'll be apple-cheeked again. You'll see." Lately, there was a faint odor when she entered a room, not greatly noticeable, but definitely there. It was, if there is such a thing, a sweet, rotting smell which Rosemary didn't understand at all. Her mother was fastidious about personal hygiene and instilled the same standard in her children. "It's true what they say now and don't forget 'Cleanliness is next to Godliness.'"

Doctor Petrukonis and Rosemary King walked down the stuffy hallway in identically paced swift steps. The doctor's shoes were gum-soled and quiet, Rosemary's high heels, a strident rat-a-tat-tat, and then there was carpet.

"Please, have a seat, Miss King."

"No, thank you, Doctor. I'd rather stand."

Tall, tow-headed, prematurely balding Doctor Jonas Petrukonis had glasses perched on the tip of his long nose and a stethoscope dangling from his coat pocket. He was the first in his Lithuanian family to graduate from college and was supported through medical school by his parents, aunts and uncles who worked at laboring jobs as lineman, hotel maid, factory worker, seamstress, butcher, rubbish man, and baker. He tried his best to stay detached but couldn't, and feigned looking for Norah's records in order to regain composure. "I don't know what I was thinking. Her file would still be at the nurses station."

He closed the cabinet drawer and slowly made an about face. "Miss King, there's no easy way to say this." He took a couple of steps toward his desk and stopped. "I'm afraid your mother has cancer. We did an exploratory procedure after the tumor removal, and it's spread considerably. Apparently she's had it for some time now."

Rosemary put her hand to her mouth. "Oh my God." She felt lightheaded and took a seat.

"Are you all right, Miss King? I can have someone bring you a glass of water."

Am I all right? The dearest person in all the world to me has cancer. "Thank you. I'm not thirsty, Doctor."

"I know this is hard to believe, but trust me, I've seen enough to identify a malignancy when I see one. And the decline in your mother's health these last months has been alarming. I'm confident your family will do all they can to make her as comfortable as possible."

"Of course we will." Rosemary's answer was curt. She wasn't angry, she was anxious.

"The pain will be fairly intense toward the end, and we'll admit her again if necessary. In either case, I'll prescribe something to see her through. At best, your mother has about three months."

Rosemary sat up even straighter, as if her improved posture could improve the situation. *Wait a minute* "What exactly do you mean?" She knew. It was perfectly clear that her mother was dying. Rosemary was stalling and hoping for a better answer.

He understood; he'd seen it before. "Is there some way I can get ahold of your father?"

Norah's first born, the one she depended on to co-parent, cooperate, and set a good example, began to tremble. "This can't be happening. How can you be so sure, Doctor?"

"Your mother has every symptom to support our advanced sarcoma diagnosis, and I'm certain the biopsy will be conclusive. Believe me, Miss King, if I thought there was a ray of hope we wouldn't be talking as we are."

Doctor Petrukonis leaned to one side of his chair. "How can I get ahold of your father?"

"That won't be necessary, Doctor. I'll tell him. It'll be best that way."

"Very well. Here's my number." He reached for a pen and pad of paper. "Please tell him not to hesitate to contact me. That goes for you and the rest of the family too."

"Thank you. I assume my mother doesn't know yet."

"She knows, but didn't know how to tell you. She's quite a lady, your mother. It was old home week when Mrs. King showed up in the woman's ward again. The nurses love her." This was the first time his face looked less than grave.

However, Norah's fatal diagnosis still hung in the room like a wet sheet, heavy and dripping with sadness.

Dr. Petrakonis saw tears stream from Norah's beautiful daughter's eyes, and he waited for Rosemary to make the next move. When she got up to leave, Jonas Petrukonis, also from Southie, whose own mother was only ten years older than Norah, with five children in eleven years as opposed to Norah's nine in fourteen, who knew the same kind of hard work and scrimping ways but not a minute of domestic abuse or alcohol-related adversity, came out from behind his desk and took Rosemary's hand. "Miss King, I promise to do everything in my power to see your mother through this with the least amount of suffering."

CHAPTER 15

Most all the other beautiful things in life come by twos and threes,
by dozens and hundreds.
Plenty of roses, stars, sunsets, rainbows, brothers and sisters,
aunts and cousins,
but only one mother in the whole world.

KATE DOUGLAS WIGGIN

THE WREATH ON THE FRONT door of the three-decker's main entrance, its black ribbon blowing in the early October wind, told passersby that someone was being waked within.

Elderly, white-haired Peg Hennessey, clothed in dark colors, kerchief on her head and hankie in hand, sat on a straight-backed chair just inside the door and directed visitors upstairs. "Second floor. Mrs. King, God rest her soul." It comforted the old woman to do so.

In South Boston, known or not, everyone waked the deceased. To pay your respects was part and parcel of "being a decent human being."

Tradition called for a two-day wake at home with a Rosary said on the second night. Funeral and burial were on the third day. Drawn drapes and black ribbons announced the loss, and doors opened wide to the sympathy of family, friends and caring strangers.

At one point, a line of people went from the Kings' apartment on Eighth almost halfway up to I Street. Visitors carried flowers, food, spiritual bouquets, and tired children. Hushed conversations hummed with lament, and when some spoke in normal voices, sad eyes stared them down. They continued to arrive well into the dark, and those still waiting left only after Peg Hennessey said, "The family's exhausted as you can only imagine. They need to be closin' up for the night. God bless you for comin', and please come back tomorrow."

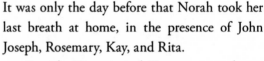

Spiritual Bouquets are similar to secular greeting cards but have religious images such as saints, the Holy Family, Blessed Mother, or Sacred Heart, and sometimes a spray of flowers, such as lilies or roses. The sender pledges to pray a Rosary or Novena, or to attend Mass on behalf of the recipient or their loved one. Or they may sponsor a devout order to do the same.

It was only the day before that Norah took her last breath at home, in the presence of John Joseph, Rosemary, Kay, and Rita.

Patrick, Timmy, and Tommy were downstairs eating breakfast in the landlady's apartment. Marie Flynn thought it was the least she could do under the circumstances. *I can't believe Norah King is in her final days now, last rites and all. God bless her dear soul.* She told Rosemary, "Send your brothers to me right after Mass, so you can have some peace and quiet with your mother. I'll make 'em pancakes and eggs."

Rita and Rosemary were on either side of the bed, each holding their mother's hand, and Kay stood by Rosemary with one hand resting on Norah's knee.

John Joseph remained at the foot of the bed, stiff as a statue.

The room was quiet, and Norah lay completely still, her flannel nightgown buttoned to the very top, faded, auburn-gray hair in one long braid, and face so pale there was little contrast with the pillowcase, and then she moved. Norah reached for Rita's face, and her gasping words began. "For the love of God . . ."

She closed her eyes, coughed deeply, opened them again and looked first toward her husband, then to her two oldest daughters. "Please promise . . . you'll look after each other."

John Joseph supposed she was speaking to the girls only and said nothing as all three leaned in one at a time and kissed her. "We will, Mum," Rita answered, patting her mother's hand, while Rosemary barely got the words out, "Please don't worry, Mum," and Kay urgently followed with, "Mum, you can depend on . . ." and that was it.

Norah was gone.

The sisters looked at each other in disbelief, and Kay cried, "The doctor said she had a few more days," and then they looked at their father. "Dad," Rita pleaded, "Dad, do something."

John Joseph tightened his crossed arms and mumbled, "I'll go get Mr. Gorham."

∞

Middle-aged, second-generation undertaker, Francis Xavier Gorham—no one in Southie ever remembered seeing his tall, corpulent build in anything other than a dark suit—sat in the Kings' living room late that Sunday morning, and explained to John Joseph and Rosemary all that would be taking place for the next few days. "First of all, Mr. King, Miss King, thank you for giving me the privilege of serving your family at this most difficult time."

John Joseph let out a huff, and Rosemary delicately held on to her hankie as Mr. Gorham continued. "Mrs. King should be arriving at the funeral home any minute now, and you can rest assured my staff will take good care of her."

Rosemary's unused (and it would remain so) hankie was the R-embroidered Irish linen she'd discovered in a pocket of the red coat. Today it brought back the memory of that afternoon in the kitchen when Norah surprised her with the elegant garment. She could see herself twirling and her mother gleefully clapping as she said, "It's as if it was made for you darlin'."

"Your kindness is very much appreciated, Mr. Gorham. Thank you," Rosemary said with dignity, her expression composed.

"Some of my fellas will come by before dark with the coffin table, extra chairs, and a kneeler." The experienced undertaker respectfully continued with specific protocol for an at-home Irish wake. "We'll need to have Mrs. King's casket in a prominent place in the living room, and of course, the kneeler in front of it. People like to see their flowers so all arrangements should be as close to the casket as possible, and the rest should be in plain sight. Now, to the right, you'll need one immediate family member or more, other than the spouse, to receive visitors and move them along. There'll be kneelers and standers alike, but you'll soon notice that everyone says a prayer. It's a natural progression. People generally know what to do."

"Do they now?" John Joseph barked.

Francis Gorham, accustomed to the erratic behaviors of grief, was completely unaffected by the irascible husband and quickly engaged his usual strategy under such circumstances. He spoke in a quieter, compliant tone. "Yes, Mr. King. Now, as the spouse, you'll be sitting in a chair directly to the left of the casket. People don't expect you to stand at a time like this, sir. So please don't feel you must."

"I don't give a horse's arse what people expect." John Joseph's hand tightened on the arm of the couch.

"That's understandable, Mr. King." The undertaker paused and looked down in order to give the room a chance to breathe; it was something his father taught him about the business years ago.

"All right then, where was I? Ah yes, my fellas will set up chairs along the wall directly to Mr. King's right, and that's where the rest of the family's to be seated."

Food had been coming in for days: baked beans, potato salad, platters of cold cuts and cookies, cupcakes, fish chowder, soda bread, and more. Caring neighbors used their War Ration coupons to provide for the Kings and many prepared better food for Norah's family than their own. "It pleases our Lord to no end when He sees His children sacrificin' for the good of others."

Kay was writing everything down. "Excuse me, Mr. Gorham, with all due respect, it's important that the chairs and kneeler selected are in good repair. My mother would have wanted it that way." Only a month ago she'd been at a wake where all the rented mortuary furniture was shabby.

"Absolutely. You have my word. Our best." He admired the young woman's pluck. "We're almost finished. I know this isn't easy. Now, there's no food or drink to be had at a wake, except maybe some whiskey in the kitchen for the men, and smokes too. But after the funeral you'll want a big spread with a good amount of drink. People need it, you know, to be breaking bread and seeing the sadness through together. Don't worry about providing anything. I've yet to see the deceased's family have to come up with a crumb or a drop. God bless the goodhearted people of South Boston."

Mr. Gorham wrote something down in his small, black, spiral-bound notepad. "We'll move ahead then. Mrs. King's funeral will take place at Gate of Heaven, and the burial at New Calvary. God rest her soul."

John Joseph nodded his head but looked as though his thoughts were elsewhere, and they were.

"Don't worry about providing anything." Those were the exact words Norah's employers had used all those years ago. *Don't worry about providing anything after the wedding. We'll have a grand lunch for your guests and wedding cake like no other.* He pictured his bride in her wedding finery and remembered how proud he was to be marrying such a fine young woman, hardworking and comely too. *Don't worry about providing anything.*

Without further delay, Mr. Gorham stood, pulled in, and buttoned his coat jacket. "Now, if you'd be so kind as to come to the funeral home, we'll find a suitable casket and discuss the little girl's situation too. Say, three o'clock?"

⊙₰

Rosemary, Rita, and Kay and her husband, Steve, accompanied John Joseph to Gorham's Funeral Home on Broadway, where they were graciously received by Mrs. Eugenia Gorham, a pigeon-breasted woman who softly cooed predictable sympathies. "I'm so sorry for your loss. Of course, it's much harder on those left behind, now, isn't it?" She led the family to her husband's office. "Your mother's suffering is over, and when you see her again, all will be well."

John Joseph found it difficult to stay seated in one of the several armchairs surrounding the undertaker's desk. Particularly after Mr. Gorham asked him about Noni, the forever eight-year-old who rested in a solitary grave at New Calvary Cemetery.

"Mr. King, do you want the child's casket to be disinterred so we can put her to rest with your wife? This, of course, would require a reorganization of grave sites."

"I need to go outside. Give me a minute." The bereft father, and now widower, excused himself twice before the child's arrangements could be finalized. *A reorganization of gravesites, is it? How in God's name do you expect me to come up with that kind of cash?*

The discussion and decisions brought it all back: Nonie's fatal accident, their newborn baby, Timothy, only three weeks old at the time and Norah's milk drying up while her tears never stopped, Noni's clothing, her place at the table, and after a while, the slip of the tongue, saying there was one more child in the family than there actually was. The father of nine never did know how to answer that question. *If one of your children is deceased, do you subtract them from the total sum?*

When Noni died, there was barely enough money to buy one grave, let alone the four suggested by the undertaker at the time. "Even knowing our loved ones' eternal home is in heaven, it's a great comfort having them all in the one place here on earth. I'm sorry to say it, but the day will come when you'll have need for the other spaces."

The decision was simple then. "We'll only be takin' the one." And now, the need was here.

John Joseph knew he could always borrow money for the gravesites from hoodlums, boyos who made personal loans with notoriously high interest, bodily harm guaranteed should a payment be missed. But that was of little concern. This was his chance to make it up to Noni, who lost her life because of him, or so he'd always believed, not giving any credence to the fact that the truck driver who ran over her was, as the attending police officer had said, "driving like a bat out of hell."

As far as John Joseph King was concerned, the sprite of a girl—the child who had his lean build and Norah's kind spirit—weathered winter, spring, summer and fall in the hard ground, all because she was sent to the store to buy a loaf of his favorite bread.

It haunted him. And no amount of drink would obliterate his ceaseless guilt and ongoing anger with God. *Why her? Why not the new baby? We certainly didn't need the one more, now, did we?*

John Joseph returned and gave Mr. Gorham the go-ahead. "You'll have your money tomorrow afternoon." They made final arrangements for Noni's casket to be removed from its solitary grave and buried with her mother's in what was now the family plot. "And tell those cemetery workers to watch what they're doin'. I don't want my daughter left unattended."

In all, there were four spaces, and two of them would be occupied that week.

Rosemary, Rita, Kay, and Steve remained, for the most part, speechless until the three sisters spoke of their mother's final needs. "Mr. Gorham," Rosemary spoke first, "we'll look after our mother's hair, and please ask your people not to put any makeup on her. Thank you."

Kay was next. "As you can see, we've brought a dress. It's our mother's—*was* our mother's." She looked up at her husband, who'd been standing the whole time holding a deep blue, lace-collared, long-sleeved dress on a hanger, being careful not to wrinkle it.

Steve Chalpin tenderly squeezed his wife's shoulder. "It's going to be okay, honey." John Joseph harrumphed, he thought too quietly to be heard. "Cream puff."

When Noni was waked, the undertaker slid his case of makeup under a bed in the girls' room and explained, "Sometimes, touchups are necessary, from the kissin' and all." Rosemary recalled how upset her mother had been at the exaggeration of rosy cheeks and bee-stung lips. "I understand some color is needed but I'll not have my little girl lookin' like a painted kewpie doll."

Steve squeezed Kay's shoulder again.

Mr. Gorham sprang to his feet. "I'm so sorry. My wife should have taken the dress from you earlier." No sooner had he hung it over the top of a door than the youngest King sister addressed him.

"Mr. Gorham, here are . . ." Rita didn't want to say underwear. "Some of our mother's personal items, and her shoes and stockings too." She held a Filene's bag on her lap.

"Thank you. Please forgive me for being so specific, Miss King, but your mother's legs will be covered. The stockings and shoes won't be necessary."

"Yes, they are, Mr. Gorham." Teenage Rita stiffened, and the bag crinkled. "Our mother's not walking into heaven barefoot."

The chagrined, but expressionless, undertaker didn't argue.

❧

When U. S. Navy Corpsman John Michael King walked into his father's house, fresh from the Pacific with war in his veins and mourning in his heart, he stood up to John Joseph for the first time in his life.

"Dad, there'll be no whiskey at my mother's wake and funeral. None."

John Michael was ready for a fight but didn't have to lift a hand. His father, surprisingly and shockingly, complied. And for the next three days, he didn't drink a drop of alcohol.

Word got out that the wake and funeral would be dry, but men still made their way to the kitchen like lemmings, and instead sipped strong tea in short glasses.

❧

Almost three months to the day of her diagnosis, fifty-year-old Norah Catherine Foley King's open casket lay on a long narrow coffin table in front of the bowed living room window. The fawn-colored draperies and lace sheers were, in that order, partway and completely closed, providing a lovely backdrop for the lady who did her best to make things lovely, from the way she set her modest table, kept house, raised her children, clothed her family, treated others, practiced her faith, and celebrated special events and holidays.

"Pretty is as pretty does, remember that girls," is what she'd say. "On the inside, on the outside, and all about." Norah even wrote the "words to live by" inside each of her daughter's Daily Missals:

Pretty is as pretty does.

Mary Callanan, Norah's closest friend, met visitors at the open front door of the Kings' apartment. "Thank you for coming. It means so much to the family."

Her daughter Marion took the flowers and cards, putting the former around the living room, and the latter on a doily-lined, wooden tray, while Mary's twelve-year-old son, Don, ran food back to the kitchen, where landlady, Marie Flynn, and upstairs neighbor Mrs. Flanagan were waiting to put it away. Mary's husband, Frank, was in the kitchen too, making sure the men's glasses remained full, even if it was only strong tea.

Patsy Sheehan Prescott personally created a heart-shaped wreath of white mums and other autumn flowers with nine white roses tucked in between, one for each of Norah's children. The wreath rested on a tall easel, and an ivory satin ribbon across the center read "Beloved Mother" in softest gold script.

Rosemary and Kay stood to the right of the casket greeting visitors and mourners in gentle tones. "My mother thought the world of you."

"We'll miss her too."

"Your flowers are so beautiful."

"Thank you for remembering Noni."

"Our father's in the kitchen right now."

"John Michael got home late last night. We hoped he'd get here in time to see our mother, but she went quickly. The Red Cross is still trying to locate Joe. We think in Germany."

"Sister Veronita and Sister Agnes, Rita's right over there." Kay indicated with an open hand, mindful, even now, of her mother's words about a pointing finger being impolite.

When a neighbor insisted Rosemary sit down for a few minutes, she resisted. To do so at a time such as this went against her well-raised character.

"No, thank you, I'm fine. Really."

Most visitors knelt before the open casket and said a prayer, but others stood to the side and did the same, just as Mr. Gorham predicted.

Some put a kiss on their fingertips and pressed it to Norah's cheek or forehead.

Doctor Petrukonis cupped his palm over Norah's rosary holding hands and was heard to say, "You're in our Lord's care now."

Curious Southie teenagers Lorayne Joyce and her best friend, Jane McDonough, never liked to pass up a wake. Telltale black ribbons welcomed them through unknown doorways, but this time their condolences were far more personal. Jane's father was Mr. Mac from the drugstore, and her family knew Johnny King's mother well.

Jane studied Norah's face. *Mrs. King looks just like herself.* And Lorayne asked God, *Why do you take the nicest people first?*

Norah's scrubwoman friends, eight in all, stood before her casket the longest. These women went together on buses, trolleys, and trains into the heart of Boston five nights a week, and washed the floors of City Hall and other downtown buildings, grateful for the work.

Years later, Jane would have occasion to tell her goddaughter, "The first thing I noticed at your grandmother's wake was how clean the apartment was. Everything was absolutely immaculate."

A casual observer might call them old biddies, but these were loyal ladies, sincere in their comments and grief.

"God bless, Norah. She'll never see her grandchildren."

"And after how hard she's worked all these years, puttin' up with himself and holdin' the family together." This said with the greatest discretion, when John Joseph was absent from the room.

"Sure and you can see the girl in her today. Gorham's does such a grand job of makin' the dead look good."

"Heaven and all the angels will be happier for her presence."

"Norah's the first one of us to go, and only fifty."

"Who do you suppose is next then?"

Mary Callanan stood strong by the door but at one point broke down crying and had to leave. "I beg your pardon, but I can barely talk for the sorrow I'm feelin'." However, she soon returned to relieve Kay who'd taken over her duties. "Sure and a cuppa always helps, now, doesn't it? Helps, but all the tea in the world isn't goin' to bring her back. Your mother and I have always made it our business to see things through together, and this is no different. Sure and she'd do the same for me."

Mary tenderly patted Kay's arm. "You can go back to your sister now."

John Joseph sat directly to the left of the simple, dark wood, lacquered casket as suggested, and was kinder than his older children had remembered him being in many years as he answered visitors.

"Thank you very much."

"It's good of you to come by."

"Yes, she was a fine woman."

They knew it was the absence of drink that made their father more civil, and the younger children didn't know what to make of it, other than they wanted him to be like this all the time, "a nice man."

Many times he took an offered hand in his two, but much to his children's embarrassment, John Joseph frequently left his post to visit friends in the kitchen. And when he did John Michael stood in his place, concerned the empty chair would be seen as a lack of respect.

Norah trained her brood well. Not one of them could sit comfortably in the presence of an adult and did so only when there was a lull in the line.

"Thank you for saying such nice things about my mother."

"My father is in the kitchen if you want to see him before you leave."

The little boys, who were nine and eleven, didn't say anything other than, "Thank you." Tommy kept wiping his tears away with the cuff of his white shirt, and every time he did, Timmy leaned close and whispered, "Ya gotta cut it out, Tommy. Yer gonna make us all cry again."

Rita welcomed Sister Veronita's warm embrace. "I'm glad you're here, Sister." She politely acknowledged the other nun too. "Good afternoon, Sister Agnes."

"I'm so sorry, dear," Sister Agnes said, her clasped hands hidden within the folds of her habit's sleeves.

"Thank you, Sister."

Rita tried hard to hold back her tears, and did, until Sister Veronita said, "It's a fast-fading tradition Rita, but Sister Agnes and I want to honor your mother's memory by sitting up with her these two nights. We'll return later this evening and keep vigil. She'll never be alone, and neither will you, dear. Your mother will always be watching over you from heaven."

Norah's youngest daughter, her sixth child, began to gently weep. Sister Veronita removed her glasses, wiped her own tears away, and was about to speak again when the whole room stopped, as if it were electrical and someone had pulled the plug.

All eyes looked down the hall, toward the kitchen as John Joseph wailed for the second time, "Norah, Norah, come back."

Most visitors assumed Mr. King was inebriated, and there wasn't one who'd deny him his pint or whiskey at a time like this. But he hadn't had a drop.

∽

Early the third morning after Norah passed away, shortly before it was time for Mr. Gorham to close Mrs. King's casket, the family privately said their final goodbyes with kisses, pats, tears, and in John Joseph's case, questions and edicts. *Why are you leavin' me now, Norah? Haven't we still children to care for? And if you think I'm ever takin' another step into the house of God after today, you're sadly mistaken. He's got you, and that's all the more He'll ever get from me.*

Timmy bided his time and quietly asked Rosemary's permission to leave something with the person he knew loved him more than anyone else in the world.

"Yes, of course you can," she gently answered, pulling him toward her for a hug, "but be sure Dad's not looking."

The determined eleven-year-old reached in his corduroy trousers pocket for the ribbon he'd lifted from the heart-shaped wreath the night before. And by the grace of God, "Timmy, who, God bless him, has the best heart," as his mother said time and again, was able to tuck his final goodbye, *Beloved Mother*, under Norah's satin pillow without being noticed.

∽

When Norah King's funeral procession arrived at New Calvary Cemetery, the two caskets were already side-by-side; a spray of red roses sat atop Norah's and Noni's was covered with a white, cross-embroidered, linen cloth that gleamed in the intermittent autumn sun. One lady was heard to say, "Why, it's as bright as an angel."

Rita walked up to the site with her father, followed by Johnny and Pat, then Timmy and Tommy, behind them Rosemary and Tony, then Kay and Steve. Everyone else followed. Rosemary and Kay reached for each other at the sight of the two caskets and held on. "Ro, it's as if our Noni was waiting for Mum."

The little boys stood close to the casket, and Tommy whispered hurriedly for both of them, "We didn't know you, but you're still our sister, and we wanted to say hello."

Rosemary thought she would fold, just fold with the sorrow of it all. "Now she won't be alone anymore."

A cold wind suddenly came up, and several people looked toward the sky. The Irish-born priest in attendance slowly walked over to John Joseph and whispered, "Do you want the child's presence acknowledged, Mr. King?"

The beleaguered widower took his hat in his hands. "Just get it over with, Father."

Father Seamus Michael Casey did a heartfelt graveside ceremony as his long vestments blew about and those in attendance shivered. "You'll also want to please remember Noni King, Norah's namesake, in your prayers."

Thunder rolled. This time all eyes turned heavenward and the few people that had umbrellas became stations of shelter for those who didn't.

The astute, old priest silently prayed as everyone regrouped. *Dear God, forgive me, but I've not a lot of confidence in the father lookin' after his children. Protect them from harm and please keep each one strong in the faith of their dearly departed mother.*

Father Casey took one step forward and cleared his throat. "It's said in the book of Isaiah that, 'a little child shall lead them,' and isn't this little girl," he turned toward the smaller casket, "leading the way home to heaven for her own dear mother, perhaps at this very moment?" A fierce downpour sounded hard on the umbrellas and on the canvas canopy over the gravesite, almost drowning out the priest's remaining words. "Eternal rest grant unto them, O Lord, and let perpetual light shine upon them. May they rest in peace. Amen."

Out of seemingly nowhere, the sad cry of a bagpipe was heard through the downpour, and its sweet refrain took refuge in the hearts of all present.

The staff at New Calvary Cemetery often saw Father Francis R. Burke, S. J., or Father Frank, as he was known to his students at BC High School, slowly walking among the gravestones, where he earnestly played his bagpipes, thinking this was a place where no one would object to the noise. And it was there on consecrated ground that God led him to provide musical closure for grieving families, unannounced.

This stormy day, for the mother and child, it would be, "Ave Maria."

We slumber safely til the morrow . . .
O Maiden, see a maiden's sorrow,
O Mother, hear a suppliant child!
Ave Maria, gratia plena,
Maria, gratia plena,
Maria, gratia, plena,
Ave, ave dominus,
Dominus tecum,
Ave Maria

CHAPTER 16

You can shed tears that she is gone,
or you can smile because she has lived.
ANONYMOUS

TONY KNEW ROSEMARY NEEDED TIME to collect her thoughts. She'd had to make some difficult decisions lately and was eager to "get the house back in order," her coping phrase for the heartbreaking task ahead. Taking the King boys out on Saturday would give her and the two nuns who were coming to help almost a whole day to do so. Tony had "just the ticket, Ro," and invited the King brothers to the movies and gave them candy money too.

Red Sox loyalties clearly understood, there wasn't a boy in Southie who didn't want to see *The Pride of The Yankees*, starring Gary Cooper as baseball great Lou Gehrig, now showing at the Strand Theater.

"You've got a nickel each, so be thinking of what you want."

Tommy already knew he wanted a Sugar Daddy, because the big caramel lollypop lasted so long. Timmy thought Necco Wafers would be his best bet. "You get a lot, and if I suck instead of bite, maybe I'll have some left over." Pat asked for a box of Cracker Jack and gave the prize inside to Tommy.

A few days earlier, when Tony suggested the idea to Rosemary as they strolled along Pleasure Bay, she was disappointed in his lack of judgment. "Absolutely not. What will people think if my brothers show up at The Strand so soon after their mother passed away?"

"Listen, Ro, I don't want to do anything improper, but these kids have been through a lot. Who'd deny them? Besides, do you really want three wild fellas around when the good sisters from Saint Augustine's arrive?"

When they stopped to enjoy the view, Tony put his right foot up on the park bench, leaned on his knee, and gave Rosemary his best pitch and a beguiling smile too. "Come on, hon, let's give them a break."

Tony liked these kids. Teenage Pat had an easy smile, strong skinny build, good-looking dimpled face, golden-brown hair just this side of kinky, and his photographic memory made him one of the best students in the family. Twelve-year-old Timmy was just as lean but more muscular and quick on his feet, and he had an Irish tenor voice that had made his mother proud. "Sure and my Timmy has the makin' of another John McCormick," Norah had said. His chestnut hair was tight like Pat's, and he too had dimples; all the King kids had dimples. And all the King boys had tempers as well, while only one of the girls did.

When Irish dance insructor Moira Brennan saw Timmy King playing kick the wicket on E. 8th Street, his agility astounded her. "You've the same light step as your sister, Noni. Aren't we always in need of dancin' boys? Won't you give it a try?" Certain his friends would call him a "sissy" or even worse – they'd labeled Donal Mulligan "Prancin' Prince," and he was forever known as "Prancin'Mulligan"—Timmy politely declined. "Thanks anyways, Mrs. Brennan."

As he grew older, Timmy's looks were, according to Peg Hennessey, "nice enough but not movie-star-good-lookin' like the others." The attentive old woman seldom lacked an opinion, and she considered rascally ten-year-old Tommy "the most handsome," with his deep dimples, sapphire-blue eyes, and abundance of wavy brunette hair. Thomas Augustine was an avid reader, and his genuine love of people made the baby of the family irresistibly charming.

It was the thought of her rambunctious brothers and the two serene nuns all in the apartment at the same time that changed Rosemary's mind.

"Okay, but no monkeyshines." She gave Tony a peck on the cheek. "Don't think that smile's always going to work Mr. Williamson." Rosemary got serious again. "They're to behave like perfect gentlemen out of respect for our mother."

Tony grinned and promptly saluted.

Rita did her best to get off work so she could help too, but Mr. Schultz, the manager of W.T. Grant gave her a hard time. "Saturday's our busiest day. There are plenty of girls who'd like to have your job, Rita. Just let me know if it's too inconvenient for your schedule, and I'll hire one of them in your place."

Mr. Adolph Schultz, who changed his name once the war broke out and now went by Al, was a small, difficult man and his position of authority made him even more so, ironically earning him the name of "Little Hitler," which employees said kiddingly behind his back.

As World War II progressed and many Southie servicemen lost their lives in battle, "Little Hitler" ceased to be amusing and stopped being said.

Dot Reardon, a seasoned waitress who worked the lunch-counter, overheard Mr. Schultz's disgruntlement, and later, when Rita was taking her lunch break, Dot said, "He's a small man with a big stick. What can you do?" As she slid a hamburger and a coffee frappe across the counter to the pretty, auburn-haired teenager, and then fumbled through her order pad. "Sorry doll face, I can't seem to find your check."

Norah's coat hung right where it belonged, on the third peg of the coatrack by the back door, and more than one family member had hugged it when they thought the others weren't looking. It still smelled of her favorite fragrance, "soap and water, the best perfume in the world."

Rosemary looked at the white, child-sized rosary beads hanging on the seventh peg and remembered when Sister Bernadette, who helped all grieving families in Saint Augustine's parish, had removed Noni's jacket from that peg and kindly replaced it with the holy beads.

Although the King family had been going to Gate of Heaven for years now, Sister Bernadette offered to help again, "when you're ready, dear," with what she knew was one of the most difficult things there is to do after a loved one dies, care for their personal belongings. She was expected any minute now "to help tie up a few loose ends, dear." They were the only words she could think of for such a mission.

Sister Eugenia, who some thought a mute because of her quiet ways, would be with her.

John Joseph was seldom around, other than to sleep and demand "a change of clothes, decent breakfast, and have me lunch pail packed. It's the least you can do, seein' as I'm payin' the rent." Still, Rosemary thought it best to ask his permission for the nuns to help. *It'd be just my luck he'd be home on Saturday, and God in heaven if all hell wouldn't break loose.*

Last Sunday, she approached her father right after his nap and meekly explained everything, which went against her grain but played into his. "That is, if it's all right with you, Dad?"

John Joseph sat in his armchair with the bearing of a king and bluntly granted Rosemary's request. "Fine then. It needs to be done sooner or later, now, doesn't it?" He characteristically ran his hand over the top of his head, looked away and back at her with glistening wet eyes. "I just don't want 'em doin' it when I'm here. Have 'em come on a Saturday when you're home from work. Hear me, Rosemary? A Saturday. I'll wait it out at the pub."

◌

When Sister Bernadette and the much younger Sister Eugenia entered the Kings' apartment, a sense of well-being entered with them.

Their calm presence and flowing black habits emanated cleanliness, holiness, order. Their movements were purposeful, peaceful, and the soft click-click-click of the beads that fell from their waists seemed to say to Rosemary, *Don't worry, don't worry, we're here now, don't worry, don't worry you're not alone.*

Sister Bernadette quietly explained, "This is a little sooner than usual, dear, but we want to be of assistance and you sounded somewhat anxious on the telephone."

"Thank you, Sister Bernadette, Sister Eugenia. Yes, I need to get things in order for my family as soon as possible." She couldn't say the reason why. She wasn't ready yet.

"Oh, Rosemary! You're engaged!" Sister Bernadette had spotted the ring. "I had no idea! Congratulations! Have you set a date?"

"Yes, early June. Right after my husband-to-be graduates from Boston College School of Business Administration, then we're off to New York." Rosemary looked down at her ring and up again. "He has a Navy commission,

"Fiancé" wasn't a word used in South Boston. "Future husband," "the person I'm going to marry," or "my intended," were. When Rosemary read fiancé in a wedding etiquette booklet Jordan Marsh gave to all their registered brides, she liked it. But she knew better than to use a term some people in Southie might consider "puttin' on airs," or worse yet, "uppity."

and his first assignment is in the Big Apple. I'm so thankful he doesn't have to ship out right away."

"And who is this fortunate young man?" Sister Bernadette pleasantly asked.

"His name is Tony Williamson."

"Italian?" The nun comically raised one eyebrow. "I'm surprised your father approved."

"He's not Italian, and I can't convince my father otherwise so we've had a time of it. My Tony is actually Scotch-Irish."

"Well, God bless you two." Sister Bernadette, despite her almost daily task of helping the living with the aftermath of their dead, was an incredibly cheerful person. "Oh Rosemary, if you won't be the most beautiful bride." Her habit and beads swooshed and clicked as she gaily turned to Sister Eugenia. "Beautiful! Beautiful!" Sister Eugenia easily agreed. "Absolutely beautiful."

"Thank you, sisters." Rosemary was eager to get started, concerned her father might come home early, but she didn't want to be impolite. "May I get either of you a cup of tea?"

"Later, thank you, dear. We'll do what needs to be done first and have that to look forward to," Sister Bernadette answered.

Without further delay, Rosemary led the nuns to her parents' bedroom, where they made the sign of the cross before entering and calmly removed Norah's clothes from the closet, and her folded garments from the bureau drawers.

It was evident these humble Sisters of Notre Dame had done this together many times. Their dutiful movements corresponded in sync as Sister Eugenia folded longer items on the bed and Sister Bernadette folded shorter ones in place before stacking them in one of the large cardboard boxes they'd brought along.

Rosemary gathered Norah's shoes from the closet floor, and when she reached under the bed for her mother's house slippers, the nuns glanced toward each other with knowing looks of compassion.

Sister Bernadette waited until she could see Rosemary eye to eye again. "Usually we launder and iron these donations before giving them to the poor, but that won't be necessary this time. You should be very proud, dear. Your mother was quite orderly."

Sister Eugenia glanced around the neat-as-a-pin bedroom. Its white walls were free of fingerprints or spots, sheer white curtains covered the two windows, the yellowing shades were pulled halfway down, and faded green print drapes were precisely pushed back so all four panels were the exact same width. A large crucifix hung over the neatly made bed, where both pillows were perfectly lined up and tucked under a worn, off-white bedspread.

The floor was dust-free and highly waxed, and there were two unmatched braided rugs, one on Norah's side of the bed, and the larger on John Joseph's. A wide dresser took up most of one wall, and several saint cards had been slipped into the frame of the mirror above it. The dresser scarf was starched so stiffly it almost looked like paper and a statue of the Blessed Mother stood front and center, the back of her graceful image reflected in the mirror. The dresser also held photos of the King children, and a slip of palm was still where Norah had placed it, beneath the oval frame that held Noni's first-grade image.

The only light, other than natural, came from two small lamps. The one on the dresser shone brightly and the one across the room, next to the bed was comparatively dim. A stack of Norah's books, a pad of paper, pencil, and pen were neatly piled on the seat of a simple pine chair that took the place of a night-stand, and the sturdy short table on her husband's side of the bed held an alarm clock, a clean ashtray and book of matches, water glass, and a memorial card from Norah's funeral.

Rosemary lined Norah's shoes up just so in another box: the sturdy, black, low-heeled lace-ups her mother wore every day, rubber galoshes and Norah's treasured dancing shoes, brown, crisscross-laced ghillies the immigrant girl brought from Ireland so long ago but couldn't bear to part with, and her wedding shoes, ivory satin Louis-heeled pumps, now discolored and crumbling with the signs of time. Her daintier, perforated, black, lace-up pumps, reserved for Sundays and special occasions, had been taken to the funeral home.

Norah's slippers remained tucked in her daughter's apron pocket. "Excuse me, please, Sisters. I'll be back in a jiff."

Rosemary went to the bedroom she shared with Rita, sat down on one of the beds and held the backless scuffs against her heart. *I'm so sorry Mum. I hope you understand. I have to leave this house. I have to.*

When she returned to the task at hand, the good sisters suggested Rosemary save something of her mother's for each of the children. "It's been our experience dear, that having even one small item from a lost loved one provides a certain comfort."

For herself, Rosemary selected the crucifix Norah wore every day. How many times had she seen her mother seek its solace with a light touch, as if making sure the Savior was still with her?

Kay was given their mother's sewing-basket because she was the most interested and skilled when Norah brought her daughter's together one afternoon for instruction. "Sit down now, girls, and I'll show you what to do with a needle and thread." It was a flip-topped natural wicker table, lined with fabric pockets for scissors, thimbles, odds and ends. Norah's last mending project was still inside, a pair of boys trousers in need of patching.

Rita received Norah's pure white with scattered roses tea set for four, a wedding gift from her mother's employers at the time, the Collins family.

All the King sisters adored lovely things, but Rosemary felt Rita deserved the fine china set because she'd have the hardest time, being so young without a mother. There was one more item, more precious than the first, which she would give to Rita privately. Kay had Steve and Rosemary had Tony. Who would look after Rita? Certainly, not their father.

For her brother Joe, Rosemary chose a photograph of their mother, taken shortly before she married. Her abundant tresses were arranged Gibson-girl style on top of her head, her complexion flawless, and expression gently self-assured. The high, lace-trimmed collar of her long-sleeved, pleated-bodice blouse held a cameo broach centered above a medium length string of imitation pearls and made the Irish colleen appear almost aristocratic. But overall her look was undeniably one of a young lady in love.

The sepia portrait was found among other old photographs in Norah's seen-better days-valise, stored on the highest closet shelf. A golden imprint on the cardboard frame said,

Bigelowe Portraits, Tremont Street, Boston

and written on the back, in Norah's fine hand:

To Mr. John Joseph King,
My own sweet, handsome Joe
With all my love,
Miss Norah Catherine Foley.
September 1917

Norah's private pet name for John Joseph came early in their courtship. It seemed even when she spoke his name softly there was always another John close by who answered or looked her way. Joe didn't seem to be quite as common, and more so, was "very American."

Rosemary prayed those written words of affection, although intended for her father, would resonate some kind of blessing for her brother Joe, who was so isolated and needed one in the worst way.

John Michael, at his own request, took possession of Norah's Daily Missal and returned to war in the Pacific with it safely packed in his Navy-issue duffel bag. In the distant future, after he became a father, each of his daughters would reverently carry the holy book beneath their wedding bouquets.

Sister Bernadette approached Rosemary who'd been gathering more of her mother's possessions on the kitchen table. "If you don't mind me suggesting one more thing, dear."

"Of course not Sister, shoot." Rosemary practically choked on her last word. *Did I really just say, "Shoot" to Sister Bernadette?*

The amiable nun grinned. "Very well, dear. I think it would be best if you kept any remembrance for the younger boys in your personal care until they're older."

"That's a good idea, Sister, I'll do it." Rosemary put the teakettle on a low flame, and returned to her parents' bedroom.

Rosemary would forever regret not taking her mother's wedding photo for herself that day. It would have been so easy, but for some reason she believed it would always be available when, in fact, she was devastatingly wrong.

For all three, Pat, Timmy, and Tommy, she chose the same thing, Norah's gloves.

Her mother's black wool winter gloves would go to Pat, spring/summer white cotton lisle gloves to Timmy, and the buff-colored kid leather pair with three tiny buttons at the wrist that Norah purchased as a young woman and hadn't worn for years, went to Tommy.

Rosemary reasoned. *They're boys who'll one day be men who may not want a remembrance until I explain, the hands that cradled you, fed you, bathed you, worked for your keep, washed your clothes, led you to church—these gloves held those precious hands. Please take them and may you never forget how very much you were loved by our mother."*

Too-Ra-Loo-Ra-Loo-Ral
That's An Irish Lullaby
Words & Music by J.R. Shannon

Over in Killarney,
Many years ago,
Me Mither sang a song to me
In tones so sweet and low.
Just a simple little ditty,
In her good ould Irish way,
And I'd give the world if she could sing
That song to me this day

Too-ra-loo-ra-loo-ral,
Too-ra-loo-ra-li,
Too-ra-loo-ra-loo-ral,
Hush, now don't you cry!

177

CHAPTER 17

Bless the four corners of this house,
And be the lintel blest;
And bless the hearth and bless the board
And bless each place of rest;
And bless the door that opens wide to strangers as to kin.
THE MIRTHFUL LYRE
ARTHUR GUITERMAN

ROSEMARY KING NEEDED TO TALK to someone older and wiser, but the very person she needed was gone now. She went to the next best.

Mary Callanan shooed her children away as soon as Rosemary arrived. "You're to stay out of the kitchen until I tell you differently. There's a piece of chocolate cake and glass of cold milk for those who obey and you're not to disturb your father." Despite all the activity in the house, Mr. Callanan was sound asleep in his easy chair with *The Boston Globe* sports section sheltering his face like a tent.

Mary saw Norah in the young woman's demeanor. She sat straight like her mother and had the same pleasant manner, but concern pooled in Rosemary's eyes like soft rain. *She's a burden beyond the loss of her mother. I can feel it. Dear God, guide me to help as best I can.*

"Would you like a little somethin' to go with your tea, Rosemary? There's of course the chocolate cake, but I have some cold cuts if you're hungry for a sandwich. Can I make you a bologna sandwich? Or are you starvin' yourself for the weddin' day? There isn't a bride that doesn't. Lookin' your best on the most important day of your life is of utmost importance. So you're not to feel queer about it now. What'll it be then?"

"To tell you the truth, Mrs. Callanan, a bologna sandwich sounds delicious."

"How about I fry it up with some onions, and we'll make a hot meal of it?" Mary smiled, and opened one of the two side-by-side iceboxes required because of the size of her family. "No, thank you, Mrs. Callanan. A little mustard and lettuce would be more than appreciated."

Rosemary thought how different Mary Callanan looked from her own mother. Norah hadn't been overweight but she was robust, at least until the illness took over.

Mary, on the other hand was, as Norah used to say, "thin as a rail" and tall. From the back, she looked like a young girl, and moved like one too, as she bounced from icebox to stove to sink to the table. "I'll have the whole business done in no time and keep you company. Isn't it just as easy to make two sandwiches as it is the one?" Mary pleasantly reasoned.

The Callanans were considered "lace curtain Irish" because they owned their own home. Early on, they'd lived in an apartment, and Mr. Callanan's widowed mother offered, "I've a small amount of money your late father put aside. If you wouldn't mind an old lady livin' with ya, I think we've enough for a down payment."

Rosemary cleared away the dishes, and Mary Callanan poured each of them another cup. "So what is it you really wanted to talk about? Not that I don't find your weddin' plans or job down there at Social Services fascinatin', but it's apparent you've somethin' more on your mind." The kitchen door opened slightly, for about the fourth time, and then all the way to reveal three of Mary's twelve children standing in a row. The girl in the middle said, "Ma, we're hungry. How much longer?"

Mary turned to Rosemary. "She's my cheeky one." And back to the children. "'How much longer,' Eileen? Until I say otherwise. Meanwhile get your little fanny outta here, and that goes for the rest of ya's too. And close the door."

Rosemary pulled her chair closer and lowered her voice even though it was still just the two of them in the large, warm kitchen.

"Mrs. Callanan, I'm a light sleeper, and a few times now, I've awakened to see my father standing in the doorway of our bedroom."

Just thinking about the stench of his drunkenness and stillness of his being put a lump in her throat. "A couple of nights ago, he went to the side of Rita's bed, and when he bumped against it, she woke up and asked, 'Is anything wrong Dad?' My father said, 'The only thing wrong is some rotten young bloke is goin' to have you all to himself one day, and you're mine. You hear me? Mine.' Mrs. Callanan, he reached for Rita's covers. But she pulled them up around her neck, and begged my father to go back to bed."

Mary put her hands on either side of her face, and shook her head. "God in heaven."

Rosemary said, "I know." She leaned in again. "Please promise you'll never repeat any of this, let alone what I'm about to tell you next."

For the first time in her life, Mary Callanan was speechless and nodded her head.

"My father yelled, 'Rita, you're tellin' me to go back to bed? What makes you think I've been in me bed? Isn't it your beauty that keeps me awake at night, and your sister's as well? But Rosemary's already taken.' He stumbled backwards and kept saying, "The bed's cold. The bed's cold.'" Rosemary was visibly shaken; her typically assured voice quavered. "Finally, thank God, he left."

Mary Callanan was angry, and her face grew redder by the minute. "You and Rita have to get out as soon as possible. Please God that your dearly departed mother can't hear anythin' we're discussin' down here from her home up there in heaven."

"Oh, I'm on my way, Mrs. Callanan. Before any of this happened, Tony thought it would be a good idea for me to live someplace else until we got married, which I happened to mention to Patsy Sheehan, and two days later, her Aunt Alice invited me to live with her. I just wanted to run the whole situation by you to be sure I was doing the right thing. But I'm concerned about my sister."

Mary Callanan crossed her slender arms over her heart with her hands resting on her shoulders and looked toward the ceiling for answers; it was her way. "Has that man no decency? I'll stop there. He's still your father." She looked at

Rosemary. "This is how it's goin' to be. Rita can live here. And won't my Marion be happy as a clam to have her best friend under the same roof?"

Rosemary sighed with relief, and the tears she'd been holding back fell. "Thank you. I didn't know what to do. I've wracked my brain with all kinds of possibilities, and none of them seemed quite right. I even considered asking Aunt Alice if Rita could live with her too."

"God in heaven, Rosemary, I know Patsy's Aunt Alice's place, and there's barely enough room to turn around, let alone take in the two of ya's. It doesn't matter now, does it? Your sister's new home is here with us."

"Thank you, and don't worry. Rita can pay her own way. She gives my father money every week."

"What difference is one more mouth to feed when you've got the twelve? Though I must admit every little bit helps. I won't be needin' much from her."

"You're such a good person, Mrs. Callanan."

"'Good person?' No, Rosemary. I'm not a good person, not on me own I'm not. But I learned how to be from your late mother, God rest her soul. I think it's somethin' to do with goin' to daily Mass, bein' on me knees before the Almighty and seekin' His intent for me days. Didn't your mother get me started? And now it's as natural as breathin'. I wouldn't miss goin' to Mass every mornin' if the Pope himself showed up on me front doorstep. I'd say, 'How'd ya do, Holy Father? I'm on me way to church. You can join me if you want to, Your Holiness or make yourself comfortable 'til I get back.' As God is my judge, that's what I'd say rather than miss what feeds me soul and keeps me heart right. Norah was a saint, and that's the God's truth."

" . . . if there was one thing that drew the people of South Boston together and gave the neighborhood a distinctive quality of life, it was the Catholic Church . . . Many people went to daily Mass in the dark hours of the morning before going to work."

South Boston: My Home Town by Thomas H. O'Connor

Rosemary had forgotten how much Mary Callanan talked. Her mother had enjoyed telling how Mary could go on and on about anything and everything that had nothing to do with the matter at hand. "Not to say she doesn't know how to tell a good story. It's just aggravatin' when you're tryin' to get to the bottom of things."

Rosemary shifted gears. "Mrs. Callanan, Patsy Sheehan has a car and she offered to help me move. May I use your telephone to give her the latest news?"

"Now Rosemary, seein' as you're about to become a married woman and you've been lookin' after your mother's house as your own, wouldn't you be grown enough to drop the Mrs. and call me Mary?"

"I would if I could. But you'll always be Mrs. Callanan to me, Mrs. Callanan."

They both smiled, and Mary cautioned, "Do the movin' today, Rosemary. Fair warnin.'" She squeezed Rosemary's hand. "You're so like your dear mother with all the lookin' after. Now follow me to the telephone."

Patsy was more than ready to help. "Stay where you are, Ro. I'll be right there."

Rita was still at work and had no idea her head would be resting on a different pillow from now on. Rosemary and Patsy headed straight for W. T. Grant & Company.

Patsy "Ann" Sheehan Prescott, who'd only had her driver's license for three months, did a spot-on job of parallel parking her husband's big black Buick right in front of the small, economical department store. The two friends went inside under the watchful eye of the store's manager, who was excited about the obviously prosperous young women selecting Grants for their shopping needs.

Manager Adolph "Al" Schultz still had the habit of smoothing down his recently shaved off moustache, and continued to be stunned every time his bony fingers met bare skin. Today was no exception as he primped for the smartly attired young, lady shoppers, reached for his phantom mustache, buttoned his suit coat, straightened his bow tie, and adjusted his ostentatious boutonnière. This was after all, Grants in Southie, not the posh, R. H. Stearns in downtown Boston.

However, his carefully calculated efforts to look appealing were in vain. Mr. Al Schultz was repulsively squirmy, touching this and that excessively. His thin stringy locks constantly fell forward under the weight of too much hair tonic, and he smelled strongly of mothballs, an acrid repellent not only for fabric eating creatures but for discerning humans as well.

Rita was standing right where Rosemary knew they'd find her, behind a counter in the lingerie department where she went from being nicely surprised, "Hey, you two? What's new?" to sudden despair and just-round-the-corner tears, when Rosemary told her about moving out.

"But what's going to happen to me? I can't live with the Callanans forever."

Her older sister did her best to make it sound good. "Look on the bright side, honey. You'll be sharing a room with Marion now."

"I like sharing a room with you, Ro!"

"Okay Rita, let's get down to business. You know my plans for moving in with Aunt Alice, and I'm not leaving you home alone with Dad."

Rita's cheeks instantly flushed. *I can't believe this is happening. If only my mother was still here. Mummy, please help me.*

Patsy was well aware Mr. King wasn't the best father in Southie but her friend's urgent tone told her this was more than she needed to hear.

"Hey girls, I'll be over in the notions department. Norman's mother asked if I'd pick up some common pins the next time I went shopping."

Rita pointed Patsy in the right direction and said under her breath to Rosemary, "Thank you. He scared the life out of me the other night."

"I know. He scared the life out of me too." Rosemary looked at her watch. "Patsy and I are on our way to 8th Street right now, Rita. We're going to get your things and mine out of there as fast as we can. I want everything safely in place before I tell Dad."

"What about the boys? Won't they tell him?"

"Possibly if he was home, but he won't be until later. Meanwhile, I'll send them to Morris's Drug Store for a soda."

Patsy bounced back. "Got them!" She held up an accordion pleated card of W. T. Grant Superior Common Pins ~ One Hundred Count. "What time do you get off work, young lady?"

"Six o'clock on the dot, madam," Rita said with a smile despite the lump in her throat.

"We'll be back to pick you up, Miss." Patsy winked at Rosemary. "Oh, and let's go to Howard Johnson's for fried clam dinners. Okay?"

"Only if I pick up the check," Rosemary answered.

Rita said, "I can almost taste those clams and French fried potatoes now," and led by the strong smell of mothballs, briefly looked over her shoulder then said it all by rolling her eyes.

Mr. Schultz lurked close by and pretended to be straightening some flimsy merchandise as he took each pastel colored piece, shook it out and laid it back in place just so, sometimes with a pat, pat. The fact that it was ladies' panties didn't occur to the myopic manager, and his fidgety fingering of the delicate under-things made "Al" Schultz look absolutely obscene to the parochial-school-trained young ladies.

Rita came out from behind the counter and did her own pretending as she showed Rosemary and Patsy a new selection of quilted robes. "This color is very popular." She pointed it out to Patsy. "It's called turquoise. Have you ever heard such a word? Turquoise?"

"Why no, I haven't." Patsy spoke louder for Mr. Schultz's benefit, should he take issue with Rita for personal visitors. "It's very pretty, Miss, but I'd prefer it in that yummy yellow, please."

Rita removed a size small from the rack, and whispered, "Do you really want to buy this, Patsy?"

"Of course," she whispered back. "We're not going to give your manager the satisfaction of finding something wrong. What a creep."

Rita wrapped the robe in standard tissue and placed it in a paper bag. "That will be eight dollars and ninety-five cents, please, madam."

Miss Rita Margaret King wistfully watched newly married Patsy and Rosemary, her *could she get any prettier* sister, who was soon to be wed, rush to the other side of the store. The rich sheen of Patsy's "Ann's" black curly lamb jacket, and happy hue of Rosemary's red coat bobbed in and out of each department along the way until they reached the men's, where both bought a package of Best Quality Gentleman's Handkerchiefs before dashing to the car. *If only I had a sweetheart of my own.*

CHAPTER 18

*I think my father is like the Holy Trinity with three people in him,
the one in the morning with the paper, the one at night with the
stories and the prayers, and then the one who does the bad thing
and comes home with the smell of whiskey and wants us to die.*

ANGELA'S ASHES
FRANK MCCOURT

I T WAS PATSY AND ROSEMARY's third trip downstairs when Peg Hennessey
opened her apartment door and stood there drying her wet hands on a dishtowel just taken from over her shoulder.

"So what goes on here, girlies? You've been movin' stuff out like the house
is on fire."

Rosemary didn't want to explain, nor take the time to talk, but so loved
Mrs. Hennessey for all the kindnesses she'd shown to their family through the
years. Like when she'd say they had too much of this or that food and asked
wouldn't the Kings take it off their hands, and the great interest she took in the
children's special occasions, celebrating each one with a small gift, let alone how
she'd sat sentry in the entry hall for days when Norah was waked, respectfully
directing visitors upstairs.

"Truthfully, Mrs. Hennessey," Rosemary confided, knowing this was a coup for the older lady who loved to be in the know, "Rita and I are moving someplace else. I'll be boarding with Patsy Sheehan's Aunt Alice, and Rita is going to live with the Callanan family. My father has no idea this is taking place so please don't tell him. Please. I really can't say any more, Mrs. Hennessey."

The old woman left her doorway and said to Patsy, "It's not my intent to be rude, darlin', but I've somethin' private to discuss with your friend."

"Oh, please don't think twice about it, Mrs. Hennessey. I was on my way to the car anyway." Patsy reached for Rosemary's bundle. "Give it to me, Ro. I can manage."

Peg Hennessey was barely audible. "There's no need to explain a thing. For isn't me bedroom right below yours and Rita's, and haven't I heard him stumblin' to and fro at all hours, though not beyond the doorway 'til the other night but with a fast turnaround, thank God. Are you girls all right?"

"Yes, Mrs. Hennessey. Nothing happened." Rosemary felt a knot in her stomach.

"Rosemary, it's the liquor that makes your father less than the good man God Almighty made him to be. Now you must remember that. It's the liquor talkin', beatin', cursin', not your father in his natural state. He loves you girls. By leavin' home you're avoidin' all kinds of trouble and savin' him when he's sober, from a life of regrettin' ever layin' a hand on either one of ya's."

Rosemary had no desire to clarify whether Peg Hennessey was talking about violence or the absolute unmentionable. She was, in her own way, taking over where her late mother left off. Norah had been not only loving parent, but also constant guardian of her three daughters' virtue, running interference between her husband, when he'd been drinking, and the girls' budding beauty. The drunkenness was hard enough, but John Joseph's subsequent lechery was worse, and he'd hideously sing away, "My wild Irish rose, the dearest flow'r that grows. And some day for my sake, she may let me take the bloom from my wild Irish rose."

Norah King's unrelenting defense indubitably meant she'd suffer a physical blow, but in the end, victory was hers. John Joseph never achieved his drunken objective. Not once.

"Get out while the gettin's good, Rosemary King, and may God bless your way, and Rita's too. I'll keep an eye out for the boys."

"Thank you, Mrs. Hennessey."

Rosemary gave her favorite neighbor lady a quick hug and ran up the stairs again.

Norah's crucifix rested beneath three layers of Rosemary's clothing—slip, blouse, and wool suit jacket—but she could still feel its comforting silhouette against her fingertips. *It's you, Mum, isn't it? You and the Sacred Heart of Jesus are watching over us. And it was you last Saturday too. Wasn't it, Mum?* Rosemary shuddered at the thought of what had taken place less than a week ago. *Tony and I could have been burned or trampled to death.*

The happy couple had gone to the Boston College versus Holy Cross football game—a favorite and fierce rivalry—and had planned

On the night of November 28, 1942, Boston's Cocoanut Grove Nightclub exploded into flames, in what remains one of the deadliest fires in U.S. history. A total of 492 people were killed and hundreds more were injured. The popular club was filled to overflowing capacity with 1,000 plus customers, wait staff, band and other entertainers. It was a tragedy that shocked the nation and for a time, replaced World War II news headlines. The devasting blaze led to a reform of fire codes and safety standards across the country, prompted a seminal study of grief and led to innovative medical treatments for burn victims. The club's owner, Barney Welansky was eventually found guilty of involuntary manslaughter.

to join friends afterward at the wildly popular Cocoanut Grove nightclub on Piedmont Street in the theater district, but never made it. *Whatever possessed me to agree when Tony said, "Maybe we'd better call it a night. There's nothing to celebrate." Even if the Eagles did lose the game, we still could have enjoyed dinner and dancing.* Rosemary sighed aloud. "I miss you, Mum." She crossed the threshold into the apartment.

Patsy said, "Ro, we don't have anything to carry all this stuff in." Rosemary ran and got pillowcases from the hall closet. "Hurry. We can use these."

This wasn't easy, her mother having been gone only weeks, leaving her father's house without his knowledge or blessing, and taking her younger sister with her. *God in heaven, what happened to our family?*

Rosemary longingly recalled her blissful early childhood when the whole family would sit in the kitchen listening to John Joseph play his fiddle, dance and sing along too. She missed the times when her parents would gather all their children in the living room on weeknights to say the Rosary, and especially the final bedtime tuck-in when John Joseph would delay their night's rest with just one more story and Norah would chide with a dimpled smile, "And won't they all be class dunce for lack of sleep? You've got to say goodnight now, Mr. King." *What happened to our happy family?*

Rosemary sat down at the kitchen table for the last time to write her father a letter. Patsy could see her from the hallway, where she was ready to take the last armload of items down to her car. "Make it short and sweet, Ro. It'll go over better that way."

Dear Dad,

When you read this, I will have moved to Patsy's Aunt Alice's apartment. As you know, my wedding date is only a month away now and Tony thinks it best if I live someplace else until then. Dad, I don't want to be disrespectful in the least but your drinking and yelling and the threat that you'll strike one of us again has become more than I can bear. I'm a wreck, and I don't want to begin my new life jangled let alone walk down the aisle that way.

Rita is going too. She'll be living with the Callanan family from now on. I don't want to put to paper the reason for this, but please don't go after her, or I'll tell my boss at Social Services why I needed to get Rita away from you.

Pat knows how to cook, and I think he'll do a good job. But you and the little boys will have to chip in and help. I'm sorry Rita and I had to leave home like this, but it's for the best.

Your daughter,
Rosemary

When the time came, her omission of love didn't go unnoticed.

The two determined young women moved everything to the Buick in record time and were about three streets away when Rosemary screamed, "Stop the car! Oh, Patsy, you're never going to believe this? I left my red coat in the living room. You and I ran up and down those stairs so fast I never got cold enough to miss it. We have to go back. I'm so sorry for the trouble."

"No trouble at all. What's a U-turn between friends?"

"An illegal act, a traffic ticket, better safe than sorry."

"Okay." But Patsy made the U-turn anyway. "A small price to pay. You love that coat."

There was an air of relief and caution as they pulled up in front of the three-decker. "Hurry Ro. You don't want to run into your father."

But she did.

∞

"You're goin' to live with Patsy Sheehan's aunt, and I'm goin' into the goddam priesthood. Do you honestly think I'm fallin' for that line? You're goin' off with the Dago, aren't you? It's a good thing your mother's not alive to see her 'pure as the new fallen snow' Rosemary livin' in such a way. Aunt Alice!"

"I'd never do a thing like that, Dad. I just can't live here anymore." Rosemary could feel her heart beating faster and faster. *Please God don't let him come after me.* "And Patsy's Aunt Alice says she could use the company."

"And don't think I don't know your possessions have already left this house. For didn't one of the neighbors ask why you were movin' out and I might add it was mortifyin' to be told me own business by that snoop of a woman, Mrs. Delaney, who doesn't know her arse from the top of her head but manages to know all the goins on of the people around her."

Downstairs, Peg Hennessey was well aware of father and daughter in the apartment at the same time. *Old lady or not, I'll fly up those flights should I hear even one shouted word or misplaced footstep.*

"Let me leave in peace, will you please, Dad?" Rosemary pleaded.

"'Let me leave in peace, will you please, Dad?'" John Joseph sing-sang in the mocking high-pitched tone she knew only too well. "Who the hell do you think you are?"

"Who do you think you are?" might as well be tattooed into the forehead of certain old Irish Catholics, they ask it so much. "Too big for your britches," too.
Object Lessons by Anna Quindlen

Rosemary walked toward the living room, and John Joseph followed after her. When she reached for the red coat, which was laying over the back of the sofa, her father lunged and grabbed it first. "You wouldn't be needin' this, now, would you? Your fancy I-talian college boy can buy you a new coat. Cheap at twice the price if he's to get a beauty like you for himself." John Joseph pulled a jackknife from his pants pocket and flipped it open with the aid of his adroit right thumb. "Maybe we could cut it up into little pieces for aren't you too proud for your own good when this coat's on your back?"

"My mother gave me that coat. Don't do it. Please don't." Rosemary grabbed for the garment that, to her, represented all that was good and generous and prosperous. "Dad, please don't."

Her father, who smelled of ale and cigarettes, held the coat up high—almost in effigy. "God only knows how much your late mother paid for the goddam thing."

He moved quickly and waved her much-loved garment like a toreador. "You're not gettin' it unless you apologize for bein' so goddam uppity. Say it. 'Dad, I'm sorry for bein' so uppity, especially when I'm wearin' the red coat.' Say it, and the coat goes with ya. Hold back and I'll cut it in shreds before your eyes."

Rosemary sat down in a nearby chair. "You really want me to say that, Dad?"

"You bet your life I do, and you'll do it standin' up when you talk to me, or there's no deal."

The lithe young woman stood on her feet, nervously brushed her golden hair back, paused and said, "Dad, please forgive me if I've ever offended you when I'm wearing that coat. It wasn't my intent."

John Joseph taunted her and pushed the tip of the knife through a button-hole. "You've got it all wrong. I'll be needin' the uppity part if you're to take this coat away in the one piece."

"Dad, please forgive me for being uppity when I'm wearing the red coat."

"That's more like it. Here's your costly rag, Miss High and Mighty." He threw the red coat across the room.

Rosemary ran to catch it. He laughed and tossed the pocketknife in the air a few times while she hurriedly put the coat on and rushed to the front door.

John Joseph followed, and his laughter got louder.

Rosemary's legs felt like they would buckle right out from beneath her as she turned around and stared her father straight in the eye. "I never want to see you again in my life." She walked out the door and firmly closed it behind her.

Peg Hennessey pulled the lace curtain slightly back from the bowed front window in her daughter and son-in-law's living room and watched as Rosemary swiftly got into Patsy's car. *She'll do fine.*

∞

That night when Rita entered the Callanans' orderly, noisy, children-in-every-room home, Mary welcomed her with open arms. "If it isn't me lucky charm? Rita King, your livin' in this house makes the number of offspring a full baker's dozen now. Sure and you're a sign of more good things to come."

Mary gave the bewildered teen a hearty hug. "Have you had your supper yet? We've still a couple of fishcakes and some beans, which is nothin' short of a miracle seein' there's seldom a crumb left after this bunch sits down."

"No, thank you, Mrs. Callanan. I've already eaten."

Patsy and Rosemary overheard the conversation as they carried Rita's possessions inside. "Mrs. Callanan, we stopped at Howard Johnson's for clams. Ro's treat," Patsy said and playfully pinched her friend.

Just then little girls' voices rang out from upstairs. "Say the magic words, Marion, and we'll let you pass."

Eileen, Sheila, and Sheila's twin, Patricia, who the Callanans nicknamed Pansy because there were so many Patricia's in Southie, were blocking Marion's way.

"Pretty please," Marion sang, and the trio giggled as they let go of each other's hands and she ran past them.

"Rita! You're finally here! Can you believe it? We're going to be roommates now. Well, you and me and two of my sisters."

Norah's youngest daughter did her best to appear cheerful, her dimpled smile a ready cover as she echoed back, "Can you believe it, Mar?" *Can you believe that your best friend is an orphan now?*

Someone was whistling a muffled "Boogie Woogie Bugle Boy" from the other side of the cellar door. When it burst open, a blonde, blue-eyed preteen boy appeared. He stopped mid-tune and addressed the newest member of the household. "Hey, Rita, Ma says ya gonna live here now." *Please God, when I'm old enough to have a girlfriend, I want her to look just like that.* "Glad to have ya!"

"Thanks, Don. I'm glad to be here." *No, I'm not. I want to go home. But I can't go home. Ever.*

Marion walked over to her mother. "Ma, you're terrific."

"Oh, I think Rita King's the terrific one, seein' she's brave enough to sleep in the same room with you, Jean and Eileen." *Poor girl, havin' to leave her home on account of. . .God help me, there'll be no mention in thought or speech.* "And I trust everythin's in order up there, Marion Louise?"

"Yes, Ma. And I changed the sheets like you asked me to."

Mary put one arm around her daughter. "Good girl." She reached out to Rita with the other. "And now Miss Rita King, you're one of my girls too."

Much later that same night, John Joseph returned from the pub drunker than usual. He pulled Pat, Timmy, and Tommy out of bed, and beat all three boys, with Pat getting the worst of it. After everything calmed down and their father turned in, the three brothers tiptoed to the kitchen and made a snack of toast and milk.

Tommy said, "Does it hurt, Pat?"

His brother didn't say a thing.

Timmy said, "Do you want me to get a facecloth and put cold water on it?"

Pat remained silent, kept his head down, and didn't even glance at his brothers. Then Tommy got up from the table, being careful not to scrape his chair, leaned his head on top of Pat's and said, "I'm sorry Dad did this to you."

Patrick sniffled and wiped tears from his cheeks with the backs of his hands. "I'll be all right."

The next morning as John Joseph was "sleeping it off," fifteen-and-a-half-year old Patrick Henry King shyly walked into the Naval Recruiting Office with a swollen-shut black eye, got the necessary papers for enlistment, left and came back an hour later with the forms filled out, his father's signature looking very much like his own and his supposed birthdate, extremely doubtful. Mercifully no questions were asked as Pat joined the ranks of countless other young boys from across the nation who preferred the fields and seas of war to what was going on at home.

The savvy recruiter informed him, "To be perfectly honest son, you don't need anything other than the clothes on your back, and you can leave for boot camp first thing tomorrow if you want to. There's already a bus scheduled. Or you can leave a week from now."

Patrick's stomach jumped at the haste of it all but he didn't hesitate. "What time tomorrow, Mister?"

"You're in the Navy now, son. You'll want to be calling me, sir. Six a.m., will we see you then?"

"Yes, sir."

∞

Pat went straight to the Flynns' apartment and asked Peg Hennessey for refuge until his take off at dawn. "You're safe here, Patrick, and welcome any time ya return." It was just the two of them. Her daughter and son-in-law had gone to Nantasket Beach in Hull for a couple of days to enjoy the ocean and popular Paragon Amusement Park.

Peg served the exhausted, bruised teen a simple lunch of tuna sandwiches. He ate two, along with bread and butter pickles, tomato soup—he had two bowls full—several glasses of milk, and a big bowl of raisin, nutmeg, molasses and cinnamon-laced Indian pudding with whipped cream for dessert.

She taught Patrick how to play solitaire and encouraged him to take a nap in her son-in-law's soft chair. "It'll do you good, and here." She pushed a dog-eared burgundy leather hassock in his direction. "Put your feet up. It'll be more relaxin' that way."

That night Peg Hennesey served Patrick huge portions of beef stew, corn muffins, and red Jell-O filled with fruit cocktail. She tucked him in on their sofa for the night. *God love him.* Then she began watching for his brute of a father to arrive home, peeking out the apartment windows, "until God knows how late," as she later told her daughter.

As was John Joseph's habit when entering the three-decker apartment house "durin' the wee hours," he came in through the common back door, into the shared hallway crowded with a baby carriage, scooter, two pairs of roller skates, a snow shovel, plunger, mop, bucket, broom, and box of redeemable bottles. Peg Hennessey was waiting for him.

"Good evenin', Mr. King," she said at the top of her voice with all the courage of someone who knows they have the upper hand. "May I have a moment of your time, please?"

John Joseph was inebriated, but not so much that he didn't catch the seriousness of her request. "And what can I do this fine evenin' for a good lookin' woman such as yourself?"

"You can begin by savin' that blarney for those who'd believe it." She folded her arms and inclined her head toward the stairway. "When you go up, Mr. King, you'll find Patrick's gone."

The boy's father frowned. "What do you mean, gone?"

"He's joined the U.S. Navy, and if you interfere, I'll call the police and tell them exactly how you've been treatin' those children—let alone the carnage I heard comin' from your apartment last night."

She greatly regretted not going up, but home alone, there was no back up, and fear of "physical harm or permanent injury from that raging drunk demon" held her back.

"Leave him be. And a word to the wise, I'm also toyin' with the idea of tellin' Father Delaney about the whole sorted mess, but your lack of interferin' with Patrick's plans could persuade me otherwise."

John Joseph started to address the older woman by her first name but stopped himself. "Peg, ah, Mrs. Hennessey, sure and you'll agree there's nothin' wrong with puttin' them in their place." John Joseph walked unsteadily toward her. "And what makes you think I'd go chasin' after that snivelin' ingrate? Haven't I put up with Mr. Patty Cake's mopin' about since his mother's death?"

The Aran Isles of Ireland are home to a very distinctive type of sweater. Made from natural, cream-colored wool and hand-knit into combined patterns of knots, ropes, braids and basket weaves—each island family had their own unique design. In the event a fisherman was lost at sea, once found, he could easily be identified by his "Aran sweater" pattern.

"Don't come one step closer, John King." Peg shook her index finger. "And from now on you'll not lay a hand on those that's left. If I see one hair out of place on either Timmy or Tommy's heads, it's out the door and into the hoosegow you'll go." Peg pulled her bulky, hand-knit Aran sweater closer around her. "Now go get some sleep so's you can be a better man tomorrow and stop disgracin' your family. Go on now!"

John Joseph was woozy but managed to get upstairs, muttering all the way. "Wait and see. You'll all be sorry. You just wait."

Mr. and Mrs. Williamson
Maid of Honor, Rita King.

Within months, Rosemary and Tony married at Gate of Heaven Church where Aunt Alice stood in for the bride's mother but didn't take her place in the first seat of the first pew on the left. She sat directly next to the open space where Rosemary had laid a nosegay of white roses in memory of Norah.

Patsy happily arranged the flowers for Rosemary's wedding although her mother-in-law had discouraged her from doing so. "Ann, dear, that kind of occupation is behind you now. Does South Boston have a good floral shop, or shall I recommend one here in town?"

With the older boys away at war, well, two of them anyway, only Rosemary and Tony knew where Joe really was, Patsy Sheehan Prescott's father gladly stepped in and walked Rosemary down the aisle.

Rita was her sister's maid of honor, and Kay was a bridesmaid along with Patsy.

Don Campbell stood in as best man, and Tony requested that John Michael and Patrick be added as groomsmen in absentia.

Tony's parents were deceased, so he asked Don if he thought his would be willing to take their place. "If it wasn't for your family's Christmas party, I wouldn't have met Rosemary."

Mrs. Campbell told her friends, "You'll never guess what this coming Saturday holds for us! An Irish wedding in South Boston, and we're to be honorary parents for the groom. Isn't that positively delightful?"

Rosemary felt certain her father wouldn't allow Timmy and Tommy to attend and was thrilled when she saw both boys immaculately dressed and sitting in the second row, one on either side of Peg Hennessey.

The day before the wedding, Peg informed John Joseph that Timothy and Thomas would be escorting her to the church and reception. "I'm here to see if their clothes need washin' and ironin'."

He blocked the doorway. "They're not goin'."

Peg pushed past him. "Don't even think of stoppin' me. I believe you're aware of the waitin' consequences, Mr. King."

The wedding reception took place at Patsy's parents' large, two-story home on Farragut Road, where white paper honeycomb bells swayed on the porch and decorated the rooms inside. Delicate spring green ferns crowned each bell-top bow, and satin ribbons streamed out from the big one over the dining room table, creating a grand bridal canopy.

Although it looked like April showers, there was no rain in sight so people spilled out onto the front porch and enjoyed the ocean view, with one of the guests saying as he raised his glass to the sea, "It doesn't get much better than this. Here's to love, friends, food and drink. *Sláinte!* To your health!"

Three Callanan brothers were put in charge of the record player. Big band tunes laced the air with popular tunes while Kate Smith, Bing Crosby and Frank Sinatra sang of romance. But most often, at the urging of countless adults, the boys chose Irish tenors and uplifting reels. People loved singing along and many danced, but the majority of guests simply tapped their feet to the pleasingly familiar tunes.

This was the last time they would see Ensign James Frances Sheehan, who fought valiantly in the Pacific and was killed aboard an aircraft carrier when a Japanese Kamikaze pilot crashed into the deck and took sixty American lives with him.

James Sheehan kissed the bride's hand and shook Tony's. "You've got me to thank for this, Williamson."

"And I will. Thank you, Mr. Sheehan, for bringing the prettiest girl in Boston to that Christmas party in Milton. I am forever in your debt."

"I'll remember that, Williamson." James patted Tony on the shoulder. There were no hard feelings.

Rosemary and Tony had originally planned on having their reception at a local hall for hire, but Patsy's father wouldn't hear of it. "Why Rosy, you're like one of our own. It'll be at the house."

Rosemary had been saving every penny she could to avoid what was known in Southie as a "Protestant reception," with cake, fruit punch, and pastel-candy covered almonds. But Tony, prudent beyond anyone else she'd ever known, said, "Ro, there's absolutely nothing wrong with simple fare."

"Tony Williamson, what are you thinking? We have enough money for a nice buffet and limited alcohol. Enough to be hospitable, but not too much. I don't want anything to ruin our day."

The young couple profusely thanked Mr. and Mrs. Sheehan for offering the use of their home, and Mr. Sheehan said, "Use of our home? What are you talking about? We're doin' the whole shebang from beginnin' to end."

Rosemary politely proposed a cake and punch reception out of consideration for the Sheehan's pocketbook, and Patsy's mother, who had the reputation of "puttin' on a good spread," was horrified. "Over my dead body you two are havin' a Protestant reception. Don't worry about the money, honey. We get everythin' wholesale cause of the store and all. You're havin' a proper affair, and that's all there is to it." Mrs. Sheehan smiled and brushed her hands back and forth. "All there is to it, beautiful girl."

"It" was a lavish buffet meal of cold meats—roast beef, ham and turkey—a variety of breads, rolls, butter, assorted condiments, several relish trays of radishes, pickles, olives, celery and tiny onions, a large serving bowl of Harvard beets, and even larger hot dishes of macaroni and cheese, Boston baked beans, scalloped potatoes, and a cavalcade of jewel-colored Jell-O salads in an array of shapes, sizes and flavors.

Mrs. Flanagan, whose family lived on the top floor of the three-decker that Rosemary called home until recently, made arrangements with Mrs. Sheehan to provide her famous lobster salad. "Reserved for the special occasion only, Mrs. Sheehan, and now it's here."

The couple insisted on paying for their three-tier, frosting roses-laden wedding cake—from Helen's Bakery, of course—and it was, as the bride's sisters said several times over, "really gorgeous, Ro."

There was plenty of liquor, thanks to Mr. Sheehan's brother's Sunday bootleg business. "What the hell. I make enough money as it is. Everything's on the house." But no one had too much, and the entire afternoon went smoothly.

Mr. and Mrs. Williamson honeymooned for one night at Boston's Parker House Hotel, which was the first time Rosemary had slept any place other than her parents' home or Aunt Alice's apartment. The bride and groom arrived in their wedding attire, and Rosemary blushed when the desk clerk said to Tony as he signed the register, "And this I assume is Mrs. Williamson."

The next day, the newlyweds returned to Southie where their personal belongings were piled high in Aunt Alice's apartment. They packed it all in a second-hand car Tony bought from "a fella at BC who wanted to get rid of it before he went overseas."

The new Mister and Missus drove straight to New York City, where Tony began to fulfill his Naval commission and Rosemary went to college full time while working part time for Lord & Taylor. She had applied for the advertised sales position in lady's pocketbooks and accessories but the personnel director offered her a better paying job. "We have an immediate opening for a fashion model. Interested?"

∽

It was two weeks after Tony and Rosemary left for New York that the Kings apartment seemed too quiet. So Marie Flynn went upstairs with one of her seed cakes as an excuse to see if all was going well. Never could she have expected to find what she did. The curious landlady soon learned Timmy and Tommy had been living all alone for more than a week.

John Joseph had left them without food or money, but Timmy tried to keep up a good front. "We'll be fine, Mrs. Flynn, really. I'm sure our father will be back soon. I think maybe he had a job somewhere's else for a while."

"Have you checked his closet, Timmy? Are his clothes still there?"

"I don't know, Mrs. Flynn."

"Well, let's go see then." The concerned landlady opened the bedroom closet door to find it completely empty except for a few wire hangers haphazardly strewn on the floor.

Timmy panicked. "Ahm, I didn't know. Ahm, Mrs. Flynn, you don't have to worry. He'll be back. Hey, is that cake for us?" As soon as she handed the seed cake to Timmy, he pulled the waxed paper off and called, "Tommy, come in Mum and Dad's room!" Timmy broke off a piece and with a full mouth said, "Thanks, Mrs. Flynn."

Tommy came running from the kitchen where he'd been desperately looking for something to eat. He had found a container under the sink of what he thought was flour, and he ate some.

"What in the world's all over your mouth, Tommy King?" Marie Flynn asked.

"I'm not sure, Mrs. Flynn, but it tastes awful." He complained, "I don't feel so good," and Timmy handed him a hunk of the cake, which Tommy pushed into his mouth without taking a bite.

"Show me where you were, Thomas," Marie demanded and seconds later identified the white substance as laundry starch, rushed both boys downstairs, and called Mr. McDonough at the pharmacy, who told her straightaway what to do.

"Give the sorry bugger castor oil, and make him drink lots of water. He'll be fine."

Her next call went to Social Services.

Eleven-year-old Timothy Matthew King and nine-year-old Thomas Augustine King were taken to The Home for Destitute Catholic Children, where they got three meals a day, went to school, said their prayers, and slept peacefully every night in a dormitory with twenty-eight other orphan boys.

Later, the brothers were transferred to The Home for Little Wanderers, where they got more of the same until Mary Callanan's childless

The Home for Destitute Catholic Children

relatives, Loretta and Doyle Garvey, adopted the boys, presumably to fill the void in their lives for a family.

In truth, the penny-pinching couple thought this would be a good opportunity to get help with their thriving plumbing business in exchange for the orphans learning a trade and having a roof over their heads. But they'd overlooked the fact that Timmy and Tommy were still children in need of clothing, food, school supplies, and more, and the Garveys resented it. They barely took care of the two orphans.

All the while, Loretta Garvey rode around town in a shiny Cadillac and quite often wore a mink stole, while the only shoes each boy had was a pair of canvas sneakers, even in the dead of winter.

There was no love lost between the four, and after graduating from high school, each boy quickly moved out.

Timothy found work in a meat market, where he learned the butcher trade, and spent most of his spare time at a local gym, where an impressed boxing coach observed his natural gift for pugilism. "You've got the making of a champ, pal. A real, bone fide champ!" The coach offered to train him free of charge in exchange for a career-long commitment. "Boston Garden here we come!" Lightweight boxer Timothy A. King won all sixteen of his professional bouts.

Timothy A. King
"The Quincy Chiller,
knocks 'em out cold,
every time."
THE BOSTON GLOBE

Tommy joined the Navy, where he learned about small business from a senior officer who enjoyed the personable young enlisted man's skill at chess and took him under his wing. In time, Tommy owned his own plumbing business and a couple of successful Laundromats.

John Joseph King faded into the woodwork of men who don't keep their obligations and get away with it. The wry, middle-aged widower and father of nine now lived agreeably alone in a small, upstairs apartment in Southie's Thomas Park neighborhood. He continued his job as a steel worker, spent free time at the pub, and in his own despicable words, "got on with the ladies."

He had in his possession almost every photograph ever taken of the King children, as well as photos of himself and Norah, which he refused to relinquish, even when Mary Callanan discovered where he was living and went to him on behalf of Rita and her siblings.

∞

"Would these be what you're lookin' for?" John Joseph held up Rosemary and Kay's high school senior portraits in his strong but shaky hands, giving Mary a glimmer of hope that quickly faded when he folded one of the photos in half vertically and despite her gasps did the same to the other, marring the beauty of his daughter's faces. "They take up less room this way," he said, slyly slipping the tinted matte 8×10s into a nearby drawer.

"What good are the photographs to you, John?" Mary Callanan plaintively asked.

"It's the only thing I've got left that they want, and it's how I'm gettin' the last goddam word."

"Fine then, John King. The Almighty has ways of dealin' with your kind. I've nothin' more to say."

"Right this way then, Mrs. Callanan." He motioned with a long sweeping gesture toward the door that Mary insisted remain open during their conversation. As she rushed down the steep, narrow wooden stairway, no handrail on either side, her scampering footsteps had the sound of hard rain on a windowpane. Although her back was to him, John Joseph got what he wanted, what he always juggled for, schemed for, fought for, come hell or high water . . . the last word.

"And never darken my door again."

PART II

CHAPTER 19

After the ball is over, After the break of morn —
After the dancers' leaving; After the stars are gone;
Many a heart is aching, If you could read them all;
Many the hopes that have vanished After the ball.

"AFTER THE BALL"
CHARLES K. HARRIS

CORDELIA PARKER WAS UNWED.
Norman Prescott, the boy she thought she would marry, much to his family's bewilderment and Cordelia's devastation, wed an Irish girl from South Boston. Trying to make the best of what she considered a very unfortunate situation, his mother described Patricia "Ann" Sheehan to friends and family as "particularly pretty, polite, bright and petite, but from South Boston nonetheless."

Two and a half years later, Cordelia continued to ruminate over the series of events she truly believed took Norman away from her that Christmas season two years earlier.

∽

From the moment of introduction, Norman Prescott kept a close eye on Patricia Sheehan, despite Cordelia's cunning attempts to distract him. "Oh, there's Beatrice and Paul. Do let's say hello" she told Norman, and "Be a good sport and take me outside on the terrace for a sec. It's so stuffy in here." Later that night, when she spied the way Patricia seemed to be looking for someone and stopped searching when Norman came into view, Cordelia cannily requested, "Would you mind very much if we called it an evening, Norman?" Not wanting to seem a wet blanket, she cheerfully said, "What a fabulous Christmas party," as she leaned on his shoulder and then sighed. "Mmmm, I'm delightfully exhausted."

But just as they were about to leave, Cordelia said, "Let me powder my nose. I'll only be a minute." That's when Norman dashed off to find that cute little number again, politely declining other guests' attempts to connect with him along the way.

"Norman, haven't seen you since—"

"Yes, it has been a while." He extended his hand for a quick shake. "Merry Christmas." Norman kept moving, and other friendly inquiries came as he paced his steps to the tune of "Deck the Halls," which someone had turned up, once again, to almost full volume on the phonograph. *Fa, la, la, la, la . . .* The laughter and conversation reached an even greater level of merriment.

From time to time Mrs. Campbell serenely entered the fray and amiably turned down the volume. But it never lasted very long.

"Hey Norman, how are you pal?"

"Terrific. And you're looking well." His feet never stopped. "Merry Christmas."

"Norman Prescott, international relations field of interest, you're just the fellow to settle our difference of opinion about the unrest in Europe."

He was growing impatient, but remained jovial, and then he spotted Patsy and swiftly patted one of the debaters on the shoulder. "It's Christmas, no difference of opinion allowed."

'Tis the season to be jolly.

Patsy pretended not to notice Norman approaching and coyly stood on tiptoe with one foot poised behind her while reaching to put an ornament that had fallen off the Christmas tree back in place.

The music changed. *Hark! The herald angels sing, glory to the newborn King...*

"Patricia." Norman lightly tapped her on the shoulder. "May I help you with that?"

The dainty, dark-haired beauty felt butterflies in her stomach at the nearness of him. *Keep calm. Keep calm.* "No, thank you, I've got it." Patricia turned about-face.

Joyful, all ye nations rise; join the triumph of the skies.

"Oh, it's you again." She gave the tall Brahmin a shy smile. "Norman, right?" *He's even better looking than I remember, and heaven forgive me, I bet he kisses well.* At that thought, her cheeks lightly flushed. *Patsy Sheehan, what in the world are you thinking? Stop!*

Patricia wasn't the only one who felt pleasingly on edge. Norman seemed uncertain of his name. "Why yes, yes, Norman . . . Norman Prescott."

"Hmm, are you positive?" She smiled, and although a bit embarrassed, so did he.

Hark! The herald angels sing.

"I'm sorry, Patricia, I should have begun by introducing myself again. Surely you've met dozens of people tonight."

She observed his tall, sandy-haired, brown-eyed good looks for the second time that night and noted his charcoal jacket had patches on the elbows, which she considered very academic looking. The length of his dark slacks seemed to go on forever, and a hunter-green vest, white dress shirt and simple striped tie, which actually belonged to his father, completed the conservative, old money appearance.

"Yes, so many names to remember, but I believe our introduction ended with an interrupted invitation, something about my brother, Rosemary, and me joining you on the Common for ice skating tomorrow?"

Joy to the world, the Lord is come.

"Coincidentally, that's why I'm here. It will be great fun. There'll be about fourteen of us meeting at the Frog Pond." He was surprised to hear himself speaking so fast. "My family lives close by, and we're going to my house afterward for a casual holiday buffet, including our Dutch housekeeper's famous hot chocolate." Norman stopped talking for a minute. "Patricia, I really want to see you again, and I'm doing a terrible job of trying not to appear too eager."

Let every heart prepare Him room.

Patsy glanced to the side before folding her hands and looking up at the tall, gentleman. "What time, Norman?" *Dreamboat.*

"One thirty, Patricia."

And heaven and nature sing, and heaven and nature sing.

When Cordelia returned to the entry, Norman was nowhere to be seen. She assumed he was saying his last goodbyes and decided to retrieve her coat on her own to save time. Mr. Campbell was ready to help and asked, as he reached in the guest closet, "The long velvet, right, Cappy?"

Cordelia approached the lively gathering in the parlor only to find Norman and Patricia standing side by side, laughing at the antics of two freshmen who were circling the room waving mistletoe and looking for coed kisses while at the same time being summoned by other young men who wanted to get in on the act. "Hey fellas, got any to spare?"

Norman looked at Patsy and teasingly began to raise his hand as if in preparation to call upon the revelers himself.

"Norman Prescott, do that and tomorrow you'll ice skate without my company."

Cordelia suddenly stood before them, her elegant needlepoint evening bag held in both hands and royal-navy velvet coat over her shoulders, where Mr. Campbell had placed it.

"Oh, Cappy, there you are," Norman said. "I believe you two ladies met earlier this evening."

"Yes," the two young women answered simultaneously, and they extended their hands for a light ladylike handshake that ended with Patricia excusing herself. "Please forgive me for rushing off, but I really need to get back to my friends. You're welcome to join us if you want."

Norman turned and said, "Your call, Cappy."

Cordelia slipped her gloved hand into the crook of Norman's arm. "I'm afraid we've already planned to make our exit. Thank you just the same, Patricia, isn't it?" Not waiting for a reply she cordially added, "Another time, maybe," and gently tugged Norman. "Shall we go?"

Bing Crosby's crooning rendition of "I'm Dreaming of a White Christmas" saw them out the door, and it seemed everyone at the party was singing along. They continued to hear its sweet refrain all the way to the car.

Six months later, at Patricia and Norman's June wedding reception in his parents' Beacon Hill home, days before he left for active duty in the U.S. Marines, Cordelia's family were preferred guests. Thus, they were seated at one of the tables closest to the bride and groom, where, with great embarrassment, Cordelia listened to her father's soft-spoken advice. "Be pleasantly congratulatory and no one will be the wiser. But if you insist on going around with that long face, Cappy, I'm afraid you'll look the fool."

Cordelia obligingly rose to the occasion and warmly waved to the happy couple. She was, after all, her parents' daughter and brought up to keep personal feelings "close to the vest," as her father strictly stated. Her mother very firmly insisted, "There's no dignity in airing one's emotions or private business."

∽

That wedding was two years ago, and even after all this time, Cordelia still believed the absence of the red coat sealed her spinster plight. Just last Sunday, as she and her closest friend were serving coffee and donuts at the U.S.O. in downtown Boston, Cordelia visited her heartbreak again.

"Oh, Abby, if only I'd had an opportunity to wear my lovely red coat once more in Norman's presence, I'm certain the enchantment of that long ago evening walk home would have returned. You can't imagine what it meant to have his arm around my shoulders." She broke away and asked the Army private standing before her, "Cream and sugar, soldier?" As he walked off with a cup of steaming black coffee and two donuts, Cordelia didn't miss a beat of her previous conversation. "And I still don't understand why Mother was so cavalier about giving my lovely coat to that Irish scrubwoman."

Abigail Adams Dubois Remington discreetly overlooked the tears that welled up in Cordelia's deep blue eyes and changed the subject. "Slow down,

Cappy. If you continue to give every serviceman two donuts right off the bat, there won't be enough to last the day."

"Abby, have you seen what's in the kitchen? There are so many where those came from. Don't worry, we won't run short."

"And the same can be said for good men, Cordelia. There are plenty of fish in the sea."

"So they say." Cordelia turned away, wiped her eyes with a paper napkin, and spun back again to see a dozen or more soldiers and sailors standing in line. "Okay, fellas, who's next?"

Abby had known Cordelia for years. They'd been girlhood friends and college roommates at Radcliffe, and Cordelia was the only bridesmaid in Abby's wedding that wasn't her sister. How many times had Abby listened to these words? She wanted more for her friend. *Enough is enough. What might have been and if only has been eating her alive for too long now, and that simply won't do.*

Abby and Cordelia were both thankful for the next interruption and turned their attention to three friendly WACS who came back for a second cup of "the best joe in Boston." The one in the middle quipped, "Well, maybe in Boston, but the best Joe in Seattle is six foot one, serving Uncle Sam stateside, and waiting for me to come marching home."

The Women's Army Corps . . . WACS Over 150,000 American women served in The Women's Army Corps during World War II . . . Both the Army and the American public initially had difficulty accepting the concept of women in uniform . . . However . . . by the end of the war their contributions would be widely heralded.

The Women's Army Corps:
A Commemoration of
World War II Service
By Judith A. Bellafaire

When Cordelia reached across the counter to offer the sharply uniformed trio more donuts, the Seattle WAC was taken aback to see someone so beautiful and classy without an engagement or wedding ring.

"Now, don't take off for the Northwest, duchess, and steal my Joe."

"Wouldn't think of it. Besides, I don't think I'd have a chance."

All the women, on both sides of the counter smiled and nodded in agreement.

It was a moment that would resonate with Cordelia for years as she wondered what became of the personable young WACS. Did they make it home? Did the brunette's Joe wait for her? *What uncertain times.*

Abby and Cordelia were restocking the napkins, cups and saucers.

"Well, if there is indeed such a thing as a broken heart, Abby, my days are numbered."

Abby, cute as ever with her high-spirited ways and sable-black Buster Brown haircut, which she would still have when her locks turned middle-aged gray and even later when they were entirely white, began to laugh. "What in the world did you just say, Cordelia?"

"Okay, a bit melodramatic, I'll admit."

Abby was pleased she at least got Cordelia to smile.

"But, Abby, you of all people know how difficult this has been for me." She opened her eyes wider to keep the second round of tears from falling. "And after Doris's wedding, I'll be one of the few in our gang who still isn't married. What will become of me, Abby?"

⸎

"Honestly Mother, if Pip says one more time, 'always a bridesmaid.' How in the world is that supposed to be anywhere near acceptable?" Cordelia stood on a firm, towel-covered (to protect the crewel upholstery) hassock in her parents' sunny bedroom while her mother pinned up the hem of yet another bridesmaid dress.

"There's no ill intent, dear. It's merely an expression." *If only I could believe that myself. I'm afraid our Cordelia is destined for a life much like her aunties, no husband, no children. Oh my. We'll need to make some changes to our will, so she'll be well provided for. Perhaps the house should be hers alone. Yes, that's it. Pip, of course, will come into the family business, but I think it would be very appropriate to leave the house to Cappy. The aunties found tremendous consolation in never having to leave their own family home. Yes, that's it. I need to speak to Price.*

"Between 1940 and 1943, more than a million more couples married than would have been expected in "normal times." For some, marriage offered hope of deferment; for others, a hasty wedding meant more time together before the husband entered the military. Furthermore, the 1940s saw the median age at first marriage for women reach an all-time low of 20.3 years.

Clarence Holbrook Carter's
*War Bride and the Machine/
Woman Fantasy* by
PATRICIA VETTEL-BECKER

"And, Mother, will you look at this dress. What in the world was Doris thinking when she selected such a color and style? It's positively dreadful."

Simply stated, Doris, heiress to a railway fortune and the only child of enormously doting parents was thinking, *I don't want anyone to outshine me. I'm the bride, and this is my day.*

Caroline didn't dare articulate her agreement. *Whoever heard of such a color indeed and for bridesmaids' gowns?* "Well, dear, you are after all Doris's bridesmaid and that means humbly tending to her needs and whims even if it means wearing a less than favorable frock." *Unless the young man in question is blind, Cordelia certainly won't be catching a husband at this wedding.*

The dresses were long, loose, and puce, with short, puffy, triple-ruffled sleeves and a shapeless waist that left enough room for any future early pregnancy. The bride told her "girls" exactly where to purchase the shoes she'd selected for their ensemble. "Low heels have such a look of ease, don't you agree?"

One of them lied out loud. "Oh, Doris, we've already purchased our bridesmaids' slippers. It was supposed to be a surprise and give you one less thing to think about, dear, but please don't be concerned. They're very appropriate." The others silently consented, and the next day, all the girls met downtown and shopped for the most outrageously attractive, open-toed, high-heeled pumps they could find.

There was seldom a time at the wedding or reception, when Doris's girls didn't have the hems of their gowns raised, appearing to demurely lift them so as not to trip, but in truth doing so to reveal their; pretty pumps, polished toenails, well-turned ankles and in one bold instance, shapely calves.

Caroline helped Cordelia step down from the hassock. "Just remember, Cappy, you've a beautiful complexion and a neck like a swan. Merely hold your head high, dear." She took her daughter affectionately by the shoulders. "And you're more than welcome to wear my pearl-drop earrings if you wish."

Cordelia Ann Parker admired her mother's ability to make everything seem better than it was and took pride in quoting Caroline's optimistic wisdom later that day to her two remaining single girlfriends, who were also in Doris's very large wedding party of eight bridesmaids and groomsmen, a matron of honor, best man, a little boy ring bearer, and two flower girls. "My mother says not to worry about being the last of the unmarried. That God saves the best for last. We need only be patient and pleasant during the wait."

Cordelia's parents found themselves going to more weddings than they'd ever remembered occurring in so short a period of time.

"My goodness, darling," Mrs. Parker said. "We'll break the bank with all these gifts. Mr. Atkinson at Shreve, Crump, and Low said I've become one of their best, if not most frequent, customers."

Caroline Parker selected the same exquisite gift for every couple. A cut crystal vase, from one of the most prestigious, old guard stores in Boston. And with each purchase she reasoned to the clerk at hand, "It goes with absolutely everything, no matter the couple's china pattern, furniture style, or preferences, and thankfully, I'm spared all that bother of wondering what to give."

Price Irving Parker III had been excused from active military duty due to a congenital health problem. Nothing serious, but his erratic heartbeat was cause enough for concern according to Uncle Sam's Massachusetts medical advisor, who said, "We can't take a chance on you having a heart attack in the middle of battle, son. Your country will be better served if you remain in your father's employ and keep those commissioned ships in good repair for the war effort and running on schedule."

World War II was escalating, and by now, most of Cordelia and Pip's male friends were commissioned, drafted, or had readily enlisted in the armed services. Those who had a steady girl, or in some instances, with young women joining up too, a steady fellow, were more than ready to tie the knot before saying goodbye for who knew how long. For sweethearts left behind, the romantic song "I'll Be Seeing You" was more than a pop tune. It was a sympathetic and comforting wartime anthem. But for Miss Cordelia Parker, every tender word applied to her loss of Mr. Norman Prescott. Indeed, she was forever *seeing* him, from family homes to church, the Cape, and every other familiar place they had ever spent time together.

CHAPTER 20

There was about the house a stillness, which rendered spoken
words louder and more pointless than at all other times.
LOUISBURG SQUARE
ROBERT CUTLER

THERE WAS NOTHING UNUSUAL ABOUT the front door of the house at number ninety-one, Mount Vernon, being left ajar. The Beacon Hill property's black, cast-iron fence and at-all-times latched gate, provided a certain sense of inaccessibility and safekeeping from the world outside.

But today the intricately ornate gate was left wide open for arriving guests, and if a passerby were to steal a glance beyond the doorway or at the downstairs windows, they'd observe a large gathering of black-clad men and women, their conversations streaming out to the sidewalk in a respectful low-toned dirge.

Price and Caroline Parker were gone.

The shock of their untimely deaths left Cordelia so bereft she spoke only when absolutely necessary, and losing their parents had sent her brother, Pip, straight to a bottle of his father's select Scotch and then some. But through it all, the adult children of Price and Caroline Parker maintained a sense of dignity and propriety beyond their sorrow.

Cordelia stood in the parlor, her back to the dormant fireplace. From this location she could see everything and be seen, making herself available for the condolences of those who wanted a personal connection and most times taking an extended hand in her own two. "Yes, they will be tremendously missed. Thank you for being here."

Pip positioned himself in close proximity to his sister, next to a Bombe chest that held a sizeable, slightly tarnished silver tray of crystal decanters he seemed to be tipping endlessly. "My parents had a very high opinion of your family, and were they able to speak for themselves would be extremely grateful for your presence here today. May I pour you something, Scotch, sherry, brandy?"

Together, Cordelia and Pip had planned the service, gathered pallbearers and selected their parents' coffins. The burial arrangements had been in place for generations. Mr. and Mrs. Parker would be put to their final rest in the family crypt at Mount Auburn Cemetery, in Cambridge. These distressing but very necessary decisions were the last time Cordelia and Pip would agree on anything, ever again.

The Parkers' stately home was filled with people, but noticeably missing was the light and love of Mr. and Mrs. Price Parker, mourned not only by family and friends but also by the City of Boston and the Commonwealth of Massachusetts.

The couple was renowned for graciousness, foresight, and generosity through their charitable trust for the preservation of numerous Massachusetts historical sites and papers, ever-increasing grants for higher education, and frequent backing of city cultural events. Their home was at all times open to visiting dignitaries, available for fundraisers and most recently for special events related to the war effort, such as A Midsummer Evening of Classic Chamber Music ~ Light Repast to Follow - for the establishment of a Back to School Clothes & Christmas Fund intended for widowed wives of soldiers with dependent children.

Irish Catholic Mayor Maurice Tobin and former Mayor James Curley, of the same persuasion and presently a congressman, had tremendous respect for the Brahmin couple, whom Curley, long-time Protestant critic, uncharacteristically esteemed many times as "sweethearts to each other and the Commonwealth as well."

Both politicians hastened to meet with Governor Saltonstall and proposed the State House flag be flown at half-staff on the day of Price and Caroline's funeral.

Leverett Saltonstall a close, deeply grieved friend of the Parkers, was in complete agreement.

The governor and Price Parker had been classmates at the exclusive Noble and Greenough School, went on to study business and law at Harvard, crewed for the same championship team, and after a stint in the service during World War I, stood as groomsmen in one another's weddings, celebrated their children's births,

The "sweethearts" quote appeared in a Boston Globe article about "Curley's way with words." Price Parker was mortified to have his wife and himself referred to in such a "highly personal, appallingly sentimental, and thoroughly Irish manner."

and through the years, managed to consistently meet once a week for lunch at their alma mater's private club on Commonwealth Avenue.

"Absolutely gentlemen, half-staff, from dawn to dusk. Thank you for taking the time to come out in this hellacious heat wave," he said rather loudly, in an effort to be heard over the whir of a desktop fan in his office.

The governor of Massachusetts shook each of their hands and then pulled a handkerchief from his pocket as he walked them to the door of his office. "Excuse me, please." He blew his nose and said, "Thank you, gentlemen. It will be done."

The circumstances that led up to Mr. and Mrs. Parker's untimely deaths were relatively routine. Who could have known?

It was an ordinary Friday summer afternoon when Caroline and Cordelia returned from the Red Cross offices, where they'd been helping to package cookies, magazines, candy, and chewing gum parcels for servicemen and women overseas. Both women were glowing from their long, arm-in-arm walk across the Common.

Price was already home, sitting in a comfortable club chair in the parlor, feet propped up on the matching hassock, working a crossword puzzle. "My, my, what do we have here?" The proud husband and father removed his glasses, pinched his nose, and put them back on again. "Two very diligent and patriotic citizens standing right before my eyes."

Caroline Parker had long legs and nice ankles. Although she was a matron during World War II, one day, while taking a walk through the Public Garden, several sailors whistled at her, and one called out, "Hey, Betty Grable, I got ya picture in my locker." She was aghast, quickened her step, and didn't go anywhere alone for a week.

Price Parker rose, crossed the room and gave his wife and daughter, each, a kiss. "I'm very honored indeed to be associated with such noble ladies. Now, what's for dinner?" he asked, tongue in cheek, and sat down again.

"Oh, Daddy." Cordelia seldom called her father "Daddy." It just slipped out, but this time day after tomorrow, she'd be glad she did. Cordelia preferred "Daddy," but after college her father said it seemed rather juvenile. "How about Dad or Father?"

"Men," Caroline said. "You're all alike. When everything is said and done, it's what's on the table that matters most." The attractive matron pushed her husband's feet to the side and sat down on the ottoman facing him. "I'm sure you'll be happy to know we're having Yankee pot roast with mashed potatoes, fresh green peas—imagine, Hilda and Rolf grew them in our very own garden—and of course, Lina's delicious gravy and buttermilk biscuits. We'll have the leftover Waldorf salad from yesterday's C.M.S. luncheon for our first course, and dessert, my darling, will be black walnut ice-cream with shortbread cookies."

The Parkers' Swedish part-time cook, Lina, only prepared evening weekday meals, with the exception of some holidays, and special daytime occasions, the City Mission Society of Boston luncheon being one of them.

Cordelia excused herself to freshen up for dinner. It was in that fateful window of time that her parents spontaneously made plans to take a drive to the Cape on Sunday, just the two of them. It was something they'd done many times before, but not recently.

Price was weary from all the red tape involved since the government had commissioned a few of Parker Shipping's vessels, and his wife was, as he liked to tease and did presently, "the best tonic for a tired old man." For weeks now, Caroline had been longing to have some time alone with her husband. *Still,* she thought gazing at the only man she'd ever kissed, *my darling.*

"Wonderful idea, Price, and we can have lunch at that charming little restaurant in Hyannis Port with the huge lobster tank. You know the one."

⚬⚭⚬

The call came just as Cordelia was sitting down to an early Sunday dinner with a good book as her only company. "Hilda, please don't bring the food in until I'm off the phone." She lay the open book face down, spine up, in order to keep her place and impishly considered the countless times her mother had cautioned her not to do so. *Cappy, honestly, you know better. Whatever condition will that book be in for future readers? We've dozens of bookmarks in this house.*

"Hello, Parker residence." Cordelia answered.

"Who am I speaking with, please?" a male voice on the other end inquired.

"Whom am I speaking with?" Cordelia curtly replied.

"I'm sorry, Miss, if I have that right, but I'm with the Massachusetts State Police, and this is a call of some urgency. I need to speak with a relative of Mr. Price Parker or Mrs. Caroline Parker. Would you be such a person?"

Cordelia's stomach tightened. "Yes, I'm their daughter."

"Forgive me for asking this, Miss, but are you there alone?"

"No, not exactly. Our housekeeper is in the kitchen. Officer, what is this about?"

But Cordelia knew. In the deepest part of her being she knew. And she slid down the wall next to the small telephone desk. "Please, Officer, tell me what has happened to my parents."

"Miss, it might be better if you asked your housekeeper—"

"Officer, I'm not a child. Please, continue."

"Miss Parker, your parents were in a terrible automobile accident. And they're both . . . deceased."

His words fell into a space of complete silence that lasted for what seemed to the young officer at least five minutes, when in fact, it was less than two. "Miss Parker?"

Cordelia closed her eyes. *You need to be strong, Cordelia. No hysterics. No demonstrative hysterics . . . talk, talk.* "What happens now, Officer?"

"Miss Parker, are you sure you don't want someone else to take care of this? Do you have a brother or an uncle who can assume responsibility?"

"I have both, Officer, but I assure you I'm quite capable. Please, tell me what's next."

"You'll need to drive down here to Hyannis and identify your parents before we can release the . . . them to your care."

"How did it happen?"

"Apparently the driver of the other car fell asleep behind the wheel, and he hit your parents' automobile head on. All appearances indicate he was hung over, and as is usually the case, this joker survived, although he's in pretty bad shape. But if it's of any comfort to you Miss Parker, I believe your parents, if you'll excuse the expression, never knew what hit them." There was that long stretch of quiet again.

'Never knew what hit them.' Why, yes, Officer, I'm tremendously comforted by that.

"Miss Parker. Miss Parker, are you all right?"

"Yes, Officer, as right as can be expected under the circumstances." She took a breath. "Will you please tell me where I can find my parents?"

Cordelia remained on the floor. She slowly put the receiver back in place and looked all about her. *They were just here, and there's still a hint of Mother's fragrance.* Her father's briefcase lay on the entry settee, and she crawled toward it. *Daddy, why didn't you see it coming?* But she stopped herself. *This can't possibly be happening.* She looked toward the front door, half expecting them to walk through it. *I'll never see my parents alive again.*

Cordelia immediately picked up the receiver and phoned her brother, her rival, her only sibling, the person in her circle of relationships for whom she had the least respect and a great deal of conflicted love. There was no answer. *Wiling the afternoon away with his latest conquest, no doubt.*

Cordelia pulled herself up, put the phone back on the desk, looked about her again, walked over to the settee and picked up her father's briefcase. *Daddy.* She gently put it down and walked toward the kitchen.

The housekeeper, who'd looked after the Parker family since Cordelia was a baby, covered her mouth with one hand and cried out through parted fingers. "Oh, my God!" She put both hands over her ears and cried out again. "Oh, my God, oh, my God!" And straight from her supposedly Protestant heart, she uttered words of solace from her one true faith, "Blessed Mother of God, oh, my most Blessed Mary, Mother of God!"

The young lady of the house and the long-time housekeeper fell into each other's arms and wept. Cordelia was the first to break away and did so abruptly. Hilda pulled her apron skirt up and buried her face in it. Cordelia took a seat at the kitchen table where her mother's grocery list lay with a pen placed horizontally across the top third of the note pad, creating a facsimile of a cross, and she prayed, *God be with us,* as tears streamed down her cheeks, but she got right to business.

"Hilda, I want Rolf to come with me, and you're to keep phoning my brother's apartment. Please. Do not tell him about Mother and Father on the telephone. Make him come over here. Tell him he needs to come home. I don't want Pip to be alone when he finds out. Do you understand, Hilda?"

The housekeeper was wringing her hands within the folds of her apron. "Yes, Miss Cordelia. But if you don't mind me saying so, wouldn't you rather have one of your relatives go with you?"

"No, this is going to be difficult enough. I don't want to burden them beyond what's ahead of us all. Now, do you understand, Hilda? Cordelia picked up the pen and tapped what could have been Morse Code for S.O.S.: tap-tap-tap, pause, tap-tap-tap. "Your only responsibility is to keep trying to get ahold of my brother." Tap-tap-tap. She hurriedly wrote down his number.

As it turned out, Cordelia endured what seemed like an endless drive to the Cape. She identified her parents, along with Rolf, who respectfully supported her elbow during the viewing. Her mother's golden-gray hair was matted with blood and her face barely identifiable, save her unharmed closed eyes and the small screw-sized mole on the right side of her jaw, which she many times had referred to as "holding me together." Cordelia's father, although just as injured and bloodied, was still wearing his glasses, which were completely intact.

She returned home, and this time Rolf drove. Cordelia phoned the funeral home her family had used for generations and made the first of many arrangements. Pip still hadn't been located. *Where are you, brother?*

Cordelia decided to lay her head down for the night, but did so fully clothed, despite the stifling summer humidity, fell into a deep sleep, and dreamt of her parents in childhood days. Eventually, Norman entered her restless dreams too, carrying a huge Red Cross flag across the Common, with Patsy marching beside him wearing Cordelia's beloved and long-lost red coat. Cordelia herself was ice-skating on the Frog Pond, making every effort not to trip on the long, tattered bridal veil that surrounded her. And Pip was watching from the sidelines, laughing along with several of his old girlfriends. "That a girl, Cappy, keep going . . ."

Cordelia forced herself to wake up rather than bear the torture of such agonizing images, and because it was close to dawn, took a bath and dressed for the painfully long day ahead. The aroma of coffee told her Hilda was already in the kitchen, and Cordelia speculated it had been a restless night for her as well.

"Miss Cordelia, you're going to need a good breakfast to keep you strong,"

Despite the housekeeper's recommendation, she had only a single cup of coffee and a triangle of toast before walking the short distance to her elderly aunts' home.

The cool early morning air helped to clear Cordelia's head, and the walk provided time to gather her thoughts.

Aunt Agatha answered the door in a long, Colonial-blue cotton pique dressing gown. "Why Cordelia, what in the world are you doing here at this early hour?" The tiny old woman reached for her hand. "Cat got your tongue?"

"Auntie, I simply don't know how to tell you what I have to say."

"Whatever it is, it can wait, dear. You're just in time for breakfast. Come in, dear, come in."

Cordelia loved this ancient brownstone mansion that her great-grandfather had bequeathed to his two maiden daughters. Time seemed to stand still within its high-ceilinged walls, and the profusion of indoor plants, mostly ferns, filled it entirely with a pleasantly musty green smell, which presently had an overlay of frying butter.

They went straightaway to the kitchen, where Aunt Martha was preparing French toast in a big, black, cast-iron skillet.

"Oh my, Cordelia! What a pleasant surprise. You'll stay for breakfast, of course. Agatha, would you mind very much setting another place at the table?"

Aunt Martha flipped the toast and asked, "Well, my favorite niece, to what do we owe this crack of dawn visit?" Cordelia recommended they take a seat, though each declined. "Honestly, Cordelia." The two platinum-haired ladies— Agatha's long braid not yet wound up at the nape of her neck and Martha's coarse curls unruly without the aid of the two dark brown cloisonné combs that usually kept them pulled back and in place—amiably nodded toward each other, and one gaily inquired, "Might this have something to do with a beau?"

"No, Aunties, it's nothing like that." And for the first time in her life, Cordelia assumed a responsibility that typically would have been her parents', imparting important family news.

"There's been a dreadful accident . . ."

Aunt Agatha began to sob, looked as though she was going to faint, and caught herself on one of the rickety ladder-back chairs. Aunt Martha didn't shed a tear, but Cordelia noticed her frail body slightly shivered when she offered to compose a list of names and begin making telephone calls. "Don't worry about the bill, Cordelia. We're not counting our pennies at a time like this." She emphasized "at a time like this" with a waving spatula, then pulled a chair up next to her sister and sat down, spatula still in hand, butter dripping onto the floor without notice.

Cordelia used her aunties' telephone before departing and called Pip's apartment. No answer. She dialed the family business next, where the receptionist sang her usual salutations. "Parker Shipping. May I help you please?"

"It's Cordelia Parker?"

"And how are you today, Miss Parker?"

The boss's daughter avoided answering and directly asked, "Bernice, is my brother there yet?"

Pip had his own posh apartment on Commonwealth Avenue, and the family seldom knew what Price Irving Parker III was doing when he was away from his responsibilities at the offices of Parker Shipping.

Shortly after graduating from college, he'd taken on the reins of company controller and, at the same time, was predictably being groomed for company president in light of his father's pending retirement.

During a tour of Boston soon after World War II, Winston Churchill proclaimed Commonwealth Avenue to be "the grandest boulevard in North America."

"No, Miss Cordelia, neither your father nor brother are here yet. Would you like me to leave a message?"

"No, thank you, Bernice." *Bet he's still in bed. Bet dollars to donuts it's not his own. Pip, where are you? Where are you? Where are you?*

Miss Cordelia Anne Parker of Beacon Hill, second born and only daughter of the late Mr. and Mrs. Price Irving Parker II, walked through the city of her birth for the next hour, alone, saddened, fearful of a future without her parents. *Who'll give me away when I get married? Certainly not Pip . . . and what about Christmas . . . This can't be happening.*

Early on she found herself in the North End, the Italian section of town, and the patrolman on duty thought she looked strangely out of place at that early hour when delivery truck drivers accounted for most non-Italians. "Are you lost, Miss?"

"Perhaps I am, Officer." *Perhaps I am.* She fiddled with the flap of her shoulder bag. "Forgive me, I was thinking out loud. Thank you. I'll be fine." And she looked both ways before crossing the dew-dampened street.

"Take care now," the patrolman cautioned. If he'd been a betting man—with five children, a mortgage and live-in mother-in-law, he dared not be—Officer Canavan would've wagered: *This attractive young lady is down in the dumps. Maybe she just lost her fella in the war, yeah, that's it, and these Wasp types keep it tight, poor gal.*

Cordelia could barely stand the thought of entering her family home again. Once inside, she'd have to deal with everything, right away, and apparently without the help of her brother. But as soon as she crossed the threshold, he was there, sitting on the third step of the spiral staircase, bent over with his face in his hands.

When Price Irving Parker III raised his handsome head, it was apparent he'd been crying. With puffy eyes, mussed hair (running his hands through his hair when troubled was a habit Pip's parents weren't able to thwart), and slumped shoulders, he crossly asked, "Cordelia, where in the world have you been?"

She closed the massive front door behind her, secured the lock and without saying a word, met her brother halfway.

CHAPTER 21

I went downstairs and scrubbed the kitchen floor! Then I felt better.
Who was it said, 'Blessed be drudgery'? I used to laugh at the idea.
There's nothing like it to heal our frazzled nerves . . . so long as our
bodies aren't frazzled, too. That day, after the floor was finished, I
set to work and got a big dinner for the family-a hard dinner . . .
I was tired enough to drop, but I was myself again.

THE KINGS OF BEACON HILL
CHRISTINE WHITING

T HEY SAT THERE AT THE kitchen table, the two most important women
in Robert Donnelly's life, his mother and his wife.

At age nineteen, Rita Donnelly was pregnant with her first child
and carrying the baby close, according to the only three people in the world who
knew about it, other than her husband. And that meant she "hardly showed," as
Rosemary assured her.

"Which," Kay remarked, "is fairly surprising, for a girl as small as you are,
I'd think that baby would be leading the way, right away."

Today, the expectant mother chose to wear her navy-blue suit to Sunday
Mass, since the jacket still buttoned, and more importantly, it hid a chain of

safety pins used to expand the waist of her now too-snug skirt. A baby was coming, and soon she'd have to buy maternity clothes, but until then, safety pins, coats, and jackets would help to hold her secret a little longer from everyone but her husband's mother and her two sisters—none of whom were particularly thrilled when they first learned she was expecting, because, at the time, the couple's May wedding day was still weeks away.

❧

It was only a few months ago, on a blustery, rainy, early April afternoon, in Quincy, as several inside-out umbrellas led their owners down the Chalpin's puddle-strewn street, and other brave souls clung to each other for surety, that Rita King and her intended, Robert Donnelly, met with his mother and her sisters in Kay and Steve's cozy upstairs apartment. Rosemary had taken the train in from New York.

All three women assumed Bob's last minute request for "just the five of us, okay?" had something to do with the couple's upcoming wedding plans. It did, and it didn't.

After all the hellos and hugs, removal of hats and gloves, coats, and lastly rain boots, which were lined up outside the apartment door, next to open, dripping umbrellas, everyone came inside. Bob, a broad-shouldered five foot eleven, wearing his best slacks and sport coat, remained standing. While the ladies, clothed just as nicely in day dresses and stockings and high-heeled shoes for the younger women, lower-heels for his mother, sat down before the coffee table. It was laden with platters and bowls of delicious choices: a variety of precisely stacked, cut-in-fourths sandwiches, mixed nuts served with a nutcracker and picks, pastel mints, and Rita's favorite dessert, "lady finger" slices of Drake's raisin pound cake. Kay pertly offered additional refreshments.

"I've got hot water on for tea, no coffee, sorry, and some ginger ale in the icebox."

Before anyone could answer, Bob spoke up. "If you don't mind, Kay, I have something to say first."

His mother noticed the tips of her son's ears were red, a sure sign he was nervous, if not guilty of something. *I bet they've run out of money. Well, I have*

228

some tucked away, not much, but it's theirs for the asking. Without question, I'll want every penny back. Money doesn't grow on trees.

"I'm going to cut to the chase and say I love Rita with all my heart, and I can't believe she'll have me."

The women smiled at each other, and Rosemary said, "You make a really nice couple."

There was an awkward pause as they waited for Bob to continue. He looked down, punched his right hand into his left, and took a deep breath.

Rita got up from where she was sitting on the couch next to Rosemary, walked over to her intended, and faced the curious women. "I'm in a family way."

Bob's mother gasped. "God Almighty. I knew something was wrong, but I never thought it'd be something like this."

Rosemary looked as if she was going to cry. "It can't be true." She fell back on the couch from her attentive, sitting-on-the edge position, folded her arms and said, "After all we've been through, Rita, and you end up like this. Dear Jesus."

Kay untied her organdy hostess apron, threw it on the couch, glanced at Rosemary, and glared at Rita. "Thank God Mum didn't have to hear this."

The future groom sheepishly looked at Rita's sisters and, not quite as cowed, at his mother. "I'm sorry it turned out this way, but we are getting married. Father Kenney already knows, and under the circumstances, our ceremony should be taking place in his office, but he wants Rita to have the Saint Augustine's wedding she's always planned on. He's really stretching his neck out for us, Mum. Monsignor Shea doesn't know a thing."

Father Kenney had a long-standing soft spot for the bride that began two weeks after her birth in November of 1925, the day he baptized her "Rita Margaret" at Saint Augustine's.

After the initial shock and shame, it was Rita's future mother-in-law who began to calm everyone down and set everything in the right direction. "Let's make the best of it. Keep the whole business under our hats and get on with the marriage." She clapped once as if to clear the air. "Does that wedding dress still fit you, Rita?"

The future bride's hands instantly went to her stomach, one on top of the other. "Yes, it does, Mrs. Mac," she said, having tried the borrowed gown on recently for her own peace of mind.

When Rosemary and Tony were married at Gate of Heaven, the majority of guests were women and children. World War II was in full swing. Rita would invite many of the same people, wear the same gown and same veil, and borrow the same bridesmaids' dresses for her attendants, but this bride would carry a much larger bouquet.

Rosemary had been ecstatic to loan her baby sister the wedding gown and veil but presently felt uneasy about the pure white garments being worn under such circumstances.

"Oh, I'm very disappointed in both of you," she said. "And you know what, Bob? Your 'I love Rita with all my heart' really doesn't mean much when I consider everything my sister will have to go through now."

"Ro!" Rita pleaded. "This is my future husband you're talking to. Please stop!" Her cheeks were crimson.

When Rosemary caught Rita's distress, her first thought was to comfort. "It'll be okay, honey. You're not the first and you certainly won't be the last." She had nothing more to say to Bob. *What a cad.*

Kay wasn't so kind, and her disdain was directed at Bob Donnelly alone. "You should be ashamed of yourself."

His mother wisely put a stop to it. "There's nothing's to be gained by that kind of talk, although I'm inclined to agree with you." She looked at her son and shook her head. "You've broken my heart." Later on, when mother and son were alone, she mercilessly lit into him. "What in God's name were you thinking? Doing a thing like that to a nice girl about to become your wife?"

⚭

On this sleepy Sunday afternoon in July, almost two months after the wedding, her suit jacket removed, a borrowed apron donned, the mother-to-be was helping her mother-in-law with the lunch dishes, when the older woman insisted she sit down to dry the rest of the silverware. "Here, let's put it all in this bowl." Bob's mother gathered the wet utensils from one end of the drain board. "It's not good for the baby, Rita, you being on your feet for long periods of time." She pulled a sturdy oak ladder-back chair away from the kitchen table, her water-wrinkled fingers curled around the top rung's heart cutout. "They'll get just as dry with you sitting down as standing up."

The table, both extensions in at all times, held a divided drawer for silverware, and after turning back the white, fruit-bordered tablecloth, Rita pulled the drawer open, slipped each dried utensil into its proper section, and alternately observed her mother-in-law's busy-bee movements. She dipped her hands in the sink, swiftly washed dirty dishes, pots, and pans, gingerly balanced them on the drain board, reached up, down, and sideways to put various items away, and in between, watered her prized African violets, lined up like beauty queens—some ample, some slight, all very sweet—on a yellow metal utility cart.

Rita wondered how her mother-in-law, despite having such a large household to care for—husband, George; disabled young adult son, Buddy; teenage son, George Jr.; teenage daughter, Jane; nine-year-old son, Dicky; dog, Blackie; and parakeet, Peety— managed to cover the table at all, let alone with a pressed cloth. Then she remembered her own mother, Norah, used to do the same thing, and she remembered why.

"It's one thing to be short of money, darlin', but a bare table makes you poor. Food tastes better when the table's properly set."

The bride—she'd been married such a short time, bride still applied—felt gratefully at home in this sunny kitchen that smelled strongly of good food, faintly of cigarette smoke and coffee, pleasantly of soap. The floor was gray linoleum with a colorful rag-rug in front of the sink, and the humming icebox was filled to capacity with items such as homogenized milk, Canada Dry ginger ale, eggs, butter, oleomargarine, bacon, Hershey's chocolate syrup, Vermont Maid maple syrup, horseradish, Lee & Perrins, Heinz mustard and Hellmann's mayonnaise, red Jell-O with sliced bananas, Spam, and deviled ham. Her husband's mother frequently said of the last two items, "God only knows what they're made of." There was cream cheese, American cheese, and whatever was left over from the three meals a day she served her family; nothing ever went to waste.

Stale bread became bread pudding. Cold chicken, roast beef, or fish, cut into pieces, were combined with sautéed celery, onions, and white sauce for noodle casseroles, or finely chopped along with potatoes for hash. Even sour milk was saved and used in a delicious, old, German cake recipe that specifically called for the curdled ingredient.

There always seemed to be something cooking on the big, black, iron stove that still smelled of this morning's baking, egg custard and banana bread. And their friendly cocker spaniel, Blackie, forever napped in front of it, even in the summer heat.

Every cupboard was bursting with a topsy-turvy variety of dishes, glasses, serving ware, pots, pans, and non-perishable groceries. Bread and crackers were stored separately in a green, black-stenciled breadbox placed on top of the icebox. Their parakeet was perched in his freestanding birdcage, next to four wide-open windows, where thankfully, a breeze of fresh air was coming in, while the café curtains flew up and about like the hems of pretty dresses on a windy day.

The kitchen table was conveniently central and used for a wide variety of activities. Homework, bill paying, food preparation, and understandably all meals, and most times, it was where family and friends preferred to visit, with a cup of tea or coffee, glass of Kool-Aid, Zarex, water, milk, or tonic, along with a bowl or plate of "Mrs. Mac's good cookin'."

Alcohol was forbidden in Mrs. Mac's house. Milk and Hershey's chocolate syrup was the only mixed drink permitted, made especially for nine-year-old, Dicky. Curiously, the triangle punctures on either side of the syrup can were always made with a beer can opener, "Gorwin's Packaged Goods Store" embossed on both sides.

Rita's mother-in-law, Ethel McDonough, formerly Donnelly, and before that, Murphy, known by most people in Southie as "Mrs. Mac," had finally decided to take a seat too, and she began writing a recipe on the back of a used, "perfectly good" envelope in her very distinctive swirled handwriting: *Ethel McDonough's Irish Soda Bread.*

In her day, Ethel Louise Murphy had been the belle of the ball, with a wavy blonde bob, shapely, five-foot-five figure, icy blue eyes, and fashionable clothing lovingly sewn by her mother. Ethel tended the finishing touches—buttons, hemming, and pressing—on her own "custom-made" wardrobe.

Mrs. Mac put her pencil down and raised her blonde-faded-to-gray head. "Doesn't every Kate and Eileen want this recipe? And I'm not one bit reluctant to say no when asked. It's a family secret, and that's where it's staying, in the family. And now that you're one of us, Rita King," she presented the envelope with great flair, "I'm happy to give it to you."

Mrs. Mac's Irish Soda Bread

2-½ cups flour

2 teaspoons baking powder

1 teaspoon salt

½ teaspoon baking soda

¼ cup butter or margarine, at room temperature

¼ cup melted butter

½ cup sugar

1 egg slightly beaten

1-½ cups buttermilk, at room temperature

1 cup raisins

2 teaspoons caraway seeds (optional)

Sift together flour, baking powder, salt, and baking soda. Set aside.

Cream butter and sugar. Add the slightly beaten egg and buttermilk. Blend well.

Add the liquid mixture to the dry ingredients, and mix by hand until well moistened.

Fold in the raisins and caraway seeds (optional).

Pour into a greased 1-½ quart glass casserole. Or you may divide the dough between two smaller casseroles.

Brush top generously with the melted butter, and sprinkle generously with sugar.

Bake in preheated 375-degree oven for 30 minutes. Then reduce oven temperature to 325 degrees and bake an additional 30 minutes.

Bread is cooked when a knife inserted in the middle comes out clean. Let cool for 10 minutes, slice and serve warm with butter.

Next day the bread may also be toasted.

Ethel Louise Murphy and John Joseph Donnelly, ironically with the same first and middle name as Rita King's father but never called anything other than Jack, had married at Saint Ambrose's Church in Dorchester, in autumn, 1922, moved straightaway to Southie, and eleven months later, "Et" gave birth to a healthy baby boy they named Robert. Two years later, their second son, John, nicknamed "Buddy," was born and pronounced "perfect" by the attending physician. But in the following months, it became evident to one and the same that Ethel and Jack's new baby had cerebral palsy. His inability to roll over or sit without support (initially attributed to slow development), jerking movements, and gaping, crooked smile were dead giveaways. And giveaway is exactly what Jack Donnelly had in mind.

"Institutionalize him, Ethel, or else I'll leave."

"Jack, Buddy's our own flesh and blood. Mother of God, how can you even think of doing such a thing?"

After weeks of his wife pleading for Buddy to remain in their home, Jack Donnelly wouldn't budge, and neither would she.

In Irish Catholic South Boston, marital infidelity was the only socially and barely acceptable reason for leaving a spouse. Abandoning a good wife and his own two children, one of them "with something wrong, God bless him," as all the neighbors could see, would make outgoing, prideful Jack Donnelly a social pariah, and he knew that only too well. So the scheming husband and father deigned to spread a disgraceful rumor that the "crippled toddler" wasn't his baby after all. And he left.

Ethel Donnelly spent a great deal of time and money at the local pharmacy because of Buddy's special needs, making regular purchases of aspirin, cough syrup, glass straws, mercurochrome, diaper rash medicine, castor oil, cod liver oil, Vaseline for his dry lips, and penny candy for both little boys. Bobby liked bull's-eyes, caramels with powdered sugar in the centers, and Buddy enjoyed lollypops, held by his older brother or mother until the last bit was sucked away.

Pharmacist George McDonough took a kind interest in Buddy. "How's the little guy today?" He admired the way Buddy's mother looked after him, saying, "There's a special place in heaven for people like you." When George heard the rumors, he knew they were false and defended Ethel Donnelly's honor whenever the opportunity presented itself.

"Mrs. Donnelly is a good woman. Have you seen the way she cares for those children? Why, most mothers would give up. It's Jack Donnelly's pride we're talkin' about here. He doesn't want the shame of an infirmed son nor the responsibility. Lay off Mrs. Donnelly. She's blameless."

Six months after her divorce from the handsome Jack Donnelly, who people likened to movie idol Robert Taylor, George McDonough proposed marriage.

George Mac was good looking too, with dark hair and eyes and light olive skin, and he more than met Ethel Donnelly's preferences in a man, by being a gentleman with a dry sense of humor, even temperament, keen intelligence, and over all fastidious grooming. Years later, she would say, "It was the package that got me, the way that handsome bugger wrapped himself up, with his spiffy bow ties, French cuffed dress shirts, and just enough sandalwood aftershave to reel me in."

George's obvious lack, what some would call a flaw, was that he stood about three inches shorter than Ethel Donnelly, who only saw his high character, big heart, and kind smile.

It was tremendously comforting for Rita Margaret King Donnelly to be here in Mrs. Mac's kitchen like this. Particularly because it was just the two of them now, with the rest of the family out and about, napping, or in the case of Dicky and his father, playing checkers in the living room, the game board precariously balanced on George Mac's knees.

It had been two years since Norah King passed away, and Rita still missed her more than anyone could know.

When it came to the kitchen, Rita and her mother had their own spick-and-span dance for washing and drying and putting away. Every day times, doing the ordinary, would hold some of Norah's youngest daughter's most cherished memories, but closest to her heart was being in the kitchen and the rare instance of having a cup of tea alone with her mother.

Exactly like Mrs. Mac, Norah King was forever doing—doing dishes, doing laundry, doing the ironing, cleaning, sewing, making bread—and because of the doing, it seemed to Rita she saw more of her mother's back than anything else, except the glance.

Norah's doting glance most often came over her shoulder and because she was one of the legions of mothers "with eyes in the back of me head," Norah knew whenever Rita entered the room.

"What are you up to then? Is it something to eat that you're after?"

"Now, don't keep your sister, brother, whoever waitin'," was what her mother said all too often because Rita was "running just a little late" most of the time.

A good deal of Norah's sentences were questions because she had the inclination of heart to anticipate needs, forever looking after whoever or whatever was in her path.

"Can I help you out then?"

"Wouldn't that be needin' a little spit and polish?"

"She's down with the scarlet fever, and isn't it strong beef tea that will bring back her strength?"

"He's only just here from Ireland and doesn't have a penny to his name. Do you think you'd have some work for him then?"

"Isn't Christmas a busy time over there at the church? Don't you suppose we should go to them and see what we can do to help?"

"Isn't she after havin' her seventh, and the delivery a hard one at that? How about we each take a couple of children for the two or three days and give the worn-out mother a well-needed rest?"

And on and on Norah's inquiries went, even in the end. "Do you know what's goin' on here, children? Do you understand you'll all be needin' to look after one another? It won't be long now. There's no one more important than your own sisters and brothers. Don't be losin' each other. Please say, honest to God, Mum, we won't be losin' each other. And will you make me the promise of goin' to confession, sayin' your prayers, and attendin' Mass, even though I'll not be around to make sure you do?"

All at once, a feeling of belonging fell over Rita King Donnelly, like a sweetheart's arms during a slow waltz, here with the treasured Irish soda bread recipe at her fingertips and her mother-in-law up on her feet again, putting the kettle on.

"Are you ready for another cup, or do you want a glass of ice water instead? What am I saying? You, mother of my first grandchild, may have both."

After Rita requested, "Ginger ale too, please?"

Mrs. Mac teased, "Anything else, my lady?"

Repositioning her five-foot-two-and-a-half, pregnant body, Rita delicately asked, "Mother, what was the name of your baby girl who passed away?"

Although Ethel McDonough's children called her Mum or Mumma, Rita never did. Norah was the only person she'd ever call by that name. But out of respect for her new family she addressed Mrs. Mac as "Mother," and only as "Mother."

By now, Mrs. Mac had already moved on to her next task and was hurriedly scrubbing potatoes before putting them on to boil, as a first step to making potato salad. She turned and didn't say a word at first, giving Rita reason to think maybe she'd made a mistake in asking. Then Mrs. Mac leaned back against the sink, wet hands dripping on her daily uniform, a simple housedress (it was her way to change out of "good clothes" as soon as she got home) covered with a print apron, which reminded Rita of her own mother's daily dress.

Mrs. Mac was taken by surprise. Nobody ever talked about "the baby girl we lost," and she assumed Bob must have said something.

Ethel McDonough was extremely fussy about aprons. "I like the straps to button at my neck. The criss-cross kind drive me crazy with the way they always slip off. I have no time for such nonsense."

The answer came as she stared somewhere above Rita's head. "Her name was Ruth Ann."

The wistful woman dried her hands, walked across the kitchen, sat down and with her right hand smoothed the bare table surface back and forth, as if sweeping something away, perhaps the last crumb of sorrow. "Ruth, because I've always loved that name, and Ann for my sister, Anna." A tear appeared on the back of Ethel McDonough's blue-veined hand. She wiped it away, and without hurry, put the tablecloth back in place. After all these years, tears still fell for the baby girl named Ruth, "because I've always loved that name." Ann, "for my sister."

Rita's well-kept secret soon began to show, and tongues began to wag. "I bet she's in a family way."

The new baby came "early" at Harley hospital in Dorchester, first grandchild on her father's side and second on her mother's.

Young uncles proudly passed out cigars, and one was promptly shooed out of the building for smoking in the maternity ward. Young aunties, after they'd finished cooing, tried to determine who the baby looked like, with the conclusion being her mother.

Rosemary, just in from New York, was shamelessly specific. "She's a King all right. Look at those dimples," and she rushed out to buy something frilly and pink. Kay beat everyone to the punch weeks earlier, when she took a chance and sewed a pink, dotted Swiss skirt for the same bassinette that cradled her baby boy the year before.

"Listen, if I'm wrong, I'm wrong and Stevie's blue will have to do. But mark my words. You're carrying a girl."

Ethel McDonough's gift had been a christening gown all the way from Ireland, purchased months ago at Pober's children's shop in Perkins Square, because infant baptism was utmost on her mind. She wanted to help bring Rita and Bob's baby into the church as soon as possible. "God forbid, another Ruth Ann should spend her days in limbo and the family never know if our prayers got her into heaven." The first Ruth Ann never made it to church.

Limbo could be called the Catholic Church's grace land, a spiritual realm between heaven and hell where prayers of petition have the potential to deliver a deceased, unbaptized baby straight to heaven, despite its tiny soul being marked with original sin.

Ruth Ann Donnelly was born the day before Thanksgiving 1945 and christened eleven days later on a Sunday afternoon at Saint Peter's Church, in Dorchester, Rita and Bob Donnelly's new parish. Bob carried the baby up the steep cathedral stairs, while Rita, still not quite up to par, firmly held onto his arm. When she shivered, having worn the only outfit that presently fit, a charcoal cotton, white-collared-and-cuffed maternity dress, Rosemary worried that the new mother would catch her death in the crisp autumn weather. Without delay, she unbuttoned her red coat and took it off. "Here, honey, this will take care of that chill."

"I'm fine, Ro, and it won't fit me anyway."

Rosemary laid the coat over Rita's shoulders and patted them, one, two. "Of course it does."

Mrs. Mac was now "Grammy," and she stood in close proximity to the marble baptismal font, with Rita and Bob and her immediate family, including fifteen-year-old daughter Jane, the baby's godmother, and most of Rita's family too. John Michael—recently and honorably discharged from the Navy—was the baby's godfather. Father York held the infant securely with the length of his sturdy arm, her head sup-

Saint Peter's Church
278 Bowdoin St
DORCHESTER, MASSACHUSETTS

ported by his wide-open palm and poised over the font to receive holy water and blessing. It was in that very moment that Mrs. Mac stepped closer and silently petitioned heaven. *Please, dear God Almighty, let this christening be for my baby Ruth Ann too.*

All my growing up years and to this day,

I have been explaining my two names–first name,

Ruth Ann.

A middle name would follow at Confirmation but it lagged behind like an afterthought. People always want to know why I'm not Ruth, but Ruth Ann, "two words, one name, and no e on the Ann please. No, Ann isn't my middle name. My middle name is Marie." In third grade, Sister Cecelia insisted I write it as Ruthann, and when my mother learned of the alteration, she rushed to Saint Gregory's School, baptismal certificate in hand. "Sister, she was christened, Ruth Ann." The name game litany is what my mother and grandmother began that long ago day in the kitchen.

God bless them.
Ruth Ann Marie Donnelly

CHAPTER 22

To speak frankly, I am not in favour of long engagements.
They give people the opportunity of finding out each other's char-
acter before marriage, which I think is never advisable.
OSCAR WILDE'S THE IMPORTANCE OF BEING EARNEST

O LD BIDDIES AND YOUNGER ONES too, began counting backward whenever a baby came sooner than nine months after the wedding.

"Preemie, my eye! She was expecting way before they got married."

"When a girl loses her mother, anything can happen and did!"

"Wasn't it Jean Adair, housekeeper over there at Saint Augustine's, who told me all about it? Shortly before tyin' the knot, Rita and Bob met with Father Kenny, and the pair of 'em left in tears. You can only imagine what the poor priest had to deal with, her without parents and him just out of the service with his newfound worldly ways."

∞

It all began innocently enough, more than two years ago, when the McDonough family came to Norah King's wake to pay their respects, even palsied Buddy, who was being carried in Bob's arms when they got to the door. Their brother, George Junior, followed closely behind, carrying a wheelchair, which Rita and Johnny helped to position beneath the personable, but nonetheless helpless, young man.

Bob remembered seeing Johnny's younger sister around the neighborhood, but who knew she'd turn out like this? *What a doll.*

Rita remembered him too, but always thought of the boy with the baby-blue eyes as too old for her. And besides that, he was her brother's friend. She liked keeping things simple and separate.

"Rita, you know Bob Donnelly?" Johnny asked quietly.

And Rita answered even more softly, "I'm afraid not, but thanks for coming."

On that saddest of days, she didn't give Bob Donnelly a second thought, and he couldn't get her off his mind.

Bob reluctantly waited a decent amount of time before contacting Rita. But time was of the essence, and shortly before leaving for Navy boot camp, he went to Morris's Pharmacy and asked George Mac, away from the ears of the rest of the family, if he thought Rita King would go out with him for a bite to eat.

His stepfather stopped counting capsules, looked up, and chuckled. "What in the world are you asking me for, Bob? Why don't you ask Rita? Pretty girl. Hear she's living with the Callanans now. Got their number right here, and you can use this telephone if you make it short. Aw, forget it." George handed Bob a nickel, so he could make the call from a phone booth in the far corner of the store. "I know you kids like your privacy."

Bob had plenty of change in his pocket, but he knew George Mac would have been insulted.

"Now, don't tell your mother. She'd skin me alive if she thought I'd spent a nickel that could've been saved."

Their first date was for a late lunch and an early movie, starting at Joe's Spa (grilled ham and cheese sandwiches, with a vanilla frappe for Rita and Moxie soft drink for Bob) and then on to The Broadway Theater.

Rita knew everyone at Joe's Spa, or so it seemed as guys and gals called out.

"How are ya, Rita?"

"Will your brothers be comin' home soon?"

"Cute outfit."

"Hey, I didn't realize you two knew each other."

Bob saw familiar faces too, but never ventured far as he said hello up close or signaled it across the cacophony of music, exclamations, and laughter with a show of two fingers and a nod. The soon-to-be sailor couldn't believe his luck. The prettiest girl there was with him, and if things went the way he hoped, she'd be with him always. *Always.*

Rita was so distracted she hardly noticed how smoothly Bob took care of everything—got them a booth by the window, folded her coat so as not to crush it, and waited patiently for her to finish talking. That is until he brushed crumbs from the red vinyl bench seat before inviting her to sit down. *Nice.*

Mindful of how quickly the movie theater filled up on Saturdays, Bob made sure they left in plenty of time to get good seats downstairs. He didn't want to get stuck taking Johnny King's sister up to the balcony, also known as "Lover's Lane," giving her the wrong idea and having to answer to her brother once he returned home from the war. Not to mention he'd already determined this was the girl he was going to marry, and everything needed to be completely above-board. *Completely.*

Their seats were perfect, middle aisle, middle row, and at Rita's request, closest to the end, "I don't like being hemmed in." Like everyone else around them, they chatted while waiting for the movie to start.

"So, how soon do you leave for boot camp, Bob?"

"First of the month."

"You went to South Boston High, right?"

"Yeah, you too?"

"Are you serious? My mother wouldn't let us go to school with Protestants. I went to Gate of Heaven."

"No kidding? Did you know—"All at once Bob thought of something. "Rita, I'm sorry I didn't ask earlier, but would you like something from the snack bar?"

"No, thank you. Mmmm . . . yes, please. I'd love a box of nonpareil chocolates."

He made it back just in time, slipped into his seat, opened the package of candy, and handed it to her. A minute later, the lights went out, and you could have heard a pin drop when the newsreel flashed up on the screen. There wasn't a person in the theater that didn't know someone who was in the armed services. People were hungry for news from the front, and all eyes were glued to the tumultuous scenes before them as the announcers gripping, drawn-out pitch reported,

"Innnvasion of the Solomon Islandsss gets under waaay, U.S. troops go overrr the side of a transport ship to enter landing bargessss at Empress Augusta Baaay, Bougainville."

When it came to selling war bonds, newsreels from the front opened people's wallets like nothing else. Subsequently, most theaters had a table set up in the lobby ready for business. And if good-looking girls ran them, increased sales were a sure bet.

The feature film was *Road to Morocco*, starring Bob Hope, Bing Crosby, and Dorothy Lamour. "The boys find themselves in hot water, or rather hot sand, coping with the Bedouin and a beautiful Arab princess." It had the audience in stitches most of the time, but when Bing tenderly sang "Moonlight Becomes You" to exotic beauty Dorothy Lamour, Bob Donnelly couldn't help but think of the pretty girl sitting next to him.

At one point Rita and Bob found themselves staring into the glare of a bobbing flashlight, as a skinny, long-necked teenage boy suited up in an elaborate, red, gold-trimmed usher's uniform with matching cap inquired, "Youse two doin' okay?"

And Bob said good-humoredly to his friend's younger brother, "Scram, Doyle. You're making us miss the movie."

"Geez, Bob, I'm just tryin' to do my job."

"I understand, and we're just trying to watch the movie."

Undaunted, the usher sauntered down two more rows and beamed another couple. "Youse two doin' okay?"

Rita laughed. "Give Jimmy Doyle a uniform, and he's practicing to be a cop on the beat."

Bob added, "Don't forget the flashlight," and a wave of "shhhhhh" came from all directions. They both raised an index finger to their lips and silently shook with hilarity at the mutual gesture.

He wanted to hold Rita's hand in the worst way but didn't dare. It'd been hard enough to get that first date. Rita only accepted his third invitation because so many of Southie's boys had already gone off to war, and the one she'd been seeing, though not on a serious basis, at least not on her part, had joined the Marines.

Before Bob left for boot camp, he and Rita went out together a few more times. Their last date ended on Mary Callanan's front porch with nearly nonstop kissing, until Mr. Callanan flicked the outdoor light on and off before coming out in his stocking feet. "Come on, you two, break it up."

The embarrassed couple stood still and didn't say a word.

"Rita, I'm leavin' this door open and I expect you to be on the other side of it in five minutes." With thumbs tucked under the wide, single-stripe suspenders on either side of his substantial stomach, Mr. Callanan turned to Bob. "And I expect you to see that she is."

"Yes, sir, I will."

The protective father of twelve slammed the door, and remembering what he'd said only moments ago, opened it abruptly and flickered the porch light again.

Bob immediately brought Rita's hand to his lips, kissed it, and held on. "I know it's kind of early to say something like this—"

"It really is, Bob."

"Rita, I'm crazy about you."

"I care for you too, but let's just wait and see how things go after you get back. Okay?"

"If you say so, I guess it'll have to be."

Rita's caution was merited. Her friend Barbara "Bunny" Keeley had experienced a similar situation with a quick, pre-boot camp courtship and pledge of true love that she believed with all her heart meant eventual marriage when her beau declared, "You're the only girl for me." Bunny gladly saved every penny she could, bought a wedding gown, and swooned over her soldier boy for the next two years, only to have his final letter explain why an English girl would soon become his war bride. "It sure isn't something I'd planned on but you're going to love her, Bunny. I call her my English rose. Sorry about the way things turned out."

Rita and Bob both promised to write, and he walked her to the door promptly but not without one more kiss and one last note. "I've picked out a song for us. Want to know what it is?

"Of course, but hurry, please. I have to get inside."

"'I'll Be Loving You Always,' . . . always."

Rita gracefully stepped over the threshold and looked back; the diffused light from inside created a soft halo around her petite silhouette.

"Goodbye and God bless you, Bob Donnelly."

"Goodbye and God bless you too, Rita King."

⚬⚭⚬

It was when Bob Donnelly sent a three-page letter home to his mother, Mrs. Ethel McDonough, 548 E. Fourth Street, South Boston, Massachusetts, and spoke of how much he missed the kids, her, and George Mac, and gave a detailed description of what he was learning and eating, and then slipped in, "Rita King's been writing to me. She's a swell kid!" That Ethel McDonough began to prepare herself for what she'd dreaded most of her adult life—the day her first-born son, Bobby, preferred another.

Lastly, Bob wrote he didn't miss his job as cabinetmaker in the least, having seen one too many "men down at the shop lose a finger or two" and planned on "getting into another line of work" as soon as he got out of the Navy.

When the time came for Electrician's Mate Second Class Robert F. Donnelly to return home from the war, he and Rita would have already covered with steady correspondence most of what each one wanted to know about the other: likes, dislikes, hopes, dreams, who they mutually knew, who they didn't, favorite foods, colors, movie stars, music and sports, childhood shenanigans, teenage infatuations, and their shared Catholic faith. Bob told Rita what he knew she'd want to hear, "Sunday Mass is mandatory in my book." And all of it was written with increasing affection.

Dear Rita, Love, Bob

Hello Bob, Yours truly, Rita

Sweetheart, All my love, Bob

Dear Bob, Fondly, Rita

To my one and only, All my love always, Bob

Dearest Bob, Affectionately, Rita

CHAPTER 23

May the nourishment of the earth be yours;
May the clarity of the light be yours;
May the fluency of the ocean be yours;
May the protection of the ancestors be yours;
And may you be buried in a casket made from the
wood of a century old oak I shall plant tomorrow.
IRISH BLESSING FOR A NEWBORN

RITA KING AND BOB DONNELLY met again, more than a year later, at South Station, where he was among hundreds of returning sailors and soldiers leaning out train windows, waving and shouting elatedly to their families, friends, and sweethearts waiting on the platform. Several windows of young men sang a rousing version of "Southie Is My Hometown," arms slicing the air for happy emphasis.

The troops disembarked in record time, shining faces expectant and duffle bags slung over their shoulders. When they entered the fray, war-separated families and couples fell into each other's arms, many sobbing, some composed, most simply ecstatic, all grateful.

One injured soldier slowly made his way down the train steps, crutches in one hand, the other clutching a porter's arm, until his three brothers rushed up, raised him on their shoulders, and pressed through the crowd.

"Comin' through, comin' through. We gotta get this hero to his welcome home party. They can't start without him. Comin' through, comin' through."

At the same time, another family circled their returning son and prayed, eyes wide open; they didn't want to lose sight of him. "Thank You, God, for bringing our boy home." The father took notice of a teen sailor wandering and looking for his people, with no one there to meet him. He made a long reach and pulled the appreciative young man into the loop. "Thanks for bringing this one home too, God."

Bob spotted Rita right away, alongside his family, and how could he miss her? She was wearing the red coat and standing on tiptoe, but still didn't see him. Rosemary's visit home was perfectly timed for Rita's need to look her best for Bob's return. "Ro, could we please trade coats for a day? Mine's not so bad, but yours is stupendous and red for goodness sake."

She's here. my girl is here. Bob dropped everything, ran straight to her but turned his head and said, "Hi Mum," as he picked Rita up. His cap fell off in the process.

Eight-year-old, towheaded Dicky put it on and turned around to see his oldest brother locked in a kiss. "Aw, mush!"

There was no doubt about the young couple's love for each other, and days later, after Sunday Mass, they walked arm in arm down the steep steps of Gate of Heaven Church onto the icy sidewalk and up the street, so animated in conversation they stopped a couple of times along the way, despite the freezing January weather. Rita's fair beauty was never more radiant as snowflakes collected on her hat and coat. "I can't believe you're here, Bob. This is like a dream come true."

Icy crystals glistened on the sandy blonde crown of Bob's hatless head and wool topcoat. "For me too, Rita. I want it to be like this always." His adoring eyes were irresistible.

She leaned closer, both hands holding on to his left arm, and they continued walking in the direction of greatly anticipated hot coffee and honey-dip donuts as he laid out his plans for the future. "I'm taking a test for the Boston Police Academy next week. And after that, who knows?"

"I'm sure you'll pass it with flying colors, Bob Donnelly."

He kissed her cold nose. "Stop right there." Without warning, Robert Padraig Donnelly, having first asked Mr. and Mrs. Callanan the day before for her hand, got down on one knee in the newly fallen snow and proposed marriage to Rita Margaret King. "Will you do me the honor of being my wife?"

"Bob, what are you doing? Your trousers will get ruined."

"I'm asking you to marry me, and I'd like an answer before I get frostbite."

They both laughed and Rita brought her gloved hands together. "Yes, yes, I can't wait to be your wife." And he said, "I can't wait either."

Bob Donnelly's bended knee didn't escape the attention of people waiting in line outside Mae's Donuts, one of Southie's favorite af-ter-church stops. And when he and Rita joined

Bob was so nervous when asking Mr. Callanan's permission to marry Rita, he continuously jingled the coins in his pocket without thinking. "Tell you what, Bob, stop makin' that racket with the change and you've got our blessin'."

them, a gaggle of giddy teenage girls sang, "The bells are ringing for me and my gal!" When it was clear they intended to sing the entire song, a few others joined in "Everybody's been knowing to a wedding they're going."

Bob used all of his mustering-out pay for the down payment on a "de-cent-sized diamond ring," and he nervously asked Rita would she mind if he put off their engagement celebration until he had a couple of paychecks under his belt, grateful to have secured work at the shipyards, until he found out if the Boston Police Department was going to work out or not. She assured him the ring was enough, but he wouldn't hear of it.

Bob Donnelly went all out and made reservations at Blinstrub's in person, to make sure they'd be seated in a booth, and politely stressed to the affable host, Stanley Blinstrub, who had heard it hundreds of times before, "This is a really special occasion, sir."

That special night, Southie's claim to fame featured Les Brown and His Band of Renown, starring songstress Miss Doris Day, and opened with a local group, The Harmonettes, who sang traditional tunes for the older set.

The newly engaged couple had their picture taken at the table, and Bob held Rita's hand front and center, so the ring showed; they ordered one photo for themselves, one for his mother, and one more for Rosemary.

Blinstrub's jolly photographer wore his fedora tipped back, a photo-price sign tucked in its brown band and he kidded, "You two certainly don't need me to say smile. Count of three, okey-dokey?"

They were thrilled to tell his mother, "We got a gift for you. It'll be ready in a few days," and every happy detail of the previous evening's celebration. "You should have been there, Mum. The food was delicious, and the music was fantastic! There's nothing like a big band!"

"Honestly, Mrs. Mac, I've never seen anyone with hair as blonde as Doris Day's, and her emerald evening gown was all sparkles. She said she chose green because rumor has it there are a few Irish people living in Boston."

Unable to keep her opinion to herself a minute longer, after stewing over it for days, Mrs. Mac asked, as she looked up from the ironing board, reached for a water-filled tonic bottle capped with a clothes-sprinkler stopper, and dampened her husband's white dress shirt, "Don't you think it was a bit over the top, you two going to Blinstrub's? Wouldn't that money have been better spent on things you'll need to set up housekeeping?"

Rita got a lump in her stomach and couldn't believe the nerve of the question but managed a fairly pleasant attitude for Bob's benefit. "Honest to God, I don't mean any disrespect by this, Mrs. Mac, and I realize we're just getting to know each other, but…"

The future mother-in-law loathed the "but." She'd never heard anything good follow a "but."

"It would make me a nervous wreck to think you'd be throwing your two-cents in like that about everything we do."

The older woman was fuming inside. *The cheek of that one!* But she remained calm in spite of her tendency to melodramatic outbursts, which, up until then, had been reserved for her family. Mrs. Mac worried she'd lose Bob if she didn't curb her moods when Rita was around, at least for the time being, and she surrendered. "Enough said."

Mrs. Mac put the iron down fairly hard, hung the starched shirt over a doorjamb with other freshly pressed, clean smelling items, and asked, "Would you two like something to eat?"

One month later, and after absolute abstinence, the engaged couple passionately went against all reason. Much to their regret, Rita would now have to walk down the aisle on her wedding day with a baby secretly resting beneath her heart.

When the time came to find a place to live, the soon-to-be Mr. and Mrs. Bob Donnelly hastily rented a charming one-bedroom apartment on Boudoin Street, in nearby Dorchester, for the lone reason of thinking they could hide her delicate condition longer that way. But after

Rita's family had never lived more than a street away from their church, and the Donnellys' apartment was only a stone's throw from Saint Peter's. Norah's influence was clearly at work. "God makes the best neighbor."

the baby was born, Rita longed to move back to Southie. "We never should have left."

Within days, they put their name on a waiting list for the fairly new Old Colony Housing Project across the street from Carson Beach and hoped. Meanwhile, Bob made arrangements to meet with a friend of a friend who had connections down at City Hall, and having been told prior to their appointment, "He smokes Camels, if you get my drift," he bought a carton and a bottle of Four Roses whiskey too, trusting the expense would pay off.

His contact, a middle-aged man, South Boston born and raised, had himself moved to Dorchester, earning his family the next-step moniker. "Yeah, we're lace curtain Irish all right. It's what the wife wanted, but then you know how that goes." He shook Bob's hand and wondered at them going backwards. *But who can blame 'em? There's no place on earth quite like Southie.*

"I certainly do, sir."

Bob handed him the gifts. *Butts and booze, Jesus, what a guy has to do.* "Thank you for seeing me at such short notice."

"This wasn't necessary, really." The portly official opened a desk drawer, placed the cigarette carton next to two others, took the Four Roses bottle out of the gift box, swung his chair around, secured the whiskey in his briefcase, and spun back. "Tell you what, Bob. Mayor Curley's got a soft spot for vets, and he sent word out to all city employees, 'Vets first, whatever you're dealing with', so don't worry, you'll get in soon. Mark my words."

The call came when the baby was two months old.

"Mr. Donnelly, this is Joe Dombrowski from the Boston Housing Authority. A two-bedroom apartment has opened up at Old Colony. Do you happen to know where Pilsudski Way is?"

Generations of Irish, Polish (the street Rita and Bob would be living on was named for a Polish general), Lithuanian, Italian, German, Czech, Albanian, Armenian, and other ethnicities called South Boston home. But by and large, it was mostly Irish. And so like the Ireland many of them left, Southie had small shops, big families, the sea close by, cafés, pubs, bakeries, street vendors, love of sport, and more Catholic churches per capita, seven in all, than any other city in the state of Massachusetts.

And this is what Rita missed—stores she'd gone to with her mother, sisters and brothers; people she'd known all her life, even "Looney, Miss Rooney;" fried clams at Kelly's; that golden-yellow, frosted raisin bread from Helen's Bakery; Pober's for the baby's needs; Woolworth's for this and that; Mrs. Rosengard's store for quality discount clothing; and Carey's Furniture, where she and her girlfriends used to walk around imagining how they'd one day furnish their homes. Thanks to Carey's "Easy Payment Charge Account Plan," she and Bob were in possession of a beautiful three-piece bedroom set, cute solid-wood kitchen table with matching chairs, and an elegant roll-armed dark green couch.

"A number of Jewish merchants came into South Boston every morning to open their clothing shops, variety stores and meat markets….and did a thriving business….But every evening they… returned to their homes in the Jewish district of the city, along Blue Hill Avenue. Since blacks had neither business or commercial interests in South Boston there was little reason for their coming into the peninsula except… the beach at City Point or a picnic at Marine Park."

South Boston: My Home Town by
Thomas H. O'Connor

Furthermore, there was Morris's Drugstore, where Mr. Mac, now her father-in- law, always had a kind word and even reliable medical advice.

But what she loved most was the sound, smell, and presence of the ocean; and the two churches where she'd been christened, made her First Holy Communion, was confirmed, laid her sister and mother to rest, worshipped with her family, and married: Saint Augustine's and Gate of Heaven. Rita was going home and couldn't have been happier.

There was a wonderfully caring and close-knit spirit to be had in South Boston, with fund-raising bazaars, raffles, dances, and myriad other events pulled together at the drop of a hat (not to negate actual hat passing for cold cash) when some deserving person was in dire need. No one closed ranks like the loyal citizens of South Boston when it came to looking out for their own—past, present, and future.

However, Southie's striving, hard-working, church-going citizens put a high value on high morals, and God help the boy or girl who even came close to sullying his or her family's good name with improper conduct.

Standards were so prim that one incident during World War II sent a crew of French sailors straight to jail. Dick Callahan (not to be confused with the Callanans) was a teenaged lifeguard on Carson Beach at the time. "I couldn't believe my eyes, and another lifeguard said, 'We've got to get these perverts off the beach.' They were wearing those small, tight-fitting European bathing suits and positively indecent. We told them to leave, and they wouldn't, so someone called the cops, and off they all went in a paddy wagon."

Even though Rita and Bob were married, the baby in question born and christened, they weren't out of the woods yet. Their reentry road would be fairly bumpy—but not forever.

‍‍

௸

Biddies in the know formed their own mock Celtic court when it came to purity, virginity and early births. With judgment declared in any number of ways: the silent treatment, cool greetings, brief conversations, that certain look, sighs, or harrumphs, but primarily they kept "an indiscretion of that degree" front and center, so no one thought wool could be pulled over their eyes, and as fair warning to anyone who thought they possibly could. There was very little mercy for a girl who made a mistake.

However, the twenty-year-old new mother went about her business in Southie, head held high, just as her mother had taught every child in their family to do on the other side of "misbehavin'," after first making things right with God. "Sure and there's shame to be had by us all, but isn't that why Jesus Himself died on the Cross? That we might have forgiveness and a new beginnin'? Go to confession now, say your Act of Contrition, do your penance, and get on with it. For if you don't, it will eat you alive, guilt will. No mopin' about over old business!"

How could Norah King possibly have known when she was teaching her own children about life and faith, propriety and purity, economy, endurance, and "makin' a decent appearance" that many of her lessons would resonate for generations, right into the next century? How could she have known? It would have made her happy. It would have made her proud. It would have made everything all worthwhile. And it did.

∽

Mary Callanan had been completely ignorant of Rita's premarital dilemma, until the untimely birth of what she'd assumed all along was a honeymoon baby. Mary loved Rita King like a daughter and was heartbroken about the whole state of affairs but never took her to task. *What's the point? It's all water under the bridge now. And Rita really is a good girl, God love her.* And she chose to look the other way whenever anyone else brought the subject up.

It was on a busy Saturday afternoon at Helen's Bakery—when people were lined up three deep, buying bread, rolls, cookies, cakes and pies for Saturday's supper and Sunday's dinner—that Mary Callanan reached her limit with the gossip. And she was reminiscent of the Blessed Mother herself with "full of grace" words that began to turn everything around for the well-intentioned couple.

"Listen, ladies, will you?"

She pleaded with her cronies after they brought up the "Donnelly situation" yet again in hushed tones while at the same time keeping a watchful eye on the bakery's cases and shelves of quickly disappearing baked goods, as the line slowly inched to the front.

"God in heaven, don't you think it's high time for us to help them be a family and stop rehashing what He's already forgiven?"

The bakery was noisy, stuffy, and hot from the ovens, too many people, and frantic activity on both sides of the counter. Mary unbuttoned her weighty melton wool coat. "Jesus, Mary, and Joseph, between the heat and your condemnation, God save us."

"Now, Mary—," one of them placated.

Norah's faithful friend held her hand up and kept her voice down. "I'll thank you not to 'now Mary' me, Peggy Burke." Then she perused the entire group. "We've got to ease up on talkin' about those two out of respect for Norah King's memory if nothin' else."

Peggy Burke had a look of "who do you think you are?" but flabbergasted everyone when she meekly said, "Thank you for stoppin' us," and looked at the other women who were hanging on every word. "Mary Callanan is absolutely right. This is Norah's daughter we've been talkin' 'n' talkin' about, and in her blessed memory, I myself am not goin' to say one more thing about the whole unfortunate episode. Are you with me then, girls?"

After a bit of looking down at the marbled gray-green linoleum floor, across the bakery, and toward the bell-topped door that seemed to ring endlessly, one by one they answered.

"Absolutely."

"Wouldn't think of havin' it any other way."

"Whose ready to stop talkin' and start sippin'? Tea at my place everyone?"

It went without saying that the cups of strong, steaming hot-tea served with milk and sugar would be thoroughly enjoyed, but only after they'd all done what they came for, the well thought out selection and purchase of Helen's delicious "fresh today" baked goods.

"Give me a dozen of those hermit cookies, will ya, hon?"

Before long, bygones were bygones, and the Donnellys were well on their way to being a "good Catholic family." However, there's always one.

And this one was Edna O'Halloran, who made it her business to be in the know about other people's shortcomings. If there were a backhanded way to punish the accused, Edna would find a sweet, left-handed complimentary way to do so, seeing the former as sin, and justifying the latter as her personal responsibility.

Edna Theresa O'Halloran felt she'd been shortchanged in life, with her "lummox of a husband" and three children who never met her

"Moral Aspects of the Irish-Catholic Community of South Boston—The importance of unqualified sexual abstinence outside the formal married state was both a social and religious tenet of the community, and the virtues of purity, modesty and virginity were accepted as articles of faith without question or condition. Perhaps because of their special devotion to the Blessed Virgin Mary, they adopted an unusually unyielding attitude regarding matters of a sexual nature..."

South Boston: My Home Town by Thomas H. O'Connor

expectations. Her daughter, God bless her—so dull even the nuns wouldn't take her in as a postulant—dashed Edna's utmost aspiration to one day say, "My daughter is married to Christ."

Her sons, "jugheads" too young to enlist, dropped out of school, got jobs at Gillette, and became yet another generation of blue-collar O'Hallorans. Hadn't she had higher hopes? Yes, Edna felt life had shortchanged her, and she was dearly making others pay for it.

Edna's observations about the Donnellys, which she told anyone willing to listen, "and that poor baby of theirs, comin' into the world before her proper time," got to Rita's ears through a delivery system more reliable than a Western Union telegram, the busy-body connection. No details were spared.

Rita didn't sleep well that night, and when Bob asked, "What's wrong? You seem restless, honey?" she drowsily answered, "It's just part of getting used to listening for the baby," because he, more than she, cared very much what people thought. But the next day, she couldn't get to Kay's counsel fast enough.

"Evidently, Edna O'Halloran is making it her business to broadcast our business. So the baby came early? What skin is that off her nose?" Rita's cheeks flushed. "Tell me, Kay, why would a holier than thou woman who serves on the Altar Guild stoop to such mean spirited talk?"

Pragmatic Kay had her own take on Edna. "Listen, I think it's because the poor woman is incredibly dim and doesn't know any better. Don't let her get to you." Kay bounced her chestnut-haired, doe-eyed toddler son on her knees. "It isn't like she's lying, Rita. You must have known you'd have to pay the piper sooner or later."

"Kay Chalpin!" Rita looked at her baby, peacefully sleeping on a blanket laid out on the living room rug.

"Mark my words, Rita, before long everything will blow over." Kay's hands went in the air for emphasis and Stevie tried to slip off her lap. "Where do you think you're going, little man?" She stood the tot on his soft-soled saddle oxfords, kissed his chubby hands, and did what she did best, set her sister straight. "Honestly, it'll be fine. Just remember what Mum used to say, 'Only those without a thought of their own find pleasure in discussing other people's business.' In my opinion that means dim."

Girded by Kay's encouragement, Rita was no longer avoiding Edna O'Halloran. She was ready.

Norah's youngest daughter knew beyond any accusations and unkindness that God saw the night when she and Bob gave in to temptation, his entire family visiting relatives in Cambridge, leaving no one at home when they returned after a romantic Italian dinner, including Chianti. God knew they loved each other and God forgave. He didn't expect her to do penance for the rest of her life, of that Rita had no doubt, but she wasn't without regret and ruminated for God's ears only, the same thoughts over and again. *I was so foolish to go against everything my mother and the Sisters taught me about staying pure. I wish everyone would just forget and let it be, not only for my sake but for the baby's. Please God, protect her from any consequences, please.*

Despite her dismay about the gossip, Rita was determined not to let Edna, or anyone else for that matter, steal her happiness. And at that moment her happiness looked back at her with blue eyes and a dimpled baby smile. "Come on little girl, let's go see Grandpa McDonough at the pharmacy."

Mr. and Mrs. Mac, along with the aunts and uncles, had pitched in and bought Rita and Bob a lovely carriage, the kind nannies on Beacon Street pushed their little charges in, a Perambulator, the very best. That was the way of South Boston's Irish, to scrimp and save so new mothers in the family could have a carriage to be proud of, and join the parade of "mummies" strolling their little ones all over Southie—up and down Broadway and Dot Ave, along the Strand, and around Castle Island—winter, spring, summer and fall.

Rita Donnelly pushed the carriage at a quick clip down Broadway; it was still cold, and she didn't want to keep the baby out too long. She'd just dropped Bob's shoes off at the cobbler and spotted Edna O'Halloran walking so fast in her direction you'd have thought Rita was holding out a hundred dollar bill for the taking.

Edna's mousy-brown, over-permed hair and primarily drab clothing, along with a build that was little and plump—like an overstuffed kitchen mouse—did nothing to make her memorable. But one thing did: Edna O'Halloran incongruously sparkled. She had a weakness for rhinestone jewelry and wore at least two pieces on any given day—bracelet, pin, necklace, or earrings. This showy penchant often prompted curious inquiries about the fanciness, but Edna didn't care and said time and again, "It's my only real pleasure."

"And Rita, how would you and the baby be this fine, crisp afternoon?" she asked, out of breath.

"We're doing very well, thank you. And how are you, Mrs. O'Halloran?" Rita held on tightly to the carriage handle.

"Oh, for heaven's sake, you're a married woman now and a mother to boot. Please call me Edna." She grinned cunningly from ear to sparkly ear.

Rita's auburn curls tossed about in the February wind, and she pushed the unruly locks back from time to time. A large kerchief had covered her head earlier but slipped off and was presently tucked in the collar of her tan wool swing coat that stylishly concealed any extra baby weight, making Rita appear smart and svelte.

Edna calculated. *She's got it made. Pretty as ever, and married in spite of her wrongdoing. Well, let's just see what this newborn looks like.*

"I can't wait to get my eyes on your baby. Everyone says she's real King-lookin'."

Edna peeked into the well appointed carriage, its mattress and pillow were covered in pure white linens, the baby's name, *Ruth Ann,* embroidered on the upper left corner of the pillow in petal-pink with tiny matching ribbon flowers kitty-corner. A pastel pink blanket covered most of the carriage opening and was secured around the edges with silver-plated clips from Pober's on Broadway.

The baby was bundled in a long, white cotton sack with two teeny-tiny buttons at the neck (a crossover, snapped, long-sleeved undershirt, diaper, and rubber pants beneath that), pink knit bonnet, a matching sweater and booties that were out of sight beneath a white, hooded bunting zipped up to her chin, all of which made the infant look like a frosted confection, her rosy button nose the cherry on top. Lastly, a small white blanket was stored beside the baby and folded in such a way as to make sure the satin winking lamb appliqué showed.

Baby Ruth Ann's wide-awake eyes were focused on Edna's rhinestone Scotty dog pin, and Edna's squinty eyes curiously focused on the baby's features. *She's even got an adorable . . .* Edna slowly turned in Rita's direction, folded her arms, and declared, "My, what a healthy little preemie. Heard she weighed in at nine-and-a-half pounds. God bless her!"

With one swift step, Rita pushed the stop on the carriage wheels, folded her own arms, and said, "Yes, she is healthy, Mrs. O'Halloran, and she's not a preemie. I know what you're driving at, and I'll thank you not to. What kind of satisfaction could you possibly get from saying something like that?" And then Rita Margaret King Donnelly let down her feisty Irish guard and became a protective, solicitous mother. "She's a baby, Mrs. O'Halloran, an innocent baby. Let's give her a good start. The baby did nothing wrong." Rita reached in the carriage and covered her daughter with the extra blanket.

There was something in the guilelessness of Rita's plea that made Edna feel ashamed. She'd been direct but also gentle. Didn't her manner remind Edna of Norah? *Not that she's quiet and calm like Norah, but it's there, her mother's good sense. And isn't Norah's pride there too?* "Honestly, Rita I didn't mean anything—"

They were interrupted by a former high school girl friend of Rita's that happened by. "Oh my God, Rita, I didn't know you had a baby."

"Yes, it's a girl. Maybe all this pink gave you a hint?" Rita said sweetly.

After introducing her former classmate to Mrs. O'Halloran, the friends continued to catch up, and Edna, being Edna, contemplated as she put her pinky within the baby's grasp. *The way Norah King went around holdin' her head high, herself a scrubwoman and him a regular steelworker. Who did Norah think she was anyway? As far as I'm concerned, just havin' good-lookin' children isn't reason enough to think well of yourself. Then, she was a likeable woman. Maybe her pride wasn't quite that bad. No, I was right the first time, no reason for her to walk around like she and her family were somethin' grand. But then I'd have to say they all are grand and smart. Look at Rosemary and Kay, both married to college men . . . and beautiful . . . and full of pride too, just like their late mother. May she rest in peace.*"

If Rita's late mother had a fault, it was indeed pride.

Norah Catherine Foley King was proud of being Irish, proud of her church, proud of Southie, proud of the city of Boston, proud of getting a bargain, proud of doing a good day's work, proud of her ability to put a decent meal

Norah Foley and her sister Mary looked after their dewy, fair-skinned beauty with the greatest of care, as instructed by their mother, Barbara Addley Foley. "Girls, you're to wash your faces, mornin' and night, finish with the cool rinse and when the sun is shinin', never let it get a peek at your fair prettiness. Don a hat."

on the table, and when needed, a fine-lookin' suit of clothes together, proud of keeping a spotless apartment, proud of her flawless complexion and that her daughters also possessed "the creamy Foley glow," proud that her children went to parochial school, knew how to say an Act of Contrition, do their penance, and take the body of Christ into their hearts.

"God has blessed me with nine beautiful children," is what she would say. "No woman is richer, not even Mrs. Vanderbilt herself. She can have her furs and cars and lovely clothes. I've got my nine million dollars: Rosemary, Catherine, Joseph, Nonie—God bless her darlin' soul—John, Rita, Patrick, Timothy, and Thomas. And aren't my children rich too, for isn't every one a King? Now I never knew a poor king. Did you?"

Early shadows of day's end, played tag with the fading light and Rita turned back toward the carriage to see her nemesis adjusting the baby's blanket.

"Her little hand pushed it aside," Edna reported.

"Thank you. We'll be on our way now."

"I'm sure your husband will soon be looking for his supper."

Rita left Edna O'Halloran behind her and headed home to Old Colony, her pride and joy intact.

CHAPTER 24

In a word, I was too cowardly to do what I knew to be right,
as I had been too cowardly to avoid doing what I knew to be wrong.
GREAT EXPECTATIONS
CHARLES DICKENS

THAT AFTERNOON HAD BEEN PRODUCTIVE and peaceful with Hilda busy in the kitchen, preparing Pip's favorite foods, and Rolf in the basement, shoveling more coal in the furnace at Cordelia's specific request.

"You know my brother, Rolf. Anything less than seventy degrees, and Pip's certain he's a candidate for frostbite. He's so seldom here, let's make the house as comfortable as we can to his liking."

His liking also included tunes of the times (as opposed to the soothing stream of classical music brother and sister had grown up with): crooners, big bands, and satin-voiced young ladies he called songbirds. Sultry soloist Miss Peggy Lee was his favorite and "in a league all her own." Presently, a recording of Benny Goodman's big band performing, "I've Got a Gal in Kalamazoo," filled the house with a sense of gaiety. Pip was coming home.

Hurrying, so everything would be ready when her brother arrived, Cordelia's swift footsteps sounded click-click on the hardwood floors as she scampered back and forth to the dining room, lit the fireplace herself, and fussed with the table setting, where she pinched napkin folds just so, straightened silverware, and placed two pewter candlesticks in straight-line symmetry on either side of an heirloom blue willow bowl filled to overflowing with early hothouse tulips and greens. But the table still wasn't quite right. Her parents' place settings were sorely missing. *When will I stop expecting them?*

∞

"It's great to see you, sis."

Pip hugged Cordelia, hat in hand, before taking a tartan plaid scarf from around his neck and removing his snow-dusted camel hair topcoat. "Whew! I don't know if it's colder outside or in here." He tossed all three items on the entry settee, rubbed his hands together, and asked, "Where's ol' Rolf?"

"In the basement stoking the furnace. It'll be warmer before you know it."

Cordelia gathered Pip's garments from where they'd already left a faint, damp impression on the settee's new upholstery, and she hung them on a bent-wood coat rack by the staircase.

Price Irving Parker III looked about him. "The house looks good, Cappy, very good."

"Thank you. I've made a few changes since you were here last. When was that? Three, four weeks ago?"

"Come on now, you're not going to make me feel guilty, are you?"

"Of course not. It's just been a while, and the house is happier when you're in it." Cordelia gave him a peck on the cheek. "Welcome home, Pip."

He looked around again. "Mother would be proud." Pip walked up to a golden Regency mirror and tamed his hat-mussed, sandy hair while talking to Cordelia's attentive reflection directly behind him. "I see this is one of your changes. Very nice Cappy, much more elegant than the old Chippendale, but then you've always had an eye for décor."

"Come on, handsome. Let's not waste our precious time together looking in the mirror." Cordelia put her arm through his, but he smoothly pulled away. "I'll be right back." He started to run upstairs, and his long legs easily took two at a time. "I need to get a few things from my old room, so I don't forget them later."

"Can't it wait, Pip? Dinner is just about ready to be served."

He stopped halfway up and spun around. "It can, but don't let me forget." His smile was mischievous as he slid down the banister and landed, just as he did when they were children, right in the center of one of the black-and-white marble tiles.

And this is the man in charge of Parker Shipping?

"Is that Hilda's roast chicken with apple dressing that I smell?"

"Yes, and she's terribly excited about cooking for you, but we'll let the rest of our menu be a surprise."

Cordelia rarely saw her brother these days, and although he annoyed her considerably with his questionable lifestyle and vain antics, she missed him. But with his increased responsibilities at Parker Shipping and preferred activities of Harvard alum events, spectator sports, sailing, squash at his club's gymnasium, various girlfriends and night life, there was little time left for Sunday dinners with his "spinster sister."

Cordelia's days were also full as she faithfully kept track of her parents' charitable endeavors, which though independently managed, she felt duty-bound to show an ongoing interest in, as well as volunteer work at the Red Cross and U.S.O., keeping up with friends and family, particularly her elderly aunties, and her pursuit of other interests as well including church, the D.A.R., The Women's City Club of Boston, and what Cordelia called "my saving grace—lunches out with the girls."

Shortly, the two siblings would take their seats at the dining room table directly across from each other, as they always had, with Pip closest to the fireplace. Their father's chair at the head of the table and their mother's at the opposite end would remain empty.

The Women's City Club of Boston

Price Irving Parker III was what some would call a man about town. Others less cordial branded him "a womanizer, a gambler and thirsty," so unlike his

263

father, Price Irving Parker II, his reputation impeccable apart from penny pinching and the rare second brandy. If father and son had been in a contest of contrast, surely they would have taken top prize. The father was conservative, deliberate, surprisingly sentimental at times, and a one-woman man. His son lived for the moment with a charming, cavalier here today, gone tomorrow, "love 'em and leave 'em" way of thinking.

The safety net of family money and his parents' favor left little accountability for Pip, with the exception of one irate father, who demanded his daughter's reputation be saved with a wedding ring, but eventually accepted a sizeable check in its stead. Pip, handsome, persuasive, enchanting, debonair Pip, was, in a word, a scoundrel.

Women, he loathed their "Do you love me?" And "when we get married" always rang in the end of a relationship. Women, he loved them: blondes, brunettes, redheads, there was no preference; showgirls, society girls, shop girls. He did, however, feel particularly attracted to women with what he called "substantial physical assets." And Scollay Square, home to honkytonks, burlesque houses, bars, restaurants, small businesses, and big hotels seemed to hold a bevy of them.

Shirley Simonson—the latest in a string of beautiful young women Pip entertained in his posh apartment—was a showgirl at the grand Old Howard Theater, which featured the biggest names in show business, presented "high class strippers," and drew customers from all walks of life: sailors and soldiers, rowdy frat boys, couples of every class looking for a naughty night out, businessmen, politicians, blue-collar workers, traveling salesmen, and more.

Many Bostonians, though they'd hesitate to articulate such a thing, considered sneaking into the famous burlesque theater a "healthy" young man's rite of passage.

❧

Pip and Cordelia lingered at the table over coffee and a dessert of devil's food layer cake, catching up with the news each had to offer, until he suggested they retire to the parlor, and reached across the table for a black lacquer, Asian-inspired cigarette box, taking it and a close-by silver lighter with him.

Upon entering the comfort and warmth of their mother's favorite room, and before either one sat down, Pip lit up and said, "Cappy, I need to talk to you about Parker Shipping."

"We're having such a nice visit. Can't it wait, Pip?"

"I'm afraid not, sis." He raised an eyebrow, and Cordelia sighed. They both continued to stand and silently stared out a large French-paned window at the falling snow.

Cordelia particularly liked the way it collected on tree branches in pristine puffs. "Is it any wonder this room was Mother's favorite place to be? It's like having a moving picture of the seasons. Lovely."

What happened next changed everything, everything as they'd known it.

Cordelia, stoic by nature, felt sick to her stomach when she heard Pip's updates. Her brother was in trouble, and more specifically, the family business was in trouble because of her brother. Parker Shipping was going down unless he raised some capital at once.

Neither one moved from where they were as Pip discussed the gravity of the situation, and Cordelia wondered how he could have kept it to himself this long as he droned on with excuses. "Unfortunately, much to my disappointment, without Father at the helm, the war has taken its toll, it's just a matter of time, didn't want to trouble you" and so on.

She remembered how accommodating their mother had been during several of his crises, stepping in and covering Pip's tracks before things became worse, and very often, before her husband got wind of it. *Is that what he expects? But how could I possibly? Our parents gave him complete power of attorney, and he alone owns the company.*

They continued to converse in an eerily calm manner. The fireplace crackled loudly, and what smelled delicious earlier now made Cordelia's stomach churn that much more. She was definitely out of patience with the music her brother preferred. "Just One of Those Things" played next.

Cordelia couldn't turn the phonograph off soon enough. "I think this will go better without the distraction of Miss Lena Horne." She felt like screaming from the tension of it all, but didn't. However, the distraught young woman did resort to sarcasm, an untoward habit she'd tried to curb at her late mother's urging, much to the disappointment of her friends who depended on its jab for pithy entertainment.

Caroline Parker felt so strongly about her daughter's random caustic speech she jotted down a list of antonyms for sarcasm and Scotch-taped it to Cordelia's closet door. "In your coming and going, please determine to make these exemplary terms more representative of your charming character than they presently are—Friendliness, Good Humor, Kindness, Sweetness." Cordelia's sarcasm was typically a cover-up for her anxiety.

"You're to be congratulated on such expeditious mismanagement, Pip. What took generations to build you've managed to tear down in a mere eight months. Extraordinary!"

"It wasn't quite as bad as that, Cappy." Pip was, to her amazement, smug. "In truth it's taken me two years and eight months to do so." He didn't flinch.

"I don't believe it. Father would have known." She held one arm over the other.

"Not necessarily. As company controller, I had many opportunities. Let's just leave it at that." Pip was speaking so fervently, Cordelia couldn't get a word in.

"Do you have any idea how unbearable it is to have all your days numbered and precisely planned by someone else? Father never once, not once mind you, asked if the salary he was paying me was sufficient. My expenses are far greater than his were at my age. Thus, he had a completely unrealistic estimation of what an adequate income would be for a man in my position."

Cordelia clearly recalled overhearing her parents discuss the matter one evening when she came home late from a Boston Pops summer concert on the Esplanade, tip-toed past the parlor, and hesitated at the foot of the stairs, undetected. Her mother had amiably implored, "Pip seldom seems to have enough money, dear."

And her father firmly replied, "Caroline, the boy has too much as it is. No more. It's not in his best interest. Why, Pip makes double the amount Charles Thayer's son does, and he's practically running their textile mill." The information had been exchanged by both fathers during a good meal at the Somerset Club.

Cordelia looked her brother straight in the eye. "My God, Pip! Where did all the money go?" *I don't understand how this could have happened. He had every advantage.*

"I'm not finished yet, Cappy," her older brother continued. "I approached father several times about an increase, and his answer was always the same, 'In time, son, in time.' He simply left me no choice but to draw on my inheritance. It was coming anyway. I just moved things along." Pip drew on his cigarette and exhaled slowly. "I didn't take anything that wasn't coming to me."

"Yes, you did, Pip. You stole from the family's share of the profits. If there's no Parker Shipping, there can be no dividends for us, the aunties, our cousins."

"Shall we take a seat?" he asked.

"Not yet, please." Cordelia's arms remained folded, her whole being solidly in place.

"I knew you were gambling, Pip, but assumed you were doing so with some discretion, apparently not." Cordelia tried to hold her anger in check. "And I'm well aware you had to pay off someone's father, that couldn't have been cheap—although the girl undoubtedly was—and your frequent visits to Scollay Square must cost a small fortune, and who knows what you spend on other romantic interests?" She picked up her pace. "How could you possibly have such degenerate values? Mother and Father were sterling. Their prudence protected our interests and their philanthropies provide enormous advantages for who knows how many people."

Cordelia was pacing so furiously several strands of her fine, ash-blonde locks slipped from beneath a russet silk headband and she brushed back the wispy annoyance without thought. "Your carousing and gambling are your business, but when they threaten the security of Parker Shipping and our very survival, they become my business. How bad is it, brother? Tell me the truth, and we'll deal with it together. Before you have a chance to do any further damage."

"My, my, haven't we become the little mother?" Pip grinned, sat down in his father's chair, leaned to one side, tapped the ashes off his cigarette into an ashtray, laid it down in the same, and sat back, elbows on the arms of the chair, and fingertips to fingertips slowly moved his hands in and out. "Need I remind you that I hold all the financial strings, Cappy? It would behoove you to use a more respectful tone when we're discussing family matters."

"You are absolutely delusional. Family matters, indeed." Cordelia sat down in a straight-backed Windsor chair. "If you don't face facts today, Pip, today, we're apt to find ourselves completely ruined."

He remained absurdly calm, still holding his hands in the same position. "Not if you sell this house."

Cordelia couldn't believe her ears and sat forward. "What did you say?" *He couldn't possibly expect me to do such a thing.*

"Not if you sell this house." Pip pushed the hassock in front of him out of the way with one foot so he could cross his legs. "It should bring in a pretty penny, Cappy."

"A pretty penny? This house is all I have. You know that." Cordelia was devastated by her brother's cavalier suggestion, but determined not to cry.

"The house is much too big for one person. You could get a smaller place on the hill for a fraction of the proceeds."

"This is insane."

"It would be most unfortunate, Cappy, if the situation had to go to court. Most unfortunate."

"Mother and Father's will clearly stated the house is mine. There isn't a judge in New England who'd side with you." Against her resolve, hot tears welled up. "What's done is done and I'll do whatever I can to help you, but I'm not going to sell this house."

He offered her his handkerchief, but she refused to take it, her hand held up like a crossing guard. "Which by the way, I intend leaving feet first. If you outlive me, Pip, you're welcome to it."

"Cappy, you've left me no alternative but to offer Parker Shipping to the highest bidder, and do you really want that on your conscience?"

"Oh, Pip, please don't do this. It's just the two of us now, and frankly, conscience is the bottom rung of your argument. Conscience indeed, you of all people."

Their voices were moderately raised, and Hilda appeared, thinking maybe they were calling for her. "Is there something I can get for you?"

Cordelia quietly replied, "No, thank you, Hilda. We're fine for now."

Pip's hands gripped the arms of the chair. "Cappy, why won't you support me?"

She ran to his side and stooped down. "It isn't that I don't want to support you, Pip. This house is all I have, and it's all we have of Mother and Father. Don't you see, if we sell, it will be like losing our parents all over again? I'm doing it for both of us, Pip. Come back to Mount Vernon, and save the expense of your apartment, just for now, all right?" Cordelia rose slowly, but her mind was racing with possibilities. "Have you considered selling your share of the Martha's Vineyard property to our cousins?"

Pip snapped, "You know how much I love Woodleigh. Giving up my portion is absolutely out of the question."

"I do too, but I'm willing to sell my share if it would help. We're talking about survival." Cordelia sat down again, this time on the soft velvet sofa, which was closer to him.

Pip spent more time at Woodleigh cottage than all the cousins put together. Balmy weather, sailing, racing, and a pretty girl on board was Pip's idea of a perfect day. His family belonged to the Edgartown Yacht Club, where he learned to sail as a child and later won the EYC Annual Regatta two years in a row.

Pip lit another cigarette. "Cordelia, have you no heart?"

"Perhaps I should ask the same of you, Pip. Your disregard for the family's welfare seems fairly heartless to me."

"All right, Cappy, that does it." He bolted out of the cushy chair. "Clearly you've no intention of cooperating. Parker Shipping goes on the block this week. And don't worry. There'll be a small amount of capital left for the family's, as you say, 'welfare.'" He crushed his cigarette out in the ashtray. "I'm truly sorry it had to be like this." Pip stormed out of the room.

"Pip, please." Cordelia followed him. "Pip, listen to me."

Pip called, "Hilda, Hilda, where are you?"

The housekeeper answered from afar, her German accent resounding from some place upstairs. "I'm coming, sir."

He about-faced in his sister's direction. "Please, save your breath, Cordelia."

"Just a few words, Pip. I don't want you to leave like this."

"The only words I want to hear from you are, 'I'll put the house on the market right away.'" He hastily buttoned his topcoat.

Cordelia calmly replied. "I'm sorry. But I won't. Ever." And she handed him his hat.

"Hilda, at last." Pip gave the housekeeper a saccharin smile. "Thank you again for the delicious dinner."

"The pleasure was all mine, Mr. Pip." She nodded and made a slight bow.

"Please, give Rolf my best, and thank him for bringing some warmth to this house." Pip pulled kid gloves from his coat pocket. "And Hilda, I'll be sending a courier over tomorrow with a list of personal and family items I need you to pack up for me. He'll return later in the day to collect them." The perplexed housekeeper looked toward Cordelia.

"It's all right, Hilda. Pip can have anything he wants from my house."

Price Irving Parker III smoothly navigated his luxury sedan through the snowy streets and dismal darkness while flurries danced off the windshield to the beat of each wiper's scrape, swoosh, scrape, swoosh.

Pip's carefully scripted visit hadn't gone as planned, but instead of being distressed he was actually relieved and sang, sometimes whistled, the same cheery song again and again in route to his overheated apartment on Commonwealth Ave. Everything was looking up now that he knew what direction to take.

Tomorrow he'd pursue his back-up plan and get the wheels in motion to sell Parker Shipping before there was no company left to offer, subsequently dispense adequate sums to the relatives to appease their loss, and take what was left with no further thought of his sister. *Cordelia's a smart girl. She'll figure out how to take care of herself. She did a damn good job of it tonight.* He'd pursue his dreams: warm, sunny weather, endless sailing, and all those gorgeous movie stars.

"California, Here I Come."

CHAPTER 25

Après la pluie, le beau temps
After the rain, beautiful weather

CORDELIA'S MONEY PROBLEMS LEFT HER no choice but to cut back on expenses.

"Hilda and Rolf, there have been some unforeseen complications with my parents' estate, and I'm no longer in a financial position to employ you. But rest assured you'll have a home on Mount Vernon for as long as I do."

The far side of middle-age couple was left aghast as they stood before the lady of the house in her father's study. Cordelia was standing behind his desk. She couldn't bring herself to sit at it. *Someday perhaps, but not yet.*

"Miss Cordelia, what does that mean exactly?" the caretaker asked while crunching a tweed cap that moments ago topped his platinum-haired head, having just come in from touching up paint on the property's surrounding black iron fence and gate.

"It means, Rolf, that you and Hilda are free to secure day jobs. I've no doubt you'll find suitable employment straightaway considering how often people have said I'm very fortunate to have the both of you looking after everything. It also means that, out of gratitude for your years of service, the apartment over the garage will continue to be yours, no rent, no condition, other than please don't leave. I couldn't bear to lose one more person."

Hilda had to stop herself from stepping forward and comforting Cordelia with a hug. She knew better; the familiarity would be a breach of domestic etiquette. Though she did do that very thing when they got the terrible news of Mr. and Mrs. Parker's fatal accident, but that was different, a sudden shock with no time to think. *I'll say a couple of Hail Marys for the poor girl instead and ask the Blessed Mother to ease her grief and send her someone to love, a good man like her father.*

"Miss Cordelia, I feel sure I speak for Rolf too when I say we'll still look after things, as best as we can, in exchange for our apartment. The lady with the three children, you know the one, she walks by the house at the same time every afternoon on her way to meet them at school. She stopped me at the florist the other day and asked if I was available to do some housekeeping. Naturally I said no at the time."

Rolf spoke next. "What I think my wife is trying to say is the only change will be the lesser amount of time we'll be spending in this house, but things will be taken care of, Miss." The corners of Rolf's mustached mouth slowly turned up. "Out of gratitude to your family for all the years Hilda and I have had the best jobs in Boston and a nice place to live too."

Keeping the family residence was worth more to Cordelia than her pride, and she'd get a job. But what, and where? *How does one go about gaining suitable employment without making a big to-do of it?*

"Cappy, I have something pleasantly shocking to tell you!"

Cordelia brushed her hand along the softness of a fringe-piped sofa cushion and looked back at her friend Abby, who was selectively plucking a few drooping blooms from an otherwise fresh flower arrangement, but stopped to make her point.

"I'm opening a linen shop on Newbury Street. Can you believe it?"

"Finally your dream is realized. Good for you, Abby. I can't wait to see it."

Cordelia was the picture of casual refinement in a gray flannel, pleated skirt suit and flowing blue silk-print scarf as she secretly fidgeted, all ten toes wiggling within the confines of her sensible walking shoes, and eagerly patted the sofa. "Come over here right now and tell me everything."

"Oh, you're simply going to love it." Abigail Chandler, whose shiny Dutch-boy cut swung slightly every time she moved, was a chic study in black and white, reminiscent of Coco Chanel. Her long-sleeved white blouse, the two top buttons undone, afforded a minute peek of ecru lace, while a short strand of pearls rested against her pale skin, and a longer double strand bobbed across the bodice. Her black pencil skirt was tailored to perfection, while a pair of "outrageously ex-pensive" black alligator pumps anchored the ensemble. But the *pièce de résistance* that Abby insisted every outfit needed was a vintage, diamond-stemmed wrist-watch held in place with a bow-tied, black, grosgrain ribbon.

Abby gracefully fell into the down cushion's comfort, landing both palms on her lap. "The space was formerly a millinery boutique, so it has a fair amount of charm already. I'm sure you'll recognize the building when you see it, brick, with a steep, elaborate, iron-railed stairway that leads directly to my shop on the right, and on the left a posh stationery store, mirror image of mine. Both have showcase bay windows, which of course are excellent for business."

Abby explained that the owner of the building on Newbury, although keen to rent the space, refused to do so without her husband's signature on the lease as well. "It's routine," he said. "There's nothing to take personally here."

Abby bit her tongue. *If my husband were renting the space, would you require my signature as well?*

Cordelia enjoyed every minute of Abby's enthusiastic report. "Please, continue."

"Well, the stationers are two rather persnickety but adorably debonair gen-tlemen, and you can't begin to imagine how remarkable their window displays are. I shall do my best to follow suit. Why, with all the foot traffic on Newbury we've a thoroughly captive audience."

Abby's next-door-neighbors, Carleton Cross and Howard Ambrose of Ambrose & Cross – Fine Stationary – Invitations – Writing Instruments, were more than pleased about the new tenant. Mr. Ambrose said, "Refinement is written all over Mrs. Chandler," and Mr. Cross added, "Love the Chanel touch."

"What perfect timing, Abby. Once you and Edwin begin a family . . . "
Cordelia arched one eyebrow; they had, after all, been married for three years.
"I'm afraid adventures such as this will be too ambitious. Meanwhile, a linen
store, how marvelous!"

"And how perceptive of you, Cappy. As it happens our bundle of joy is on
his or her way already."

Cordelia brought her hand to her heart. "You're kidding!"

"Oh, no, I'm not. Trust me, I've never felt like this before in my life, nau-
seous twenty-four hours a day. I thought it was only supposed to be morning
sickness. Thank goodness for saltine crackers."

"Congratulations! How long have you known?"

"Well, as luck would have it, the day we signed our lease, I felt somewhat
queasy and completely credited my malaise to nerves." Abby, as always, spoke
with her hands as if they were exclamation points. "Actually, Edwin and I just
found out a couple of days ago, which brings me to my next point. Would
you consider helping out with the store, just to get it off the ground? You have
such exquisite taste, Cappy, and the best way with people. I'll make it worth
your while."

Abby desired a certain atmosphere in her upscale store, and she knew
Cordelia's sensibility and sophistication would greatly assist in making it welcoming but not familiar, well-designed but not stuffy, serene but not dull, and
definitely aromatic with seasonally appropriate potpourri, *muguet de bois* (lily of
the valley) toiletries, lavender sachets, and at all times, light refreshments, coffee,
tea, water with lemon, and an assortment of petite cookies. There would also
be, at background volume, recordings of chamber music or light opera, from
time to time, Edith Piaf's enchanting French tunes, and during the Christmas
season, traditional carols in English.

"Why, I believe you're serious, Abby." Cordelia selected a milk chocolate from the Limoges candy dish on the coffee table. "Do you suppose this is
a caramel?"

The fledgling business woman felt concerned that her request and subsequent claim that she'd make it worth Cordelia's while were received as insults,
but she couldn't imagine taking on such an enterprise without the benefit of her

trusted friend's organizational ability and winning presence. *Cordelia could sell ice cubes to an Eskimo.* Abby decided to forge ahead.

"You have absolutely the best taste of anyone I know, Cappy, and your way with people is extraordinarily persuasive. Think back to our Radcliffe days. Why, hardly anyone in our crowd ever finalized plans until they'd run them past you."

Abby became comically theatrical as she slinked across her parlor, a breeze of Chanel No. 5 wafting behind her, and reached for the French-inspired telephone on her cherry writing desk. "Has anyone asked Cappy yet what she thinks? Let's give her a jingle."

"Oh for heaven's sake, Abby, no need for the charade. I'm not in the least offended. To be completely honest, I find your proposition rather intriguing, if not tempting. It sounds like great fun and on Newbury no less, how lovely."

"Now, you're kidding!"

"No, I'm not."

Cordelia couldn't believe these next words were about to come out of her mouth. "When do I begin?" But she was incredibly grateful for the opportunity. *There is indeed a God and thankfully He values my pride.*

Abby clapped her hands in rapid succession. "Oh, I'm so happy!" And she straightaway shook her first employee's hand. "We'll make a great team, and I'll certainly need your discretion in hiring one or two other people to join us in this endeavor. I simply can't believe you said yes. Thank you, thank you."

The last three years had held many unforeseen changes for Cordelia— losing the love of her life to a person she deemed unworthy at best, her parents' sudden deaths, and a conflict with her only sibling that severed all relationship to the point of not even knowing where he was living.

After the ill-fated dinner with Pip, she continued to live life almost as she'd known it: quietly, comfortably, predictably. Her days were filled with volunteer work, cultural events, family, and friends. Sundays were, as always, for attending services at Park Street Church, where she gained strength and solace from Pastor Ockenga's hope-filled sermons.

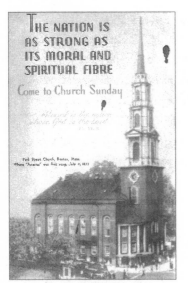

Park Street Church
BOSTON, MASS.
Where "America" was first sung,
July 4, 1832

Quite unexpectedly, upon learning her trust fund had run dry, the financial freedom and protection Cordelia Anne Parker had been accustomed to was gone. The presumed amount squandered to a vastly lower sum by her trustee brother. His betrayal broke her heart.

Price Irving Parker III neglected to tell his sister about the adjustment, and here she was, certainly not without assets, but definitely in need of steady income if she was to keep her house. Monetary difficulties were uncharted territory for the Beacon Hill heiress, who feared she might have to sell the only home she'd ever known.

Cordelia loved every square inch of 91 Mount Vernon: the way it smelled slightly of evergreen the minute you walked in the front door, due to a cedar-lined entry closet; and the inevitable squeak of that door no matter how often Rolf tended to it; the rippled, divided, window panes, several randomly aged to an opulent violet; and the way she felt when approaching the house at night, light within glowing safekeeping and welcome. Her cozy bedroom, even now with the choice of three others, remained a private retreat, its familiar atmosphere a comfort like no other when she slipped into one of the twin beds at night.

Above everything else, there was the sense of her parents' presence all about the house. Price Parker's pipes remained on a rack in his study, and from time to time, Cordelia would cradle one in her hand and breathe in the piquant tobacco aroma. Her mother's special touch was everywhere, most things unchanged from when she'd systematically managed house and garden with optimum grace and skill. Cordelia's bittersweet joy was to follow in her mother's footsteps, and she often drew on the memory of her sage advice.

"No matter what may take place in the world as time goes by, always remember these three things about good housekeeping. Good food, good mattresses, and a good deal of loveliness—flowers, candles, books, and music—all of which make for a happy home."

It was Cordelia's way to visit each room before locking up the house at night, and when it came to the bedrooms, she lingered. Her parents' was just as they'd left it, Caroline and Price's nightclothes neatly laid out. Pip's room, with missing photos and other absent framed items, had phantom ovals, rectangles, and squares on every wall. The guest room, as always, remained ready. Her decidedly feminine room stayed unchanged, and Cordelia wondered whatever was to come.

Providence truly did step in when Abigail Adams Dubois Chandler finally decided to take hold of her long-time dream of offering quality domestic selections and specializing in European imports with an emphasis on French linens and a modicum of Irish. The wealthy young matron was briefly tempted to call her store La Vie en Rose but ultimately chose something much more "New England-sounding," *Chandler's Linens ~ 33 Newbury Street, Boston, Massachusetts.*

Abby's father was "a frog," as her maternal grandfather jovially called him. And she grew up visiting Grand-mère and Grand-père at their elegantly eccentric, Parisian apartment and simple summer home in Provence. An observant girl, she took in every enchanting detail of French style, housekeeping, food and linens.

Abby needed help, and Cordelia appeared to be a lady of leisure. Productive, yes, but nonetheless perceived as a single woman with time on her hands.

Cordelia saw Abby's offer as a *Godsend* that required no clever explanation about her new working status other than "I'm helping a close friend out for now."

It pleased Abby her store would coincidently be opening in May, a time of year when the French customarily purchase a bouquet or plant of Lily of the Valley as a token of love and good wishes for family, friends, and even themselves. The tiny, bell-shaped, white flower is literally known as a *porte-bonheur,* or "bringer of happiness," or what some prefer to call "good fortune."

CHAPTER 26

We make our choices, and our choices make us.

PRICE IRVING PARKER II

TIME AND AGAIN, OVER THE past few months, Cordelia was stunned to discover she actually enjoyed the routine of regular working hours and adjusted with relative ease, considering she'd been raised with a silver spoon in her mouth, household chores and cooking left to the care of hired help.

She'd grown quite accustomed to preparing her own breakfast: set the table at night with dishes, cup and juice glass turned upside down just as Hilda had done "to keep the dust and germs away, Miss," and got the coffee pot ready. So next morning when she meandered into the kitchen half asleep, these days rising two hours earlier than usual, a mere twist of the wrist got things underway.

There was a quick bath while the coffee was perking and a dash downstairs again, with Cordelia half-dressed in full slip, skirt, stockings, slippers and a long dressing gown that billowed behind her. In short time, she'd enjoy a light but nutritious breakfast of juice, a soft-boiled egg, and whole-wheat toast or oatmeal and fruit, followed by dishes washed at once, dried, and put away—the thought of an unkempt kitchen intolerable. After breakfast it was upstairs again to finish getting dressed and then an invigorating walk over to Newbury Street, where

Cordelia Parker opened Chandler's Linens with such aplomb a passerby would take her for proprietress rather than wholehearted employee.

She particularly enjoyed pulling up the store's sizable window shades and looking out on the new business day, Newbury Street still shimmering from the damp of dawn. Cordelia absolutely relished what she came to refer to as fluffing: She made sure water in vases was fresh, pillows on the French Provincial, wood-accented settee and two armchairs of the same design were arranged just so. She double-checked that every single thing in the store was artfully, temptingly, irresistibly in place: from bed linens to towels, a few unique kitchen items and books, handkerchiefs, lingerie keepers, sachets, silk tassels for cabinet doors, soaps and fragrances, petite-point accessories, coin purses, glass cases, bookmarks, and cigarette cases, among numerous other luxury items.

A turn of the burnished brass key in its antiquated lock, and Chandler's was ready to serve, suggest and sell.

Cordelia had taken to wearing her reading glasses on a chain rather than to hunt all about Chandler's and keep customers waiting. Caroline often came to mind, *like mother like daughter,* and prompted within Cordelia a recurring longing to be in her much missed mummy's company just one more time.

Surrounded by beautiful things and given free rein by Abby to do whatever she deemed best for business, Cordelia was in her element and flourishing, as was Chandler's Linens.

At day's end, she left the store with a great deal of personal satisfaction from a job well done. But as she set her course for home and saw people meeting up along the way, presumably en route to have dinner together, a feeling of forlornness often crept in, as did the reality of returning to an empty house, eating alone and going to bed without another soul to say "good night" or "see you in the morning."

But Cordelia resisted dwelling on such thoughts, as the result of a childhood lesson. Her father was the type of man who frowned on his children ever missing school, and when she, often at her mother's urging, wanted to stay home because of a minor malady, such as a cold, runny nose, or "tummy ache," he greatly objected.

"Cordelia, life isn't always easy, and you must learn to steel yourself against dallying, dwelling, and giving in. We make our choices and our choices make us."

Although Cordelia had sold back her interest in the Martha's Vineyard property under the guise of consolidating when it was, in fact, to help prolong her stay on Mount Vernon, the cousins insisted she regard the eighteen-room cottage always as her home away from home.

The stoic young Beacon Hill woman's life had become much more solitary than she'd ever expected. Certainly there were friends, neighbors, and acquaintanceships, tradespeople, Chandler's staff, and of course, Hilda and Rolf, but when it came to flesh and blood, there was an aching absence of family. Cordelia seldom saw the cousins, her late father's deceased brother's children, and their families, except for weddings, funerals, and Christmas, and they never missed the Fourth of July fest on Martha's Vineyard. Her mother had been an only child.

The aunties were gone now, having passed away only a month apart. Symbiotic endearment kept them going all those years, and then there was one, but not for long.

Aunt Agatha and Aunt Martha had been enormously grateful for Cordelia's assistance as old age caught up with their robust Yankee health. She escorted them to doctor and dentist's appointments, biannual beauty shop dates for "a quick clipping" and "low upkeep, if you please," social obligations, and any other need that required a helping hand or the comfort of a car. Walking about the city and public transportation had become daunting challenges for the aunties' frail limbs.

Much to the family's shock, and more severely, disappointment, the spinster sisters bequeathed their brownstone mansion and a good deal of money to three different *societies*.

The Society of Arts & Crafts ~ "Owed to our admiration of the crafts movement and particularly Mr. William Morris's colorful, yet subtly elegant designs of wall coverings, draperies and upholstery, which we have a great deal of in our home, due to our parents mutual fondness for one and the same. We are privileged to contribute to the furtherment of such extraordinary and altogether pleasing design."

The Boston Historical Society ~ "We must preserve the past in order to establish firm foundations for the future. Society learns, be it alarming or disarming, inspiring or convicting, educational or dumbfounding, from previous wisdom as well as former foolishness."

The Society for The Prevention of Cruelty to Animals ~ "Living in the city all our lives we've come across any number of unfortunate four-legged creatures scrounging for food and shelter. Godspeed to the *S.P.C.A.* and the resources we impart to their most worthy cause."

Believing Cordelia financially secure, they deemed to give their favorite niece and "best relative" not property or cash but select pieces of family furniture, art, china, and crystal; all the personal jewelry they had between them, a modest maidenly collection; their father's solid gold pocket watch and his Abstinence From Alcohol pin, given to him at age fourteen after taking the pledge in Sunday school; their mother's cameo broach, dainty locket watch, and wedding rings, as well as her mother-of-pearl lorgnette; and family photos in well-kept albums or encased in fine frames.

A smaller number of family items went to the other Parker relatives. Martha very much wanted to leave them a note beginning, "Had you taken the time to visit us more than once or twice a year . . ."

But Agatha wouldn't have it. "That's not the way we want to be remembered, sister. You make us sound like two bitter old woman looking out the window. Let's leave them with Godspeed, and a few more things as well." And they did.

Last was Cordelia's most beloved bestowal from "the dearest Aunties ever," a partially moss-encrusted garden sculpture of two graceful Greek maidens in flowing gowns, one poised holding a shallow, open, water-filled vessel, the other carrying an armload of grain. The sisters had commissioned it in a rare moment absent of their customary frugality, prompted by introduction to a sculptor turned soldier who'd tragically lost one eye to a Nazi grenade attack in North Africa.

"Damn those Germans," Martha said upon learning of his permanent plight, the very reason he wore a black patch, and she decided there and then that she and her sister would become his first post-war patrons.

Cordelia had often admired the work, and now it stood in her own garden, *Peace & Prosperity* carved in the stone banner beneath the two maiden's feet. The graceful sculpture's subjects bore a striking resemblance to the aged Brahmin sisters in their younger days, but any reference to the likeness was forever met with a change of subject. When the statue was being prepared for the move to Mount Vernon and tipped on its side, what should Cordelia spy but the names of each of her aunties chiseled on the bottom surface.

Agatha Camellia Parker ~ Peace
Martha Hepatica Parker ~ Prosperity
Papadakis
MCMXLII

∞

"Yoo hoo, Cordelia. Do you have a minute?" Eleanor Brewster called from in front of her home a short way down Mount Vernon from where Cordelia was walking.

Cordelia waved and mouthed, yes—she abhorred calling out like a fish wife—to her neighbor who was only five years older than her, which seemed like twenty when she was in college—Eleanor, wife and mother, Cappy, carefree coed.

The two women had, out of their mutual loss of Caroline Parker as mentor and mother, become close friends. Eleanor was, as Cordelia confided to her recently over coffee, "the only person on earth, save Pip, who knows my true financial situation."

"I feel certain Abby thinks of my helping out at Chandler's as a temporary lark for a woman who otherwise has too much time on her hands. If she only knew how every penny I earn is accounted for, and to tell you the truth, Eleanor, it's still not enough. Something's definitely got to give." A rush of emotion and the lump in her throat limited Cordelia's explanation to ten words. "If I'm to keep the only home I've ever known."

Presently, Cordelia's hands were full. Her walk home from the linen shop at that golden time of day, just before twilight, involved a couple of stops for groceries and dry cleaning. "Eleanor, how are you?"

Eleanor relieved her of the dry cleaning, and Cordelia reluctantly let go. *Oh my, this has all the look of a long winter's nap, conversation. I just want to get in my house, take a hot bath and heat up some of this vegetable beef soup from the deli.*

"First of all, good evening, Cordelia. I simply adore Indian summer, don't you?"

Eleanor briefly took in the spectacular yellow-green, russet and crimson leafed trees as if to be sure they were still there.

Cordelia smiled. "It's my favorite time of year, and I'm looking forward to Thanksgiving dinner with your family. Oh, that it wasn't still weeks away. I pine for that scrumptious pumpkin pie of yours."

"Well, speaking of food, Cordelia, we'd love to have you to join us for dinner tonight. There's a pot roast in the oven and apple crisp for dessert. Are you game?" The "we" was in reference to her husband, Sinclair, son, Jonathan, and daughter, Blythe.

Before Cordelia could answer, a male voice interrupted.

"Good evening, ladies." The young policeman tipped his hat and asked, "Do you need help carrying those packages, Miss?"

"No, thank you, Officer." Cordelia said, deeming that was the end of it. Her unadorned ring finger didn't escape the officer's overall observation of the situation at hand.

Eleanor coolly inquired, "Where's Officer Tierney? Why, I haven't seen him for days."

"Oh, he's moved on to police headquarters. We call him Detective Tierney now. I'll be covering this beat, and if there's any way I can be of assistance, please don't hesitate to contact me at Station 3 on Joy Street." He reached in his dark navy, double-breasted, brass-buttoned uniform jacket pocket, pulled out a pen and pad of paper, wrote his name and the police station's telephone number down twice, folded each one and handed them to the two ladies. "Patrolman Bob Donnelly at your service." He courteously tipped his hat for the second time.

Cordelia tossed the paper into one of her shopping bags now resting on the first step of the brick walk to Eleanor's home.

The policeman's arresting blue eyes followed it and caught hers on the way up. "I hope you'll say yes. I can smell that delicious meal all the way out here." *Thank God I can hold my own with these snobs. Although I had my doubts when the single one threw the station's number in that bag, but her eyes told me otherwise.*

Cordelia couldn't quite put her finger on it, but there was something about the way the dashing policeman said, "I hope you'll say yes" that felt fairly and unsettlingly flirtatious. She bid him a slightly less than civil adieu. "I'm sure we've taken too much of your time already, Officer. Have a good evening."

Bob Donnelly was from Southie, where people gave it to you straight, and he found her style of ending their conversation interesting. *Jesus, this must be high class dame talk for "Get lost, Bud."*

His grin, firm "Good night, ladies," and subsequent swagger as he walked away whistling the happy tune of, "Blue Skies," all told Cordelia her reserve hadn't phased him in the least.

As for Bob Donnelly, he enjoyed a great sense of accomplishment after all the hard work of two jobs, moving Rita, himself, and the baby back to Southie, and getting into the police academy and out again as a top graduate. He'd made it—badge, gun, billy club, and uniform. Bob was proud to be a member of the Boston Police Department, and as a rookie, amazed to be assigned to Station 3, Joy Street. The best. "God Almighty," he'd said to his mother. "Imagine a fella from Southie spending so much time on Beacon Hill. It's terrific, Mum."

The two women promptly resumed their conversation. "Cordelia, I've an idea regarding what you said last week about something's got to give. Come for dinner, and I'll disclose my fiscal brilliance as soon as Sinclair leaves for his evening constitutional around the Common."

That early Indian summer's eve, as the straight-backed, W.A.S.P. women stood within the

Beacon Street
BEACON HILL, BOSTON, MASS.

privileged confines of Beacon Hill's rich dewy palette of red brick, dapple-gray cobblestones, and green trees yielding to autumn glory, Cordelia accepted her neighbor's invitation. She was glad she had on the one hand, because Cordelia enjoyed the company, and grateful on the other, because of Eleanor's unappealing, yet simple solution to her dire financial situation.

"Why not open a couple of the bedrooms in your home to medical students? Goodness knows they have no time for tomfoolery, and you'll get a certain quality of boarder that way."

CHAPTER 27

*I had three chairs in my house:
one for solitude, two for friendship, three for society.*
HENRY DAVID THOREAU

"HELLO, MY NAME IS DAVID Miller. I'm a medical student at Tufts, and I understand you have a room to let."

It had been less than a week since Cordelia submitted her ad to the Tufts University School of Medicine and the Tufts School of Dental Medicine as well.

Two furnished bedrooms, each with fireplace and private bath
Limited kitchen privileges, solarium, and garden. Reasonable rate.
91 Mount Vernon, Beacon Hill.
Applicants must be full-time students and
provide two local references.
Shown by appointment only — COmmonwealth 6-2407

"Yes, I do. Another interested party is coming by late tomorrow afternoon. I'll have to leave work early, and it would be more convenient if you came at the same time."

"Tell me when, and I'll be there, Mrs. . . ."

"Miss Parker. Four o'clock sharp, please. Oh, and Mr. Miller, before we waste your time or mine, this is a quiet house, and I fully expect it to remain so. No parties or gatherings, the kitchen and garden are available for your use, but everything else would be off limits. Do you think you'd be content with such an arrangement, Mr. Miller?"

"Yes, Miss Parker, perfectly content."

"Very well, then. I'll see you tomorrow."

Cordelia slowly put the receiver back on the hook. *He sounded nice enough— that my livelihood has come to this. I suppose I should be grateful for the interest. Oh, for goodness sake, so I'm letting out rooms. If that's what needs to happen to keep this house, then so be it.* A slight smile slipped across her lips. *Taking care of business.* She made a beeline for the kitchen. *I think I'll have a cold plate of leftover chicken and pickled beets for dinner, enjoy my privacy while I still have it, and a slice of bread with butter. And perhaps a glass of port by the fire later, or perhaps not. I don't want to get in the habit of spending my evenings with spirits. Hot chocolate will do for now. I'll save the port for company.*

Chandler's Linen Shoppe in a very short time established itself as *the* place in Boston to purchase exceptionally lovely merchandise of a certain superior quality. This happened in no small part due to Cordelia's innate sense of style and creativity, let alone hard work. She was, after all, a descendant of Puritans. Due diligence was in her blood.

On any given afternoon, countless numbers of women—socialites, matrons, working girls, homemakers, even students who primarily purchased hankies and petite perfumed soaps—could be seen admiring Chandler's window displays, with many sooner or later sashaying up the stairs and into the store for that item or items they simply could not live without. Cordelia was frequently, precariously poised while plucking a requested "last one" from the window, or a member of her staff could also be seen doing the same.

There were two additional staff members now. Mr. Percival Clark was a middle-aged gentleman of independent means, who'd never married and lived with his elderly, "sharp as a tack" mother. She was a good friend of Abby's family and one day pleaded of the new store proprietress, "Abigail, Percy drives me mad with his well-intentioned but too frequent inquiries after my health, incessant reading aloud newspaper articles of interest to him alone, and over-attentiveness to every aspect of anything to do with the house and larder. Do you suppose, Abby dear, that you could use an extra pair of hands in your lovely new establishment? I do believe he'd be quite flattered and leap at the chance. Oh, to get Percy out of the house for even a short period of time."

Then there was Miss Alice Lochrie, a young lady new to Boston from "the wilds of Maine," and she lived at the Franklin Square House.

Coincidently, and many years ago, Cordelia's maternal grandparents helped establish the direly needed haven for young women. Thanks to the dream of their dear friend Reverend George L. Perin, who'd envisioned "not an alms house but affordable, respectable, out-of-harm's-way housing." The Reverend had seen firsthand, in the course of his city ministry, many an innocent girl suffer untoward tragedy at the hands of unscrupulous lodging-house keepers and residents. Subsequently, he petitioned wealthy, socially conscious Bostonians and dubbed his generous sponsors "my team of dreamers."

It was actually Hilda who suggested Cordelia give Franklin Square House a call and ask if there was a nice, refined girl who's in need of employment.

The three of them, Cordelia, Percy, and Alice, were well matched.

Percy's attention to detail began with his dapper appearance, from the tip of his highly polished shoes to his interesting array of bowties and only bowties, to the top of his well-clipped partially bald head. He kept everything in the store pristine, pretty and presentable.

Alice's gentle ways led patrons to purchase more than they'd anticipated as she serenely placed one enticing item after another before them. "I know you could live a long life without this, but then again, would you want to? Why it seems ideal for your needs, don't you think so? I'm not sure we'll be able to acquire this again. That's just the way it is with imports. You understand, I'm sure."

Alice, golden-haired, lithe, and poised, moved through the store like a prima ballerina and was brilliant at creating a felt need out of any customer's passing want. "What excellent taste you have."

It wasn't long before Chandler's needed to add a fourth member to their staff.

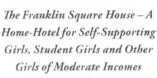

The Franklin Square House — A Home-Hotel for Self-Supporting Girls, Student Girls and Other Girls of Moderate Incomes
11 East Newton Street
Boston, Mass.
"The idea of the Franklin Square House was and is to meet a conspicuous need. We undertake to furnish for girls living away from home a dwelling place, which is morally safe as well as comfortable and sanitary, and to give them food that is both palatable and wholesome. We undertake to care for them in sickness and to do it all at a cost which the young women can pay. During the last year, we have accommodated about 600 girls on a permanent basis."
Reverend George L. Perin Founder
New York Times, June 1913

Miss Florence Morton came by way of R. H. Stearns, one of Boston's best regarded retailers. She'd been a long-time employee but pined for something new in her very predictable working life, and fate met desire when she walked into Chandler's looking for a house-warming gift. She immediately recognized Cordelia Parker as a valued customer of Stern's, and it occurred to Miss Morton she hadn't seen the Beacon Hill socialite for quite some time. And now, could it be, Miss Parker was a clerk like herself?

Florence Morton perused every fascinating inch of Chandler's and found just the type of gift she was looking for, a French oil and vinegar cruet set housed in a pewter ring-topped holder. "Perfect," she exclaimed to Cordelia, and placed her find on the highly lacquered counter with a finely gloved hand.

Florence, a thin, prim, lady wearing a perky, hunter-green, Robin Hood-styled hat with a golden feather on one side, looked vaguely familiar to Cordelia, but she couldn't quite place her, and to be on the safe side, was more than friendly. "Good afternoon." Cordelia paused hoping for a response that would give her a hint, but there was none. "I'm delighted you found something suitable and must say your hat is so smart." She picked up the cruet set. "Would you like me to gift wrap this for you?"

Florence was stunned by Cordelia's warmth; she didn't remember her this way.

"Oh, yes, please, gift wrap."

"Won't you take a seat, and I'll have Alice bring you a cup of tea, or would you prefer coffee, water?"

"Coffee, thank you."

Cordelia still didn't know who this well-dressed woman was, and then Florence Morton said, "You're so fortunate, Miss Parker, to have found work in such a unique and elegant place. Why, I'd give my eye teeth to work in a store like this."

For goodness sake, this is the saleslady from Stearn's special occasion department. Oh my, what's her name? Well, Miss, whatever your name is, you're about to be offered a job. How well I remember your efficiency and courteous manner. "Actually, I'm temporarily managing the store for a close friend." And then it came to her. *Morton, that's it! Yes, I remember because of Judge Morton, my father's friend, and when I asked if there was any connection, she said,* "I'm afraid my Mortons were the ones being judged," *along with that wonderful smile of hers.* "As it happens, Miss Morton, we have a full-time opening for a woman of excellence such as yourself."

Abigail Adams Dubois Chandler was beyond pleased with the store's success and urged Cordelia to consider staying on permanently.

"With the baby coming any day now, and all that Edwin requires of me, I don't have enough time to do Chandler's justice, Cappy, and I'm not too proud to say that you are Chandler's Linens. Without your panache, we'd simply be another specialty store on Newbury."

Cordelia was cagey, not wanting to give her affluent friend the wrong impression, or more truthfully, the right impression, that she desperately needed the money. "Abby, after giving the situation some thought—"

"Yes, Cappy?" Abby nervously blinked her eyes as she leaned in closer for the answer.

"After giving the situation some thought, I'd have to agree with you. I am Chandler's Linens." Abby looked perplexed, if not a bit affronted, and blinked again.

"I'm kidding, dear. This venture wouldn't be half what it is without your vision. You're a brilliant merchandiser and have made my job easy. Why, look what I've got to work with. I adore this store and I'm not going anywhere."

"Cappy, you've made me not only the most fortunate businesswoman in Boston, but the happiest as well. Whatever did I do to deserve you?"

Abby kissed Cordelia on both cheeks in the European fashion, and Cordelia turned pink. "That may bode well in Europe, madam, but please, let's restrict our friendly affection to light hugs and handshakes. Agreed?"

∝

Cordelia could see them in the distance, standing in front of her house, and the first thing that came to mind was salt and pepper.

"I'm terribly sorry to be late and keep you waiting out in the cold. It absolutely couldn't be helped. The store I manage had an after Christmas sale, and it was utter pandemonium. What a day! Shall we?"

In a polite effort to compensate for lost time, the about-to-be landlady swiftly navigated her recently shoveled walkway, snow banks piled high on either side, quickly opened the unlocked front door, and welcomed her would-be roomers in with one sweeping but close-in gesture. "Gentlemen." A brief tour ensued.

The two graduate students, on the verge of a new semester, felt grateful to find lodging in such a nice place, and they said so. Fair-haired Richard Malmgren, a shy dental student from Minnesota, spoke up first, fearful the rooms had been shown to others before them and perhaps there was only one left.

"Miss Parker, I realize you'll need time to check my references, which I assure you are in perfect order, and if you otherwise find me an acceptable tenant, I'd like to move in as soon as possible. Student housing is wild, and the peace of this house far surpasses anything I'd ever hoped to find."

David Miller, a monochromatic study in chestnut brown, with hair, eyes, and a herringbone topcoat all the same color, picked up where Richard Malmgren left off. "This future dentist took the words right out of my mouth. Hopefully the two rooms are still available. I like the idea of living next door to a man who appreciates peace. As far as references go, I trust the professors will have a good word to give you. Meanwhile at the fear of seeming too forward, does any of this seem feasible, Miss Parker?"

Cordelia knew she'd led an extremely sheltered life, but sheltered or not, she knew people. She just did, and she was convinced these were two very good men standing before her. She had only one reservation: David Miller did not appear to be a student. He seemed too old, not by much, but still too old for her ad's requirements.

"Mr. Miller, I may have misunderstood. Are you teaching at Tufts?"

"No, Miss Parker, but thank you for the vote of confidence. I was finishing law school back in New York when the war got under way, and after serving overseas as a medic, realized I was studying for the wrong profession. Tufts made a place for me, and here I am, one of their more mature medical students. The only thing that consoles my parents about all that tuition is the G.I. Bill. Uncle Sam is paying this time."

Cordelia walked toward the front door, and the two baffled men followed her, with David raising his eyebrows at Richard and Richard shrugging his shoulders.

"Gentlemen, I trust you'll respect this house and abide by my requests. Your bedroom, bath, the kitchen, solarium, and garden, as I've said before, are within limits. Everything else is off, and it goes without saying, but just so it's perfectly clear, no mixed company in your rooms. You are however free to invite a friend or two to join you for visits, within reasonable hours, in the common areas. If this is amenable to your needs, and of course pending references, you both have a place to hang your hat." And with that Cordelia opened the door once more for her soon-to-be tenants, only to find Officer Donnelly standing before her with a snow shovel in hand.

"Hello, Miss Parker." He spotted the two men. "Evening, fellas." *They look decent enough, wonder why they're here.* "I found this close to the sidewalk. It could get clipped in a minute, even on Beacon Hill."

Officer Donnelly and Cordelia Parker were now on speaking terms. At first, she was put off by his "too forthcoming manner," but soon realized he truly was concerned for the safety of the neighborhood, and she enjoyed their almost daily hellos, when he'd tip his hat and say, "Looks like rain," "Have a good day," "The Common's all ready for Christmas," or "Happy New Year."

One brutally cold afternoon not so long ago, Cordelia had invited Officer Donnelly and the other equally good-looking policeman, who as it turned out, was his brother-in-law, Officer John King, in for a cup of hot cocoa, which they drank in the kitchen absent of her company. "Officers, please help your-selves to more if you wish. I'll return in a few minutes." Although Cordelia and the policemen were about the same age she assumed a senior, if not superior, role when addressing them.

The house felt alive again, with the three occupants coming and going at various hours. Richard Malmgren was seldom seen, and with Cordelia's consent, he frequently brought coffee to his room where he studied day and night at a desk with a peek-a-boo view of Mount Vernon through the trees outside his window.

David Miller chose to hit the books at the kitchen table, where he drank copious cups of hot tea, most often laced with honey. From time to time, he lit up a cigarette only to take a puff or two until it burned itself out, a study habit reserved for when he needlessly feared he'd bitten off more than he could chew.

Rolf and Hilda were in and out almost daily but couldn't help Miss Cordelia as much as they'd hoped. Outside employment took most of their time and energy, but they did manage to do a bit of housework and minimally maintain the grounds. Cordelia was grateful they even did that and didn't mind cooking simple meals for herself, or baking even, when she had a minute. Cordelia followed recipes in The Fannie Farmer Cookbook to the letter and baked brownies more than anything else, due to her success rate.

Otherwise, the increasingly self-sufficient Brahmin bachelorette depended on modest eateries located between Chandler's Linens and home, or take-out deli dishes, and once in a while she enjoyed sitting down to a meal of Chinese or Italian food in their respective parts of Boston, Chinatown and the North End. Jordan Marsh's blueberry muffins were practically a staple.

David Miller thought Miss Cordelia Parker one of the most enigmatic women he'd ever almost known. Their verbal exchanges were limited to polite greetings, comments on the weather, and inquiries and answers concerning household business. Miss Parker obviously owned the house, but seemed significantly young for such a grand possession, and curiously, she worked in a linen shop. Not what you'd expect from someone of her caste, unless the business was theirs, and even then it was unusual. Although she appeared to be extremely self-possessed, he perceived vulnerability in the way she avoided eye contact until absolutely necessary. There were numerous family photographs and portraits throughout the house, and he often asked himself, *where are those people now?*

She spent her at-home evenings in the library or parlor, and when they did encounter each other, she continued to address him as Mr. Miller, and never once indicated he should address her as anything other than Miss Parker.

He observed how much she enjoyed giving occasional, small dinner parties with the assistance of the older couple who lived over the garage, and he never ventured downstairs on those nights, out of respect for her privacy. Nor did Richard Malmgren.

However, Richard Malmgren didn't seek Cordelia's consent to eat in his room and enjoyed Swedish *skorpa*, pieces of oven-crisped bread, plain or cinnamon sugared, with his coffee, sent on a regular basis by his *mormor*, his grandmother, in well-wrapped tins from Minnesota.

David and Richard both knew they had a good thing going and didn't want to do anything to wear out their welcome. The same consideration took place when Miss Parker was on the telephone in the entry hall. When Cordelia needed absolute privacy the extensions in her bedroom and the study provided their own seclusion.

Cordelia soon concluded David Miller must come from a fairly nice family because whenever she entered the kitchen, no matter how engrossed he was in the books and papers before him, her lodger would jump up and ask, "Can I make you a cup of tea, Miss Parker?"

And without waiting for an answer, did so every time, not in the least offended when she'd take it to another part of the house where she could keep to herself.

"Thank you, Mr. Miller."

PART III

CHAPTER 28

You are the peace of all things calm
You are the place to hide from harm
You are the light that shines in dark.

Celtic Praise

L IFE WAS GOOD ON PILSUDSKI Way, and many of Rita and Bob's neighbors were people they already knew. There was the Logan family downstairs, long-time Saint Augustine parishioners, mother, father, three children and the old grandfather. Across the hall from them was the John Egan family; John had been a schoolmate of Bob's and was on the force too, and they often passed each other coming and going to respective police stations. One in a hurry to get to work on time, the other ready to call it a day—but neither to the omission of courteous recognition.

"Goin' well, Bob?"

"Good, and you, John?"

Their Old Colony apartment building was basic, brick, and substantial and connected to one exactly like it by an arched passageway that led to a large asphalt paved area, with at least ten long clotheslines suspended from wobbly metal poles. Here and there, scruffy patches of irrepressible crabgrass and dandelions escaped through cracks in the blacktop, in search of better ground. Any number of mothers threatened, "God help the child who dirties my laundry." They warned playful children to keep away from the temptation of grabbing, hiding behind, and running between rows of sheets, towels, underwear (always a thing to giggle about), and a sundry of other washables.

"The people in the village (Housing project) seemed to share a common bond, a closeness that couldn't and can't be explained — just felt."

That Old Gang of Mine:
A History of South Boston
Patrick J. Loftus

It was communal living at its best, each family with their own private living space but greatly caring of the others. It was run of the mill for neighbors to borrow eggs, milk, sugar, laundry soap, and whatever staples a household might run short of, or to "spot" one another with a coin or two, which actually meant borrowing dollars, until pay day.

The public grammar school, Perkins, was just up the street, which was of no consequence to Rita, since her children would go to Saint Augustine's parochial. A public library was around the corner, and they could catch the train at close-by Andrews Station. Carson Beach and the great Atlantic Ocean were directly across the road. Best of all, for many families living in Old Colony, was the fact that they could, if they were very careful, save money and move up to a three-decker or nice duplex and maybe, as some vets were able to do with the help of the GI Bill, even buy a home of their own.

The Donnellys set their sights on eventually getting a bigger apartment away from Old Colony, so Rita took a three-nights-a-week waitress job at Steuben's downtown, where, according to newspaper reviews, movie stars, famous sports figures, and entertainers chose to go for late night dining when visiting Bean Town.

Colorful street vendors could be heard all times of day as they hawked their wares to Old Colony residents from specially outfitted open trucks with rolled-up tarps, graduated wooden shelves, baskets and boxes brimming with goods. Closed panel trucks typically carried products that required ice, but once they stopped, the doors were flung wide open.

"Come getcha Italian ice. We got every flavor."

"Fresh fish, fresh fish. Flounder special today, fresh fish."

"Fruits and vegetables. Bananas, grapes, apples, turnips, potatoes, carrots, and onions. Bargains ya don't wanna miss! Fruits and vegetables, fresh fruits and vegetables."

Housewives leaned out windows and called from the top of their voices, "Hey Mister! Hey Mister!" They waved frantically to catch the vendor's attention, or they'd send a child ahead with a message. "My Ma says to tell ya she'll be right down."

The ice cream man needed no words. His truck's familiar jingle conjured up visions of Hoodsies, Fudgsicles, Popsicles, Dreamsicles, Drumsticks, and ice cream sandwiches that sent every child within hearing distance straight to their mother's apron pocket.

"Please, Ma, please just a nickel, Ma, please, please Ma, please, I've been good."

The ragman's distinctive Eastern European accent could be heard near and far as he shouted from atop his horse-drawn wagon, the last of two in Southie, with the other belonging to Mr. Segal, the potato man.

"Rags and bots. Pennies for your rags and bots and newspapers. Rags and bots."

There were other tradesmen who came to the front door. The Fuller Brush man with his brushes, combs, and cleaning products "guaranteed or your money back"; photographers who could take the children's picture right there in the apartment; and the lady who peddled scarves, caps, and mittens she knitted herself and who also took custom orders. "You're welcome to take care of it with three payments if need be," she'd pleasantly offer while pulling a spiral notepad from the depths of her big canvas bag.

The life insurance salesman appeared like clockwork once a month. "Such a small price to pay for your family's peace of mind," he assured everyone.

Mr. Green's colleagues questioned just how much insurance business he could drum up in the working-class neighborhoods of South Boston. His answer was "plenty," as long as he was willing to personally collect the payments. That's how it worked in Southie. You knocked on the door, made nice with the family, and left with the money in hand. He enjoyed it. The people were friendly and eager to do what many considered a step up from the last generation, invest in their loved ones' financial protection, and they generally reasoned, most times aloud, "Should the man of the house go before his time, God forbid."

Today it was Old Colony, beginning with Pilsudski Way and he had to give credit where credit was due. This had nothing to do with insurance and everything to do with self-respect, Mrs. Rita Donnelly's.

The last time Mr. Green visited the second-floor, two-bedroom apartment, he blithely referred to Mrs. Donnelly as a housewife in the course of doing business with her husband. Rita heard what he said from the bedroom, where she was ironing Bob's police uniform shirts to perfection, and marched out, still holding the iron as a precaution from having it fall on her child. But the insurance man didn't know that.

"Hello, Mr. Green, just for the record, I am not married to my house. I am the maker of a home for my husband and children, a homemaker."

Bob Donnelly was speechless but proud. Didn't he love Rita's feistiness and the way she held that iron, punctuating each point of protest with its shiny plate!

"Mrs. Donnelly, please forgive an ignorant man's words. 'Housewife' is no longer in my vocabulary."

Mr. Green had to agree with Rita Donnelly as he looked around the modest but immaculately kept public housing apartment; she was indeed a "homemaker."

The living room drapes hung just so, and the Venetian blinds behind them were free of dust, as was the mottle-patterned linoleum tiled floor. There wasn't any clutter to speak of, but there was a collection of three miniature porcelain horses on the mirror-backed mahogany shelf that hung over a small telephone desk and chair, now relegated to a child's use—coloring books and a box of crayons on top, Golden books neatly stacked beneath, with titles facing out, including *The Pokey Little Puppy*, *Mother Goose*, *The Alphabet A-Z*, *Nursery Songs* and *Prayers for Children*.

The furniture in the living room, where there was still space for more, consisted of a nicely upholstered couch and one armchair, two mahogany end tables and one coffee table, one floor lamp, one table lamp, and a two-sided magazine rack with a handle on top. The kitchen was directly adjacent, and a honey-colored wooden table with four matching chairs and tidily tied seat cushions helped to set the two rooms apart.

Rita put the iron down on the drain board and politely asked, "Mr. Green, may I get you something to drink?"

"If it's not too much trouble, Mrs. Donnelly, a glass of cold water."

She ran the faucet, stepped over to a small, blue worktable next to the sink, and plucked a ruby-red glass from one of two rows of upside-down, jewel-toned aluminum tumblers next to a set of also inverted red, blue, and yellow, carousel-themed children's glasses. "Are you sure you don't want ginger ale, Mr. Green?"

"Water is good."

Rita's prized philodendron trailed halfway to the floor at one end the blue table, and a yellow wall clock above it kept perfect time between everyday items and a portrait of the Sacred Heart.

Mr. Green rightly assumed all of the Donnellys' furniture had been purchased with a charge account. *How else could they afford such nice things on his patrolman's salary? By the time it's all paid off, they could have bought everything twice, with interest rates being charged these days.* So far the likable couple hadn't missed one insurance premium, and that was the bottom line for Mr. Green. *There'll be a day they can't. Sooner or later there's always a day with these people. So, there's a day. Most of them are good for it.*

On the following month's visit, Mr. Green clearly caught the thumping echo of his own heavy footsteps—*a Fred Astaire I'm not,* as he ascended the apartment house's inside stairway. He was a large, egg-shaped man and frequently wore more clothing than the weather called for, just in case there was a change. Delicious aromas from a variety of meals already underway for that night's supper mingled in the air, and every whiff made his mouth water, even if it was primarily "Mick food": potatoes, boiled meat, fishcakes, frankfurters, beans, and he could have sworn fried eggs too.

He looked forward to his own evening meal, as promised by Mrs. Green that morning. "So, my dearest, tonight, for your dining pleasure, we'll have brisket with pearl onions, roasted potatoes, red cabbage, green peas, challah, and for dessert, *apfelstrudel.*"

As he knocked on the Donnellys' sturdy metal door with a gentle hand, it occurred to Mr. Green that he spent almost as much time in these Southie dwellings as he did in his own sizable Tudor home in Brookline. *But then, without the one there wouldn't be the other.* The door opened, and there she was, the homemaker, apron clad with a little girl at her side. Two sets of dimples greeted him, and he smiled back. "From my mouth to God's ears, if it isn't the best homemaker in South Boston. How are you and the children doing today, Mrs. Donnelly?"

And then there were two, five-year-old Ruth Ann, and hiding behind his mother, four-year-old Bobby.

Robert Padraig Donnelly Junior was born only fourteen months after his big sister, and the extended family fondly referred to them as "the Irish twins." Rita's next pregnancy almost claimed her life, if not her soul. It was tubal, threatening unbearable pain and eventual hemorrhage. Her doctor said the fetus needed to be removed within two weeks at the latest. Rita protested it was against their mutual Catholic faith to do such a thing. He single-mindedly suggested she discuss her situation with the Church then. "It's a matter of life or death."

Rita and Bob agreed to keep the heartbreaking news to themselves, "at least for now."

The troubled twenty-five-year-old mother, her two children in tow, walked to Saint Augustine's Church nearly every day, lit a candle, and knelt before the flickering votives at the foot of a statue of Mary, the Mother of God, made the sign of the cross, and prayed, always addressing God the Father first.

Dear God, thank you for giving me two healthy children. Jesus, please perform a miracle and let the doctor be mistaken. Most Blessed Mother, please send a sign, so I'll know what to do about the baby, my baby. Blessed Mother, what am I supposed to do about my baby?

Each time, the hopeful believer said three Hail Marys and three Our Fathers and wondered what her mother would have done if this had happened to her.

Ruth Ann and Bobby were kneeling too, but on the floor, facing the back of the church, using the pew closest to Mummy as a table for their toys, his policeman-fireman-mailman storybook and tiny tin car, her kitten-themed yarn lace-up cards.

Father Sullivan was outraged when Rita and Bob Donnelly brought their dilemma before him, and he ran an index finger between the Roman collar of his priestly garb and his pulsating red neck to help relieve the pressure he felt from such a sacrilegious request.

"Did you really think I was going to give you the go ahead to end the life of an innocent unborn?"

The clock on his desk told him it was almost time for lunch. "There's nothing to do now but put the situation in God's hands and wait for His answer."

Bob jumped to his feet. "With all due respect, Father, do you realize what you're saying? You're putting a noose around my wife's neck. If Rita doesn't follow doctor's orders, she's going to die."

"You've got to understand. This isn't my decision. It's the Church's. I'm a mere messenger." Father Sullivan looked at his clock again. The ticking stridently struck each second of the Donnellys' silence. The "mere messenger" fidgeted with his cuffs and collar, moved things around on his desk, and dismissively warned them, "It's wet out there, I hope you two brought an umbrella."

The desperate husband and father of two gently touched his wife's elbow. "Come on, honey."

Rita Donnelly gracefully rose. "Bob, just a minute, please." She addressed the already standing, resolute priest. "I don't want to go against the Church, Father. We'll wait."

Patrolman Bob Donnelly phoned Rita's older sister Kay from a public telephone on his Boston Common beat and begged her to talk some sense into his wife. She complied without hesitation and suggested they get everything in order with the doctor before presenting their case. "So Rita doesn't have time to change her mind."

Father Sullivan may have been outraged, but Kay Chalpin was furious at the Church. The place she faithfully went to for solace and worship had decreed a death edict for her sister. *Merciful Mother of God, guide me through this maze of madness.*

Two days later, she showed up at the Donnellys' apartment under the guise of just dropping by for a Saturday visit, which Rita saw through right away, and Kay suspected as much.

Bob tried to act as if he was genuinely surprised. "Hello, Kay. Where's Steve?"

Rita crossed her arms. "For God's sake Bob, don't you think I know why my sister is here?"

Kay got straight to the point. "I'm so sorry this happened to you, Rita, and if there was any chance of the baby surviving it would be another thing altogether. Meanwhile, it makes absolutely no sense to anyone other than a host of celibate autocrats for both you and the baby to die. And with or without the Church's consent, you're going into the hospital and getting this taken care of, if I have to drag you there myself."

Kay tossed a "now it's your turn" look at Bob.

"Doctor Ross is a good Catholic honey, and he's still standing his ground. Kay and I met with him yesterday."

Rita let out a mournful sigh. "Mother of God." She took her apron off and threw it at Bob. And because both children were napping, she kept her vehement voice low, "Do I have any say?"

Bob raised his voice. "We're doing this, Rita. As your husband, I'm telling you, we're doing this. The Carney won't have any part of it, so Doctor Ross has made arrangements with a hospital that's willing to help us."

Bobby suddenly appeared, sleepy-eyed, clutching a teddy bear. "Am I gettin' a spankin'?"

Rita stooped down. "No, my handsome boy." She smoothed his mussed hair. "Daddy's not mad at you." She turned to her husband and said in an even tone, for the child's benefit, "I'm calling Rosemary right now, even if it does mean paying for long distance."

"Jesus, Rita, do you think I care about the cost of a phone call at a time like this?" Bob brusquely lifted the frightened child into his arms. "Be a good boy, go back to bed." And he put him down again. Bobby looked at his mother, and Bob raised his voice. "Now!" He scooted the crying preschooler down the hall with a smack on the bum.

Kay told Bob to take it easy and took the telephone from its doily pad on an end table and handed it to Rita. "I thought you'd say that. Ro's expecting your call."

The operating room nurse at Beth Israel asked Rita Donnelly if she had any children, and when she answered "two, a girl and a boy," Rachel Maier shook her head. "What the hell were you waiting for? Two children to bring up and you took this risk."

Rita closed her eyes, softly wept, and pressed her fingers to the faintly seen scapular beneath her hospital gown. Nurse Maier took her hand and gently patted it. "I spoke too quickly. You're taking care of it now, that's what matters. I'll be with you all the way."

The hospital corridors had an acrid smell of ether, but when Rita's gurney was rolled into the operating room the sweet fragrance of roses met her. She looked around for a source until the anesthesia took hold and she saw her mother, Norah, through the haze. *Mum, you're the roses.*

Grammy McDonough kept Ruth Ann and Bobby for a few more days after Rita returned home.

Kay visited Rita every day at lunch. "Don't worry, kiddo. We'll get through this." On Friday, she brought two comforts: Rita's favorite "fish," a fried clam dinner from Kelly's, and from New York, their older sister.

At the sight of Rosemary, Rita began to fall apart. "Oh Ro, it was so horrible. Kay's been terrific. I don't know how . . . "

Norah's firstborn, the one the rest of her children looked to for advice and approval, tossed her pocketbook and a huge Lord & Taylor shopping bag on the living room chair. She rushed to Rita, who was seated on the couch in a robe and nightgown, and sat down and stroked her baby sister's arm. "I know honey, but you did the right thing. With all my heart, you did the right thing."

"Honest to God?"

"Honest to God."

They sat there not saying another word, until Rosemary sweetly whispered one phrase from the song that was their mothers. "Hush, now, don't you cry."

Meanwhile, Kay put the clam dinners in the oven and the kettle on a low flame for tea later on, set the table, including a bottle of Coca Cola at each place, and stood in the kitchen flipping through a *Photoplay* magazine until her hunger soon took over. "You two ready for lunch now?"

As was their way, the King sisters fell into an easy conversation of memories, family, old friends, movies and movie stars, economic challenges and future plans, all laced with much needed laughter, and as always, love and loyalty.

"Seems like Mum should be sitting here with us."

"Let's face it, girls. The U.S. Navy was our brothers' saving grace."

"You'll never believe who got married last week."

Kay opened *Photoplay* to a page she'd dog-eared. "Do you think Elizabeth Taylor's new haircut would look good on me?"

Rosemary got up to make the tea. "Well, baby sister, I have some good news and a surprise."

Rita stacked the plates from where she was seated, not one clam left on any of them. "By the look on Kay's face, I assume she already knows."

"Of course I do, and before Ro tells you about the surprise, please be aware that I'm completely fine with it. You'll see." *This is just what she needs, a wonderful, absolutely unexpected gift to interrupt all that sadness.*

Rita reached for the porcelain teapot that had been their mothers. "The suspense is killing me."

It occurred to Kay that this afternoon was the first time in weeks she'd seen her sister's dimples.

Rosemary put an apple-shaped, green glass sugar bowl and matching pitcher of evaporated milk on the table. "Tony's been offered a great job with United Way."

"Congratulations. Finally, you'll be back in Boston." Rita knew her sister was dying to come home and assumed a "great job" wouldn't be anywhere else but home.

"In Arizona."

"Arizona! Oh God, no, that's too far. New York is bad enough, Ro."

Rita stirred and stirred a spoonful of sugar and splash of milk into her steaming cup.

Rosemary explained, "I know, but it's a great opportunity, and this is what Tony has always wanted to do, work in social services." *If Rita cries again, I'm done for. Please, don't cry.*

Rita Donnelly's utmost camaraderie came from her sisters, and now Rosemary was moving to Arizona. It felt like she was losing her mother all over again.

Kay cleared the plates away. "Okay, kiddo, next course." She plopped a Helen's Bakery box before Rita. "Open it, please."

"God in heaven, Kay. I'm trying to digest this move to Arizona." *Pull yourself together. Ro doesn't need another round of tears.* Rita's teaspoon landed in her saucer with a loud clink.

"Open the box. It'll help," Kay commanded with a grin.

Those dimples showed again. "Barbara Catherine, you're absolutely impossible." Rita cut the thin twine with a table knife and brought her hands together at the sight of sugar-dusted cream puffs and chocolate éclairs neatly arranged in individual, pleated white papers. "You'll find clean plates in the cabinet next to the fridge."

"Are you ready for the surprise?" Rosemary asked with deliberate lightness of heart. *This should give Rita the boost she needs right now.*

Rita gingerly shifted in her chair and grinned. "I hope it's better than your good news, Ro."

"You decide." *My God, she's white as a sheet.*

Rosemary was bursting with more good news, but in light of her sister's loss, would keep her, "I just found out we're finally expecting," announcement a well-kept secret until next month. She went to retrieve the Lord & Taylor bag, and Rita admired her sister's as usual lovely appearance. Her softly waved blonde hairdo looked like she'd just left a beauty shop, the seams in her stockings were straight as arrows, and a flared tweed skirt flowed over her slim hips as if it had been custom tailored, while a tucked-in, white silk blouse subtly emphasized her spare waist. *And those movie star teeth, is it any wonder Ro's a fashion model!*

Rosemary presented the Lord & Taylor shopping bag. "For you."

As soon as Rita looked inside she knew. The garment bag within, folded precisely so Jordan Marsh would be seen at first glance, and a small vinyl window opposite the familiar imprint revealed Rita's certainty. This was Rosemary's red coat.

"Oh my God!"

The Lord & Taylor bag fell to the floor as Rita stood up and unzipped the other. Rosemary offered, "Let me help," removed the coat from the hanger, and said, "I believe this is madam's size. Now, if you'll just slip that robe off." She helped Rita into the coat and gently turned her around. "Beautiful!"

"Ro, I don't think I understand. You love this coat."

"It's yours, Rita."

"I can't believe this. Are you absolutely positive, Ro? I know what it means to you."

"What in the world am I going to do with a winter coat in the middle of Arizona?"

Kay tugged on the coat's lapel collar and quipped, "You've got to remember, little sister, good fortune comes with this coat. Plan on it." She kissed Rita on the cheek, and Rosemary kissed her on the other. Kay broke away first. "Dessert is on the table, ladies."

Rita sat down and reflected on the gift. *This beautiful coat is so much more.* Wrapped all around her were Norah's love, Rosemary's joy, Kay's confidence, and now her own comfort. *So much more . . .*

No one in either the King or Donnelly-McDonough families ever mentioned the sorrowful termination again. It was over.

∽

Much to Rita and Bob's shocked relief, Father Sullivan greeted them, however coolly, at Sunday Mass, as if nothing had taken place. "If it isn't the Donnelly family. Come in. Come into the house of God with those two beautiful children." *Forgive them Father, and if it be your Divine will, please take that innocent baby from the loneliness of limbo into Your most sacred arms.*

The Donnellys' life in South Boston was family, church, work, friends, trying to get ahead, walks along Southie's beaches, shopping on Broadway, trips into Boston and occasionally out of the city too (with a borrowed car), and an overall satisfying sense of belonging.

But all was not as it seemed. Robert had a wandering eye. And Rita tried her best to look the other way.

CHAPTER 29

For there we loved, and where we love is home,
Home that our feet may leave, but not our hearts.
"Homesick in Heaven"

Oliver Wendell Holmes Sr.

"We don't want anyone stealin' dough off the Blessed Mother. There's a sawbuck in it for both of ya's." The North End festival chairman made it his duty to secure protection for the Mother of God.

"A sawbuck between us, sir, or each?" the uncertain young policeman asked.

His older, more experienced partner stepped up and said, "He's just kiddin', Angelo. When do you need us?" The senior officer had worked these North End feasts for years and never without being paid more than agreed upon. He loved that about the Italians—everything was big and generous.

"The festival takes place in two weeks, Officers, and here's how the whole thing breaks down. I know you've done this before, Ed, but for the benefit of the rookie."

"Rookie." Bob Donnelly had been on the force for four years now, but decided to let it go.

"There'll be marchin' bands and wall-to-wall people, so lots goin' on. The Blessed Mother's statue will be carried through the streets on a platform by ten of our most honorable men. People will be pinnin' money on her clothin' and the ribbons too. Every cent goes to the church, and I don't mind tellin' ya it's my own mother who made Our Lady's beautiful clothes."

It was a sticky, warm, June day, and courteous, fastidiously groomed community leader Angelo Cassasa reluctantly removed his expensive linen sport coat. "Excuse me, but I don't want to ruin this with sweat stains." He handed it to the hostess at his well-known restaurant, Villa de Italia. "Unfortunately, Officers, some lousy, small-time crooks are willin' to pull greenbacks right off the Mother of God and hide 'em in the palms of their hands while tryin' to look like they're pinnin' money on. Anyway, if there's trouble, I don't want ya's makin' any kind of scene. Just take trouble away. *Capiche?*"

"You can depend on us, Angelo. Thanks a million."

"We'll be there."

All three men shook hands, and Angelo offered, "Come in some night with your Missus. You too, Rookie. On the house."

The two peace officers continued on their beat, past meat markets with freshly cut chickens hanging in the window, sweet-smelling bakeries, busy tailor shops, family-owned grocery stores, delis, restaurants and colorful flower stalls, and gift shops of every variety: souvenirs, luxury leather goods, Italian pottery, fine fabrics, and decorative glass.

Old men seated on stoop stairs tipped their hats or gestured hello in a manner that looked like a priest blessing his flock. Old women peered down from their eagle-eye view in apartment windows above and very often informed *agente di polizia* of supposed crimes in progress. "Those boys onna the corner looka like they up to a no good."

More often than not it was a false alarm. The North End was one of the safest places in the city. Recently, Officer Kane advised a lady who asked him for directions to Paul Revere's house and timidly inquired, "Is that area safe for my little girl and me?"

"You have nothing to worry about, Missus. It's the North End, and they'll kill anyone who tries to harm a mother and child."

Bob liked walking the beat in the North End where the people were full of life but not much trouble. And the food was delicious. Both cops continually touched the visors of their caps in respectful greeting to passersby.

Officer Kane said, "Jesus, Bob, you could have blown the whole deal for us. This kinda work is helpin' me put together a down payment for a car. Listen, pal, and I'm only sayin' this for your own good, no offence, but you'll get a lot further if you take the humble route, especially with these guineas. We're in their territory, and that makes them boss. The guy's offerin' us good dough to keep an eye on the Blessed Mother. In my book, it doesn't get much better than that." His usual smile returned. "*Capiche?*"

"No offence taken, Ed. I'm used to those Beacon Hill types who nail down everything, especially if a buck's involved." Bob stopped walking, and Ed followed suit. "Just last week a wise guy over on Acorn asked, 'Officer, could you help me with these jammed window screens? It shouldn't take much of your time, only two are stuck, and please don't expect any compensation. I understand there are people who tip public servants, but I'm not one of them.' Can you believe the gall of that guy, Ed?"

Despite tightfisted Brahmins, summers so hot "you could fry an egg on the sidewalk" and bitter "Jesus, it gets colder than a witch's heart out there" winters, Bob Donnelly loved his job. Oh, he had plans for getting ahead, "But for now," he told someone, "it's a helluva good situation."

Where else could a "regular guy" enjoy the freedom a beat allowed as he patrolled through "the greatest city in the world," even if he did have to check in with the station every forty minutes from a B.P.D. call box or work overtime without further compensation?

"The call boxes were accessible only by an officer with a key. Most of the officers were on foot and had no radios. They were to make their rounds, open and pull the lever in the boxes every forty minutes or so. This connected them to a signal desk and let the station know they were where they should be. The station could also send a signal to the box, and a flashing blue light on top would alert the officer they were looking for him. And every box had a direct phone line to the station."

Where else could a regular guy have a decent amount of respect for the work he did, wear a fine-looking uniform and spend day after day with the policemen of Station 3, who were like fraternity brothers to him? They worked together, ate together, drank together off-duty, played cribbage and covered each other's backs for whatever reason needed: a medical emergency, death in the family, new baby, wedding, house or apartment that needed painting or some other kind of attention, a move to "new digs," loan until the next pay period, switching shifts, or providing a valid excuse for unaccounted time away from home to stop for a drink or a game of cards, or venture to Scollay Square.

Officers Donnelly and Kane ducked into Finocchi's Italian Market & Deli for a quick sandwich. When they finished ordering and pulled out their wallets, the proprietor wouldn't hear of the two *carabinieri* paying for the spuckies, fresh coffee, and mouth-watering Italian cookies. "Put your money away. It's no good in here." Mr. Finocchi then spoke in rapid Italian to Mrs. Finocchi, who warmly led them to one of three tables crowded into a small space by the window. "Please, please sit down. Give your feet a rest."

"So, Bob, how's it going with you and Rita and the kids?"

Bob Donnelly was meticulous about his uniform, taking extra care to brush it free of lint, polish his shoes to a mirror finish, and see that the badges on his hat and chest were smudge free.

Bob Donnelly really appreciated Ed Kane, who wasn't hesitant to help bring his game "up to snuff." George McDonough was a good stepfather, but George Mac was a guy with lily-white hands, a pharmacist. What did a pharmacist know about the streets, about getting ahead in the police department? Ed was a seasoned veteran and a good guy in Bob's book. He used to be at the Joy Street Station but was transferred a while back, and covered the North End now. When there was a shortage of patrolmen, Bob was detailed out to work right alongside him, and he never left Ed's company without knowing more than before.

"Great, except with the new baby, we definitely need a bigger place."

"You're kiddin' me. I was just gettin' ready to ask the fellas at the station if anyone's interested in a reasonably priced apartment in Jamaica Plain. My mother has a three-decker and the top floor is available first of the month. Would seven rooms be big enough for you?"

"What's the rent and when can we see it?"

Jamaica Plain wasn't Southie, but it was close enough, and the Donnelly family would now have the space they so desperately needed.

They'd been through some hard times with the tragic end of Rita's pregnancy, her subsequently missing work and back for only a short while when she found herself in a family way again, which was good news in the long run. Another baby was coming, "thank God growing in the right place." It was also not so good news; she'd miss more work. But Rita was determined to get their family out of the project, and she continued working at Steuben's until two months before the baby arrived. The white half-apron that covered her black skirt helped to hide what the other waitresses kindly called "barely a bump, honey."

The owner of Steuben's was a benevolent man and never short of good help for that very reason. He deduced Rita was in "a delicate condition" and discreetly made sure she was the only one on her shift permitted to fold napkins and refill salt and pepper shakers, a coveted sit-down job.

The new baby was a healthy, auburn-haired, blue-eyed porcelain doll. Catherine Louise was the apple of her mother's eye, her father's pride and joy, big sister Ruth Ann's "baby doll," and brother Bobby's "lil' sister." For the time being, Rita and Bob firmly agreed they'd be more careful when tracking the only birth control sanctioned by the church, the rhythm method.

The third-floor apartment on Arcola Street in Jamaica Plain was so large, Bob's mother coined it a barn, but the Donnellys relished every square inch: a living room, three bedrooms, small eat-in kitchen with a big, old-fashioned, black iron stove that Rita had to learn to master, walk-in pantry, formal dining room, large bath with a claw foot tub, pedestal sink, and pull-chain toilet, and a big back porch the entire width of the apartment.

The formal dining room remained empty until the Donnellys bought a walnut table with two leaves, six chairs, and a small buffet from a regular customer at Steuben's, a widower who was moving to Florida and, as Rita told Bob in order to justify the purchase, "was practically giving it away, honey."

Blessed Sacrament Church was within walking distance, and there were two mom-and-pop grocery stores, one on each corner of the entrance to the Donnelly's street, which dead-ended against one of the top sledding hills in the neighborhood.

Each grocery store had its own specialty. One featured a butcher shop, while the other provided fresh packed ice cream and ice cream cones, "Jimmies extra," and a pay telephone booth.

Ruth Ann Remembers

W E KNEW THE FOOTSTEPS IN the back stairwell to our third-floor Jamaica Plain apartment were his. We knew the sound of heavy, shiny, black policeman's oxfords, and we knew the repeat of his quick pace; each step barely landed on as he flew up the stairs. My brother Bobby and I would shout, "Here he comes! Daddy's home!"

As soon as we said it, Mummy would appear with baby Catherine on her hip and join us at the top of the landing.

In preparation for Daddy's homecoming, and to calm things down a bit, Mummy would always set us up for quiet play. When it was at the kitchen table, we knelt on the matching honey-colored chairs. Our choices were crayons and coloring books or modeling clay, one box each, with different colors lined up in perfectly scored rows, ready for sculpting, or as my mother used to say, mayhem.

"You're to keep everything on the table this time, kids," she warned, remembering when we'd rolled clay worms and placed them all over the kitchen and hallway, where they were unknowingly stepped on and dragged throughout the apartment. "I'm still picking up those worms."

"We won't do it again, Mummy," Bobby said as he squished two hues of clay into a muddy-colored ball.

"Or do you want to play Pick Up Sticks?" She'd set us up on the shiny, waxed but worn, red linoleum kitchen floor. That too came with a warning: "And stay on the rug. I don't want you two catching cold."

We loved to play, but nothing could completely distract us from listening for Daddy and the squeak of the downstairs back door when his huge hand turned the old-fashioned, brass doorknob. Every step of his homecoming was a kind of dance that produced its own music and varied with the seasons.

Tap, tap, tapping meant he was getting the snow off his boots; shuffle, ball change, meant shaking spring rain from his umbrella and placing it opened next to baby carriages, roller-skates, and bicycles on either side of the stairs. My father seldom moved slowly, but in the humid summer, he waltzed. One, in the door; two, pause; three, grab the railing for support. One, two, three, and slowly he would ascend those three flights. The crisp air and vibrant colors of autumn energized him, and many times he opened the back door with such vigor it banged against the wall, a percussion prelude to his quick, long-stride tango, two smooth stairs at a time, into the arms of his waiting family. There wasn't a car to listen for because we didn't own or need one. Our father took the train from Park Street Station in Boston to Jamaica Plain and walked home from the subway, passing Blessed Sacrament Church, Al's Shoe Store, Gambon's Liquors, Busy Bee Cleaners, Friend's Food Shop, and other small businesses along the way.

Sometimes he stopped to pick up a quart of milk, dozen eggs, can of Franco-American spaghetti or whatever other provision my mother had asked for when he took the time to call from a public telephone somewhere downtown or on the vast city park, Boston Common.

The Common, one of the places in the Beacon Hill area where five and sometimes six days a week my father went to work as a cop on the beat. At night, he went to school at U. Mass because he wanted "something more, something different than three-family apartment houses, a cop's beat, and winter."

Those sounds of the back door opening could have come from any of the other families living in that three-decker.

There was the O'Day family on the first floor, best described to you in my mother's words. "Dan's a milkman for Hood, grew up in Medford, and Ginny's from Southie. We went to Gate of Heaven together. They have five children, four girls and the youngest is a boy."

The pretty O'Day sisters were older than me. During the week, we all wore navy-blue Catholic school uniforms, but I was in awe of their weekend petticoats, poodle skirts, twin sets, and pert hairdos. Their brother, Danny, was, in my mother's words, "such a good boy." I remember Mr. O'Day coming home

Boston Common and State House

from work during a scorching heat wave and telling his daughters and me, as we all sat outside on the front stairs, fanning ourselves with pleated *Seventeen* magazine pages, "Very clever girls." Then, with the gentlest of smiles, he shook the red-and-white cardboard box he was carrying and announced, "After supper, Hoodsies for everyone in the building!"

Or a member of the Ed Kane family could have turned that doorknob. When Grammy asked about them, my mother answered, "Ed's on the force too. His mother owns the building. That's how they got the middle floor, cooler in summer and heated by the other apartments in winter. You'd think they were Protestants though, with that small family of theirs. Imagine just the two children."

Mr. Kane was tall and thin, Mrs. Kane short and pleasingly plump. In less charitable moments, my mother would say, "Jack Spratt could eat no fat, his wife could eat no lean, and so between them both, they licked the platter clean." Their children were built just like them, the oldest, a boy, short and chubby, the girl, as tall as a high schooler, although she was only in fifth grade. What I remember best about the Kane family is they were very quiet and kept to themselves, except for fleeting hellos and touting Mr. Kane's mother's handmade braided rugs. "You won't find a better price for the quality." My mother bought two, one at a time as she could afford them, for each of the children's bedrooms.

Unless we had company and my father was running downstairs to answer the door, our family seldom used the formal, winding staircase in the well-kept front hall.

The three tenant wives took turns washing and waxing the entry and stairway and scrubbing the white granite steps outside. Sweeping the sidewalk was relegated to older children.

When our doorbell rang, my father would hit a security button inside our apartment that released the door lock to the building with a loud buzzing sound. And he'd proclaim, as if for the first time, "Rita, I'll go see who it is."

To which she repeatedly replied with a certain exasperation, "Bob, you're supposed to look out the window and see who it is first, then ring the buzzer."

"Rita, will you stop making a goddam federal case every time I go to open the front door."

To us, the back staircase above the second floor was like the entrance to a private club, *The Donnelly Family - Members Only Please.*

And we only had to hear two or three footsteps to know it was Daddy. "Daddy's home!"

Bobby and I would dash out the kitchen door, lean over the stair rail, our hands poised on top to lift us just enough so we could peek down at Daddy coming up.

When we heard the rustle of a paper bag, which he did intentionally, it meant presents: a ball and jacks, balsa wood airplane, bubbles, brightly swirled lollypops, a kaleidoscope, or storybooks.

"I've got surprises," echoed up the stairwell, landed in our hearts, and settled there for a lifetime. I cherish these memories, although I learned years later Daddy wasn't always eager to "get home to Rita and the kids."

CHAPTER 30

CORDELIA PARKER LOOKED OUT ON the torrential downpour and grew increasingly impatient with herself for such inordinate care. *Good heavens. He's a grown man and not your concern. Mr. Miller survived World War II. Surely he can navigate a New England storm.*

Earlier that night, she'd puttered around Chandler's Linens after hours, while waiting for the storm to subside before walking home, but when she turned the radio on to catch the latest forecast, listeners were warned the worst of the blustery nor'easter was yet to come.

Cordelia telephoned Rolf. "Please secure whatever you possibly can." He replied, "I took care of that all late this afternoon, Miss."

She called for a taxi, though she detested paying for one, always mindful of the meter ticking, but thought it better than taking the risk of being blown into injury or, heaven forbid, struck by lightning.

The Yellow Cab slowly swooshed up to the curb in front of Cordelia's Mount Vernon home. "Here we are, Miss."

She already had the fare in hand and hopped out before the driver could open her door. He rushed to her side and shouted over the wet, windy weather. "Jeez lady, at least let me carry your packages," and he grabbed all three.

Cordelia quickly opened her umbrella and covered both of them. "Yes, yes, thank you, but please, let's hurry."

They dashed through the shadows and puddles, the house completely dark save a desk-lamp glow from the second-floor window in Richard Malmgren's room. She opened the front door to more darkness, flipped a light switch on, and instructed the driver to put her wet packages on the rug inside. "Thank you."

Lately, it had been Cordelia's experience to return home from work to the warmth of the porch lantern and once inside, a small hall lamp too, as well as

Dining room
91 MOUNT VERNON,
BOSTON, MASS.

the distant kitchen light that made its way to the entry in dim, beckoning beams, David Miller forever sitting at the kitchen table with his medical books, tea and partially smoked cigarettes. But not tonight, the house was dark. David Miller was not there.

How fortuitous. Now I won't have to bring my dinner to the dining room. Good. I'm much too tired for all that rigmarole.

She took a leftover macaroni and cheese casserole from the refrigerator and put it in the oven at a low temperature. *This will give me time to put everything in order first.*

Her few dinner dishes washed and put away, the teakettle steaming, flame below it turned off for the third time, there Cordelia stood, worried about a man she hardly knew. *A boarder, for goodness sake . . . I'll be completely worthless tomorrow unless I get my rest.* "Go to bed," she heard herself saying out loud, and it concerned her. *Now I'm an old maid who talks audibly to herself.*

As Cordelia donned her Parisian-blue, white-piped cotton pajamas and contrasting white, blue-piped, monogrammed robe (a birthday gift from Abby this last spring) it dawned on her it must be David Miller who made sure the two lights were always on when she returned home. *Surely he has no personal need other than the hall light when it's time to retire, very thoughtful.*

She'd been home for three hours now, and still no sight nor sound of her other boarder, except a sliver of light from beneath his bedroom door and the ever-present whiff of coffee. Richard Malmgren was shy, and that was fine with her. *This isn't a social club.* He needed a place to live, and she needed the income.

Cordelia decided to go downstairs and have that last cup of tea after all but detoured to the parlor first, to peek out the window one last time. The storm was still fierce, and she cherished the feeling of safety her well-built, ancestral home provided as raindrops pummeled against the windowpanes and tree branches blew to and fro, one wrenched from its trunk.

Inexplicably her unrequited love, Norman Prescott, and his Irish wife, Patsy, came to mind, and an only too familiar ache returned with her "if only" recollections. *It was snowing. I was wearing my beautiful red coat.* She envisioned herself as she was in those days, blithe, with not a care in the world save winning the heart of her lifelong love. *Norman had his arm around me.*

And then she saw him. David Miller was clutching his hat, head down, and rushing toward her front door.

Oh my, he can't see me like this. She rushed to the stairway but didn't make it in time, so she quickly turned around, secured the tie on her robe with a double knot and faced the door. "Oh there you are, Mr. Miller. I was just about to make myself a cup of tea. My goodness, you're absolutely drenched."

"Very observant of you, Miss Parker," he chuckled. "I can't remember the last time I was in such fierce weather." He remained on the entry rug, removed his soaking wet shoes, and looked around for where he might deposit them, as well as his dripping hat and coat.

"Just put your things on the hall tree for now. This marble floor has seen its share of water, not to worry. And you can place your shoes by the cellar door in the kitchen. They should be dry by morning."

The slightly embarrassed, pajama-clad landlady headed for the kitchen first. David Miller entered minutes later, carrying his soppy shoes. As he was washing his hands in the sink, she said, "Mr. Miller, you look as though a cup of hot tea would do you good right now."

"At least a cup, Miss Parker."

"Well, I've made a whole pot."

And without any fanfare, announcement, invitation, or awkwardness, Cordelia Parker set two places for tea with family-acquired, old-fashioned, floral-patterned china relegated to the kitchen years ago. She sat down and poured a cup for each of them.

Meanwhile, Rolf and Hilda spied the late night "tea for two" through the kitchen window of their over-the-garage apartment. "Come, come," Hilda beckoned Rolf. "Look. Miss Cordelia is sitting at the table with that nice doctor."

"If you don't mind my asking, Mr. Miller, what in the world kept you out on such a night?"

He was ready for a second cup but warmed hers first. "To answer your question, one of my professors and his wife invited me to their home for dinner, but unbeknownst to me, they also had a bit of match-making in mind."

"And were they successful?"

"Their daughter's an intelligent and, I might add, very attractive young lady." He held his cup steady and stirred in two teaspoons of honey. "But she's not the one for me," he said as he brought the cup to his lips.

"Well, Mr. Miller, it's good to know you're safe and sound. Excuse me, please, but I'm afraid it's way past my bedtime."

David Miller stood when Cordelia did. "And mine as well. Thank you for the tea, Miss Parker." When she began to clear the table, he insisted, "Please, allow me," and accidentally brushed her hand when he took the teacup from it. Her subsequent blush surprised him.

"Thank you, and good night, Mr. Miller."

"Good night, Miss Parker."

He didn't budge until she was completely out of his sight.

Cordelia inadvertently caught David Miller's standing-still reflection in a large mirror over the sideboard as she passed through the dining room. *Good night, Mr. Miller.*

The next day, Miss Cordelia Anne Parker awoke to a clear, sunny, glorious Boston morning, went straight to the kitchen as part of her usual routine, and directly looked toward the cellar door. David Miller's shoes were gone. *My, he had an early start.*

However there was a piece of folded notebook paper, addressed to her, on the table.

Dear Miss Parker,

Last night's hot tea hit the spot. Thank you for your kindness.

Sincerely,
David Miller

When she went outside to collect the newspaper, a fresh, luxuriant breeze of green, earthy scents came toward her. Green grass, green trees, and green foliage, some just changing color, all tossed and washed clean to their utmost beauty by the unexpected storm, wet soil, wet cobblestones, and wet bricks all contributed to the overall enchanting ambiance of Beacon Hill after the rain.

I'll never leave this house. Feet first, isn't that what I said? She opened the newspaper and folded it up again, much too distracted to read headlines. She couldn't get David Miller off her mind, from the minute he opened the door last night to their parting in the kitchen.

Maybe I should ask my boarders to call me Cordelia. She tried to imagine how the gently handsome medical student, who forever seemed to possess a five o'clock shadow, might say her name, or would he prefer to continue with Miss Parker? *Thank God Eleanor came up with such an agreeable way for me to keep on living here. Boarders, whoever would have thought?*

∽

That same morning in Jamaica Plain, Rita Donnelly, still in her pale-pink, long-sleeved nightgown, white chenille robe, white bobby socks, and moccasin slippers, was busy cooking breakfast for her husband. He sat at the kitchen table partly dressed for work in stocking feet, his dark uniform pants, and a full white undershirt, drinking hot coffee and reading *The Boston Globe*.

She loved looking at him. Even on his days off, he was clean-shaven, hair combed just so, and chose to wear comfortable yet presentable clothing.

And more often than not, when Bob donned the rest of his B.P.D. gear, she would say with a beguiling smile reserved for him alone, "Oh how I love a man in a uniform," despite her certainty there were other women who thought the same thing of him.

It was little things, like the smell of perfume on his coat a while ago. When she questioned it, he claimed, "Some old woman hugged me with gratitude when I helped her get on the trolley." Rita wanted a happy home for her children, so she accepted his "ridiculous explanations," but she knew in her heart it would have to be faced sooner or later. For now, she chose later, hoping for the best. *My husband is a philanderer. God help me.*

She placed a plate of bacon, eggs, and two slices of buttered toast before him, popped a tiny sampler jar of Trappist orange marmalade on the table, and returned to the stove to stir the children's oatmeal. The marmalade was part of a gift sampler given to Bob by a Boston Miss on his beat, but he told Rita it came from a "nice family" on Beacon Hill.

"Well, I don't think it's going to rain anymore, so I'll go shopping today instead. Who knows what tomorrow holds?" Rita was nervous about the announcement and attempted to waylay her husband's usual inquisition with inordinate cheerfulness. Bob tried to keep a tight rein on her, and his interrogations about the amount of money she spent were very often the beginning of yet another fray.

"I'm taking Ruth Ann with me, and your sister already agreed to babysit Bobby and baby Catherine." Rita's dimples were showing.

Bob was under the impression that all of Rita's part-time waitress earnings went directly from her pocketbook to the Whitman's Sampler candy box "bank" in the top drawer of his dresser. Yes, what was in her pocketbook, but not the little bit she secretly tucked in her shoe before leaving Steuben's.

"What are you going to buy?" He drank more coffee and put his cup back in the saucer with a fairly forceful hand. "Do we really need anything?"

The diligent homemaker stopped stirring. "Listen, I don't question the way you do your job. Please give me the benefit of the doubt. Okay?" *I knew he was going to do this.* "Listen to me, Bob."

He'd returned to reading the paper and put it down in exasperation. "Go on."

"Everyone says how well-dressed our family is, and how do you suppose that happens? Looking and looking for the best markdowns in Filene's Basement, that's how it happens. And I need to buy a gift for your mother. We're celebrating her birthday on Sunday at Aunt Jean's." *God knows he won't deny his sainted mother a gift.* Rita pressed on her pin-curled hair as if the escalating confrontation may have loosened one or two pins. "And I have to find out when Jordan's and Filene's will be getting their First Communion dresses in. I don't want to shop for Ruth Ann's when everything's picked over."

"Jesus, Rita, its fall. Isn't First Communion in the spring?"

"Jesus, Bob, this is the most important day of her life, and I don't want to leave anything to chance."

Bob drummed his fingers on the table. "Seems like you're looking for excuses to stay downtown longer. If Ruth Ann wasn't going with you it could look suspicious. She's absolutely going, right?"

"You listen to me, Bob Donnelly. Don't you ever accuse me of a thing like that again. Jesus, Mary, and Joseph, I can't believe you'd even think it." She threw the oatmeal-covered spoon on the table, and some of the cereal stuck to her husband's undershirt.

He grabbed her wrist. "Pick it up."

"No."

He tightened his grip. "Pick it up, Rita."

"No." *I'm not going to put up with this kind of nonsense.*

He shot out of his chair still clutching her wrist. "Pick it up."

With her free hand, she grabbed a frying pan. "Unless you want to show up at the station with a flat face, you'd better let go of me."

He forced the pan out of her hand. "Nice breakfast," he said, and banged the pan down on the stove.

She rubbed her wrist and grinned, "Want another cup of coffee, honey?"

"You're a real piece of work sometimes, you know that." Bob reached across the kitchen floor for his sturdy, black police shoes right next to Rita's black high heels and Bobby's black-and-white saddle oxfords, where they had been placed on newspaper the night before, after he'd painstakingly shined each pair. "I have to finish getting ready for work."

"Send the kids back, okay?" Rita pulled the highchair closer to the table. "I'll get them started and take the baby out of her crib in a minute."

Bob stepped into the long hallway with his heavy-footed "Jack and the Beanstalk" giant walk and bellowed, "Fee, fi, foe, fum! Here I come!" to the playful screeches of Ruth Ann and Bobby.

CHAPTER 31

The times may be gone when children accompany their mothers
downtown for a day of shopping and lunch in the tea room . . .
and when the personality of a city or town can be read in its big
stores. But those days are far from forgotten and they still have
power to influence how we shop today.
SERVICE AND STYLE: HOW THE AMERICAN DEPARTMENT STORE
FASHIONED THE MIDDLE CLASS
JAN WHITAKER

RITA DONNELLY ADORED SHOPPING IN downtown Boston with all the hustle, bustle, and beauty of the city—stately buildings, elaborate store window displays, and vast choices. She had a well-known flair for finding the best bargains in Filene's Basement; Ruth Ann almost always accompanied her, and they followed the same path every time. First came a visit to one or two posh stores on Newbury Street, just for fun, where upon inquiry, beautiful linens, eyeglasses, china, stationery, lingerie and stockings, hand-dipped chocolates, and many other fine items were taken from exquisite cabinets, display cases, drawers and shelves for Rita's unabashed perusal. And if a little something affordable caught her eye, she made the purchase and proudly carried the uptown bag that said she could shop in such places. Just walking in the door of these stores—usually a highly lacquered red, black, or dark green, with brass handle, kick plate, and numbers—was a pleasant experience.

"Good afternoon, may I be of some assistance to you?" the toney clerks would tout.

This all stood in stark contrast to the bargain battleground of Filene's Basement, where it was every woman for herself.

"Are you gonna get that or not?"

"Hey, that's really cute. Where'd you find it?"

"The line starts back there, lady."

"Are ya all set? I'll ring it up for ya's right over here."

Jordan Marsh Department Store
Washington Street
BOSTON, MASS.

After Newbury, came a quick walk around fashionable department stores, including Jordan Marsh, where they'd stop for a snack of Jordan's blueberry muffins, or have a half dozen boxed up to take home, and visit departments of interest. Then on to Filene's, where the expensive upstairs tour always came before the downstairs bargain, treasure hunt, the very reason Rita came to town in the first place.

Jordan's and Filene's had select merchandise enticingly displayed in massive sidewalk-level windows and on well-dressed mannequins strategically placed throughout the enormously popular stores.

The female variety had long eyelashes and petulant smiles. Most were in classic fashion-model poses with one foot forward and an arm raised at the elbow. Its open-palmed hand with a perfectly manicured index finger pointed delicately toward the potential customer as if to say, "This way, please. You'll find your size right over there."

The eye-catching, impeccably ordered displays of goods throughout the stores were practically irresistible, as was the clothing on mannequins of every size: men, women, and children in seasonally smart outfits and winning postures. To post-war shoppers, the perfect, pretend people represented peace, prosperity, and the good life.

Whatever went unsold in Filene's upstairs, eventually made its way to their bargain basement and into the hands of discerning shoppers with, as Rita's mother-in-law, Mrs. Mac, said to nobody in particular, one too many times, "champagne taste and beer pocketbooks."

Although Bob was a good provider, his policeman's wages could hardly cover the cost of many upstairs purchases, but in Rita's hands his paycheck was a passport to the land of good appearance, leaving anyone who ever saw their

Jordan Marsh and Company combined an elegant atmosphere with excellent personal service and a wide range of merchandise...the store drew shoppers from the city as well as from the growing "streetcar suburbs." Once at the store, consumers could do more than just shop. Jordan Marsh offered fashion shows, a bakery famous for its blueberry muffins, art exhibitions, even afternoon concerts.

Mass Moments-
www.massmoments.org

flawlessly dressed family of five believing they were fairly well off. For Rita, it meant she was in the running, not the orphan teen left behind, not the bride "in trouble," but the lovely lady her mother intended. Just like her older sisters, Rosemary and Kay.

And even though it was a bit of a walk, across the Common and past the Public Garden, Rita always went to Newbury Street first. "We don't want to look like ragamuffins carrying bargain basement bags all over Boston," she explained to Ruth Ann.

Each and every time, the self-respecting wife and mother approached her shopping experience with great care and tactical planning. She instructed her daughter, "Being properly dressed is a must, if you want the salesladies to treat you well." Rita would never think of going downtown without wearing high-heels, gloves, and most times, a suitable hat.

This morning, with or without her husband's approval, Rita Donnelly would soon be off to enjoy what she considered the equivalent of a vacation on the Irish Riviera, Scituate, Massachusetts, shopping with only one child at her side.

As usual, New England's fickle autumn weather bordered winter with pleasant Indian summer one day, bone-chilling wind and overcast skies the next, or a sudden rainstorm. And Rita couldn't quite decide which coat to wear. *The raincoat is out, too ordinary, and my navy boucle still looks nice but not nearly as good as Rosemary's red coat.* She would forever refer to it that way. *Then again, I can't stand being too warm, but the red's so sophisticated. No, I'll wear the navy.*

It was almost noon when Rita and Ruth Ann glanced up at what the young mother considered to be the prettiest store window she had ever seen on Newbury Street.

Suspended in the center of the oversized bay—giving it the look of an enormous work of art—was a harvest-gold tablecloth, bordered with pumpkins, curly vines, acorns, and autumn leaves. A walnut sideboard featured a folded damask tablecloth on the diagonal, topped with pewter candlesticks and three hurricane lamps, each with fall-colored tapers. A variety of small gifts were artfully arranged in front of them, while a few decorative pillows were on point at the foot of the piece.

Directly opposite, an antique breakfront with scalloped carving was lavishly filled with French faience, ivory-colored dishes; cups dangled from top shelf hooks, and saucers beneath them were propped against the backboard, as were dinner plates on the next shelf down. A bounty of gourds filled a cornucopia at one end of the buffet top, while fanned white and ivory napkins spilled out of drawers and stacks of coordinating linens filled the open shelves below.

Both pieces of furniture held huge, informal, fresh flower arrangements. And whimsically displayed in the middle of the window, on what looked to Rita like a small farm chair, *of all things,* with its rush seat, were matching mother-daughter aprons in pure white. She took Ruth Ann by the hand. "Let's go inside." They gleefully ascended the stairway to Chandler's Linens, for the very first time.

As soon as Rita opened the door, every one of her senses met with something enjoyable: a fresh scent somewhere between clean laundry, honeysuckle and pine; pleasing colors and elegant textures could be seen high and low, mostly in creams and whites, a bit of blue, yellow, red, and green, and dashes of black. One of two shelved armoires, what Rita called a "wardrobe," was filled with pastel merchandise: crisp linens, fluffy towels, silky pajamas, lavender sachets, pink and blue baby sweaters, as well as petite nursery music boxes with doorknob-sized, ribbon loops. One was winding down *"Frere Jacques."*

Ruth Ann pointed, "Look, Mummy."

The child was quietly but sternly chastised by her mother. "For the hundredth time, it's impolite to point. Do it again and you'll be very sorry."

The furniture, cabinets, and display cases were primarily higher end, but a small pine table and three chairs in the corner reminded Rita of those in storybooks she read to her children, something Hansel and Gretel would sit in. She remembered the chair in the window and suddenly realized, *oh, this is all part of a cute set.*

The table's top held kitchen items: big bars of Savon de Marseille soap; tea towels; crocheted, blue onion storage bags; sel and poivre shakers; and two French book titles, one for cooking, the other, housekeeping. The chamber music was soothing and, at the same time, cheerful, while the middle-aged male clerk's "Welcome to Chandler's" was stuffy, but nonetheless engaging, even though he sashayed directly towards the back room, straightening this and that along the way. "Someone will be with you shortly, madam." Rita had heard her husband refer to men like this as "light in the loafers."

In Chandler's Linen Shoppe the sales clerks had a tendency to hold their chins high while looking down their noses, but graciousness still prevailed. A pleasantly reserved saleslady close to Rita's own age invited Rita and her daughter to sit on the French provincial sofa and offered to bring them refreshments. It was more attention than the "just browsing" shopper anticipated or even wanted, but before she knew it the saleslady asked, "May I get you a cup of tea or coffee and perhaps some milk for the little girl?"

Rita, who knew how to hold her chin up too, replied, "Tea, thank you, and can my daughter please have her milk in a teacup?"

Rita caught the woman's name when a willowy salesgirl glided up. "Pardon me, please."

It has often been asked, "How in the world did so many poor Irish immigrants ever come up with such distinctively good taste and proper manners?"

The Bridgets and Kathleens, Norahs and Marys certainly learned about "behavin' in a suitable manner" back in Ireland, but they closely observed the way things were done in the homes of their affluent American employers. It was an acclimating standard of measure, diligently applied to the best of their emulating ability, in the way they made a home, spoke, dressed, addressed, conducted themselves, and raised a family.

Never forsaking their Irish pride and traditions, and forever faithful to the Roman Catholic Church.

She softly inquired, "Miss Cordelia, did you want those schiffli pillowcases stacked on the shelf or hanging up in the armoire?"

Ruth Ann felt so grown up in these downtown situations and carefully followed her mother's every lead. Rita had the most elegant way of removing her gloves, each fingertip pulled just a bit as her green eyes perused the store, a look down, then all glove fingers were gathered and pulled off ever so deftly, both gloves held in one hand for just an instant before being placed in her imitation Grace Kelly pocketbook. The clasp had a crisp snap that her daughter never forgot; click open, crisp snap closed. Ruth Ann did the same and tucked her own gloves into a plaid, Scotty-dog shoulder bag, which she put down beside her mother's pocketbook.

Before adding sugar and milk to her tea, Rita removed two spoonfuls from her teacup, stirred them into Ruth Ann's milk, and added sugar too, exactly as they did at home, to the seven-year-old's delight. "Tea with milk for Mummy, and milk with tea for me—milk tea."

"That's a little lady in training you have there," the male clerk commented.

And an older saleslady cordially chimed in, "Isn't she cunning, remembering to place the napkin on her lap like that?"

Rita wasn't completely comfortable, thinking maybe she was in over her head this time. *God help us, it's a whole new ballgame. Sitting down with refreshments?*

However, she was her mother's daughter and had been taught gracious deportment and self-respect repeatedly from a young age. "Sure and your standin' in society has less to do with money and everythin' to do with the manner in which you conduct yourself—if you act like a lady, you'll be treated like one. Remember that darlin', and you'll get along fine in this world, not havin' to kowtow to anyone."

Store manager Cordelia Parker observed something very sweet and confident about the way the well-put-together mother proceeded. *Not your typical harried young mother by any means. And the child appears to be quite content. Lovely.*

All of this took place while a parade of fine, Swiss, high-count cotton sheets were being presented to Rita. She'd sip her tea, look up, sit back, and enjoy, and decline the purchase, but not for lack of interest. "Yes, they're very soft, and the faggoting is nice," she said. "I'm just not sure I need them."—The cost was equal to one week of her husband's salary. She chose instead two surprisingly affordable French linen guest towels, which the older saleslady touted as "a charming addition to any bath, particularly when one is entertaining."

Ruth Ann tugged on her mother's sleeve.

Rita said, "Excuse me, please," and bent her ear toward the fidgety youngster.

Cordelia took the towel treasures, "an excellent selection," into the back room for packaging, and Ruth Ann slowly followed her with a detour to the powder room. Never once was it called the bathroom, lady's room, rest room or God forbid, lavatory. In Chandler's Linens, it was "the powder room," and situated directly on the other side of one of its walls were the wrapping desk and a kitchenette, where associates prepared their own simple lunches and hot tea or coffee trays for the clientele.

And it was in the powder room of Chandler's Linens, with whisper-yellow striped wallpaper, four pale green, moiré-matted botanical prints on the far wall, a pedestal sink, round, burnished gold mirror hanging above it, brass sconces on either side, each with a celadon, C-embroidered, off-white silk shade, which cast a soft glow on everything—it was in that beautiful golden room Ruth Ann first became aware of an ugly reality. In some circles of 1950s Boston, being Irish might be considered less than. She could hear almost everything said on the other side and impishly tried to hear more.

With her right hand cupped around one ear (a trick she'd learned from the O'Day sisters), which was up against the wall, requiring the curious child to lean over a small, double-tiered, towel-laden, bamboo table, Ruth Ann did her best to make out what the lady was saying in between the rustling of associates packaging and moving things about.

R. H. Stearns & Co.
140 Tremont Street,
BOSTON, MASS.

Although Florence Morton's speech had a gentle tone, some of her words were startlingly harsh.

"About that customer with the little girl, when I suggested perhaps she'd like to have those towels monogrammed and asked what letter would suit her surname, she very proudly said, 'D for Donnelly, but no, thank you. I like them just the way they are.' It takes a lot of nerve for someone that Irish to walk into an establishment of this caliber and act like she belongs. There was a time in this city when people knew their place." Rita's classic colleen coloring—auburn hair, emerald eyes and the fairest of complexions—was a dead giveaway to her Celtic roots, something a person of Flo Morton's ilk took to task. "Donnelly" only added fuel to the fire.

The uppity saleslady held old guard Yankee families in the highest esteem. All others were secondary at best, unless they were people of means. "She's not shanty Irish. It's obvious she has some class, like Grace Kelly or the Kennedy's, but . . . "

At age nineteen, pretty Stella Florence Sippi, of light skinned Northern Italian descent, gained an English surname from a regrettable marriage. She kept her husband's Morton moniker after the annulment, seeing it as a chance to be "more Boston mainstream. Mama. Flo Morton is better for my new job at Stearn's. Who's going to listen to Stella Sippi when it comes to advising rich people about expensive clothing?"

If only Florence Morton knew the classy lady before her currently waited tables two nights a week at Steuben's on Boylston Street—only a stone's throw away from Chandler's.

Ruth Ann lost her tiptoe footing and almost knocked the table over but regained balance and once again cupped her ear. She heard the nice lady, Miss Cordelia say, "Oh for goodness sake, Flo. I like her spunk and the way she attends to the child. Let's give Mrs. Donnelly one of these lemon guest soaps, say it's a gift for her little girl."

To which Flo Morton sighed. "Poor thing," she said, "crossed eyes, glasses, and Irish to boot."

As young as she was, Ruth Ann knew her eyes were unattractive, but she always thought it was a special gift from God to be an Irish girl, because that's what every adult in her family had led her to believe. "Sure and the angels kissed you because you're Irish and left those darlin' dimples as the proof."

Rita and Ruth Ann had gathered their pocketbooks and put on their gloves. Miss Cordelia handed Mrs. Donnelly her prettily packaged purchase, wrapped in tissue and placed in one of the store's signature dark blue bags, Chandler's Linens scrolled across the middle in ecru script with their simple, bow-tied, wheat-sheave logo centered beneath it. Next Cordelia presented a jonquil yellow drawstring sachet bag to Ruth Ann. "You've been so good," she told her. "It's a miniature soap just for you."

In her haste to receive it, the child dropped the delicate item and apprehensively looked at her mother, but before Rita could say a thing, Cordelia stooped down and handed it back. "It was an accident, honey. Look. It's fine."

Ruth Ann peeked inside. "Thank you."

Rita looked at her watch. "Oh, we have to get going. Thank you."

Cordelia held the front door open, and just as mother and daughter approached the stairway, Ruth Ann ran back and hugged her. "Thank you for my present."

This caught the woman, who spent very little, if any, time with children, completely off guard, but not so much that she didn't speak what she'd been thinking. "You're welcome, dear, and Mrs. Donnelly, I hope you'll both visit us again, soon."

"You can plan on it, Miss Cordelia."

RUTH ANN REMEMBERS
FILENE'S BASEMENT

I have written this song, for you to take with you when you go away
Something to sing and slowly swing to on your colder days . . .
"DIAMOND DAYS"
JIMMY MACCARTHY

EVEN THOUGH IT HAD BEEN almost fifty years, instinctively my hand went toward the sturdy metal railing of Boston's famous Filene's Basement at Washington and Summer Streets.

At first, I simply stood at the top of that stairway, stared, and remembered. When I was ready to take the first step down, one leather-gloved hand held the rail tightly, but my heart held on with a little girl's mitten. The other hand gripped my shoulder bag strap, but reached back through time for maternal protection. I remembered how firmly my mother would hold my one bare hand, mitten off for a better grasp, when we went down those same steep stairs all those years ago.

"Ruth Ann, leave that other mitten on. I don't want you getting germs from the railing, and don't let go of my hand, no matter what."

These were her carefully laid battle plans for the bargain hunter's combat at Filenes' famous month-end sales, where wise women always brought an ally. Even if the ally was only a child.

It was my job to guard whatever bargains Filene's held that day for the invading forces of my mother's good taste and her talent for finding the very best for the very least. I could be depended on to follow orders because I really loved to please my mother. I felt so grown up when she saw me as capable, almost her peer, and trusted me to guard bounty collected for consideration and placed in my arms. "Don't let go of this angora sweater . . . tweed skirt . . . adorable baby blanket . . . shirt for daddy . . . shoes for your brother."

Once, I actually saw a bargain basement confrontation between my mother and another woman who was after the same baby-blue, pullover, wool sweater that sat atop a pile of cardigans and crewnecks on a giant square table. In short, my mother reached for the sweater and the other woman did too, a beat behind her. They both tugged. My mother said something like, "I had it first, and I think you know that."

The other woman pulled. "I'd say we both have it now."

My mother gave her a look that meant business, and the other woman let go. Right away, it was handed to me for safekeeping. My mother offered to help the woman find another and pulled a melon-colored duplicate out. "With your pretty olive skin, this will be much nicer."

The woman gladly took it. "Thanks, sister. You're okay."

Later, my father heard the whole story at the supper table and got my mother's bottom line. "I wasn't about to let that grabby guinea take it away from me."

Although shopping meant spending, my mother had a "less is more" sensibility. "Better a few good pieces than a lot of cheap choices" was her strategy and timeless advice that came straight from her own mother, the grandmother I never knew. Norah King.

But what I remember best and with great joy is how I would anticipate and delight in my mother's consultations when she'd say things like, "What do you think, Ruth Ann? Would Aunt Marion like these slippers for when she goes to the hospital to have the new baby? Should we get them for her?"

This afternoon, five decades later and two weeks before Christmas, my Grammy McDonough's long-ago Irish blessing was being fulfilled. "May your eyes see today what your heart needs to hold for tomorrow."

I really could see the two of us, mother and daughter, frozen in time: me, blue eyes peeking out of tortoise shell glasses, and Toni permanent, tightly curled, red hair trying to escape from beneath a brown beret, while a double-breasted, tan, wool boy coat "with lots of growing room" kept me warm, and cabled, green knee socks, held up by rubber bands carefully hidden beneath a top fold, covered my pale, freckled skinny legs. Sensible, brown, Catholic-school-uniform oxfords completed that autumn, "your most flattering colors, Ruth Ann," outfit and practically all of it had been purchased in Filene's Basement.

And I saw Mummy as she was in the 1950s: young, radiantly beautiful, wearing her favorite coat—its vibrant red color quickly led me to her side if we got separated—seamed stockings, high heels, and gloves. I saw her wavy, auburn, cap-cut hairdo and stylish felt hat kept in place with hidden, sewn-in combs, and her latest "steal," gracefully carried on her right arm, a black leather pocketbook styled "just like Grace Kelly's."

Women dressed up to go downtown in those days, even if they were only shopping in the bargain basement, which was, without question, our very last stop before going home because, as my mother used to say, "We don't want to look like ragamuffins carrying bargain bags all over the city of Boston." The reverse was just as true. She was proud to carry an uptown bag around town, and in Filene's Basement it gave her the look of someone who could afford to buy anything but chose to shop for bargains. She loved every minute of this type of day, and so did I.

Presently, after a quick look around Filene's Basement, I came up and out of that place of the past empty-handed, but filled with memories of what would have come next: our happy train ride home, when my mother would go over her successful shopping strategies and peruse every purchase without taking them all the way out of the bags at the risk of looking "common."

Soon the increased din of holiday crowds, piped music, downtown traffic, and a man leaning against the building and playing guitar while his tambourine-tapping partner sang a folk tune, brought me back.

Although the world is a much different place today, many downtown Boston sights and sounds are the same as they were the in the 1950s, with a cacophony of car horns and the discord of disgruntled drivers; grinding gears in big trucks maneuvering small spaces; wheezing, squeaking buses coming to a stop, and the reverberating vroom-vroom as they pull away from the curb; the booming orders of seemingly choreographed traffic cops as they shout, blow shrill whistles, and spin this way and that in the middle of busy intersections, their directive arms turning like windmills, or a single hand commanding, "Stop!" The conversational buzz of passersby; an occasional solitary whistler, or impassioned street orator; and the characteristic click of women's high-heeled shoes, although much more then than today. In the fifties, women didn't change into comfortable sneakers to get across town; they suffered blisters, bunions, corns, sore feet, and aching backs in order to look suitably stylish.

Some high-heeled clicks sounded confidently paced, while others went click-click-click in rapid succession, perhaps the footsteps of those rushing back to work from lunch or mothers running to catch the next train home in time for their returning schoolchildren, or maybe, like my Grammy, they were purposeful, task-oriented women, who simply moved quickly no matter the circumstance or time of day. I am my Grammy's girl with a pace that forces me to politely hold back in order to keep company.

But as a child, I loved to walk precisely in step with my mother. When her high-heeled feet moved forward, my small feet, in their sensible oxfords, imitated Mummy's more feminine steps, click-click, not fast, not slow, simply wonderful.

CHAPTER 32

He simply went to a place in my heart that was waiting for him.

KING'S ROW

HENRY BELLAMANN

ALONG THE WAY, THERE'D CERTAINLY been suitable young men for Miss Cordelia Parker to date, and she'd enjoyed their company, but no one of any consequence. Then good-looking, friendly Officer Donnelly came along with his attentive greetings, compliments, and inquiries after her wellbeing or possible need for some assistance. *Ashamedly,* she'd consider, *I find myself somewhat attracted to this married man.* There was absolutely no doubt in her mind about his attraction to her, especially the night of a nearby burglary.

The perpetrator was still at large, and Officer Donnelly knocked on her front door to advise, "Batten down the hatches," as he braced himself against the cold and rubbed his gloved hands together, "California Here I Come!" His warm, exhaled breath blew a hazy cloud of condensation between them. "That thief has to be an Eskimo. Who else but working stiffs like me would come out on a night like this?"

"Please, come stand by the fire for a minute," Cordelia said.

Officer Donnelly gratefully accepted her invitation and swiftly stepped over the line between outside and in. "Quite a place you have here. Thanks for giving me a chance to defrost." He removed his hat and calmly toyed with the brim.

"You're more than welcome, Officer. Now, may I get you something hot to drink? Tea, coffee, cocoa? Surely a bit of brandy would warm you up, but I'm fairly certain that must be against regulation. Is it, Officer?" She placed a bookmark between the pages of the novel she'd been reading and held it close to her like a schoolbook. "Against regulation to have a quick brandy on a glacial night such as this?"

Contrary to the presumed innuendoes the hopeful officer was picking up, Cordelia was completely guileless. She would never speak in such vaguely vulgar terms, even if her hospitable intentions had been less than honorable. And besides that, she was a sore sight for good eyes with large horn-rimmed reading glasses perched at the end of her nose, washed hair wrapped up in a towel, baggy, tan slacks, a white turtleneck under a big, loden-green, corduroy shirt her brother left behind, fuzzy socks and tatty brown velvet slippers that kept her feet toasty—hardly the togs of a would-be temptress.

However, Officer Donnelly did like the clean scent of Cordelia's Breck Shampoo and found her clothing disarray cozily appealing. "If you'll pardon my saying so, Miss Parker, that's some kind of get-up you're wearing, but on you it looks good."

Much to the wily officer's surprise and disappointment, Cordelia promptly opened the parlor drapes and turned on every lamp in the room, should any nosy neighbor or pedestrian (highly unlikely on such a wickedly cold night) get the wrong impression. *But one never knows.*

Officer Donnelly stood in plain sight before the grand fireplace's roaring flames. *Thought I had this single gal pegged.*

Cordelia stayed by the window and inquired again, "Tea, coffee, cocoa?" *Good heavens, he's a handsome man, and one might wonder why a law enforcement officer needs to wear what I detect is aftershave on the job.*

But all of this was before David Miller.

⚮

Cordelia was a changed person and practically everyone in her circle of friends, associates and acquaintances noticed the difference.

Abigail Adams Dubois Chandler: "Cappy, you were beginning to look eerily like our mothers with your chignon. Those come-hither, soft waves do you enormous justice."

Hilda: "Miss Cordelia, it's good to see you gardening again. We've been too long without the happiness of tulips and daffodils and irises."

Florence Morton: "Miss Parker, I recall when you purchased a diaphanous, periwinkle formal at Stearn's for a college dance. Whatever you're using for face cream, it's as if the clock has been turned back."

Eleanor Brewster: "Cordelia, you have the air of a lady in love. Sinclair and I have a wager. If I win, we'll go to Locke-Ober for dinner. If not, let's just say, it will be a romantic dinner at home. Intuition tells me we'll be dining out."

An article in the Boston Evening Transcript had touted: "In the Locke-Ober Café, one beholds the last bulwark of the ancien regime. Here for more than half a century wit and wine have mingled with the finest creations of culinary art and as the pageant of the years has passed Locke-Ober has come to mean more than just another eating-place. It has veritably become a high and holy temple of fine living."

Maury Sylvester of Pride & Joy Deli: "Miss, ya's look terrific. If I was thirty years younger—hope you're not insulted by that."

Cordelia's change for the best didn't escape Officer Donnelly's attention either. "Good morning, Miss Parker. That's quite a becoming outfit. In my neck of the woods they'd say," he continued with an Irish brogue, "that striking young woman's the look of a movie star."

There was a time when a relatively forward remark such as this would have offended Cordelia's sense of propriety. But with the personal losses she'd experienced these last few years, and seemingly inevitable spinsterhood, words such as "the look of a movie star" had the potential to reel her lonely heart in with a slithery bit of flattery.

Flattery was Officer Donnelly's forte, although not entirely insincere. He truly enjoyed encouraging others. And when it came to attractive young women, he pulled out all the stops.

It had happened so fast. There was that "magical shared pot of tea with Mr. Miller," his missed presence the next morning, and her first note from "David." At the end of the same day, they literally bumped into each other in the kitchen doorway, one coming, and the other going.

"I'm so sorry," David Miller's hands lightly touched Cordelia Parker's arms and let go again. "Please, excuse a man who hasn't had a thing to eat all day. I thought I'd get in an hour or so of study before grabbing a bite somewhere, but hunger got the best of me and I'm afraid you got right in the line of fire."

"Don't give it a second thought." Cordelia hadn't remembered his eyes being quite that brown. *And they're kind eyes. He'll make an excellent physician.* "Enjoy your dinner, Mr. Miller."

"Thank you, Miss Parker. I'd better be on my way. Got a big exam tomorrow, and I need to get back."

Cordelia wasn't in the kitchen two minutes before the future doctor appeared before her, his topcoat and knit muffler in hand. "Say, you wouldn't consider joining me, would you?"

"Whatever for?" As soon as the words were out of her mouth, Cordelia regretted saying them. "I mean, Mr. Miller," she began to straighten chairs around the kitchen table, "to what do I owe this impetuous invitation?" And she gave him a shy smile.

He lined up the chairs on his side of the table, having been responsible for their disorder with his temporary sorting system. Papers rested on every seat, some flew to the floor, and as he came up from collecting them he answered, "I just wanted to thank you for saving me from catching pneumonia last night. All that hot tea drowned out any possibility."

"Very well. On that basis, I'm happy to accept." *Oh my, is this wise of you, Cordelia?* She once again took notice of David Miller's cocoa-brown eyes. *For heaven's sake, it's only a quick supper.*

It was anything but, with Cordelia halfheartedly suggesting a couple of times they'd better leave the restaurant soon so he could get back to his books, and David ardently reassuring her he had a fairly good grasp on his knowledge of the respiratory system. "And I can get by with four hours of sleep. So that still leaves plenty of time to brush up later."

However, the waitress was a little huffy about their lingering. "You two gettin' anythin' else to eat or are you gonna start payin' rent on this table?" That's the way it was with every server at Durgin Park. Customers came in for the best traditional New England fare in town, knowing that sarcasm, barbs, and impatience were to be expected too. They'd have been disappointed if it were any other way. Those bristly remarks were made in good humor, and the savvy waitress proposed, "Tell you what, order dessert, and the wisecracks stop here. Deal?"

Harriett Mullins had seen a hundred couples just like them, young—well, these two weren't as young as some, she'd guess late twenties for her, early thirties for him. First, maybe second date, stars in their eyes at the discovery of a kindred spirit, and before she knew it, people like them were coming back as a Mr. and Mrs. and recalling the last time they'd seen her. Even when she didn't remember them, Harriett cheekily pretended to. "Maybe you'll leave me a better tip this time."

Menu in hand, David asked Cordelia, "Trust me?" and when she answered, "Yes, of course," Harriet chimed in. "When you two have completed your marriage vows, I'll be happy to take your dessert order."

Cordelia blushed, and he ordered, "Two home-style apple pies a la mode, please, and two hot teas, milk for the lady's and honey for mine."

"Comin' right up, Romeo."

David told Cordelia all about his family in New York, that he was the youngest of three children, two boys and a girl. The oldest, Michael, was a highly successful manufacturer of women's clothing, and his sister, Beth, a former schoolteacher, managed her husband's law practice. His parents and ninety-year-old grandmother still lived in the Brooklyn row house where he'd grown up. Both of his siblings now made their homes in New Rochelle, which his textile-salesman father referred to as "New Rich-chelle." David went on to say he tried to get home as often as he could because his parents didn't travel even to nearby Boston.

She spoke not of her family but of Chandler's Linens, with one exception. Cordelia said no female relative of hers had ever had a paying job, choosing instead to give of their time to charitable and cultural endeavors. She was the first.

"Frankly, I enjoy working. My employer is an old friend, and due to domestic responsibilities she's virtually turned the reins over to me. The store feels as though it's my own. Our staff is extraordinary. We couldn't ask for better." Cordelia was animated as she described them and sang praises of each one's contribution to the success of what was deemed in *The Boston Globe* as, "the Hub's best source of fine European linens and gifts with an abundance of French chic and pinch of whimsy." Chandler's received glowing reviews throughout the city, much to the annoyance of local competitors, upscale Howell Brothers and Makana, in particular.

David never anticipated Cordelia would be this chatty. Surely he'd made an accurate observation of her personality: *Proper Bostonian, somewhat straight-laced and tight-lipped, social yet private, and extremely attentive to household details, décor, maintenance and parameters for tenants.* But here they were, and his expectation that she'd give yes and no answers with one eye on the clock was completely off the mark. Clock? It was apparent neither one of them wanted the evening to end.

The walk home was brisk because the weather was nippy, but moreso because Cordelia never waned in her concern for David's studies.

"Now, Mr. Miller, I don't want to be responsible for you failing that exam. I hope you're still energetic enough to concentrate."

"Definitely. I feel a second wind coming on as we speak. Oh, here we are already." He reached behind her and unlatched the black iron gate. "After you, Miss Parker."

Richard Malmgren heard the pleasant cadence of their conversation outside his window and stealthily pushed the shade aside to see who it could possibly be at this late hour on a weeknight. The sight of Miss Parker and David Miller, together, caught him completely off guard, and try as he may, the introverted dental student couldn't quite comprehend that his landlady and fellow tenant had connected on a more personal level. *Boy, oh boy, I sure didn't see that coming.*

David took his key out of his pocket to open the door, and Cordelia felt somewhat awkward. This was, after all, her house. It was all so confusing—her house, yet he lived there, and now . . . *What is happening between us?*

Sensing her discomfort, David measured his steps by not getting too close, lest she think he was going to make a pass. *I don't want to do anything to jeopardize our new friendship. Who am I kidding? I don't want to do anything to scare this wonderful girl away.* Then, more abruptly than intended, he bid her, "Good night, Miss Parker," and headed pell-mell for his books and papers strewn across the kitchen table.

"Oh, Mr. Miller," she called after him, the color of her cheeks high from the cold of night, giving her the look of a fairy tale maiden, wisps of her ash-blonde locks breaking loose from their pulled back austerity and blue eyes sparkling. "I've been meaning to ask if you and Mr. Malmgren wouldn't mind calling me Cordelia. We are after all not that far apart in age, and Miss Parker does seem a tad formal."

The fatigued medical student (he'd stretched the truth about getting by on four or five hours of sleep) felt hopeful. *She wants to be called by her first name.* He rolled it around in his heart, as he'd done since the day they met: *Cordelia.*

"Miss Parker, only if you'll please feel free to call me David."

"David it is, and one day I trust Doctor will be in order."

David Miller surprised himself when he walked toward her and said, "Let's shake on it."

"Shake on it?" she asked with a slow grin. She met him halfway and gladly extended her hand. "Absolutely."

CHAPTER 33

A young lady is a female child who has just done something dreadful.
JUDITH MARTIN, A.K.A. MISS MANNERS

SISTER CATHERINE ALOYSIUS SOUNDED THE wooden clicker twice, signaling an all-stand-at-once command. "Girls in one line, please, boys in the other." The clicker was a small, pocket-sized device that directed the children to uniform perfection. Click; they stood when an adult entered the room. Click; a curtsey for the girls and bow for the boys. Click; be seated. Click; kneel for prayer. Click-click-click directed their steps and reined in their would-be antics. Sister promptly lined up her charges and pulled a package of Necco Wafers candy from within the soft-pocketed folds of her flowing, black habit.

The second grade class of seven-year-olds before her would soon practice receiving a Communion wafer with the thin, sugary pastel discs. When Sister Catherine brought out the package, not one of them was thinking of Christ. Ruth Ann Donnelly hoped she'd get a yellow one, while the girl next to her, Barbara McDermott, was wishing for pink. "All right, children, we'll have another go round. It's only the four or so weeks away now."

The Dublin-born Sister was preparing her students for First Communion and shaking the wrapped candy roll like a pointer. "It's the body of Christ Himself you'll be receivin' when you make your First Holy Communion, and your souls must be free from sin in order to receive the Son of God. Father Mulcahy and Father Ahern will be hearin' your confessions Saturday noon before the big day."

All eyes were fixed on the Necco Wafers.

What the Very Young Need to Know for Their First Holy Communion by the Most Reverend Louis La Ravoire Morrow

Sister walked closer to the children, and the wooden beads around her waist bumped up against a desk as she leaned toward them. "You can't keep secrets from Almighty God, boys and girls, and if you ever try to take Communion without having first confessed all your sins, well, let me just say this." She shook her slightly crooked, arthritic finger. "There once was a girl who tried to do that very thing, and when she opened her mouth to receive the Host," Sister had their rapt attention, "the priest gasped in horror. Her tongue, like her sinful soul was black!" Sister Catherine stood up straight and the beads bumped again. "I'm sure you don't want the same thing happening to you, so confess all your sins, say your penance, and never, never go to Communion without having done so."

Much to the wide-eyed children's disappointment, she put the Necco Wafers down on her desk and proceeded to instruct them yet again in how to give a proper confession, beginning with, as the good Sister cautioned, "goin' to your knees." A double click, and they all knelt, Sister Catherine as well. Click; thirty-eight right hands made the sign of the cross and prayed aloud, "Bless me Father for I have sinned, it has been . . . since my last confession." They continued to follow her lead with a measured recitation of the Act of Contrition, after which the watchful Sister imparted one more admonition.

"Kneel straight up. Don't have your wee bums resting on your feet in the Protestant way. Remember now, you're kneeling before the King of Kings." The children glanced sideways at each other and softly snickered at her use of the word "bums."

"We've one more thing to tend to before your practice Communion. Now, please return to your seats in an orderly manner."

There was a low murmur of disappointment.

"Open your Catechisms, please. And take five minutes to look it over before I quiz the lot of you."

Sister Catherine Aloysius, fresh-faced with an even disposition, the Sister whose students, past and present, called their favorite, couldn't help but grin at the whole earnest "bunch." Oh, how she loved the innocence, eagerness, and

An Act of Contrition

O my God, I am heartily sorry for having offended Thee, and I detest all my sins, because I dread the loss of heaven, and the pains of hell; but most of all because they offend Thee, my God, Who are all good and deserving of all my love. I firmly resolve, with the help of Thy grace, to confess my sins, to do penance, and to amend my life. Amen

sweetness of their burgeoning faith. These were the children Jesus talked about. *Unless you be as a little child you cannot enter the kingdom of heaven.* If it was up to her, and presently it was, every one of these little angels would fear the consequences of sin and love the Son of God.

Sister devoutly picked up a copy of the Baltimore Catechism and for a split second reassuringly patted her habit's other pocket, which held illustrated holy cards of the Sacred Heart and revered saints and small, oval Blessed Mother medals for those who answered correctly.

"Tell me now children." She read directly from the text, "What is necessary to receive Holy Communion worthily?"

The boys and girls raised and waved their hands, calling out, "Sister, Sister!" sometimes it was reduced to "Ssss," which was never recognized, other than for chastisement. Donny Roche, an A-student, cocky and stocky, dark haired, his Sacred Heart red and navy striped tie off center and poorly knotted, was the first to be called on. "Please stand, Donald."

"To receive Holy Communion worthily, it is necessary: to be free from mortal sin, to be fasting from midnight, and to have a good intention."

Sister rewarded his answer with a holy card of Saint Lawrence, martyr. "A bright boy like yourself, Donald, and beloved by all for his sacrifice and humility. Very good. You may be seated. Next question. Tell me, children, what is prayer?"

Judith Dolan, the shyest girl in the class, who only had her hand up halfway, was called upon next. She slid out of her seat, and her head was down as well as her voice.

"'What is prayer?'" She grasped the skirt of her navy-blue uniform, raised only her eyes and stated the answer as a question. "Prayer is speaking lovingly to God?"

"That's right, Judith, dear." Sister approached the slight girl with a Blessed Mother medal and pinned it on her uniform with the attached tiny, gold safety pin. "And you'll want to be holdin' that pretty head up and mind your posture while you're at it. You're a daughter of the King and must carry yourself as such. You may be seated."

The class's saving grace came right in the midst of it all when Mother Superior walked in the room with a memo, spotted the Necco Wafers and offered to help give the children Communion. Before proceeding, Mother Superior had a thing or two to say about receiving the body of Christ. "Heaven forbid you don't open your mouth wide enough, or put your tongue out far enough, and God's one and only Son fall down, in the direction of hell, from which He has saved us all."

◦≫◦

It had been an eventful last few months in the Donnelly household.

Christmas was good. The older children got what they'd asked Santa for. A Toni doll with black hair for Ruth Ann, and a red wagon and Tinker Toys for Bobby. Baby Catherine was more content to play with empty boxes than the gifts that came in them.

Rita and Bob kicked off the New Year with a rare night out. Her brother Johnny and his wife, Marion, had a party, and many of the officers from Station 3 and their wives went too. The Donnelly children were safely tucked in at Grammy's, where they fell fast asleep to the Windsor chime of church bells and woke up the next morning when Mrs. Mac's cocker spaniel, Blackie, jumped up on the bed.

But by mid-January, as Bob so aptly described it, "all hell broke loose."

Rita was changing the baby's diaper, and mischievous, freckle-faced, ever-grinning, seldom-stopping Bobby, with a cowlick sticking up on the crown of his head like a feather (Rita affectionately called him "my wild Indian") noted his mother's distraction, snatched a knife from the silverware drawer, tried to pry the top off a can of hard candies, slipped, and made a gash in his leg, requiring a trip to the hospital, stitches, and cash payment.

February held a preplanned medical expense, Ruth Ann's corrective surgery for her crossed eyes, but a week before her hospitalization the insurance company pulled back coverage due to the "corrective aspect," evaluating the often-ineffective surgery as fairly frivolous. "The child's vision is still good."

Rita and Bob went ahead as planned, and the operation was a success, but the drain on family finances almost stretched them to the limit.

In March, one of the neighbors spotted "a huge rat" in the cellar, and in a panic, Rita hid tiny red squares of rat poison in the back corners of all the apartment's closets. She was busily dust-mopping the hallway one morning when Catherine toddled up, and her scarlet mouth said it all. Hospital, stomach pumped, the last dollars, and final straw. Or so it seemed.

April brought showers of First Communion dresses. Filene's, Jordan's, Gilchrist's, and several other downtown stores were well-stocked and ready for business, while in Jamaica Plain, the second-grade girls at Blessed Sacrament School excitedly asked each other, "Do you have your dress yet?"

But the cash Rita and Bob had been putting aside for this very time was gone. Medical expenses took every penny, including Rita's secret stash. But she came up with a plan.

"Jesus, Mary, and Joseph! You pawned your wedding ring!"

"Not my wedding ring. See, the band is right here, my engagement ring."

"Oh, excuse me, your engagement ring."

She despised the sarcastic tone Bob was using.

"God Almighty, Rita, I gave you all the money I could spare for her First Communion outfit. What happened?"

"Plain and simple, Bob. It wasn't enough for everything she needed."

He disliked the way his wife held her own when they argued, and on a certain level considered it disrespectful. He was, after all, the man of the house.

"Wait a minute. I can't believe you of all people couldn't make that amount work?"

"Of course I could, if I wanted to buy her the lowest-priced dress on the rack. It looked cheap, and the veils were even worse. Filene's Basement doesn't have a thing. Communion clothes won't be there until the end of next month, when it's all over."

"Forget it, Rita. All that matters to me is that you pawned your goddam wedding ring."

"We'll get it back. They gave me six months." Rita's eyes glistened. "It's all I could think to do. I don't want to be embarrassed, I don't want you to be embarrassed, and I certainly don't want our daughter to be embarrassed. We get one shot at this, honey, and I want to give it our best. I haven't spent a penny yet. I wanted to talk to you first." She regained her composure and raised her voice. "And don't you ever call it a goddam wedding ring again."

Bob's eyes narrowed to a pensive slit, closed as he shook his head, and opened again. "What the hell." He took his petite wife in his brawny arms and, against her initial resistance, held on tightly. "I'll ask around the station about extra details. One of the fellas said he got work moonlighting in a meat packing plant. You'll have your," he hesitated, "diamond ring sooner than six months."

Rita lightly kissed his chest, and he pushed her away from him just far enough to see her face. "You and Ruth Ann better go into town tomorrow and get this taken care of. Let me worry about the rest."

The time had finally arrived to actually buy the First Communion dress. The whole family knew. Grammy and even Aunt Kay offered to go along and help with the selection, but Rita said, "Thanks anyway. I think we'll be fine."

This shopping trip, there would be no first stop on Newbury. The ecstatic mother and daughter went straight to Jordan's. It was easy. Rita knew just the style of dress she wanted, and Ruth Ann thought all of them were pretty. "Mummy, look at this one."

As Rita readied her child for "the most important day of your life" and examined rounders and racks of dresses and veils, she strongly felt the presence of her mother, Norah, in the memory of her own First Communion.

It had been the height of the Great Depression, and yet every boy and girl who walked down the aisle at Gate of Heaven Church was dressed entirely in appropriate white clothing. In Rita's case, she wore the same pretty, pristine dress Rosemary and Kay had worn, but Norah felt "Sure and this sorry-lookin' veil has seen better days," and managed to buy Rita Margaret new shoes, lace-trimmed knee socks, and material to sew a new veil. *Though only God knows how.*

Norah had wanted her youngest daughter to have brand new everything from head to toe. The original plan was for the "big girls," Rosemary and Kay, to share a First Communion dress and for the "little girls," Noni and Rita, to do the same with one of their own. But eight-year-old Noni "wore hers into heaven, darlin'," and there wasn't enough money to buy another. "We'll do well with the dress we have, Rita Margaret, and I'll give your Sunday underthings an extra bleachin'."

The Communion clothing was gone now, but Rita's Catechism had remained with her all these years, a constant source of comfort and surety, at home in her nightstand drawer.

Ruth Ann's lily-white dress had two, well actually three, layers: a full, nylon-taffeta slip; sheer, organdy dress with a delicate, lace-trimmed Peter Pan collar and short gathered lace-trimmed sleeves, topped with a scalloped hem, satin sash, bow-tied, organdy pinafore. The double-tiered, shoulder-length veil was trimmed in similar lace and fell from a dainty band of artificial white flowers. Her knee socks, Mary Jane shoes, gloves, panties, undershirt, and small pocketbook were all pure white too.

Rita was buttoning up the back of her daughter's plaid cotton dress when the perky saleslady brought a pink taffeta slip to the dressing room.

Rita Margaret's daily prayer as read from the Baltimore Catechism –

Morning Prayer

As soon as you awake make the sign of the cross and say:

Holy, Holy, Holy Lord God of hosts: the earth is full of Thy glory. Glory be to the Father, and to the Son, and to the Holy Ghost.

When dressed, bless yourself with holy water, kneel and say this short Morning Prayer,

Our Father...Hail Mary...I believe in God...

O my God, I believe all that Thou hast revealed because Thou canst neither deceive nor be deceived.

O my God, I hope in Thee and I hope to obtain from Thee all the graces necessary to my salvation.

O my God, I love Thee above all things because Thou hast first loved me and art most deserving of my love.

O my God, I offer Thee all my thoughts, words, actions, and sufferings and I beseech Thee to give me Thy grace, that I may not offend Thee this day.

All ye Angels and Saints of God, pray for me.

Angel of God, my guardian dear,

To whom His love commits me here.

Ever this day be at my side,

To light and guard, to rule and guide. Amen.

"With this you could have two dresses for the price of one." She slid it beneath the double layer of sheer organdy to make her point. "See, a pretty pink dress all ready for a party."

Rita considered it. *Bob will be furious if I spend more than absolutely necessary.* She took a chance anyway. "We'll take it." She ended up buying the entire outfit for full retail at Jordan Marsh and loved every blessed minute.

When they finally left the store, presumably headed for the subway, happily toting two bags each, the pleased mother stopped and asked her preoccupied daughter who was trying to avoid stepping on cracks in the sidewalk, "Do you want to go see Miss Cordelia?"

∽

Over the past few months, the most unlikely friendship had developed between Cordelia Parker and Rita Donnelly and her child.

The second time they went to Chandler's Linens, it truly was a "just look-ing" visit, and Rita wouldn't think of accepting refreshments for that very reason. The budget was tight with the holidays coming, but her philosophy was "You never learn anything staying at home," and she absolutely loved seeing how the other half lived.

When Rita and Ruth Ann came through the door, Cordelia put down the box of crocheted Bavarian antimacassars she was arranging in a yellow moiré-lined case and slipped out from behind the display piece. "I'm so happy to see you again. How did the guest towels work out?"

Rita said, "Oh, fine. Thanks for asking." She pictured where the luxury linens had been stored ever since, underneath bed sheets stacked on a high shelf in her bedroom closet. She was waiting for the perfect time to put them out, a special occasion when Bob might be more understanding of why exactly they needed French guest towels in the only bathroom of a third-floor apartment in a three-decker.

Cordelia couldn't help but notice Rita's familiar coat. It was the same one she wore the last time she was in, navy with a shawl collar. *Good for her.* Repeated wear mattered little to Rita as long as her outfit looked classy.

As intended, Rita declined refreshments, but Cordelia insisted. Anyone entering the store would have thought them old friends with how easily the conversation flowed. They each learned the other was an avid reader, compared titles, and Cordelia sent Rita home with a book she'd just finished. "Wait, I have something for you." She darted to the back room.

Rita left without buying a thing, and Cordelia didn't care. She hoped the personable lady and her bespectacled, cross-eyed daughter would come back again and again. And they did.

On one of those future visits Cordelia would breach the obvious in the kindest way possible. "There's something different about you Ruth Ann, no glasses this time. "No glasses and my eyes are straight too." Why, yes they are and pretty blue."

The next time Rita went to the store Cordelia wasn't there.

"I know she'll be disappointed she missed you," the gentleman clerk said and simultaneously plucked an infinitesimal piece of lint from Rita's coat while asking permission. "If you'll please allow me?"

She smiled coolly and stated her business. "Oh, I'm so disappointed she's not here. We came by to return this Francis Keyes book." Rita handed it to him. "If you don't mind." She reached in the pocket of her coat and gave him a small white envelope, a thank you note. "This too, please."

"Is there anything else I can help you with?"

"No, thank you. We have some other stops to make."

Percy Clark didn't remember seeing the boy before. "And don't you look the little man in your tweed coat and matching cap? What's your name, son?"

The boy's sapphire eyes smiled before the rest of his face did, and he reached up to shake hands, just as his father had taught him. "Bobby Donnelly, Mister."

Joy Street by Francis Parkinson Keyes, *A familial and romantic intrigue novel, many Bostonians were eager to read —replete with familiar ethnic, geographic, professional and social references to the greater Boston area and taking place primarily on Beacon Hill.*

"Well, how do you do, Bobby Donnelly? And hello to you too, young lady. Would you children like a cookie? That is, if it's all right with your mother."

Rita didn't object.

He promptly returned from the kitchenette and handed each of the happy youngsters a gingersnap and a paper napkin.

When Chandler's door closed behind them, Percy Clark joined Florence Sippi Morton, who was gazing out the window, as the mother and children made their descent to the sidewalk, and she commented, "They certainly make a nice appearance."

He blithely added, his right elbow resting on the back of his left hand, right fist beneath his jutting Patrician chin, "I've never considered red a very favorable color for women with auburn hair. However, that red coat is quite stunning on Mrs. Donnelly."

⚬

On the First Communion shopping day, Rita gaily entered Chandler's Linens and greeted Cordelia with, "I've only got a minute, but we wanted to drop by for a quick hello." She pulled a paperback book from her pocketbook.

"This is the one I was telling you about. Get ready to stay up all night. It's that good."

The Great Gatsby was new to Rita, but Cordelia had read it years ago in college, though she decided she needn't say so, and it wouldn't hurt to read it again. *Gatsby will be my dinner partner tonight.*

From the alternately shifting position of one wiggling, oxford-shoed foot pigeon-toed on top of the other, Ruth Ann said, "Miss Cordelia, want to see my First Communion dress?"

"First Communion dress? Yes, I've never seen a First Communion dress before."

Rita was a little embarrassed and a lot warm. She unbuttoned her coat, rather than remove the three-quarter, beige boiled wool she'd had since before she was married. Then she took the "most special dress Ruth Ann's ever had" out of the bag by the hook of the hanger, and held it up, thinking it was even prettier away from the bustling department store.

Cordelia was duly impressed and held the scalloped, tiny-bow-tied hem in her hand.

"Sweet, and such excellent workmanship. This must be a very special occasion, Ruth Ann."

360

Rita suddenly realized something was missing. "Cordelia, do you have any small white hankies?"

"We certainly do. I'll be right back."

"We'll follow you."

It was at that moment, in the glow of the nice lady's interest, that Ruth Ann jumped in and innocently asked, her dimples at their deepest, "Mummy, can Miss Cordelia please come to my First Communion?"

CHAPTER 34

My Dearest Savior,
Come into my heart when I receive Thee . . .
But above all, dear Savior, do please feed me (Communion)
as long as I live. . . . as the mother bird feeds her little ones.

NEW KEY OF HEAVEN: A COMPLETE BOOK OF
LITTLE PRAYERS & INSTRUCTIONS
MOST REVEREND ARCHBISHOP JOHN
CARDINAL FARLEY OF NEW YORK

RITA LIKENED HER PAST WEEK to a rollercoaster ride at Nantasket Beach's Paragon Park, with the escalating joy of First Communion fast approaching and a devastating letdown. She hadn't been looking for trouble on Tuesday morning. It was an innocent find.

Rita needed to light the stove, and when she couldn't locate any matches, she went into their bedroom and plucked a Patten Restaurant matchbook from the assorted pocket items on her husband's dresser: wallet, handkerchief, pen, notepad, Lucky Strike cigarettes, and peppermint Life Savers, right next to his empty police revolver and a saucer full of bullets. Bob was still asleep.

Paragon Park
NANTASKET BEACH, MASS.

Patten's Restaurant
Opposite City Hal Annex
41 Court Street
BOSTON, MASS.

Inside the matchbook cover, something was written in a fancy hand. Rita wasn't surprised. *Figures. He'd never take up with someone ordinary.*

Her closer inspection revealed a street address and telephone number, Commonwealth 6-2132, which she phoned right away, and a velvet-voiced woman with decidedly eloquent diction answered, "Hello, hello . . . Is somebody there? Hello."

Rita noted soft music in the background, and her mind's eye ran away with the image of a posh apartment or house, the lady of such wearing a frothy dressing gown. But she immediately banished it. *You've seen one too many movies, kiddo. Who cares where she lives and what she's wearing? A tramp is a tramp is a tramp.*

A short time later, Bob was on his way out the door to work when he asked Rita where his brown-bag lunch was. She leaned against the doorjamb, arms folded and smirked, "Why don't you 'grab a bite,' as you like to say, at Patton's Restaurant. I'm sure you'll find something there to your liking."

"Jesus, Rita, I can't be late. Where's my lunch?"

He brushed past her, headed for the kitchen.

She caught him by the sleeve. "Forget something?" Rita opened her hand to reveal the matchbook. "Or maybe you'll order a new dish. Variety is the spice of life. Wouldn't you say so, Bob?"

"What the hell are you talking about?" *Damn, what a slip up!*

Not up for his dramatics like the last time, that was as far as she took it.

❧

It was only two months ago when Rita stated the obvious. "You walk in our home late from work, smelling of Dentyne Gum, liquor, and another woman."

Bob vehemently denied any wrongdoing, but after she threatened to leave him, "I've got brothers and sisters who'll help me," he came clean, begged her not to tell them, apologized profusely and proposed they return to Southie the next evening and pray together in Saint Augustine's Church, where they were married. Once there, he cried and swore he'd never be unfaithful again, only to hold her hand tightly when Father Alphonse walked into the sanctuary and said, "We can go into my office now."

Rita was livid. *God in heaven, he arranged a meeting without telling me.*

Father Alphonse, who well remembered teenage Rita's care of aged parishioners and her mother's daily Mass attendance from the old days, counseled, "Divorce, as you well know, is out of the question. And it's your duty as good Catholics to forgive, make amends, and live in holy matrimony."

She noticed these words seemed to be directed at her alone. *Where does Bob's infidelity come in?* And questioned in her heart what should have been said out loud. *Did he tell Father Alphonse the truth?* But Rita trusted her husband had finally learned his lesson, and left in relative peace, notwithstanding her bruised pride.

Father Alphonse sadly knew of Bob's unfaithfulness but felt it was Rita's spiritual strength that would hold the marriage together, and he'd addressed her accordingly.

∞

First Holy Communion is the passage every Catholic parent looks forward to, the day their child receives the body of Christ. Rita wasn't about to let Bob's latest escapade spoil it, but she couldn't stop speculating based on the telephone number's prefix. *Why would a woman on Beacon Hill take up with a cop from Southie?*

Then again, the week was completely wonderful; Ruth Ann's special day was right around the corner. Rita's sister-in-law, Marion, to date with no children of her own but who in time would be loving mother to six, arranged to come to their apartment the night before First Communion. "Johnny said he'd drive me over, and he and Bob will make themselves scarce. Let me guess, Doyle's for a couple of pints." She smiled, "those two."

"That's fine with me. I don't care if Bob drowns himself in pints."

"That's pretty harsh. Care to tell me what's behind it?"

"No." Rita thanked Marion for helping her with all the preparation for the next day. "You're a Godsend."

They systematically set up for the celebration lunch and arranged what food they could ahead of time, on platters covered with waxed paper, and in bowls topped with appropriately sized saucers, and popped them all in the fridge. Glasses and hard liquor were lined up on the buffet, and in the refrigerator were beer, ginger ale, tonic water, and for the children, orangeade and milk, all to be brought out at the last minute with a bowl of ice. A milk-glass vase of blue hydrangeas from Marion's garden in Dorchester was centered on the white-cloth-covered dining room table, alongside a layered, white, bakery cake with First Holy Communion and pink roses prettily piped across the top.

Tall, svelte Marion, who grew up the oldest girl in a family of twelve children, had a gift for thinking ahead and helping with whatever needed to be done without a need for recognition or fanfare. She was also Rita's closest friend.

The younger children were bathed first and put to bed. Ruth Ann had her mother and auntie's undivided attention as she sat in the claw-foot bathtub filled with bubbles. Her new Communion clothes had already been laid out with the greatest of care, on the temporarily white-sheet-covered living room couch, in the order of putting them on: underwear, slip, scapulars, socks, shoes, dress, and veil. "Marion," Rita said, "I don't want to take any chances some unseen soil would stain her pretty things."

Rita tucked a prayer book, child-sized white rosary, gloves, and the Chandler's hankie into her daughter's small white purse. Earlier, Marion had spied the tiny "Made in Ireland" gold sticker and popped it off. "An Irish linen hankie, no less, nice," she said. "Bet you didn't get this at Grant's. It's very pretty, Rita. Be sure to save it for her wedding day."

Practical, not to the point of not nice, but wisely practical, Marion Callanan King never understood her sister-in-law's need for the best when "it'll do" was fine with her. But before she could give it much thought, they were out the apartment door with Ruth Ann dressed in her pajamas, robe, and slippers.

Mrs. O'Day on the first floor had a way of setting hair into perfect curls with ordinary rags, so downstairs mother, daughter, and auntie went for the last bit of preparation. Ginny O'Day was expecting them. "Is that the First Communion girl coming to my house?"

∽

Cordelia Parker had never set foot in a Catholic church and was sure if the dead could indeed turn over in their graves, today her very Protestant parents would be. Later this lovely May Saturday morning, she'd be sitting in a pew at Blessed Sacrament Church in Jamaica Plain, watching a little Irish girl receive her First Holy Communion.

And to borrow an expression she'd heard Rita Donnelly say once or twice in the course of conversation, *God forgive me. I'm looking forward to it.*

Outside, in front of the towering, twin-columned, massive, domed, basilica-like edifice of Blessed Sacrament Church, mothers fluttered, cooed, preened and flew about like maternal birds preparing their babies for first flight.

Some smoothed any stray hairs on their offspring's head with tongue-dampened fingers, and others pulled hankies out of well-supplied pock-

Blessed Sacrament Church
JAMAICA PLAIN, MASS.

etbooks, employing the same wet method for spots on faces or clothing. They bobbed and stretched their feminine necks in search of family and friends, and in quick-winged movements, made sure everything was in place with their own ensembles, adjusting gloves, spring hats, coat sleeves, and corsages, checking wristwatches, and finally guiding their charges into the church in good time, with the help of hovering husbands. "So we can get a good seat."

Cordelia joined the gathering of working and middle-class people dressed in their spring best and was pleasantly struck by the colorful array of so many flower-adorned hats. She eagerly looked for Rita Donnelly and depended on her auburn hair as a marker, but there were others with the same color. The weather was breezy, and Cordelia put a hand to her own unadorned, piped beige faille hat several times to secure it. *Where could she be?*

"Cordelia, Cordelia, here we are," Rita called to her new friend's back. "Over here."

When she turned around, Bob couldn't believe his eyes. *Miss Parker?*

And neither could she. *Officer Donnelly?*

Rita hugged the bewildered Brahmin. "Thank you for coming. Ruth Ann's already inside." With an open hand she indicated first her friend and then Bob. "Cordelia Parker, this is my husband, Robert Donnelly."

"Hello, Officer Donnelly. What a surprise."

"I'll say."

He quickly explained, "Rita, my beat goes right by Miss Parker's house."

She looked from one to the other. "You're kidding. What a small world. I can't believe this."

Cordelia responded, "And I'm pleased to report your husband keeps all safe and sound on Mount Vernon. Imagine, you're Mrs. Officer Donnelly. I simply never put the two together. You're Donnelly, he's Donnelly. How lovely!"

The eager young mother linked her arm through Cordelia's and began walking. "I'd like to keep talking about this amazing coincidence, but I don't want to miss seeing my daughter. Come on. Let's go inside."

Bob had their jumping son by the hand, and Rita was carrying their youngest.

"This is baby Catherine, and you missed Bobby the one time I took him to Chandler's."

Cordelia thought what beautiful children, particularly the little one. *Those curls and immense blue eyes.* And she said so. "Beautiful!"

Rita delicately dipped her fingers in the sculpted, alabaster angel, holy water font, blessed herself and did the same again for her two-year-old, who rubbed the moisture off with a dimpled hand. Bob followed Rita. The boy helped himself, and to a perplexed Cordelia, Rita said, "It's not expected of you."

Several extended family members had saved seats for them, and Johnny King came rushing up the aisle to guide his sister and the others. "We've got the whole third row." As they filed into the pew, he whispered out of the side of his mouth, "Jesus, Bob, what's the Brahmin babe doing here?"

Nuns in attendance glared the greeting King, Donnelly, and McDonough clans to quickly sit down and be quiet, as only they could.

Cordelia had no idea of the solemnity of the occasion and was impressed with the orderly demeanor of such young children. *So this is the Catholic Church? How in the world do they get these youngsters to behave so well?*

The children sat up straight in the pews and looked directly ahead without making a sound. And then Cordelia saw one of the nuns sound a clicker, and she was impressed beyond all reason at its effectiveness.

Click; the boys and girls were up, hands held together in front of their hearts, fingers up, thumbs crossed. Click; they filed out of the pews and lined up, boys on one side of the center aisle, girls on the other. Click; their feet began moving forward to the altar rail, where they knelt side-by-side, worshiping hands still before their hearts, and waited in turn.

When the priest appeared before Ruth Ann, she did as she had practiced for weeks—eyes closed, mouth open, tongue out, receive the Holy Host, mouth closed—and minded Sister Catherine Aloysius's careful instruction. "Don't chew. Let it melt a bit, then swallow. This is, after all, children, the Body of Christ. We don't want to be biting the Body of Christ."

That morning, Ruth Ann Donnelly had asked Jesus to, "please don't get stuck," because the O'Day sisters had scared the life out of her with stories of the Host sticking to the roof of your mouth and everyone knowing you were trying to bring Him down from there because of the funny faces you made, pushing and pulling with your tongue. Her prayer was mercifully answered; Jesus went straight to her heart.

One question remained for Cordelia. *Is this, in fact, the spiritual experience all these adults think it is? The children are so very young.*

Within moments, her question was answered, as she observed the first-time Communicants returning to their seats, each precious face undeniably alight with joy and the presence of God. Something spiritual had indeed taken place. This was so different from all the damning speculations she'd heard from her own people through the years about Catholic ritual, rote prayer, and mysterious undertakings. The statues were

Ruth Ann caught sight of her beaming mother and father, her sister and brother on either lap waving tiny waves, and held that vision for the rest of her life, recalling the day she made her First Holy Communion as her most cherished childhood memory.

unfamiliar, but then again, she really didn't understand their significance and simply chose to look the other way. Much to Cordelia's surprise, the Bible had been quoted several times throughout the service, and she found the entire experience extraordinarily reverent and worshipful, if not regal.

The church was filled with flowers, and its magnificent marble altar shone, as did the priest's elaborately embroidered white-and-gold vestments. Well-groomed altar boys, with fresh haircuts and shiny shoes, wore white cassocks trimmed with wide, red-banded cuffs and sizeable, floppy, red bows at the neckline. These were holy garments for a holy day.

The row upon row of white-clad First Communion boys and girls seemed to Cordelia a field of celestial flowers, heaven sent, heaven bound, unspoiled, radiant, one with God, their guileless childhood faith a beacon of hope and renewal.

CHAPTER 35

I am my beloved's, and my beloved is mine.
SONG OF SOLOMON 6:3

ALL CORDELIA EVER WANTED WAS to love and be loved.
Hopeful assumption had crumbled into the devastating loss of her longstanding wish to marry Norman Prescott.

A fatal car accident prematurely robbed her of both parents.

Her refusal to sell the family home, a blessed bastion and Cordelia's only security, had severed all ties with her spendthrift brother, who merely saw it as cash flow.

And then she was home alone, save former housekeeper Hilda, handyman Rolf, and two student boarders.

How could she have possibly known "Room to Let" would open the door to love?

Sundays were now Cordelia's and David's, pending his ever-increasing internship requirements at Tufts Medical Center. She went to Park Street Church in the morning while he studied, and later they sat down, Richard Malmgren included, to a simple midday dinner, usually a roast chicken, beef, or lamb popped into the oven before Cordelia left for services, followed by an outing of some sort, sans Richard. Last week it was a Swan Boat ride in the Public Garden, where they held hands like other sweethearts onboard, along with families, senior citizens, and tourists. When the boat operator informed everyone that swans mate for life, David squeezed Cordelia's hand, and after a few seconds, she squeezed back.

Swan Boats
Boston Public Garden

"Beneath this bridge and on their tours around the lake, pass the famous swan boats, the kiddies' delight. The Garden is a park of 24 acres separated from the Common by Charles Street. It contains many beautiful statues, monuments and fountains and its floral displays are beautiful." Postcard Copy

Miss Parker and Mr. Miller were "progressing quite nicely," Cordelia contentedly reported to Abby Chandler, who persistently tried to be in the know about every detail of their unlikely courtship. And because yesterday's conversation had taken place in the linen store, Abby asked quietly, "How does one go about dating a man who lives under the same roof you do?" They'd already dealt with the fact that Cordelia had taken in boarders. "Oh, for goodness sake, Cappy, what does it matter?" said Abby. "Pooh-pooh to the person who'd take issue. Pooh-pooh and adieu!"

Before reticent Cordelia could answer the question of living under the same roof—not that she had anything to hide, the courtship was hers and David's; she'd tell what she wanted to tell—Abby shot off another question from her Gatling-gun list of inquiries. "Now, Cappy is he the one, or is this just a passing fancy?"

"Honestly, Abby, didn't your mother teach you a thing about being too nosy?"

"If she did, I don't remember."

"Apparently."

"Perhaps I can answer my own question," Abby Chandler said cheerfully through a haze of held back tears. "He is the one! I haven't seen you this happy since—" she stopped herself from saying, "since Norman" and chose a better course. "In truth, dear friend, this is the happiest I've ever seen you. Shall we begin collecting your trousseau? Planning those wedding showers?" Many of

Cordelia's friends were well aware of "the dark and handsome medical student," as he was described by Abby, and hoped for the best: "At last, a wedding for our Cappy."

"Abby, you need to stop right there. We're in no hurry."

The unrelenting storeowner picked up a State Street Bank manila envelope containing the week's receipts, meticulously prepared for deposit by Percy Clark, and whispered, "Tell me, do you plan on one day having a child or two?"

Cordelia swiftly and good-naturedly handed Abby Chandler her black alligator pocketbook. "Out, Mrs. Butinski. Right now, out."

∝∾

At one point in the chance courtship, heady but cautious on Cordelia's side, eager but respectful on David's, she abruptly pulled away, confused and conflicted about their deepening affection. *What am I thinking? This is a man who rents a room from me. How can I continue to see a man who rents a room in my house? And how could I possibly have a future with a man whose background and religion are so entirely different from my own?*

In part, Cordelia's second thoughts rode in on the most innocuous incident.

From the very beginning, when David Miller first moved in, Cordelia happened to notice that he was never at home on Saturdays. Not that the genial lodger was hiding anything, what he did with his time was none of her landlady business, but when they came to know each other better and began spending time together, David brought it up in conversation. "We haven't gone out on Saturday yet because . . . " She was all ears.

This enlightening conversation took place over hot fudge sundaes, in a booth at Schrafft's on Boylston Street. The dating couple had two obvious obsessions, each other and ice cream. They frequented Schrafft's and Bailey's Ice Cream Parlor, where ice cream was served in silver dishes, set on silver plates, for sundaes and Brigham's for coffee frappes or vanilla ice cream cones with chocolate jimmies, and Howard Johnson's for single scoops of maple walnut and peppermint stick. Once Cordelia's smitten cohort learned she liked saltine crackers with ice cream, he made sure they were part of all future orders. David thoroughly enjoyed watching Cordelia eat, each bite savored, her mouth delicately

Temple Israel
BOSTON, MASS.
"Dedicated to the Brotherhood of Man.
Consecrated to the Fatherhood of God."

dabbed now and then with a napkin. So unlike his own hurried intake, shaped both by war survival and getting through medical school where every minute counted.

David Aaron Miller had been attending Saturday services at Temple Israel, and Tuft's schedule permitting, he never missed.

"You're welcome to join me if you want."

"I had no idea you were Jewish. Is Miller really a Jewish name?"

"In my family it is, for generations. After Cohen and Levy, Miller is the most common Jewish surname in America." He found her question amusing, and she found his grin, thankfully, forgiving. *What a dim-witted thing for me to say.* "I had no idea."

David continued, "My parents are devout, and to be perfectly honest, since boyhood, Judaism for me was only a matter of tradition: Temple, high holy days, Bar Mitzvah, kosher this, kosher that." He grinned and gestured with his hands. "As well as some very delicious food, but nonetheless, all of it tradition. Enter World War II. I was drafted, trained to be a medic and sent overseas. And in the hell of battle, believe it or not, I saw the hand of God at work." For a split second there was a faraway look in the Army veteran's eyes.

"Mortally wounded soldiers suddenly took a turn for the better, and my own life was spared as we dodged the enemy to collect fallen soldiers. In the thick of it all, Cordelia, the prayers of my youth came back, and believe me, I was grateful for every sacred, solace-giving syllable. Finished my tour of duty and got home on a Friday just in time for Shabbos."

David wondered if Protestant Cordelia understood what that meant. "In case you don't know, Shabbos is the Jewish Sabbath, sundown Friday to sundown Saturday." He winked and resumed his chronicle. "And for the first time in two years, I sat at the dinner table with my family." David envisioned his mother's slight, poised hands as she lit the Shabbos candles and waved in the flame's holiness with gentle circular gestures. A sacred glow filled the dining room with warmth and unity. "On Saturday I couldn't get to Synagogue fast enough. And that's how it's been ever since."

"Does it matter to you that I'm Jewish? My darling, *shiksa*." David took a drink of water but never took his eyes off Cordelia.

"No, of course not. My father used to say, 'Show me an un-churched man, and I'll show you a shallow fellow.'" *He's a Jew, and I'm a Gentile. How in the world would that work should our present fondness become a life-long commitment?*

Cordelia's growing uncertainty soon resulted in avoidance and emotional distancing with cool answers to David's warmhearted and eventually bewildered inquiries.

"Cordelia, is something wrong?" he asked

For Army Combat Medic, David Miller, it was his parents' parting blessing that resonated the most:

"Y'va-reh-ch'cha, Adonai y'yish-m'reh-cha, Ya-eir Adonai pa-nav ei-leh-cha vi-chu-neh-ka. Yisa Adonai pa-nav ei-leh-cha v'ya-seim l'cha sha-lom."

"May God bless you and keep you. May God's light shine upon you, and may God be gracious to you. May you feel God's presence within you always, and may you find peace."

on a Sunday morning after she announced there would be no midday meal or afternoon outing this week.

"Not a thing," she answered unconvincingly. "Some old friends are in town, and if it weren't for Abby's reminder, I would have missed them completely." The fact that the old friends were Abby's parents, visiting from their home in Cohasset, as they did every Sunday afternoon, stretched the truth.

"If you'll please tell me what the problem is, I'll do my best to correct it," David stated that same night when the two of them were in fairly close proximity, he hanging his wet raincoat up on the hall tree, she unaware of his presence as she came downstairs carrying a vase of tired-looking lilacs.

Her response was consistently standoffish. "Nothing needs correcting, I simply have a lot on my mind." The recurring omission of his name in Cordelia's curt answers finally said it all. *She's no longer interested. So be it.*

During this time, the house was inordinately quiet, and it didn't go unnoticed by Richard Malmgren, who did his stoic Scandinavian best to break the ice. "Would either of you be interested in a game of Monopoly?" he asked, while at the same time presenting a well-used tin of homemade cookies, for their mutual enjoyment. "This is filled with my grandmother's Swedish

Hotel Bellevue
21 Beacon Street
BEACON HILL, BOSTON, MASS.

pepparkakor, kind of like a gingersnap, only thinner." When he popped the lid off, a wonderfully pungent aroma filled the air. "But they're much better. Want one?"

"Another time, Rich, I have to hit the books. But I will take a few of those cookies."

Cordelia also declined. "Thank you, Richard. They smell delicious, but I'm meeting someone for dinner at Hotel Bellevue shortly and don't want to spoil my appetite."

These days Miss Parker made her menu choices from the column of prices before entrée descriptions. That evening she decided on the affordable
Fried Native Smelts with Bacon, Tartar Sauce, Allumette Potatoes - 75 cents
And splurged on a dessert of Baked Apple with Cream - 25 cents
Demitasse Coffee - 15 cents

David pictured Cordelia sitting opposite a well-to-do banker type, buttoned up, reserved, and WASP, but stopped himself from going any further. He got the WASP right, but not the gender or occupation. Cordelia's dinner companion was in fact a family friend from Martha's Vineyard, who happened by Chandler's Linen Shoppe one afternoon. "I'd love to catch up, dear," the older woman told her. "Perhaps we could meet for lunch or dinner while I'm still in town."

It was exactly one week later, and close to midnight, when a sleepless Cordelia sat on the side of her twin bed in total darkness and ruminated. *What to do about David?* Before long, the bedroom became too chilly for pajamas alone, so she dashed to the closet and rummaged around for her warmest robe. *Where in the world is it? I'm freezing to death.* Cordelia hurriedly pushed hangers aside, one by one, and was caught off guard as she recalled a similar hunt for her cherished red coat.

Memories rushed back as if it were yesterday: that magical snowy night with Norman Prescott's arm around her, and the following spring when she'd discovered the red coat was gone. *Blithely given away to a scrubwoman. Damn you, Norman. It would have been so easy, everything so perfectly compatible, family, friends, church.* She leaned against the wall, closed her eyes and folded her arms. *The Campbells' Christmas party, and you were lost to me forever.* A more recent memory came to mind as well, the day her heart's wound deepened.

Less than a year ago, Cordelia encountered Norman as she was coming out of the Paramount Cafe on Charles Street, after a quick breakfast of "the best pancakes in Boston." He was pushing a baby carriage, and Patsy, now known as Ann, walked closely alongside him. "Why, Cordelia, what a nice surprise," he said and politely pecked her on the cheek while his wife kindly added, "Cordelia Parker, it's been entirely too long."

Their downy-haired daughter had a Brahmin name, Priscilla, and twinkling, Celtic-blue eyes. Running into the proud parents and their pretty progeny only served as a painful reminder of what might have been.

Shivering against her will, Cordelia welcomed the warmth of a white, lambswool, satin-trimmed robe, and wrapped both arms about her, as if to keep from falling apart. She sat down again, this time in a comfortable armchair, and released her enfolding grip to the support of one elbow on the chair, slipperless feet tucked beneath her for warmth. She wistfully stared out the window at a full moon that was frequently obscured with intermittent clouds.

Thoughts of David crossed her mind like the coming attractions of a feature film: boy meets girl, polite companionship ensues, romance blossoms in the "Hub of the universe," beautiful Boston, religion and class, clash and confusion, girl runs, boy pursues.

Cordelia soon came to a final conclusion and silently spoke the phrase she'd come to use as an exclamation, but presently lamented in prayer. *God help me. I'm in love with David Miller, and I may have driven him away.* Crestfallen, she put her face in her hands and cried from the tip of her toes to the top of her being. *What have I done?*

When she at last looked up, wiping tears away right and left, Cordelia was stunned to see beams of crystal-clear moonlight streaming through the windowpanes, as if it were the break of day. *He's the one!*

Less than twenty-four hours later, Miss Cordelia Parker, hands full, strained to turn her house key in the lock, at the same predictable day's end hour, and pushed the door open to familiar scents of lemon-polished furniture, old rugs, fresh flowers, and a hint of cigarette smoke. She closed it again with a slight swing of her hip and was taken aback to see David Miller sitting on the entry settee, ashtray in hand, putting out a cigarette. He stood up at once. "Hello, Cordelia."

Tension hung in the air like billowing lines of laundry, and she knew something needed to be done before the brewing storm ruined everything, if it hadn't already.

"Hello, David," she said in a pitch softer than her usual terse tone as of late.

"Just biding time," he explained. "A fellow from Tufts is picking me up in his car any minute now. Lucky break, he's from New York City too, and we're on our way home for a couple of days."

"How nice for you."

"Yes, it's been a while."

Cordelia noted a small, timeworn valise at the foot of the spiral staircase and a black-and-white Fannie Farmer Candies bag next to it as she walked directly to the ancestral demilune table. Its nicked top held a few pieces of mail and a multicolored Chinese bowl where her family had forever tossed the keys to their Brahmin kingdom and chariots, as she did presently. Despite their pleasant exchange in passing, Cordelia felt a lump in her throat and turned back in the direction of her concern. "Oh David, I've been such a fool."

He abruptly put the ashtray aside. "I'd never call you a fool, Cordelia," he said in that calm, sure manner of his. "Cool as a cucumber maybe, but never a fool."

"I don't know what I was thinking." There was a quiver in her voice. "Well, to be perfectly honest, David, I do know." She clung to her pocketbook, gloves, an evening edition newspaper, and a small bag of groceries, as if they were a life raft. "Should we possibly have a future together, the differences in our backgrounds and religions seemed insurmountable."

"We could have worked it out."

"You're using past tense."

"Yes, I am." He remained maddeningly calm. "And you're right. Our backgrounds are different, Cordelia." He took a step toward her. "Let me tell you how differences of opinion, doubts, even heated anger, works in my family. We talk. We argue. We lay everything out on the table and make the best of it. In my opinion, you took everything off the table and closed the door. You didn't give me a morsel of truth, not one. Do you have any idea . . .? Never mind. It's not important now."

"Please forgive me, David."

"There's nothing to forgive. It was all a misunderstanding. Let's just forget everything and start all over again." His calm crescendoed to a crushing conclusion. "I rent a room in your house, and I'll do my best to stay out of the way." David looked at his watch and went to the window.

Cordelia felt heat rise in her face with every pounding heartbeat. "Won't you please say you'll forgive me?"

David turned to address her. "Didn't you hear a word I said?" He crossed his arms like a cigar store Indian. "You're fairly impossible, Cordelia."

The tears her pride had been holding back broke loose. "I know I am. But I can change, David."

He pulled a handkerchief from his sports coat pocket. "Please don't cry."

She awkwardly juggled the things in her hands and reached to take the handkerchief from him.

"Let me," he said and dabbed away her sadness.

Cordelia welcomed his touch, even if it was through folds of linen, and she had barely articulated "thank you," when a sounding horn announced the arrival of his ride.

David ignored the double beeping, and they stood before each other, still as statues but breathing in tandem. Every breath inhaled and exhaled seemed to speak: *what now?* Cordelia was completely lost for words, but David knew exactly what he wanted to say, and his arms bridged the gap between them as he firmly took her by the shoulders. "Impossible or not, Cordelia, I love you. I've loved you since that very first day, when you came rushing down the street, beautiful and apologetic, full of pride and inconvenience."

"I love you too, David. I know that now."

He took the things she'd been clinging to and promptly put them behind her. "Now where were we?"

"I think you were about to kiss me," she said, and their parted lips met as they never had before. All kisses up to this point had been pecks, busses, and light brushes. But this was the kind of kiss each had wanted all along and dared not, should it be interpreted as too fast by either party, a concern no more as Cordelia and David passionately engaged in long, unreserved kisses, despite the sounding horn and following knock on the front door.

Against every fiber of her madly-in-love desire, Cordelia politely pulled away. "Shouldn't you be getting that?"

"Unfortunately, yes."

Cordelia sent the two future doctors on their way, or so she thought, until David burst through the door all smiles. "One more kiss." He squelched any additional doubts when he said, "Did I expect to fall in love with a Gentile? No. But we'll work it out." And off he went again with two last words. "Don't worry."

That momentous night, in the softly lit foyer of number ninety-one, Mount Vernon Street, a space Cordelia had come into and gone away from since birth, another life passage began.

⁓

David arrived at his parents' home late that night, too late to tell them about Cordelia. It would have to wait.

The next morning, his mother raised open hands as if seeking God's help and cried, "Oy vey! Say it isn't so," and his father shouted, "A Gentile! A *shiksa*! A Jezebel!"

David held his hand out like a traffic cop. "Stop right there, Pop. That's the woman I'm in love with."

His father roared, "So, Mr. 'Stop right there,' what does 'in love' mean? Does it mean marriage? Is that what you're trying to tell us, David? You intend to marry this *shiksa*?" Then he blamed his wife. "This is all your fault, Esther. You're the one who encouraged him to be an independent thinker, you and your intellectual, bohemian, anarchist, Russian family."

Mrs. Miller raised her voice and delivered a high-pitched admonition. "So, you want he should be alone the rest of his life? No love, no children?"

His father shouted louder with what he deemed a righteous retort. "I want he should settle down with a nice Jewish girl. That's what I want, a nice Jewish girl and nice Jewish grandchildren."

David had anticipated every word of protest. "Pop, I'm not going to give her up. She is a nice girl. And God willing, she'll have me."

His father looked at his mother in exasperation and back again at David. "You young people just take whatever the wind blows your way without any thought of consequence. Thank God your grandparents didn't live to see this day."

He approached his wife, both hands moving in staccato sync with every word. "Esther, what would have happened if I'd presented such a situation to my father? You know what would have happened?" He turned again to his son. "He would have disowned me, and sat Shiva in the process."

David opened his arms and said, "Is that what you want to do, Pop, disown me?"

Mr. Miller raised his hands as if to God. "I should have such courage." He patted David's cheek. "I see the love in your eyes. This *shiksa*, she must be something." Hope filled the air for maybe thirty seconds, until he continued, "But is she worth you being the first in your family to marry such a person? Is she worth breaking your parents' hearts?"

Mrs. Miller, hands clasped before her, took a softer stand. "Speak for yourself. Mine isn't broken, a little cracked maybe, but not broken. So, you're going to let your son return to Boston with all of this condemnation on his head? Is that what you intend, Sam?"

"No, of course not. What I intend is to change his mind before he leaves for Boston."

Sunday afternoon dinner held delicious food and lively reunion with his siblings and their families. The table never lacked for laughter or stimulating conversation, but was sans any mention of Cordelia. David wanted to settle things with his parents first. Mr. Miller mistakenly interpreted the lack of announcement as *he's come to his senses,* and David considered his father's good mood an indication of *he's getting used to the idea.*

By midafternoon, they all left with effusive goodbyes and promises to "visit you soon in Boston," after which David sat in the living room with his parents, enjoying tea and another piece of babka cake, while waiting for his ride.

His father got up and looked out the window. "No sign of your friend." He breached the obvious. "No mention of that young woman to your sister and brother. So I'm under the impression you're reconsidering the *shiksa* situation."

David Miller put his cup down, walked over to his father, and spoke his mind. "Pop, I love Cordelia. You're either with me or against me. What'll it be?"

"I have a choice? God brings you back from the war in one piece, and I'm going to drive you away?" Mr. Miller, a big man, ponderously clapped his son on the back, momentarily gripped his shoulder, and at the same time looked about, as if the solution to "all this goy business" were hiding in a corner.

A whirl of concerns raced across Samuel Ira Miller's mind: the horrors of Hitler and devastating loss of family members in Europe, his determination to preserve hearth, home, and tradition for his own. And there was the disgrace. He could hear them now, relatives and friends, equally devoted to the beliefs and legacy of their Jewish forefathers, questioning such a union. *"I couldn't believe my ears…"*

David Miller's late maternal grandmother had a tremendous fondness for her youngest grandson. "My David, such a bright, kind boy." And she would often hold out her wrinkled, white as chalk, left hand, point and say, "One day, this gorgeous ring will be your bride's."

"We are shocked and saddened, but what can you do? They make up their minds, they make up their minds."

"It's a different world than we grew up in."

He soon came to a reluctant conclusion. *I gain a shiksa daughter or lose my beloved son, my David, my heart.* You could have heard a pin drop, until the patriarch spoke his peace.

"So we'll work it out. Am I disappointed? Yes, but we'll work it out.".

"Thanks, Pop." David took hold of his father's shoulder. "I knew this wasn't going to be easy for you, but we'll make the best of it. Just wait and see."

His mother joined in. *"Mann traoch, Gott lauch."* Man plans, God laughs. She kissed both men and inquired of her son, "I suppose you want to take Bubbe's ring back to Boston with you?"

"Yes, I do."

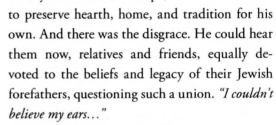

Once inside, David took his shoes off and tiptoed upstairs, not wanting to wake Cordelia or Richard. He got to the top and spied a glimmer of light beneath his sweetheart's door. *Bet she fell asleep with the lamp on.* He imagined Cordelia snug under the covers, an open book beside her.

The weary traveler removed his sports coat, unbuttoned his shirt collar, and was unpacking a few essentials when he caught sight of an envelope on the floor by the door. *I must have stepped right over it.* He saw his full name written in Cordelia's swirled handwriting. *Wonder what this could be.* David read the letter three times, every word on the personalized sheet of ivory vellum stationery spoke to his heart before he finally put it down on a nightstand. *I'll need to look at this again in the morning.* And just as soon, he decided what he needed right now was to see his sweetheart, if by any chance, she should still be awake.

A couple of light taps on her bedroom door, and there she was, Cordelia's mussed blonde hair and long, white robe only added to the overall look. *My angel.*

"David, you're back. Thank you for waking me. I fell asleep reading."

He held up the letter. "This was quite a surprise."

"Is that good?"

"About as good as it gets." He took her into his arms, her hands embraced the back of his neck, and they made up for lost time with the most passionate kiss yet.

Cordelia lightly pressed her body against his, and in the heat of the moment, he pulled her even closer. Their passion was steadily spiraling beyond reason, but Cordelia had enough presence of mind to remember they weren't the only ones in the house. She pulled David farther into her room, and with a push of his foot he closed the door behind them. Their kisses got deeper, Cordelia loosened the sash on her robe, and with some assistance from David it slipped off her shoulders and fell to the floor. The satin pajamas beneath it increased his passion, and he caressed her waist and hips as she removed his shirt, when just like that, he stopped cold.

"No, my love, not like this." He took a deep breath and stepped back.

Cordelia retrieved her robe and pulled herself together. "I'm so embarrassed, David."

"No need to be. We're in love and this is what lovers do. They make love, but not yet." He buttoned his shirt. "And no more closed doors when we're alone in the same room, at least not for now. The privacy is much too tempting. Agreed?" He smiled.

"Agreed." She stood on tiptoe and kissed his forehead.

David exited as quietly as he could and whispered, "You'll come into the hallway please?"

"I don't understand," she whispered in return and took his offered hand.

"I'll be back," he assured her and let go with a squeeze.

Cordelia stood by the grandfather clock that had been her great-grandparents and the very present tick-tock, tick-tock, under the circumstances, sounded much louder than usual, which of course it wasn't. Her racing heart seemed equally as loud, which of course it wasn't.

David returned and requested she "please have a seat" on the Hancock chair next to the clock, an exact match for the one on the other side. Another kiss, and out of the fullness of his heart, David Miller got down on one knee. "Cordelia, will you please do me the honor of becoming my wife?" His right hand unfolded to reveal a multi-diamond, splendidly vintage, gold ring.

Cordelia took his dark and handsome face into her fair Patrician hands and blissfully answered, "Yes, David. Yes."

⚮

The long-term plan was all David's doing.

Although she'd protested initially, Cordelia patiently accepted his reason for waiting to get married at a much later date than she'd anticipated. Truth be known, she admired him for it. His next decision made the waiting practically unbearable, but she was grateful for his protection personally, socially, and spiritually. *I am marrying an honorable man. Prideful but honorable, thank God.*

It was almost impossible for the couple to keep their hands off each other. Teatime now became "love to have my arms around you time" as they filled the kettle together, his body against hers while they stood at the sink.

None of it went unnoticed by Hilda and Rolf, who still delighted in keeping track of "the goings on" in Cordelia's kitchen from their perch above the garage. One night, Rolf questioned the appropriateness of such an arrangement and even speculated, "Do you think they're carrying on?"

Hilda scolded, "Not all men are like you were, Rolf. And besides, Miss Cordelia would never bring such disgrace to her parents' house."

Long, affectionate goodbyes made the determinedly chaste couple late on more than one occasion, but bedtime brought the greatest challenge of all. They'd kiss and kiss "good night," go to their respective bedrooms, pine for one another, and one would tap on the other's door for "just one more," which took place in the open hallway as agreed upon. However, one night as Cordelia lay in her bed after a particularly tempting and torrid parting, she deduced differently. *We are, after all, consenting adults.* But she thought better of it, turned over and went to sleep hugging her pillow.

It was the next day, and only two weeks into their engagement, when she rushed to meet David in the garden before she left for work as he'd asked. She could hardly wait. *Hearts unfold like flowers before Thee.*

A spring breeze blew fairly hard but the sun was warm. Rows of multi-colored pansies bordered the brick courtyard and looked as if they were sunbathing, their pretty flower faces turned toward the light; dozens of daffodils and tulips swayed to and fro behind them.

David was nervously pacing with his back to the house when Cordelia stepped outside and stared at him adoringly without his knowledge. *You are more than I ever could have asked for.* She leaned over the cast-iron stair rail. "My, my, you look fretful." Cordelia walked to the garden bench, mindful he had his eyes on her, and teasingly suggested with all the stage presence of a concerned doctor, "Let's have a seat and talk all about it. Tell me, when did these symptoms first appear, sir?"

David briefly kissed her. "This will only take a few minutes, honey. I know you need to get to the store." They sat down and he sighed. "Last night . . . "

She put her head on his shoulder and said, "I know . . . "

"I'm moving out as soon as I can, Cordelia."

She felt a knot in her stomach and faced him. He couldn't help but notice all the color had gone from her face.

"Please don't go, David."

"I have to. We can't continue like this."

"Like what? I thought we were doing just fine."

"We were until last night."

"I can't bear the thought."

"We'll be better off this way, Cordelia. At least for now."

"Maybe you will, but I won't."

"It's just not right for me to stay here any longer under the present circumstances."

David Miller stood in front of her now, straight and strong, as if lecturing. "I've waited my whole life for you. And I'm not going to disgrace our future with shame and regret, or have us be the subject of neighborhood murmurings. I love you too much for that."

Cordelia sat stiffly upright, her hands folded on her lap and both feet together, looking every inch a proper Bostonian. "Waiting to get married until you've completed your residency and found a place to practice is much too long."

"It's not quite a year, Miss Parker." He was depending on the formality for levity because they frequently laughed at how prim everything was in the beginning. "You know I can't enter into marriage with my wife bringing the only material assets to our union. Call me proud, but it's the way it has to be."

Cordelia sprang to her feet and protested. "No, it doesn't, David."

He tenderly tucked a wayward tendril back behind her ear, where it belonged and asked, "What happened to that perfectly happy young lady who already agreed to the previous terms?"

Cordelia teared up. "She's afraid to let you out of her sight, lest the whole thing be a dream."

"Dear, dear Cordelia." David took her hands into his and gazed at the family heirloom ring. "No shame, no regret, only love and honor." And he kissed it. "Forever."

CHAPTER 36

I, Robert P. Donnelly, do solemnly swear that I will bear true faith and allegiance to the United States of America and the Commonwealth of Massachusetts and will support the constitutions and laws thereof. . . . I will faithfully and impartially discharge and perform all the duties incumbent on me as a police officer of the city of Boston . . . So help me God.

EXCERPTED FROM 1940'S CITY OF BOSTON POLICE OATH,
AS PLEDGED BY OFFICER ROBERT P. DONNELLY AT THE BEGINNING OF
HIS LAW ENFORCEMENT CAREER.

BOB ALWAYS HAD HIS EYE on the brass ring and possessed a determined reach to grab hold of it. His making detective didn't surprise anyone, least of all his wife. After diligently taking night classes for the last couple of years, and striving to meet BPD requirements for the next step in his law enforcement career, Officer Donnelly's promotion brought him to Boston Police Headquarters, at 154 Berkeley Street, where the new job called for "plain clothes." His patrolman's uniform—long, weighty, winter

Bob's brother-in-law, Officer John King, liked to kid about the policemen's long, double-breasted winter coats being "so God Almighty heavy, all we had to do to apprehend a criminal was throw one on him."

coat and all—was straightaway stored in a large box between layers of tissue paper with a generous sprinkling of mothballs.

Rita gratefully tucked the last two pieces of tissue on top. *Thank God he's off the beat. Maybe he'll settle down now.*

Bob closed the lid. *God willing it will stay there.* One new detective found himself back on the beat for perceived disrespect. "All I said was, 'Imagine me, Ed Doherty, one-hundred-percent Galway, bein' stuck in Easta Bost'." A senior officer named Campesi overheard his careless comment.

Bob and Rita scrambled to town the weekend before his first day and purchased two suits, three dress shirts, three ties that were on sale, a half-dozen socks, a pair of "decent-looking shoes," and one soft hat—all with the help of their Filene's charge account, and all of it upstairs.

They enjoyed every minute. The first time Bob stepped out of the dressing room, Rita smiled and said, "Detective, you're looking very sharp." *And here's to new beginnings.*

Rita didn't want the salesman's help, other than eventually having "Dapper Dan" measure trousers that needed to be hemmed that day.

"We'd really appreciate it, and I don't mind paying extra. My husband just got a promotion and starts his new job on Monday."

It was commonplace for men's suit pants to wear out much sooner than their matching jackets, and savvy designers came up with a practical solution. Bob's new suits had two pair of slacks each.

The previously miffed salesman couldn't resist the attentive wife's proud plea and assured her all would be ready in a couple of hours.

That afternoon, the native Bostonian couple toured their city like out-of-towners. They strolled through the Common, visited the Public Garden (still a few weeks too early for flowers, but walking across the exquisite, small suspension bridge was a must) and had lunch at a reasonably priced restaurant on Bob's beat, where the waiter said, "Officer Donnelly, I hardly recognized you out of uniform. This must be Mrs. Donnelly. It's a pleasure."

He handed them each a menu and leaned in as if he was about to reveal a secret. "We've got a great navy bean soup, if you're interested, and broiled fresh scrod with buttered beets and potato croquette a la carte. Take your time. I'll be back with water."

Bob stood up. "Excuse me for a minute, hon, I need to visit the men's room."

The restaurant was packed, and Rita found the clientele fascinating as she discretely observed: a beret-donned elderly gentleman engrossed in reading a book while attempting to eat without looking, with rather calamitous results which he nonchalantly attended to absent a glance; a refined, middle-aged couple at a table for two, eating bowls of soup and staring into each other's eyes like newlyweds; and seated in a cozy booth, what appeared to be a mother-daughter afternoon out, with two of each happily talking non-stop, prompting Rita to pleasantly recall that same kind of joy with her own mother over simple, long-ago lunches at home on E. 8th Street in Southie. *Rita Margaret, you're thin as a rail. Go on now. Take another roll and put plenty of butter on it. I'll not have the neighbors thinkin' I don't give me darlin' daughter enough to eat.*

When Bob returned, all the other customers faded into the background, and the couple fell into a world of their own, talking about nothing other than the immediate.

"We couldn't have asked for better weather."

They excitedly discussed what they'd purchased. "I'll wear the charcoal-gray suit on Monday," Bob said.

Rita suggested which ties would work best with the few dress clothes Bob already owned. "The striped burgundy would go well with your navy suit. Don't you think it's good for another year?"

"Just so the pants aren't shiny, Rita."

"Of course not. Do you think I'd let you go out the door looking less than presentable? God in heaven, I thought I was particular."

"Sorry, Rit, I just want to start off on the right foot."

"From flat foot to right foot." Her dimples showed.

"Very amusing." The brand new detective nervously drummed his fingers on the table, an uneasy habit Rita disliked.

"For God's sake, Bob, relax. I'm pretty sure they aren't sending patrolmen to police headquarters for the fun of it. Honey, you've worked hard to get here. Let's enjoy it."

He took her hand and cherished the dainty fairness of it against his huge, ruddy palm. "What would I do without you?"

Later, over desserts of warm gingerbread with whipped cream and a chocolate éclair, Mr. and Mrs. Donnelly quietly declared their love for each other after Bob confessed, "I know I've been out of line too many times, honey, but honest to God, I love you so much."

Rita's stomach tightened. *You're telling me.* Her reply was an honest, "Yes, you have."

"It's never going to happen again, Rita." He cut into the éclair.

Rita had reserved the resplendent red coat for "special occasions only" out of concern it would wear out, "God forbid," if worn too often. That simply wouldn't do because in the deepest, dearest, safest place of Rita Margaret King Donnelly's heart, every button and fiber of the red coat, even the never used R-monogrammed hankie in its right pocket, forever held her mother and sisters' love, and she wanted to hold on to it for as long as she could.

Rita slowly pressed her fork through the whipped cream to the aromatic gingerbread and ate the small bite. *Holy Mary. 'Out of line' and 'I love you so much' in the same sentence.* She took a slow sip of tea and said, "I know you love me. I love you too." *But one more time, and I'm out the door.*

Bob wanted to drop by Station 3 to say hello. They doubled back to the State House and stopped to admire its gleaming gold dome. "This is a hell of a city, isn't it Rit?" They continued on to Joy Street.

Rita was elated to catch a glimpse of Beacon Hill interiors through uncovered windows when she could. "Honey, look."

Detective Donnelly and his wife were barely through the station's doors when Officer Red Driscoll, an affable bachelor, took a look at Rita, her pretty face gently blushed from the walk, eyes sparkling with contentment, and said, "God Almighty Bob, what'd ya do, rob a bank? Your better half is lookin' mighty grand in that red coat!"

Rita smiled and shook her head. "Hello, Red."

"Afternoon, Mrs. Donnelly." He lightly kissed her on the cheek. "Sure and any prettiness these neighborin' wealthy socialites may possess pales next to your Celtic beauty and that magnificent coat. If anythin' ever happens to himself—"

Bob gave Red a firm, friendly nudge. "Watch it, pal."

"Just kidding, Detective."

Red Driscoll was well aware of Bob's unfaithful escapades and never understood why. If I had a doll face like Rita waiting for me, I wouldn't be able to get home fast enough.

Other officers, coming and going, briefly engaged the couple in congratulatory, off-the-cuff conversations about Bob's promotion and wished them well, with Sergeant Mulvaney, who was instrumental in furthering Bob's career, saying the final goodbye. "Give my regards to headquarters. I've already told 'em they're getting one of our best."

Rita and Bob left Station 3 in good spirits, hailed a taxi, and ventured into the North End, where they toured the Old North Church, even though it was Protestant, and Paul Revere's House.

Old North Church
BOSTON, MASS.

The Irish duo tried to buy Italian cannoli at Michelangelo's Pastry, but the owner would have no part of it. Officer Donnelly had walked the North End beat many times and, in the course of his duties, looked after the bakery's best interests. He accompanied the owner when he had a bank deposit to deliver and made sure everything was secure after hours, trying doors front and back. "Consider these a promotion gift."

They grabbed another taxi, white bakery box in tow, and returned to Filene's men's department, where Bob's new clothing was ready to go.

When they stepped outside again, Rita instinctively looked up at Filene's famous clock.

"Oh my God, Bob, look what time it is! I told your mother we'd be back no later than five." She made a mad dash for the subway, concerned about how long they'd left their three active children in Mrs. Mac's care.

Bob ran after her. "Honey, slow down. She'll understand."

Rita's panicked pace came to a quick stop. "Are you sure?"

Filene's
BOSTON, MASS.

"I'm sure." He whisked a couple of the Filene's bags from her grasp. "Here, let me carry those." Bob added them to his own collection.

Rita rushed ahead. "Come on, slow poke."

They arrived at the platform out of breath and giddy, and Bob turned to his wife and said, "Red Driscoll was right; you are a beauty," and kissed her. On the train ride home, they held hands under the parcels on their laps, and Rita whispered to her husband, gloved hand cupped around her mouth to his ear, "I'm very proud of you, honey."

～

Detective Donnelly was thrilled with his new assignment: crime photographer and investigator. He reveled being in plain clothes and took up where he left off at Station 3 with the valued camaraderie of his law enforcement peers.

Bob wasn't on the new job more than a few months when he reached for the brass ring again. "Lots of the fellas at headquarters live in houses out in the suburbs. What would you think of that, Rita?"

"Living in a house? I'd love to, but the suburbs are out. Boston, Southie, Dorchester, Hyde Park, Savin Hill, Mattapan, Jamaica Plain—anywhere but the suburbs. I'm a city girl, and I'll always be a city girl." *God in heaven, why can't he just let things be?* Rita hadn't been waitressing at night for some time now, and she wanted it to stay that way. "And how are we supposed to afford this house, Daddy Warbucks?"

"Nice Rita, 'Daddy Warbucks.' Jesus. We can swing it. Just leave everything to me."

～

Nowhere was the statement "It's who you know" truer than in the city of Boston. Ethnicity, parish, school, profession, political affiliation, religion, region, even the street you lived on was taken into consideration when meeting someone for the first time. A great majority of Boston's citizens were the sons, daughters, and grandchildren of immigrant groups who came to America knowing virtually no one. And upon arrival, they urgently sought out their own people in the Italian, Polish, Armenian, German, Irish, Jewish, and Chinese (among many others) regions of the city. There was strength in numbers, and ethnic solidarity, above all, opened doors to jobs, housing, and special favors. With the help-

"Powers, in my opinion, was the last of the politicians who let people come right to his home for favors. He held office prior to the new wave of media candidates."

That Old Gang of Mine: A History of South Boston
Patrick J. Loftus

ful influence of venerated Irish American politician, John E. Powers, a long-time acquaintance of Bob's from the old neighborhood, the Donnelly family moved into a new, two-story, three-bedroom, brick rental house in Mattapan, only a stone's throw away from Southie. This was the first time either Rita or Bob had lived anywhere other than an apartment, and miraculously, the amount of their rent hadn't changed.

Bob couldn't believe their luck, and Rita believed otherwise. *Most precious Mother of God, thank you for hearing my prayer.*

The two oldest children, third and fourth-graders, were transferred from Blessed Sacrament School to Saint Gregory's in Lower Mills, Dorchester. Baby Catherine, at four years of age, was still at home with her mother. And for all their banter, Bob's cheating, and Rita getting even one way or another, the couple truly did love each other. He continued to admire her spunk and beauty, and she was proud to have such a handsome, hardworking husband, who went to work every day in a coat and tie. Bob's affair with the mysterious Beacon Hill "trollop," as Rita referred to her, was completely over. She was still suspicious about his possible dalliances, but unless she could prove it, Rita didn't want any more melodramatic scenes. She had her sisters and brothers, the children, the church, close friends, and a home she loved. She'd cope. Things weren't perfect, but life was good, and Rita Donnelly had steeled herself to count her blessings rather than dwell on things she couldn't change.

And then Hollywood came to Boston.

CHAPTER 37

"The Grass is Always Greener (in the Other Fellow's Yard)"
WHITING & EGAN
THEME SONG FROM BIG BROTHER BOB EMERY
CHILDREN'S PROGRAM - 1950s WBZ–TV BOSTON

"TONY CURTIS?"

"Tony Curtis! I'm telling you, Rita, he walked into police headquarters just like a regular guy." Bob laughed into the telephone. "Yeah, a regular guy with a parade coming right up behind him. Makeup, wardrobe, the director was there too, and a big guy, bodyguard, didn't say one word, just nodded. I couldn't tell you who the others were, but they definitely weren't from Boston with those suntans and California accents. Honest to God, Rita, it was something."

"I can't believe you met a movie star, let alone, Tony Curtis. Is he short or tall?" She covered the receiver and raised her voice. "You children quiet down. I'm on the phone with Daddy." Rita didn't dare ask what she really wanted to know. *Is Tony Curtis as handsome in person as he is in the movies?*

"Short or tall? I'd say average. But he's got a hell of a strong build for such a trim guy and enough hair for three men."

Her curiosity was satisfied.

"I've got to cut this phone call short, hon, there's a gang of real hoodlums coming in for processing any minute now."

"So will you be home for dinner, Detective Donnelly, or should I go ahead and feed the kids first?"

"Jesus, Rita, how many times do I have to tell you? Don't pen me in like that. If I'm not coming home at the usual time, I'll let you know."

"And?"

"I'll let you know."

"I'm not making the kids wait. Dinner will be on the table at 5:45, take it or leave it. Bye." *Who does he think he is? 'I'll let you know?'*

The abruptness of the dial tone aggravated him no end. *Goddammit!*

Though it was early in the day, Rita liked to have as much ready as possible for the evening meal. No matter what meat, fish, or fowl she served, this daughter of Irish immigrants peeled a dozen or so potatoes and put them in a pot of cold water to keep. Tonight she planned on having those hamburger patties Bob liked: ground round, breadcrumbs, minced onion, and eggs kneaded together, fried in butter, and smothered in gravy. Unless he wasn't coming home, then she'd open a couple of cans of Franco-American spaghetti. *The kids love the stuff. Bob hates it.* She'd add a jar of applesauce too, boil some frankfurters, put a plate of sliced white bread on the table, and dinner was ready. After hanging up on her husband, she took a can opener out of the drawer and slammed it down on the counter. Rita retrieved the potatoes from the stove and placed them in the refrigerator for the next day. *How do you like those apples, Detective Donnelly?*

⁓

Bob Donnelly's unlikely meeting with the famous Hollywood heartthrob had been set into motion by "the crime of the century," an armed burglary of the Brink's Building in Boston on January 17, 1950. It was the largest heist in the history of the United States up until then, netting the crooks 2.5 million dollars. And now, four short years later, the great Brinks robbery was going to be immortalized in a movie, *Six Bridges to Cross*, starring Tony Curtis, George Nader, Julie Adams, and "the Kid," sixteen-year-old Sal Mineo.

Filming on location provided authenticity, and the cooperation of the Boston Police Department was essential for getting the facts straight. Lieutenant Luigi "Lew" Cubello assigned Detective Donnelly to be the BPD's liaison and consultant. "Keep an eye on 'em, Bob, and be damn sure they make the department look good." Although "the mick from Station 3" was fairly new to police headquarters, Lieutenant Cubello thought Bob would be the best one for the job because he was sharp and had an amiable manner; everyone he knew liked the guy. And Bob Donnelly was a man's man; the Lieutenant liked that best. He well represented the force as a top marksman in shooting tournaments, hunted, drank the best of them under the table, and was known to get away with an unnamed shenanigan or two. The fact that Lieutenant Cubello was slightly put off by Bob's

The Brink's Job

"At 7:27 p.m. on January 17, 1950, the Boston Police received a frantic call from an employee at the Boston offices of America's biggest money mover, Brink's, Inc. (Armored Cars). Minutes later police squad cars squealed to a halt at 165 Prince Street in the North End. The cops on the scene found out that there had been a robbery. It was a big one . . . the biggest cash haul in history. It would take six years and the combined investigative efforts of the Boston Police and the FBI, not to mention the help of local police departments across the country, to bring the robbers to heel . . .".

**Courtesy of The Boston
Public Library**

suaveness didn't interfere with what the Lieutenant deemed would work out best with the "Hollywood people." *Hell, he's the closest thing we've got to a movie star around here, good-looking even if he does have a big schnozz and is full of himself. It's a perfect match.*

Bob rushed down police headquarters' stairway to receive the movie company and take them up again to get a mock mug shot of Tony Curtis. The tap of his well-polished cordovan oxfords bounced off the granite with each hurried step. When he actually saw the black-haired, ice-blue-eyed movie star, it seemed unreal that one and the same would be standing, big as life, in the lobby of police headquarters.

"Mr. Curtis, welcome to Boston."

"Tony, call me Tony." He affably waved away formality.

"Detective Donnelly, Bob."

The two men shook hands and introductions took place all around. Bob gestured toward the elevators. "Let's go get those mug shots taken care of." He took note of Mr. Curtis's dark, tie-less sport shirt, silk weave sport coat, and light tan slacks. *God Almighty! Are his loafers made from alligator?*

"So you had a good flight out?"

"Smooth as could be."

"I understand you want fingerprints too. We'll get that taken care of in no time."

"You're not going to throw us in the hoosegow, now are you, Detective?" one of the movie people asked tongue in cheek.

"Not if you behave yourselves."

They all chuckled, except the bodyguard.

"Here we are, gentlemen." Bob held the elevator door open. "After you."

As the movie-making entourage walked through the building, everyone stopped what they were doing to say hello or just stare. One winsome file clerk, an Irish girl if ever there was one, with flaming, kinky, red hair, freckled skin, and muscular dancer's legs, nimbly stepped forward with pen and paper in hand. "Mr. Curtis, may I please have your autograph, sir?"

The movie idol politely complied. "How could I say no to such a pretty colleen?" And as they moved along there was more of the same.

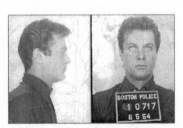

Tony Curtis
BOSTON POLICE HEADQUARTERS
154 Berkeley Street

Tony Curtis stood before the mug shot height board and measured in at five foot nine, and despite the case ID frame hanging around his neck and his pensive, in-character sneer, Bob wasn't convinced. *He no more looks like a criminal than the Pope.*

"Ready, Mr. Curtis?"

The following weeks held location visits, questions about the lay of the city and police procedure, along with a myriad of other necessary consultations. Bob was completely enamored with the entire movie-making process. *They actually say "all quiet on the set."* He had high regard for the actors and their jobs too, which, as he told Rita, "looked like a piece of cake."

When they were on location, the veteran law enforcement officer knew most of the patrolmen in the area, respectfully introduced them to whatever members of the movie company were closest, and frequently enlisted their help with spectators who seemed to come out of the woodwork. "Can you give me a hand and keep these jokers away from the cast and crew?" His request was always met with cooperation, ended with a handshake, "Thanks, Officer," and the fraternal understanding: *This is what we do, cover each other's backs.*

At the end of a grueling day of filming around inclement weather, one of the "big shots" asked where he and a few of the actors could go to get "a stiff drink and a good meal."

Bob said, "I know just the place," and highly recommended the Union Oyster House. "The food's delicious, and you won't have any complaints about the liquor either."

They invited the personable detective to come along. "That is if your Mrs. doesn't mind."

Bob said he'd need to make a phone call and returned ready to go.

Once everyone settled in at the oyster bar, he acquainted the West Coast people with New England sea fare: steamers, oysters on the half shell, and clam chowder. Later, when they sat down to a meal of whole lobsters, Bob looked around the table and couldn't believe he was actually having dinner with a Hollywood director, producer, and movie stars, each one wearing a big, white, lobster-print bib, which leveled the ground a bit for him. Their friendly din came to a halt when one of them asked, "All right, Detective, now that you've got us looking like imbeciles, how the hell do you eat this thing?" Bob took the familiar cracker, pick, and small, three-pronged fork in hand. "These are your tools, gentlemen, and this is how you separate the succulent lobster from its shell."

He cracked open a claw, dug the white, pink-tipped meat out, dipped it in drawn butter, and they were merrily on their way—laughter, lobster, colorful stories, and a few off-color jokes, which led Bob to suggest they might want to "catch a burlesque show at Scollay Square" before they left town. The entire evening was a huge success, and two nights later Bob invited whoever was interested to "get a pop at Doyle's in Jamaica Plain," so the Hollywood people could experience a genuine Irish pub.

The fact that Denis the bartender, also a Southie native, didn't recognize any of the actors, or if so, didn't acknowledge their fame, was part and parcel for a place like Doyle's, where people were friendly but not overly familiar, let alone star-struck. Robert Padraig Donnelly wrangled the obviously "you're not from around here, are you?" group of seven men, up to the bar under the watchful, if not curious, eyes of the other customers. When one crewmember ordered a martini "extra dry, two olives, please" and yet another chimed in, "Same for me, please," Bob couldn't believe his ears. *Martinis!*

The bartender growled under his breath to the only one of them he recognized. "You gotta be goddam kiddin' me, Donnelly. Who are these pansies?"

Bob answered, "Californians," made an about-face, and jovially saved the day. "This round gentlemen, the drinks are on me, and the drink is Guinness."

And so it continued for weeks, with any number of eateries and bars Bob thought would appeal to them. The few times the detective joined their company, he never had to spend a dime (with the exception of Doyle's), despite his sincere insistence, wallet in hand.

"Listen, Detective, you're doing us all a favor, getting us to these places. Consider yourself a guest of Universal Studios."

At one point, reasonably comfortable in their company and two beers later, Bob pulled out photos of his three children, and the famous director said, "These kids should be in the movies."

Detective Donnelly couldn't believe his luck. *Good move Bob.* He'd just taken those pictures of his kids at police headquarters the previous Sunday afternoon. Rita brought along an old, matte gold drapery panel to cover the boldly numbered height-board, and Bob scooted the least scratched, dark, wooden desk chair in front of it.

With an entreating, "Smile for Daddy," and a click of headquarters' "topnotch camera," he captured forever the joyful, shining images of ten-year-old Ruth Ann, nine-year-old Bobby, four-year-old baby Catherine and a place in time his eldest daughter, decades from then, would tenderly refer to as "The Diamond Days," after a contemporary Irish ballad.

The director handed the children's photos back to their proud father and inadvertently encouraged his need for a change. "Bob, we often have a need for someone like you, a guy who knows police work, an expert to do just what you're doing for us here in Boston. You'd love California."

And so it went until the movie company wrapped up production and said their goodbyes, but not before Detective Bob Donnelly, "a hell of a nice guy," was more than enticed by visions of California, where "the sun is always shining" and "the sky is the limit!"

CHAPTER 38

"I like this place," said Mrs. Mallard as they climbed out on the
bank and waddled along. "Why don't we build a nest and raise
our ducklings right in this pond? . . . What could be better?"
MAKE WAY FOR DUCKLINGS
ROBERT McCLOSKEY

THE CAMPAIGN FOR CALIFORNIA HAD already begun but Rita didn't take
it too seriously, thinking the more distance between her husband's ex-
periences with the *Six Bridges* people and real life, the less he'd nag her
about considering the prospect of moving out there. She was wrong.

Bob took every word the filmmakers said to heart. And spending so much
time with all those movie stars left the impressionable detective with what his
mother, Mrs. Mac, went on to call "Hollywood Fever."

Bob simply couldn't get "the land of sunshine" out of his mind and repeatedly tried to reason with his wife, as he did one night after their children were
tucked in bed with a kiss, "good night, and God bless you," the girls in their
frilly room with ruffled, white, Pricilla curtains, rose-pink bedspreads, and a
taffeta-dressed doll lamp on the dresser. Bobby in his "boy room" with airplane and train print curtains (one seam mistakenly sewn with a plane and

train headed for eminent collision), tan sailcloth bedspread, and trio of model airplanes suspended from the ceiling with fishing line.

"I don't understand why you're so against it, Rita. It'll be great for the kids. Remember what that director said? Honey, he's really interested in putting all three of them in the movies. And he said a real cop's input is often needed on movie sets." Bob raised an ice-filled glass of whiskey and ginger ale from his comfortable seat on the living room couch, as if toasting. "Meanwhile, I'll get a job with the L.A. Police Department." He looked away just long enough to flick the ashes from his Lucky Strike cigarette into an amber glass ashtray supported by a brass floor stand.

Rita answered his latest pitch from the other end of the couch. "I'm not worried about you getting a job, Bob. You've always been a hard worker. I just don't want to live out there. I like it here." She placed her teacup on an end table. "We have a nice home, the kids are in parochial school, and our families are close by. And another thing, I don't know how to drive. I understand you can't get anyplace out there without a car." Rita sat back with a certain resignation, crossed her navy-cotton pedal pusher-clad legs at the ankle, and needlessly adjusted the cuffs of her yellow poplin blouse. "What's wrong with our life here?" she asked and folded her arms while waiting for an answer. *Please, dear God in heaven, take this foolishness out of my husband's head.*

"Jeeesus, Mary, and Joseph, Rita! Why do you always have to make a goddam federal case out of everything?" Bob was on his feet now and pacing.

"Because it is a goddam federal case." She lowered her voice, concerned they'd wake the children, though the intensity remained unchanged. "'Jeeesus, Mary, and Joseph, Bob!'" she mocked. "Why this burning desire to see your kids in the movies? Give me a break! You want to see your kids in the movies? Get the projector out and take a look at the ones you took of Ruth Ann's Communion, Catherine's birthday, and all the others." She grabbed Bob's highball from his hand and raised it. "Featuring the Donnelly family, and starring the detective without a lick of sense, his goddam federal case of a wife, and their three unfortunate children."

Rita stormed upstairs, and Bob caught her by the arm midway. "Let me make you a drink to help calm down those nerves."

"I'm not going to California."

"I understand that. Tom Collins, gin and tonic?"

"I'll have what you're having." *And if you think this is going to get me in the mood for anything other than a peaceful night's sleep, you've got another think coming.*

Ten-year-old Ruth Ann was still awake and took in every word.

∞

The Donnellys' saltbox, red-brick home in Mattapan looked like the happy houses children tend to draw: two stories, five windows (three up, two down), with a front door in the middle, and a "just big enough," three-step, cement porch with white lattice trellises on either side. The look of a child's drawing continued with precisely centered tieback curtains on the second story, and a single, full-foliaged tree out in front, circled with whatever bloom was in season; orange, pink, and yellow zinnias were Rita's favorite. All she ever wanted was a happy home. And 97 Standard Street was so much more than she'd ever expected.

Upon entering the house, you'd right away step on a scatter rug, which protected the wood floor of the small entry space. The living room was to the right, kitchen to the left, and the cellar door was straight ahead. In winter, Rita would usher the children to "go directly downstairs" to shake the snow off and hang wet garments on a wooden clothes rack to dry. Their Nordic-patterned slipper socks were lined up on the bottom three steps, ready to warm cold little feet. She basked in the comfort and convenience of their new home. No sharing stairways, backyards and cellars.

Bob and Johnny King had created a knotty-pine rumpus room out of half the cool, cement-floored basement. The finished side was tiled with red linoleum and furnished with everything second-hand, a red-and-tan, wooden-armed couch, two coordinating chairs, and a bar the brothers-in-law had fashioned from Rita's buffet. Its roomy cabinets held variously sized glasses, and mixers, bitters and grenadine syrup, jars of cocktail onions, olives and maraschino cherries, canned mixed nuts, small plates, bowls, paper cocktail napkins, and way at the back, Bob's crispy cheese crackers from S. S. Pierce. Rita enjoyed keeping it stocked and orderly.

Where the bar butted up against a wall, two bracket-supported shelves held gift bottles of liquor arranged by size. A Zenith tabletop phonograph sat atop a non-descript cabinet, and a small refrigerator had been cleverly built into the paneling but stuck out like an uninvited guest in the laundry room on the other side, which also housed a punching bag Bob frequently pummeled in rapid succession. Pert, modern, geometric-print curtains covered the ground-level windows, and the happy homemaker was pleased to say, "I made them myself."

In the humid heat of summer, her children spent the hottest afternoons inside. "It's cooler in the basement. You can play down there for a while." Rita joined them when there was sweltering ironing to be done.

In 1954, the city of Boston had so many polio cases that parents drove their sick children to Children's Hospital and sat in their cars on the street while resident physicians decided who would go inside for care.

Massachusetts Society for Medical Research

Presently the concerned mother was doing everything she could to keep her children cheerfully isolated at home. "Who wants Kool-Aid? And Ritz crackers with Skippy peanut butter?" Rita wanted them away from what she feared most: polio.

The epidemic was at its peak, and panicked parents on Standard Street made a pact to keep their children separated, believing such a precaution would protect one and all from catching the crippling disease.

Playmates of every age could be seen waving and calling to each other across or up and down the great black asphalt divide.

"Hi, Jeannie. Hi, Judy. Hi, Francis."

"Heyyyy, Stevieeee!"

"Olly, olly, oxen, Andy!"

Four-year-old baby Catherine got a swat on the bum for getting halfway across the street before her mother caught her.

Rita and Bob's children came through the summer of 1954 unscathed, but one wandering neighborhood boy didn't. Despite everyone's sorrow, his plight validated the wisdom of "keeping kids at home 'til this horrible thing blows over."

The Donnellys' living room, observed by others as "just like you'd see in a magazine," was furnished with a pearl-gray couch piped in a green-fern print that matched the pinch-pleated drapes and round toss pillow on the "beige goes with everything" easy chair. Mahogany end tables held tall, green-based, lord and lady pastoral scene lamps with silk shades. A compact cabinet encased the strategically placed "so everyone can see" television set, and a gold, urn-shaped TV lamp on top provided low light for optimum viewing.

The green hassock with black metal legs and a black-button-tufted top improvised nicely as a coffee table. Rita changed area rugs with the seasons, sisal in summer and wool in winter. During warm weather, upholstered pieces were slip covered in a cool green print, and drapes were replaced with custom, roll-up, bamboo blinds.

Rita's modest kitchen had rich, ruby-red and pearl-white checkered broadcloth café curtains hanging from shiny brass rods, and the room extended into a dining area with a picture-window view of the Keaghan family's home. The back door window's sheer curtain was stretched vertically on tension rods, and cinched in the middle. A steep staircase led to three bedrooms and one bath.

To say the décor on the first floor of the Standard Street house was beyond the Donnellys' means would be an understatement. But they hadn't paid a cent beyond the TV set, dining set, and wool rug. The rest came from the most unexpected source. Bob had a friendly acquaintance with a newsvendor on the Boston Common.

Although Maury Lowenstein, with his wool cap, layers of mismatched clothing, bulky coat, and print-smudged canvas apron, had the look of a humble hawker, he in fact owned a good many newsstands throughout the city and philosophized, "A nickel here, a dime there, it all adds up to a pretty penny."

The well-ordered kiosk was filled to absolute capacity with magazines and newspapers of course, but also candy, chewing gum, cigarettes, cigars, aspirin, cough drops, pocket Kleenex, plastic, accordion-pleated rain bonnets, and an assortment of souvenirs: postcards, pens, key chains, combs, and miniature toys as well as Boston's cherished children's book,

Make Way for Ducklings.

Maury was beloved by his customers and had a kind word for almost everyone, each exchange an affirmation of good will on both sides, until that fateful Saturday night, at the dimming of the day, too late for afternoon business and too early for the "night on the town" weekend crowd.

"Okay, old man." A twenty-something tough guy grumbled as he pulled a gun from his jacket pocket. "Ya know how it goes. Ya money or ya life. Hand it over."

The vendor reasoned, "You don't want to do this, buddy. Put the gun away."

The mugger pushed his firearm against Maury's heart, "Don't think I haven't been watchin'. Gimme me the big money ya keep under ya coat. Or else." He put the gun back in his pocket, where it still remained pointed at his victim. Maury reached for the thick envelope of bills he did in fact keep under his coat.

Nothing about the newsvendor's expression revealed anything other than unmitigated fear as he handed it over. It was at that exact moment when the robber was watching Maury's every move that Officer Donnelly stealthily approached from the rear, grabbed the gunman's arms, and handcuffed them behind his back.

"You stupid bastard. Did you really think you'd get away with armed robbery when your intent could be seen a mile away?" Bob confiscated the weapon and roughly spun him around.

The thug demanded, "Get your hands off me, ya dirty copper," and Bob took him by the collar.

"You've got to be the slowest goddam thief this side of a moron. Gun in your pocket, gun out of your pocket, gun in your pocket." Bob shook the daylights out of him. "This is a good man, and you're going away for a long time, pal."

Maury slumped down on a stack of newspapers, wiped his sweating brow with a handkerchief, and heaved a sigh. "You saved my life, Bob. You saved my life."

⚮

Sylvia Lowenstein, well dressed in a black gabardine, straight-skirted suit, carried a leather portfolio in one hand and an umbrella, like a walking stick, in the other when she showed up at Station 3 the next day and asked for Officer Donnelly, who happened to be coming on duty.

"Hey, Bob, there's a real classy-lookin' older dame out there askin' for you. Anything you'd like to own up to, Officer?"

When Bob got to the front desk, Sylvia introduced herself and thanked him profusely "for saving my Maury's life."

"Mrs. Lowenstein, I was simply doing what the good people of Boston pay me to do, serve and protect." *How'd a crumpled up guy like Maury get a beauty like her?*

"That's all very noble, but out of gratitude I'd like to offer you my services." Several officers looked up.

"I'm an interior designer here on the Hill, and it would be my honor to give you and your family a room of new furniture and window coverings as well." She handed him her card.

Bob's first thought was, *Jesus, Rita would love that, a Beacon Hill designer.* The next was job preservation. *Damn it, if the sarge wasn't listening to every word, I might be able to take her up on this.*

"To tell you the truth, we've got all the furniture we need, Mrs. Lowenstein."

"My husband tells me you have a family. I've no doubt you'll be needing more furniture in the future."

"I don't think the department would take too kindly to me accepting your offer." He smiled now. "Thanks anyway, but I need my job more." The police sergeant's resounding double rap on a desk all but said, "You've got that right."

"Very well, Officer. 'Thank you' seems terribly inadequate but again," she extended her gloved hand and shook his, "thank you." All eyes were on the shapely matron as she exited the building.

The next time Maury saw Bob, he had a message for him from Mrs. Lowenstein. "First, let me say my Sylvia never takes no for an answer. And secondly, out of respect for your job concerns, she wants you to know this gift will be for your wife. You'll let us know when Mrs. Donnelly is ready."

When the time came, shortly after Bob's promotion and the move to a new home, it was evident the living room needed attention. Over cups of hot tea and detailed discussions about décor, Rita Donnelly and Sylvia Lowenstein enjoyed each other's company, prompting the uptown interior designer to offer window coverings for the kitchen and dining area as well. "Coordinating color flow is absolutely essential when there's an open plan such as yours, Rita."

"Thank you, Sylvia." *My home has an open plan . . . la de da.*

Rita Margaret King Donnelly ran her home with such precision you'd have thought she'd spent time in the military. The children's schedules were precise and her household was shipshape. She felt safer that way. Those days in Southie after her mother died were without provision, protection, beauty, and order. And they were terrifying.

When Norah was alive, no matter what wrongdoing Rita's father was up to, her mother made sure the children were provided for, and Norah's youngest daughter loved the memory. God only knows how she did it. There was food on the table, "It might be simple fare, but you'll not go hungry," her mother often said. The clothes on their backs were "few but fine, and decent enough to hold your head high," and there was always beauty in their home.

It was Norah's way to cover the table with a clean, pressed cloth and pop a stem of lilac or hydrangea, even pungent smelling geranium, from their landlady's garden in a glass or small pitcher, reserving her one and only vase for special occasions. "Girls," she told them, "it's a reflection on your character, the way you keep house and put a meal on the table. If there's not a penny to be had, and only a few crumbs to eat, it's still no excuse for sloth. Just ask yourself this. If Our Lady, the Blessed Mother herself, came knockin' on the door and asked to come in for a cup of tea, would I be delighted or sorely despondent with regret for the mess of the place? And you boys would do well to pay attention to what's being said. You never know that our Lord won't call you to a life of bachelorhood. Though I pray He doesn't. Unless it's the priesthood you're after."

And Rita recalled, with a great deal of pride, how she and her siblings all had household assignments from an early age, causing neighbor ladies to comment, "I don't know how you do it Norah King. All those children in a three-decker flat, and your home's as spic and span as a spinster's."

All of that went away when Norah passed away.

Replicating her mother's mode brought Norah into Rita's home. Order, predictability, and beauty—Rita held them and they held her.

RUTH ANN REMEMBERS

M Y EARLY CHILDHOOD HOME HAD a basement. The best thing about it was that our mother always had wonderful surprises hidden down there for my brother, Bobby, sister, Catherine, who we called "baby Catherine," and me.

One laundry day, Mummy called, "Ruth Ann. Ruth Ann! Come down here right now!"

I was ten years old and remember everything about that spring afternoon. I can still hear the pat of my saddle oxfords as I ran down the hollow-sounding wooden, cellar stairs. And I can still see my mother, as she was that day, wearing a yellow-and-brown mini-plaid 1950s housedress, and facing the washing machine as I breathlessly answered, "Yes, Mummy."

When she turned around, her pretty smile told me I wasn't, as I'd feared, in trouble. "There you are. Daddy and I are very pleased with your schoolwork, especially your last arithmetic test. Here's a present for your Ginny doll." She reached behind a storage box and presented a wonderful surprise: a tiny doll-sized raincoat, boots, and hat.

My mother wasn't effusive or ingratiating; she was a strict disciplinarian and nothing got past her. She wouldn't tolerate backtalk (as if we'd dare), disobedience, or poor manners. Our bad behavior always had a consequence, usually a beating with a belt, which, as hard as it is to believe today, was the norm for that time and place.

On the other hand, our good behavior seldom went unrewarded with coins for penny candy, a toy, book, or special privilege, such as going to a Saturday matinee at the Oriental Theater (with painted clouds on the ceiling) on Blue Hill Avenue in the adult-less company of a sibling or friend.

She was like that; everything was black and white, good or bad, favor or sin. Thank God, because in time I would have to draw on that good "no nonsense" childhood training, like money out of a bank.

CHAPTER 39

B OB'S TRIP TO CALIFORNIA BEGAN with one phone call.
His mother's only brother, William Murphy, passed through the Golden State as a young man when he was in the Navy during World War I, "met a cute little gal," and made up his mind there and then California would be his future home. That was over thirty-five years ago. Recently, he'd had a massive heart attack and his "cute little gal" wife phoned Boston pleading that someone from the family please come to visit her husband before he passed away. "Bill keeps saying, 'I need to see one of my own.'"

After an emergency family meeting, the Murphy, Dailey, and McDonough relatives pooled their resources and asked Bob if he would be willing to go out there as the clan's representative. They assured him all expenses would be covered.

He didn't have to think twice. "Of course I'll go."

Rita gave him a glaring look clear across the Dailey's cozy living room that needed no explanation. *You better ask if it's okay with me first, Bob Donnelly.*

"That is, if Rita doesn't mind. Honey?"

All eyes went in her direction. She was stuck and she knew it. *Mother of God. California of all places.* "Well, we certainly don't want your uncle meeting his Maker without a good sendoff. Go."

Bob smiled. "Okay. I'll go."

The family thanked him for giving up vacation days. A few of them had something to say regarding, "When you get out to California."

Aunt Blanche Murphy, who lived up to her name with chalk-white skin and white hair, and who as a nurse wore a white uniform most of her days, advised, "Robert, stay in a hotel. Irene doesn't need the trouble of having an out of town houseguest at a time like this. Even if he is a handsome charmer like yourself."

Bob chose the Ambassador Hotel in Los Angeles, home of the famous Cocoanut Grove nightclub, a favorite rendezvous for Hollywood movie stars. He thought it ironic, *we had a Cocoanut Grove in Boston too, until that god-awful fire.*

Uncle Frank Dailey, a patrolman with the Cambridge Police Department, was proud to say, after counting every dollar, "There wasn't a stingy one in the bunch, Bob. You'll have more than enough dough when you get out to California."

His wife, Aunt Jean Dailey, homemaker extraordinaire and mother of the only priest in the family, which made her royalty, chimed in, "Feel free to buy gifts for Rita and the kids with some of that money. It's their sacrifice too."

Bob Donnelly didn't for the life of him understand why they all thought it was such a damn sacrifice to go to California. *Jesus, this is the chance of a lifetime.*

Uncle Walter, a kindly, quirky, middle-aged McDonough bachelor, who lived with and looked after his elderly mother and sat with Buddy if Mrs. Mac needed to go anyplace, offered a delicious nugget of allure, which more than fed Bob's fantastic film-land dream. "Robert, you remember my cousin Mildred? Well, her sister, Ariel, lives somewhere in the Los Angeles area. I understand her husband has something to do with Hollywood filmmaking. Could be interesting. Maybe you'd like to give her a jingle when you're out there. Do you want me to get her number from Mildred?"

Bob couldn't believe his luck. "No kidding. Sure, Walter, do that, and her address if it's not too much trouble. What's her name again?"

"Ariel. I think it's from Shakespeare. That branch of the family is pretty uppity."

∞

After Bob checked into his well-appointed hotel room "with an excellent view of the Sun Club pool, sir," the first phone call he made went to Ariel. "Yes, Bob Donnelly. Your cousin George McDonough married my mother, Ethel."

He liked the warm, friendly lilt in her voice, "The last time I remember, they were still calling you Bobby." And she was delighted to hear a Bostonian accent again.

"Actually, Ariel, I'm out here on family business." He explained everything, she sympathized, and his curiosity got the best of him. "If you don't mind my asking how in the world did you happen to move out here?"

Ariel explained that as a young woman she'd visited California with her grandparents, who'd rented a bungalow in Pasadena. Their neighbors, Mr. and Mrs. Petersen of Chicago and their son, Ed, who was trying to break into the movie business, were also "escaping bitter winter for the season." Ariel and Ed fell madly in love. "We've lived happily ever after ever since."

"Sounds like it was meant to be."

"By the way, where are you staying, Bob?"

"The Ambassador Hotel." He loved the sound of it.

"Wonderful! Oh, you must go to the Cocoanut Grove. I don't know who's playing currently, but it really doesn't matter. We always have a fabulous time at the Grove."

"I definitely plan on popping my head in. Never hear the end of it if I didn't. The family has requested I make an effort to spot at least one movie star."

"I've no doubt you'll be successful. And Bob, we'll have to get together and give you a Cook's tour of Southern California before you go home."

"That'd be great. But I've got to check in with the Murphys first and see what I can do for my uncle."

Founded in the 19th century, the highly acclaimed British tour and travel agency, Thomas Cook established itself as the foremost leader of quality, dependable, well thought-out tours. Their fame for outstanding service coined the term, "Cook's tour" which promises a superior look about the place, be it a home or otherwise.

William Murphy had just come home from San Pedro Hospital when Bob visited him and he found the skin-tanned-to-leather longshoreman in much better shape than anticipated. "God Almighty, Uncle William, I was given the impression you had one foot in the grave. You look damn good for a guy who's on his way out."

As it happened, his uncle was well on the road to recovery. "Got a strong ticker after all," he told Bob.

Mrs. Murphy had jumped the gun, but Bob couldn't say he was put out or even unhappy about her exaggeration, nor his uncle's panic-stricken plea. *Hell, it all worked out for the best as far as I'm concerned. I got a trip to California, and this melodramatic character gets to see 'one of my own.'*

"Hey, Bobby, great to lay eyes on you, kid."

He handed his uncle a small, twine-tied box of baked goods. "I was told in no uncertain terms this couldn't be crushed into a suitcase. It was to be 'hand carried.' You're well loved, Uncle William."

"Call me Bill if you don't mind. Everyone out here does."

"Fair enough, Uncle Bill, and I go by Bob these days." The two men enjoyed a good laugh.

"So Bob, you carried this all the way cross country? Helluva nice thing for you to do." He sniffed the box. "I'd know that aroma anywhere. Et's Irish soda bread. Don't tell the Doc about this." He reached up from where he was lying on a bright floral-print couch and shook Bob's hand firmly. "Thanks a million. Now, have a seat and fill me in on everyone. Irene's got something cookin' on the stove. We'll have lunch before long. You like chili con carne?"

His hosts also served a tossed green salad with slices of what looked and tasted like Palmolive soap, "Mmm, what's this called?" Bob inquired. "Avocado. Isn't it delicious?" his uncle gleefully answered.

After navigating the highways and byways of Southern California from San Pedro back to L.A., AAA Club map laid out on the front seat leading the way, Bob returned to his hotel. *Think I'll catch a few z's.* That night he enjoyed a much-anticipated visit and barbequed steak dinner with the Petersens, and the next day he phoned Rita to tell her all about his "long-lost relatives."

She drew a blank.

"You remember Ariel? Uncle Walter suggested I look her up."

Rita got a knot in her stomach. *The movie people.*

Ariel Petersen was full figured and film star pretty with a short, wavy, dark reddish-brown hairdo and sparkling amber-brown eyes. She was classy, intelligent, almost old enough to be Bob's mother and, as he described her, "full of life." Ed, a good-looking, lean, fair-haired Scandinavian, personable but much quieter, was a successful lighting director, and along with their only child, a teenaged daughter, the couple lived in a grand Spanish Colonial home, which Bob referred to as "the Castle" because of its imposing turret. "Honey, they have a live-in Mexican housekeeper and a Jap gardener too. Apparently Ariel is always on the go. She's a hot ticket. I can't wait for you to meet them."

Bob let slip what Rita had already concluded. *My God, he really thinks we're moving out there.* It made her angry but she coyly bided her time. "Oh, do they plan on visiting Boston soon?" *Dream on, Mr. California. I'm not giving in to you moving us three thousand miles away, let alone pulling the kids out of Saint Gregory's. Everything's perfectly in place, Bob Donnelly, and by God it's going to stay that way.*

He flew right past her question. "It's beautiful out here, honey, and I wish you could see this hotel. There's a huge swimming pool with, I don't know, maybe fifty chaise lounges lined up all around it. And get this, they provide terrycloth robes and have cabanas just like in the movies. The lobby's huge too, with swanky, light-colored, living room setups. Everything out here seems lighter, clothing, buildings, and houses—even the general outlook. There's a barbershop too, and all kinds of classy stores, including a haberdashery and a really ritzy coffee shop. I ate there my first night, after I finally got Uncle Bill's family on the phone. I'll give you an update on his health in a minute."

She noted the change from William without comment.

∞

Ariel Petersen and Bob Donnelly were two peas in a pod. They both liked nice things, nice places and being on the go. Ariel and her friend Edith offered to take the visiting Bostonian across the border to Tijuana, Mexico. "If we get an early start, we can go to the bullfights, get lunch, do some shopping, and have dinner too. Ever had Mexican food, Bob?"

They did the Tijuana tour "in spades," as Bob said on the way back to L.A., and the "three gay caballeros" laughed over how concerned he'd been to leave the country on such short notice, even after Ariel assured him, "It's just like crossing the street. No passport required. You have nothing to worry about."

When "Roberto" got back to his room, he could hardly wait to talk with Rita. He looked at his watch. *It's nine o'clock here . . . midnight there! Damn. I'll have to wait 'til morning. He* put the receiver back on the hook. *Think I'll go downstairs, have a drink at the Palm Bar, and pop my head in the Cocoanut Grove. Or maybe I'll just have that drink at 'the Grove'.* He recalled Ariel's easy reference to the nightclub. *It all depends on the setup.*

Bob woke up ravenous, went for a quick swim, and took his breakfast of freshly squeezed California orange juice, bacon and eggs, English muffin, and a pot of hot coffee poolside before phoning home. *Whoever would have expected a working stiff like me to be enjoying the life of Riley like this? Thank you, family.* His gratitude practically sounded like a prayer as he lit his second cigarette, sat back, and enjoyed an alluring view of bathing beauties. *Thank you, family; thank you, Uncle Bill; and thank you, Rita, for holding down the fort; and thank you, BPD for the time off; and thank you, Uncle Walter, for remembering Ariel; and thank you, Aunt Irene, for calling wolf.*

Poolside – Ambassador Hotel
LOS ANGELES, CALIF.

As he waited for the elevator up to his room, Bob Donnelly certainly looked the part of a carefree, prosperous tourist, wrapped in a terry robe, his wet hair slicked back, an *L.A. Times* newspaper folded under his arm. Two young women, a tan, long-legged blonde and stunning brunette, all decked out in high-heeled sandals, bare sundresses and broad-brimmed sun hats, glanced agreeably in his direction—and he could have sworn the blonde winked as they walked by. He whistled a happy tune all the way up to his room and right away phoned Rita. *She'll get a kick out of hearing about who I saw at the Cocoanut Grove last night.* He gladly recalled sultry actress Ava Gardner in her glittering, jet-black evening gown—*quite a figure*—and her crooner husband, "Old Blue Eyes" Frank Sinatra. *Just like all good-looking guineas, dapper, smooth and damn sure of himself.*

"And you'll never guess what else, honey? I've been out of the country. Ariel and her friend Edith took me to Mexico yesterday."

"Mexico! You're kidding! What was that like?"

"First of all, I got some nice gifts for you and the girls."

"Ooooh, what?"

He bought Rita a hand-tooled, tan leather shoulder bag, and for his daughters, peacock-blue felt jackets appliquéd with sombreros, burros, and flowers, blanket-stitched in sunny yellow yarn.

Rita was pleased. "Perfect."

Bobby's gift, "a real Roy Rogers" cowboy holster with two cap guns, would be purchased the next day at a toy store in one of Los Angeles's "must see" tourist spots, the Farmer's Market. There was a knock at Bob's door, and Rita got a lump in her stomach. *Mother of God, don't tell me he's—*

"Just a minute Rit, I'll be right back." She listened closely as Bob said, "I'll be out of here within the hour. Can you come back later?" She could tell he wasn't masquerading. It was the maid.

"So are you ready for this, Rita? Ariel's husband is a lighting director. Hell of a nice guy. And today we're going to visit Paramount Studios."

"And Uncle 'Bill' too, I trust."

He caught her drift. "Jesus, Rita, give me a break. Of course I'm going to see him."

Ed Petersen had arranged for Bob and Ariel to visit the set he was currently working on, a western starring "man with the gray flannel hair," actor Jeff Chandler. He also arranged for them to meet stars Virginia Mayo and Ward Bond, who were shooting different westerns on the same lot. Bob seized the day for all time, as he snapped photos of the entrance to Paramount Studios, the set, the stars, and bit actors too. Ariel took over where he left off, and with a single click and "smile everyone," she recorded Bob, Ed, Ward, and Jeff seated at an umbrella-shaded table with the gorgeous Miss Mayo glancing over her shapely shoulder into the lens.

When Bob phoned home that night, Rita expressed how much she and the children missed him. "I miss all of you too, honey. Just a sec." He cradled the phone, lit a cigarette, and took a long drag. "Still there?"

"Waiting with bated breath."

"Are you sitting down? Because you're never going to believe who I met today."

"Who? And of course I'm sitting down. What else would I be doing after taking care of three kids all day?" She kicked off her penny loafers, put both feet up on a kitchen chair, ankles crossed, took a puff of her own cigarette, and was whisked away to Hollywood on Bob's magic carpet of enthusiasm and awe.

"Honey, they were so friendly, and Virginia Mayo even asked if I had a picture of my family. She said I have a very pretty wife. Thanks for slipping that Gloucester snapshot from last spring in my suitcase."

⁘

Bob's last call home came on the heels of a fairly sleepless night. Dreams of East and West had collided in surreal vignettes of his BPD cronies being escorted by Frank Sinatra to front row tables at the Cocoanut Grove, where Bob was waiting with Miss Gardner on one arm and Rita on the other. Ariel was frantically handing out umbrellas, and when Bob looked down, everyone was wearing galoshes. His children were out of the picture.

"Oh, and this morning Ariel's going to come to the Murphys with me. Actually, she's going to pick me up at the hotel. Her Cadillac convertible is a lot more exciting than my rental sedan. Uncle Bill is doing much better. It's not his time to go after all. And this afternoon, Ariel and Edith are taking me to the races."

"Well, Bob, I hope this trip helped get all that California talk out of your system. You came, you saw, you conquered. Now it's time to come home."

"I'd better get downstairs, honey. Be sure to give my love to the kids, and I'll see you tomorrow."

Much later that evening, when the house was at last quiet, all lights out but an overhead fixture, Rita sat alone at the kitchen table with a cup of tea and a box of milk chocolate nonpareil candies, her *Photoplay* magazine pushed aside and rosary beads that had once belonged to her mother front and center but only partway out of the small, threadbare, packet that held them.

All those years ago, Rosemary had taken the sacred beads from Norah's casket just before the lid was closed, believing with all her heart in the power of a mother's prayers. Hadn't Norah prayed for a good husband for Rosemary? And didn't Rita, more than she or Kay, need to hold the hope those tiny spiritual spheres came to represent? *Prayer and sacred praises bring comfort and peace.*

Tonight, Rita Margaret took the green Connemara marble rosary in hand, kissed the crucifix, and before saying the series of dedicated prayers, counted her blessings; Saint Gregory's was close to the top, just below Bob and her three beautiful children. The thought of losing all that she held dear terrified her. It had happened before.

Saint Gregory's School and it's ornate, Romanesque Revival-styled, twin-towered church were straight up the street from the Walter Baker Chocolate Factory, an extensive industrial property with the Neponset River rushing through it, all located at Dorchester's, Lower Mills.

Saint Gregory's Church
DORCHESTER, MASS.

An aroma of hot cocoa permeated the entire area, and Bobby Donnelly asked on his first day at the new school, "Mummy, is the Marshmallow Fluff factory here too?"

Rita's older children wore school uniforms, "a Godsend," and they each carried a green, Saint Gregory's-embossed schoolbag and a metal lunch box—red plaid for Ruth Ann and Hopalong Cassidy for Bobby.

Weekdays were blessedly routine. Brother and sister were given a hot breakfast, even if it was cold cereal with warm milk, and when they left home never failed to say, "Goodbye and God bless you" to their mother and little sister.

On designated days the boys and girls were asked to wear certain colors in honor of:

The Blessed Mother — blue

The Sacred Heart — red

and so forth. Girls wore bow-tied ribbons in their hair and on their blouses, boys, appropriately colored ties, and if they came to school without one, the good Sisters had a ready collection of big, discarded funeral arrangement bows.

The siblings walked, ran, and skipped (through autumn leaves, snow drifts, or puddles, depending on the season) down the hill and caught a public bus that dropped them off by Saint Gregory's. Sometimes, after school, they'd spend the nickel carfare on candy bars and run all the way home along Morton Street, where they'd often spy House Representative McCormick's underwear hanging on the clothesline, point and giggle, arrive home late and get in trouble— but that didn't stop them from doing it again.

On freezing days, Rita gave the Irish twins just enough money (tied in a hankie and entrusted to Ruth Ann's care) so they could buy "a hot lunch" at the corner drugstore one block away from their cafeteria-less school and kitty-corner from the chocolate factory. A bell at the top of the drugstore door rang in the youngsters' arrival. They'd gleefully slide across the slick, black-and-white octagon-tiled floor, up to a row of red vinyl covered stools at the soda fountain, where they'd sit and spin two times before taking off their coats, hats, and mittens.

Both children felt grown up when ordering their own food, even if they were following Mummy's instructions. Two cups of tomato soup, a shared grilled cheese sandwich, two chocolate Devil Dogs for dessert, two glasses of milk. "And heaven help you two if I discover you got Coca-Cola instead." Neither of them ever once ordered the preferred cola drink because their mother always found out what they were up to. "God, in his infinite wisdom, has given every mother on earth eyes on the back of her head, and only He can see them."

Mrs. Rita Donnelly assured the Sisters of Notre Dame they had complete freedom to discipline her offspring "in whatever way you see fit, Sister." She trusted the Brides of Christ.

The children of Saint Greg's learned how to be a devout Catholic, as well as duty and decorum, or else. Whatever the good Sister considered bad behavior was met with a call to the front of the room, "Put your hand out," and a whack with a ruler. Or "You're to stay after and sweep this room until every spec is off the floor," or the worst consequence of all, "Take this note to your mother. We'll be meeting at the Convent to discuss your unsatisfactory grades." Or the meeting would address rude behavior, constant tardiness, endless daydreaming, apparent slovenliness, whatever perceived sign of poor character that needed parental attention, intervention, and punishment. Rita approved wholeheartedly.

Not a day went by that the children weren't positively reinforced as well. Exceptional kindness, service, generosity, winning a spelling bee and various competitions were rewarded with a holy card or medal, and sometimes penny candy. There were school festivals: minstrel shows, Christmas parties, Valentine exchanges, spring picnics, and glorious Holy Day processions, such as the crowning of the Blessed Mother in May. These traditions were, to Rita's thinking, joyous character builders.

Just as the generation before them, girls and boys educated in the parochial schools of the Archdiocese of Boston prayed the Holy Rosary every morning. This generation, via a live broadcast over the crackling speaker in every classroom, was led by the esteemed Archbishop Richard J. Cushing. His chanting, powerful intonation kept the children's attention, and his evident happiness kept their faith. Rita believed nothing would keep her children strong in life like the teachings they received in parochial school. *The discipline of daily prayer and knowing the love of God will help get them through life's ups and downs.*

Students were expected to attend Sunday Children's Mass, where the Sisters took roll. If a child didn't show up, in addition to "the black stain of a mortal sin on your soul," there was hell to pay. Strict doctrine, "the Catholic church is the one true church," and moral responsibility went hand in hand. "Keep all those poor, unfortunate Protestants in your prayers now, children."

∞

Rita put Norah's rosary beads in their proper place for safe keeping after carefully arranging them with the crucifix at the center. And although it was almost ten o'clock at night, she lit a flame under the kettle for one last cup of tea, glanced at her *Photoplay* magazine, and wondered if cover-girl starlet Debbie Reynolds liked living in California.

CHAPTER 40

That was a memorable day to me, for it made great changes in me.
But, it is the same with any life. Imagine one selected day struck
out of it, and think how different its course would have been.
Pause you who read this, and think for a moment
of the long chain of iron or gold, of thorns or flowers,
that would never have bound you, but for the formation
of the first link on one memorable day.

GREAT EXPECTATIONS

CHARLES DICKENS

A SUDDEN SNOWSTORM FELL ON THE city of Boston the day Bob was scheduled to return home from the land of sunshine.

Uncle Frank Dailey, and his wife Aunt Jean Dailey, picked Rita up and drove her to the airport in their well-equipped Ford Fairlane, chains on the tires, a thermos of hot coffee, sandwiches and cookies packed in a brown grocery bag on the back seat, ready to go "just in case." They'd allowed more than enough time because of the inclement conditions, and the upbeat women talked every bit of the way, Frank too, teasing, "When I can get a damn word in edge wise!"

Uncle Frank and Congressman "All Politics is local" Tip O'Neill, had been fast friends since boyhood. Their speech was so identical, if you closed your eyes when Uncle was speaking, Tip O'Neill, "hell of a nice fella," was in the room.

Rita loved these two and their frugal, caring ways. Mrs. Mac's mother, "Great-Grammy," lived with their family of five, and the middle-aged couple was well known for generous, fun-loving hospitality with, as always, enough food to feed an Army.

Logan Airport was a jumble of last minute confusion as resounding announcements rattled off amended arrivals and departures one after another. "American Airline's flight number 163, Los Angeles to Boston, will be further delayed due to weather conditions." Air travel was still somewhat beyond the "average Joe's" reach, and largely for lack of experience, was often subject to exaggerated safety concerns.

Uncle Frank paced.

Aunt Jean fretted. "I hope everything's okay."

Rita looked worried, despite her hopeful, "He'll be here before we know it." *Blessed Mother of God, let me be right.*

Thirty minutes later, the Douglas DC-7 came in for approach.

Those on board could barely see the runway lights through the rugged weather, and when their pilot cautioned, "Prepare for landing," Bob Donnelly felt trapped. *No! I'm not going to live like this anymore, snow, sleet, the goddam cold! The only place I'm landing is California, and the sooner the better.*

As soon as he appeared at the top of the airplane's exit stairway, Rita put her hand to her heart. "There he is." She kissed her in-law relatives and made a dash for the door.

Mr. and Mrs. Dailey watched from the warmth inside the terminal as Rita walked quickly in her black, fur-topped ankle boots through swirling flurries, across the snow-dusted tarmac, into her husband's arms. Uncle Frank said, "What a doll. They've had their days, but that's a real love match if you ask me."

Bob's aunt agreed. "Absolutely. And I bet he didn't see one starlet in California who's half as pretty as Rita is in that red coat."

The Dailey's car slowly pulled up to 97 Standard Street, and the returning traveler noted every single light in the house was on. *What are those kids up to?* He couldn't wait to give them their gifts. *I hope Catherine's still awake.* More than anything Bob wanted to see his children. He had, after all, been gone a whole week, a whole continent away. The Daileys and Donnellys hurried to unload the car, and Bob imagined how much the kids would have loved playing in the Ambassador Hotel's swimming pool, but the cold reality of his present circumstance interrupted the sunny scene. *Wouldn't you know there'd be damn snowman in front of the house.*

Hands full, Bob walked headfirst against the storm. The front door opened and a houseful of people shouted, "Welcome Home!" He juggled the packages under one arm, brushed the snow from his hair, stepped inside, and smiled broadly. "Whoa, what's all this about?"

His brother-in-law Timmy King quipped, "Whoa? Would that be western talk for Jesus, Mary, and Joseph, what a surprise?" A gale of laughter followed.

Rita asked, "Happy, honey?" and their children ran to him screeching, "Daddy's home!"

He bent down, circled them with his brawny arms, kissed all three, picked Catherine up, and took Rita's hand. "Thanks, honey. This is really terrific." Everyone wanted to hear all about California, particularly Hollywood, but Bob said, "Give me a minute, okay?" He reached for a package Frank carried in, told Ruth Ann and Bobby, "Follow me, kids," and led the children upstairs.

His daughters put the colorful Mexican jackets on right away. "Thank you, Daddy!" He held both girls up in front of the mirror over Rita's dresser. Catherine said, "Mine has a donkey," and she petted the felt appliqué. Bobby wore the Roy Rogers holster slung low on his hips, and Bob's apt adjustment was met with, "Please, Daddy? This is how all the cowboys on TV wear theirs." They went downstairs again with an authentic cowboy leading the way, and Bob proudly paraded his children around the party. "Yeah, can you believe it? Mexico."

By the time they marched into the busy kitchen, another treasure from Bob's trip was in use. The white, red-bordered, souvenir tablecloth featured a colorfully illustrated map with the ocean, boats, waves and surfboards, missions, a plethora of palm trees, snow-capped mountains, cactus-filled deserts, flowers, grapes, and oranges. A double-reeled motion picture camera marked

Hollywood, while a big, smiling, bright yellow sun shone over the entire state with one eye closed in an exaggerated wink. California was on the table.

Throughout the lively evening, one guest after another said or asked the same things.

"So you see any movie stars, Bob?"

"Heard you found a rich relative, that so?"

"You're lookin' good, got a little sun out there, Bobby."

"Ya know, I had a friend who did basic training in San Diego, and after the war he packed his gear and bid Boston goodbye. You're not thinkin' a movin' to California now, are you, Robert?"

Bob Donnelly's mother stood at the kitchen sink rinsing party prep dishes and all she wanted to know was, "How's my brother getting along?"

Bob snitched slices of salami and provolone from a platter destined for the buffet table. "Well, Mum, to tell you the truth, Uncle William's pretty weak, but the doctor said he's going to pull through this just fine."

Mrs. Mac gave her son a wet-handed, side-by-side hug. "Thanks for going out there. I'm so glad—" she was about to say why when a tearful woman, the wife of one of Bob's fellow detectives from work, hurriedly brushed past them and made a beeline for the front door with her husband following close behind.

"Come on, hon. I was just kidding."

Rita came right on their heels, and having been privy to the husband's "idiocy," filled the curious kitchen crowd in. "Evelyn Noonan went on and on about Shirley Doyle's trim figure, and Ralph suggested to his much prettier-than-he-deserves wife, 'Maybe she'll share her secret with you, Myrna.' This from a man who manages to look like a sack of potatoes no matter what he's wearing. Not to mention the Groucho Marx stooping."

Bob took note of his own wife and thought she looked like a million bucks in her "I don't remember seeing that outfit before" latest Filene's Basement steal: a smart, gray wool, straight skirt, blouse, and coordinating beaded bolero sweater.

Another detective laughed. "That's what we call him downtown." He mimicked the zany comedian and TV game show host, holding his signature cigar, wiggling his bushy brows, and prompting contestants to 'Say the secret woid.'

Rita turned to Bob. "Please see if they're still outside and bring them back in."

Another wife humorously demanded, "But not before that louse apologizes." Rita added with her dimpled smile, arms crossed, "On one knee."

The quarreling couple sat in their idling car, windows steamed up. Bob forged through the snowstorm, wearing a striped serape and sombrero he'd bought in Tijuana, and tapped on the car window.

Myrna rolled it down. "What do you want, Detective Donnelly?"

"Hola, Señor, Señora. Do you know the way to Mexico, please?"

For some inexplicable reason his "My name is Roberto" charade diffused the situation. "Everybody at the party, miiiss you verrry much, especially the pretty señora. But the other señoras, they say the Miiister, he must apologize . . . on one knee."

Coincidently, "Old Lady Connelly" as neighbors called the somewhat senile widow, was peeking out at the storm, spotted "a Mexican" and straight away phoned her son, thus informing his speculation, "It may be time to put my mother in a home."

Ralph Sandowski bolted out of the car and did so. The freezing cold trio came rushing back inside to the catchy hit tune "Mambo Italiano" playing on the phonograph, sung by popular Irish American recording artist Rosemary Clooney and gaily accompanied by almost everyone at the party.

Quartets, duos, and singles—Pilsner glass, cocktail glass, coffee cup, cigarette, fork, or spoon in hand—tapped to the music, while swishing skirts swayed along to the beat. Many guests danced, and some simply sat back and listened. Bob mamboed across the room to Rita, twirled her around and swooped in for a kiss. "Mambo Italiano."

The "hostess with the mostest" liked her house to be full like this with people, music, laughter, and good food. It was a long way from the troubles of her teens, and she thanked God for everything as she kept food and drinks fresh, collected plates and emptied ashtrays, with the dependable help of her sister-in-law, Marion, and her sister, Kay. Guests were seated, as she looked around, everywhere, at the kitchen table, in the stairway, on the floor around the coffee table, squeezed together on the couch, and easy chair, and arms of both, some leaning against a counter, wall, or door jamb. She overheard their neighbor Charles Price ask from his party perch on an arm of the couch, one foot firmly on the floor, the other crossed on his knee, "So, Bob, what's the work situation like out there in California?"

"Funny you should ask, Charlie," he replied from his somewhat elevated position on one of three barstools brought up from the basement. "Just out of curiosity, I checked in with LAPD, and they said to be sure and get in touch when I'm ready. There's a good chance they might have an opening." Bob caught sight of Rita out of the corner of his eye and quickly added, "It goes without saying all of this was a matter of 'what if'?"

CHAPTER 41

We wish you a merry Christmas, We wish you a merry Christmas
We wish you a merry Christmas, And a Happy New Year!
Good tidings we bring for you and your kin;
We wish you a merry Christmas And a Happy New Year!
"WE WISH YOU A MERRY CHRISTMAS"
TRADITIONAL ENGLISH CAROL

THEY ALMOST LOOKED REAL, AND in fact, the Donnelly children would pretend they were. Mary, Joseph, and baby Jesus were spending the night on Boston Common, where they'd taken up residence for the season. Life-sized shepherds, wise men, angels, cow, donkey, and sheep were also nestled in the large, sheltered manger scene. Most of the time it was covered with snow, and the wooden railing that kept the Holy Family in and visitors out looked like frosted gingerbread. It was a sight to behold!

Every December, the Donnelly family made a traditional Saturday pilgrimage to visit the manger once by day and again right after dark. In between there would be Christmas shopping, lunch at the Adams House Restaurant, a visit to Santa captured with a professional black-and-white photo, and "going to see the windows," elaborate vignettes of animated figures set in captivating holiday scenes at downtown department stores.

The first window held elves wearing colorful tights, blue jackets, and striped stocking caps as they hammered strings on pull-toys, painted wagons red, dotted rosy cheeks onto baby dolls, and wrapped gifts amidst unfurled rolls of gaily printed paper and spools of runaway ribbon.

At the next one, Ruth Ann giggled at Mrs. Claus pulling a tray of goodies from the oven as a gingerbread boy ran for the door with a handful of cookies and a little gray mouse with sugar on his nose popped out of her apron pocket. The storybook kitchen held oversized candy canes, gumdrops and licorice sticks amid giant, leaning to and fro, swirled lollypops. Twinkle-toed elves, their askance chef hats flopping about, packed glittering cookies in tiny tins while a comfy sheepdog lay under the worktable wagging his tail to, *Up on the house-top, click, click, click. Down thru the chimney with good Saint Nick.* Catherine's mittened hands clapped at the make-believe scenes, and Bobby looked like an arcade game's moving target as he ran back and forth, trying to decide which window he liked best. "Mummy, look!"

The next setting featured Santa's Workshop, where seemingly every toy a girl or boy could ever want had been placed on display: Tiny Tears and Madame Alexander dolls, Howdy Doody puppets, "Kukla, Fran and Ollie" records, ant farms, Mr. Potato Head, Hopalong Cassidy pistol sets, Dale Evans Cow Girl Outfits, Captain Kangaroo storybooks, board games, crayons and coloring books, building blocks, paper dolls, Erector Sets, and Lincoln Logs.

There wasn't one piece of clothing. This was, as the piped music merrily declared, *Toy land, toy land, wonderful girl and boy land.*

Bobby had his eye on electric trains, Bob had his eye on Bobby, and on December 24[th,] Santa left an entire railroad under the Donnellys' tree. Ruth Ann spotted a golden-haired doll with a pink tulle dress and told Santa where he could find it. "She's next to the teddy bears." Catherine wanted the Tiny Tears doll "now" and cried real tears when told she'd have to wait until Christmas. "I don't want to," she said with a pout.

The last scenario featured a loaded sleigh with Santa and his reindeer prepared for takeoff, Rudolph's "very shiny nose" ready to lead the way. The

Donnelly children knew some of those gifts would be under their tree because Rudolph winked at them.

Toy Land, evergreens, and red ribbons, along with thousands of twinkling lights throughout the city meant Christmas was near. And every child on that snowy sidewalk knew the real Santa was upstairs at the Jordan Marsh department store, his ample knee poised to seat them and ear inclined to hear exactly what they wanted. It was wonderland!

This was one of Rita's favorite days of the year, being in town with Bob and the kids and enjoying the freedom of "What wonderful thing should we do next?" Although getting her family there—well dressed, well groomed, and well fed—was quite an undertaking.

Beginning the night before, she gave the girls baths, set their hair with pink foam curlers, set her own in pin curls and ironed everyone's clothing. Bob took the whiskbroom to whatever garment needed a "little brushing up," bathed his son, and polished scuffed shoes. In the morning Rita prepared a huge breakfast. "I want you kids to eat everything on your plates. Hear me? Everything." That way they'd only need to eat out once, with a late lunch. By that time the family was usually ravenous, and in an attempt to fend off all-around crankiness, Bob would hurry his brood along, like a policeman managing crowd control, as they headed to the same eatery year after year. "Let's step it up, ladies and gentleman."

Window tables at the Adams House Restaurant were always in high demand. Diners enjoyed looking out at the bustling crowds on Washington Street, and passersby could seldom resist glancing in at the delectable food. The restaurant was on Bob's former beat and had required nothing more from the patrolman than assistance with a medical emergency or rare minor offence, such as someone skipping out on the check. Whatever the situation, Bob made it right with the least amount of disturbance and maximum amount of kibitzing and kidding.

The Donnellys seldom had to wait for a table. "The next one that opens up is yours, Bob." That's how it was; people looked after each other and showed their gratitude with hospitality, generosity, and favor.

Walking into the Adams House Restaurant always felt special to Rita, with its cloth-covered tables and fresh flowers, delicious menu choices, and impeccable service from waitresses in black uniforms with white organdy aprons,

The *Adams House Restaurant*
533-535 Washington Street
BOSTON, MASS.

matching caps, and ruffled, pinned on hankies. This was the place of happy memories. "Table for five," is what Bob said every time. "Table for five, and the children will need phone books to sit on, please."

The family's arrival was a three-ring circus. First there was a big, back-slapping welcome for Bob from Leonard, the gregarious, mustached Lithuanian manager.

"In for the day?" He shook Bob's hand. "Hello, Mrs. Donnelly," he said with a slight bow. "Kids." He shook each of their hands in turn.

Then there was the job of getting outerwear checked in, no small feat with three children and Rita's hesitation to leave her treasured red coat behind. She'd grown accustomed to turning heads when she wore it and disliked giving up the adulation. "What do you think, honey? Should I leave it here?"

Bob rolled his eyes at the nubile coat-check girl and handed her some of the children's things. "I don't know, Rit. Do what you want."

"I'll wear it in." *Then there's always the possibility some idiot will step on it when I sit down.* "No, we better leave it here."

Bob checked the coat and received a reciprocal roll of eyes, and Rita didn't miss a thing. "Come on honey, they're waiting for our family."

Her ability to find the best for the least continued to defy their modest means. When the Donnellys walked into the dining room, they looked like a million dollars.

Rita led the way, prompted by Bob with a fingertip touch to her elbow. He was proud as punch when his attractive wife entered the bustling room in her fitted gray dress adorned with a rhinestone Christmas tree pin. A small black hat held her cap-cut hairdo in place, and a Longine wristwatch, purchased on time by Bob, circled her left wrist. She held her gloves like a scepter. Holding gloves while making an entrance was, in her sense of propriety, absolutely essential.

Bobby and Ruth Ann vied for the best chair while Rita and Bob turned this way and that, every move a parental dance of care and attention as they got everyone settled in. "Please" and "thank you" were sprinkled amid "sit up straight" and "put your napkin on your lap." Waitresses chanted, "Lovely family, lovely manners." Their singsong phrases a hoped-for reward, coveted by the earnest couple, who always tried their best to make a good impression.

The children's Filene's Basement outfits would be captured in a Jordan Marsh, sitting on Santa's lap, professional photo, taken later that day.

Ruth Ann's good coat was getting small, but Rita said it would pass. She got her lanky daughter's mind off the too short fit with the ten-year-old's first Christmas corsage of frosted bells, foil leaves, tiny glass balls and red ribbon. "You're a young lady now."

Bobby appeared "to the manor born" in an imitation-fur collared topcoat, and his confident "my handsome boy" smile cinched it.

Four-year-old "my baby" Catherine's princess-styled coat suited her to a tee. Its matching bonnet was off. "Let's not hide those pretty curls."

Rita looked around the festively decorated dining room and was surprised to see her in-town friend, sitting alone at a window table for two. "Honey, look, Cordelia Parker. I'm going to invite her to join us, okay?" *Where's that doctor boyfriend of hers?*

"Sure, if she doesn't mind sharing a meal with three active children." He pushed a full water glass away from Catherine's reach.

"She loves the kids. Better watch Bobby's too. I'll be right back."

Rita wove her way toward Cordelia through tables of high-spirited shoppers, darting waitresses, and busy busboys. The pleasant pitch of lilting conversations, tinkling silverware, dishes, and glassware, against a background of "Jingle Bells" provided a lively accompaniment to her deft steps and recall of the day Cordelia announced her engagement.

It was a while ago and Rita had been in town alone for what was supposed to be a turnaround trip to Filene's Basement for a few needed items, including new school shoes for Bobby. *Absolute necessities only, remember that.* And though it was a good walk, she couldn't resist stopping by Chandler's too, where a beaming Cordelia said straightaway, "I have something exciting to tell you."

She suggested they go up the street for "a quick cup of tea and pastries" at the Brittany Coffee Shop & Garden where she filled a rapt Rita in on her recent betrothal.

"I'm so happy for you, Cordelia." *Thank God she won't be alone.*

Today Cordelia looked especially pretty in a French-blue suit and ever Brahmin with her aristocratic nose a bit in the air as she perused the room for a waitress. She saw Rita right away, put a bookmark in place, and rose from the table. *What a lovely surprise.*

They hadn't seen each other for a while with Bob's visit to California and all that ensued. Rita noted her friend's radiance and was happy for her all over again. *You can tell she's in love.* They greeted one another with a light ladylike squeeze. "Merry Christmas."

Rita couldn't help but admire Cordelia's striking suit and her pearl Christmas wreath brooch, inherited from her aunties. "I love your pin." She was sorry she hadn't worn her red coat in the dining room after all.

"I hate to see you eating alone, Cordelia. Please, join us." Rita turned in the direction of her family.

The girls daintily waved, Bobby wildly sported his napkin, and Bob pushed it down. "Keep that on your lap where it belongs." He raised his other hand in a friendly half-salute.

Cordelia was tempted to accept Rita's invitation but declined. "David's meeting me. He's doing rounds at the hospital, and it could be sooner or later. It's best if we have our own table. I know he'll be exhausted." There was a respectful yet sparkling inclination in Cordelia's voice when she spoke of David Miller. Rita never considered the single woman anything other than pleasant, but since her engagement she was definitely different: sweetly, serenely, light-heartedly different.

"I hope I get to meet your mystery man soon."

"Absolutely. Let's hope it's today. Meanwhile I'm sure you'd like to return to your family. I'll walk back with you and say hello."

Without quibbling or question, everyone in the Donnelly family knew exactly what they wanted to order. For Bob it would be a steak sandwich, Rita looked forward to Lobster Newburg en Casserole, Bobby wanted a "hamburgler," Catherine asked for "mac-roni," and Ruth Ann's order customarily involved an amendment. This year she asked, "Can I please have a bacon, lettuce and tomato sandwich without the bacon on it." Bob insisted, "As is or find something else, I'm tired of this nonsense." His protest to his daughter's preference and Rita's protest to his protest, "Let her have what she wants, Bob," found their children quiet as church mice, scared they'd get caught somewhere in the middle of the escalating disagreement. "It's just a sandwich for God's sake."

The Donnelly family was ready to leave before David arrived, and Bob said, "Just as well, hon. We've got a lot of territory to cover—not the least of which is getting these kids in line to see Santa. Who knows how long that's going to take?" All three children were sent to the LADIES ROOM & MENS ROOM ONE FLIGHT UP ⇧ via the restaurant's elegant sweeping staircase with the eldest put in charge while their parents remained at the table and mapped out the rest of the day.

Truth be known, Ruth Ann would have asked permission to go to the "ladies room," even if it was completely unnecessary—and pretended, as she always did, to be Cinderella on the way up and Mummy's favorite TV lady, Loretta Young, on the way down.

Bob tipped the cheeky coat check girl generously, buckled Bobby's flopping galoshes, zipped Catherine's tiny boots, and placed Ruth Ann's pull-on pair in front of her. "There you go, big girl." Rita located mittens and hats, buttoned what needed to be buttoned, and one by one, held a Kleenex beneath her children's noses. "Blow." Lastly, Bob helped his wife into her red coat and slipped his own overcoat on as he shepherded everyone out the door. "God Almighty, Rita, it would've taken less time to clothe a damn army."

CHAPTER 42

דָּוִד

THE MEANING OF DAVID IN HEBREW IS BELOVED.

CORDELIA PUT HER BOOK DOWN and stared dreamily out the window as she sipped coffee and slowly ate a first course cup of lobster-bisque and warm rolls with butter while waiting for David. The city scene before her was reminiscent of a charming snow globe village; flurries fell, Christmas decorations twinkled and an endless parade of bundled up pedestrians moved along the sidewalk. Lately her daydreams went to the same place, forthcoming married life with David Miller at home on Mount Vernon and cold winter nights with fireplaces aglow downstairs and up. *Once the holidays are over, I'll change everything out in the master bedroom and make it our own.* She envisioned a creamy white, duvet-covered down comforter over luscious same-color sheets and pillowcases, with an ecru matelassé coverlet she'd recently put aside at Chandler's. The two of them nestled in each other's arms, their bodies bare and entwined.

Cordelia smoldered at the thought and winced at the wait, but loved David all the more for his moral restraint. It occurred to the smitten affianced she would be marrying a man very like her late father, honorable, and very unlike her long-absent brother, intemperate. She worried for Pip's welfare. *Where in the world has Pip taken himself? Please God that he's prudent.*

The Adams House management didn't at all mind how long the lovely lady in the blue suit sat at one of their best window tables. Her well-to-do appearance and obvious enjoyment of the lobster bisque served as a pretty, priceless endorsement to passersby.

"More coffee, Miss?"

Cordelia was vaguely aware of her surroundings and now realized the twice-repeated question had been directed at her. "Yes please."

She'd lifted the fresh cup to her lips and continued to enjoy the snowy view when an echo from her parents' love story drifted in. *Preposterous as it may seem, Cappy dear, your father is the only man I've ever kissed.* Along with the memory came a fleeting vision of the last time she ever saw them. Her father had opened the sedan door, held her mother's hand as she slid in and kissed it before letting go.

Oh how I wish you could see that Providence has at last sent me love. And to think—

Suddenly a peripheral column of crimson pulled Cordelia away from her musings, and Rita Donnelly came into focus. Everything paled next to her coat, and she stood out like a red rose in winter, unexpected yet familiar, unbelievable but very present. Cordelia slowly lowered her cup and almost missed the saucer. *That looks exactly like the coat I once had.*

Rita waved goodbye from the sidewalk, having just thought to do so, and couldn't understand why her usually attentive friend was so aloof and absent of a wave in return. *Cordelia looks like she's seen a ghost.*

Bob was growing impatient. "Honey, come on, we have to get going." The children pulled on his hands in agreement.

"Just a sec." Rita waved again, slower this time, with her head slightly tilted.

Cordelia was incredulous, frozen in thought at the absurdity of it all. *Rita Donnelly couldn't possibly be wearing my red coat.* She finally waved back, in a queenly fashion, stiff and formal. *Could she?*

David Miller darted into her frame of vision from the opposite direction, tapped on the window, gleamed that "I'm crazy about you" smile of his, pointed to the Adams House's double doors, and took long, fast strides to get there.

Cordelia's ambiguous expression concerned David, and he'd already decided to order her favorite dessert, a hot fudge sundae.

Rita had no doubt who the dark-haired, nice-looking man must be, but Bob called, "Rita, we need to leave, now!" She promptly gave Cordelia a heartfelt okay sign, turned on a dime and joined her family.

In that moment, Cordelia knew. She quietly gasped and jumped to her feet. *It is my coat!*

The one thing that distinguished Cordelia Parker's cherished red coat from others of the same time, place, make and style was its custom tailoring. As an energetic coed, she'd felt constricted by the too-short kick pleat and heeded Hilda's advice. "Jordan's excellent alterations department could lengthen that opening in no time." They did so quite nicely and with a bit of added flair at the top, a same-fabric, topstitched, horizontal tab "for chic reinforcement, Miss Parker."

Cordelia's eyes never left the Donnellys, and soon the family of five faded away into the snowfall, save the red coat, every thread vivid and lovely as ever, until the very last glimpse. *My red coat. Rita Donnelly is wearing my red coat.*

Although the shock of finding her missing coat on the most unlikely person still resonated, Cordelia couldn't imagine how she'd begin to tell David about the significance of it all without revealing her unrequited love for Norman Prescott and subsequent lament for the coat's return.

David, despite her scintillating "I'm so glad you're here" and gentle hand squeeze, sensed an underlying preoccupation from the moment he arrived, leading him to ask toward the end of the meal, "Are you sure everything's okay, Cordelia?" "Absolutely." She looked away briefly. "Well, there is something."

"Yes." *I knew it.*

"I've been in this restaurant far too long. Would you be open to a walk on the Common and a cup of hot cocoa afterwards?"

"Of course. Let's get out of here."

Cordelia and David's close footsteps left side-by-side sweetheart impressions on the glistening snow-covered paths of Boston Common, while sheltering overhead branches, sublime silence, and a golden day's end glow, so like that in Childe Hassam's *Boston Common at Twilight,* provided a feeling of peaceful sanctuary. But Cordelia still couldn't stop thinking of Rita Donnelly and her red coat. *How could that possibly be?*

And then it hit her, hard and fast, a vortex of loss and emotion, past and present, and in her own mother's words no less. *That Irish woman didn't ask for herself—simply wanted the coat for her daughter, Rosemary. Isn't that a lovely name, Rosemary?*

Cordelia and David were at the frozen Frog Pond, and a trio of happy, wobbly college coeds held on to each other for dear life while attempting to ice-skate. Their gaiety was contagious and onlookers, including David, joined in the laughter each time one of them screeched or slipped. Cordelia was smiling, but her mind was elsewhere as she frantically culled through past conversations with Rita and soon found what she was looking for. *Yes, yes, Rita mentioned her older sister Rosemary had moved to Arizona.* Cordelia simply couldn't believe how close the coat had been all this time, and yet so far, just like Norman Prescott, so near and yet completely out of reach.

The temperature dropped as the sun went down and a good deal of the crowd soon dispersed. David asked, "Is your offer for hot cocoa still good?"

"Of course it is." *What shall I do about the coat? Should I tell Rita? Will she feel embarrassed, or worse yet compelled to . . .*

Boston Common Winter

"Well then, Miss Parker, what are we waiting for?"

"Indeed Mr. Miller, what are we waiting for?"

They were walking up Charles Street against a cold north wind when David stopped to put money in a Salvation Army bucket and the bell-ringing, uniformed Captain smiled for the lack of a clink. "Merry Christmas, sir!"

Cordelia tried to hold her shiver in check, but David saw it and immediately took his topcoat off and wrapped it over hers. "It's freezing out here. We need to get you home." When Cordelia protested, he pulled the collar up on his tweed jacket. "Doctor's orders, my darling." He kissed her cold nose and put his arm firmly around her shoulders. "Let's hurry."

Church bells sounded the hour as they turned onto Mount Vernon, and the familiar surround of stately brownstones, black, cast-iron fences, and Christmas décor of evergreens, red ribbons, and candles in the windows all looked brand new to Cordelia, as if she were seeing her beloved Beacon Hill for the very first time. And it was in that moment of hurried steps, loving embrace, laughter, and kisses that Cordelia Parker realized Providence had been with her all along. *I never needed the red coat. I needed David, and here he is. Merry Christmas, Rita Donnelly. The coat is yours.*

CHAPTER 43

Toyland. Toyland.
Little girl and boy land.
While you dwell within it,
You are ever happy then.
Childhood's joy-land.
Mystic merry Toyland,
Once you pass its borders,
You can never return again.
"BABES IN TOYLAND"
GLENN MACDONOUGH & VICTOR HERBERT

TRADITIONALLY, THE DONNELLYS LAST STOP before visiting the manger again was to see live reindeer, also housed on the Common, behind temporary chain-linked fences painted green for the season. Bobby poked his fingers through the diamond-shaped openings in an attempt to pet the restless reindeer and would pull away just as Santa's favorite animal advanced. All the while he'd glance at his on-looking sisters, snicker, and return to his folly.

"Come on, kids, let's go!" meant the family was now headed for one last look at the Nativity scene. After dark was when it seemed most real; maybe because so many Christmas carols sang of the holy and silent night. Ruth Ann thought the baby Jesus, "wrapped in swaddling clothes," never looked warm enough and wondered if His outstretched, bare arms were reaching for a jacket or maybe a little blanket.

That night as Mr. and Mrs. Donnelly stood before the Holy Family with their own—the older children happily balanced on the bottom rail of the fence surrounding the manger, leaning over as far as they could, Catherine gleefully sitting on her daddy's shoulders—Rita Donnelly felt all was right with the world. Yes, California was still her husband's dream. *But God willing, he'll wake up soon and see how good we have it here.* She slipped her hand in his, and Bob spoke as if he'd read her thoughts. "Life's pretty good, huh, honey?"

The last observance of the traditional day trip came next when the devout young mother instructed her children to pray to the Baby Jesus. "Tell Him you'll be good from now on, thank you, and I love you." They ended by saying the family's customary goodbye. "Good night and God bless you."

Standing there in the brisk night air, mother, father, sisters, and brother, side by side beneath cerulean sky and crescent moon, strolling carolers joyously singing "Hark! The Herald Angels Sing," "The First Noel," "Adeste Fideles,"

Jordan Marsh – December 1954

and "Joy to the World" surrounded by countless others who were equally delighted in the light of the season, was Christmas. Beautiful, downtown Boston Christmas.

Rita and Bob had no way of knowing—as their young family ventured through the city, marveled at the holiday windows and lights, shopped for gifts, lunched at the Adams House, visited Santa, sang along with carolers, and adored the Prince of Peace at home on the Common—that a cherished, sustaining, never-to-be-forgotten, childhood memory was in the making. *O' holy night, the stars are brightly shining . . . and the soul felt its worth.*

CHAPTER 44

Remember, O most gracious Virgin Mary,
that never was it known that anyone who fled to your protection,
implored your help or sought your intercession, was left unaided.
"THE MEMORARE"
THE BALTIMORE CATECHISM
NO. 1
REV. E.M.DECK

"THAT'S IT, BOB. I'M NOT putting up with this anymore."

"God Almighty, Rita. Will you please let me explain?"

The New Year, 1955, had started out well enough. Ike was in office, times were prosperous and most people owned a car. Bob had recently gotten a raise and toyed with the idea of trading in his old black sedan for a new two-tone Chevy. Rita was thankful he hadn't brought up moving out West once since Christmas morning when he'd handed her a gift box from Neal's of California, a fashionable women's clothing store at 19 Arlington Street, close to the Common. However, his next bid was just around the corner.

It was a freezing cold Monday night in early January. Rita and Bob were seated on the couch ready to watch their favorite TV show. Her penny loafers had been removed for the comfort of bobby socks alone, legs tucked under and to the side. His heavy laced cordovans were replaced with fleece-lined L. L. Bean moccasins, feet propped up on the coffee table and next to a divided, ceramic clover candy dish filled with pistachio nuts, nonpareil chocolates, and discarded shells. Bob drank a whiskey and ginger, while Rita sipped ginger ale.

They were holding hands, and the opening music of *I Love Lucy* heightened their anticipation, but Rita winced as soon as the new episode's title appeared, "California Here We Come," and she let go.

Bob slapped both hands on his knees, grinned, and cocked his head in her direction. "See, honey, even the Ricardos are going out there."

"Oh, by all means, let's pack our bags right away." She reached for the candy. "You do realize this show is make-believe?"

"Beautiful, Rit, beautiful. What in God's name do I have to do to convince you?"

"You'll never convince me."

⸎

Bob's efforts were never dampened by Rita's constant refusals, and he continued to shower his wife with small gifts from Neal's of California, as if the luxury items would change her mind or at least open it to the possibility of moving out to "the West Coast," one of several phrases he'd adopted from the *Six Bridges* people and the one she particularly disdained. "No, Bob. I like this coast."

The Donnellys' life, for the most part, continued to run like clockwork, and that's how Rita liked it—predictable, peaceful, and parochial.

January was coming to an end and California tension was still in the air, but that didn't rob the couple of enjoying life as it was and enjoying each other. Mrs. Mac was happy to babysit once in a while, which freed them to occasionally pursue getting a bite to eat and going to the movies. Last year's favorite for Rita was *Sabrina*, with Audrey Hepburn. She adored the story of "poor girl makes good" and admired the pretty young star's pert elegance. *Innocent, and at the same time very sophisticated.* Bob's was *On the Waterfront*, starring Marlon Brando, whose character, a compromised boxer, missed his chance and sadly resented it. "I coulda' had class! I coulda' been a contender. I coulda' been somebody." Bob couldn't help but think of California. *I never want to be in that godforsaken boat.*

Tonight, they were going to have Chinese food at a restaurant by Ashmont Station and catch the just released movie, *Marty*, at the Oriental Theater on Blue Hill Avenue. Rita wore her Neal's of California outfit for the first time, a light tan, polished cotton, straight skirt and sky-blue blouse with a snappy gold-bar pin at the collar.

Bob was extremely pleased. "You look terrific, honey." He was also mistakenly encouraged and overly enthused. "I knew you'd like the California style. Too bad you have to cover it up, honey." He could have stopped at that point but didn't. "If we lived out there you wouldn't need a coat. Or boots. Or gloves."

Rita was tempted to change clothing and throw the entire outfit at him to the tune of: *Bob Donnelly, if you don't stop harping about California, you're going to find yourself sleeping on the couch.* Instead, weary of the struggle and thankful for a night out, she informed her children more forcefully than intended, "And I better not discover you kids got out of bed after Grammy tucked you in, or there'll be hell to pay." She grabbed Ruth Ann by the arm. "Do you hear me?"

"Yes, Mummy."

Grammy, as usual, let her first grandchild, "my pet," get up again after the others were asleep, and watch TV until they heard Bob's car pull up and Ruth Ann made a run for her bed.

It was a Saturday morning in early February. Red construction paper hearts hung in every window of the Donnellys' house and the good nuns of Saint Gregory's had already given ample warning to their students regarding the holiday of love. "You're to bring a valentine for every one of your classmates. No one's to be left out."

Rita and Bob each enjoyed a first cup of coffee while standing at the kitchen counter and looking out the window. Half-frozen, tramped over, dingy gray slush could be seen everywhere—in puddles, mounds and patches. She observed, "How could something so beautiful turn into such dismal stuff?" and he instantly came back with, "You'd never see slush out West."

As a rule, Bob did something with the kids on Saturday afternoons. Rita appreciated the break and being alone in a quiet house. In warmer weather, he took them to the Blue Hills for pony rides, Southie to visit his mother and Buddy, or out for an ice cream cone. Beach trips were always a whole-family endeavor.

In the winter, they mostly went sledding or ice-skating, and twice Bob surprised his children with a Disney movie at a theater downtown. They returned home with Cinderella and Pinocchio souvenir coloring books. "Mummy, guess where Daddy took us?"

Curiously, Bob showered earlier than usual that particular Saturday morning. He dressed nicer than usual and announced during breakfast, "I need to take advantage of the weekend and wrap up a few loose ends at headquarters."

"Like what?" Rita asked. *It better be good, pal, and will headquarters, in fact, see your handsome face?*

"What? I have to itemize everything to get your okay? Police work, nothing you'd understand."

"Oh, I understand all right."

Rita cleared the table in a tizzy, tossed utensils, plates, and glasses in the sink just this side of breaking them, and told her husband in no uncertain terms, "You'll gallivant around town. I know you, Bob. First it'll be S. S. Pierce for crackers and cheeses. Then a cold one at the Union Oyster House, and you may even stop by Station 3 to 'shoot the breeze.'"

"I said I had to take care of some things at headquarters. You know how hectic it gets during the week. I can get caught up this way."

Beyond disappointment at losing the only time she ever had to herself, Rita also felt under the weather and definitely wasn't up to taking care of all three children, all day. "Listen, Bob, I woke up with a headache and may be coming down with something. Please take the older kids with you. They can color or read while you're 'catching up.'"

"I don't want to drag two kids into police headquarters."

"And I wasn't too crazy about being left all alone with three kids when you were having the time of your life out in California." *Blessed Mother of God, now I've done it. California.*

"Fine. Have it your way." He punched one hand into the other and yelled upstairs, "Ruth Ann and Bobby, get your coats. We're going out. And make it snappy."

∝

When Bob and the children returned that night, beef stew was on the stove and the table was set. The open cellar door told him Rita was down there, and he called, "Supper smells delicious. I thought you said you didn't feel good."

She shouted back from the laundry room. "Nothing a strong cup of tea, good book, and napping child can't cure. I'll be right up."

Rita could hardly wait to crack open her latest book loan from Cordelia, East of Eden, by John Steinbeck, only to discover the good and evil tale took place in California, of all places. God in heaven!

Bobby stood at the top of the stairs holding a gold-embossed, foil-and-white-ribbon-wrapped bouquet of red tulips and smiling from ear to ear. "Here, Mummy."

"What in the world?" She rustled her son's hair. "Thank you." Rita took the flowers into the kitchen and was arranging them in a chipped blue ceramic pitcher—she hid the flaw with a leaf—when Bob came up beside her. "Am I out of the dog house now?"

"Yes," she told him, and they kissed.

The following week found the couple pressed with additional responsibilities. Catherine somehow caught pneumonia and had to be hospitalized for three days. Buddy was having trouble with his vision and every morning woke up with less of it, requiring Bob to join other family members and help transport his brother and Mrs. Mac back and forth to Mass General. Detective Bob Donnelly's testimony and extensive photographic evidence were required in three courtrooms that week. And Bobby, along with two of his pals, had set the woods ablaze down the street while attempting to bake potatoes over an open fire, and in the process, felled one tree and scorched two.

When Bob got home, he whipped his son with a belt until he thought he'd learned his lesson, as measured by the boy's tears, which Bobby stubbornly held in until he couldn't stand the pain any longer. Then he cried, "Please, Daddy, I won't do it again. Please stop. Please, Daddy."

The house was quiet after the beating, and Ruth Ann was scared to say or do anything for fear of getting the belt too. Catherine had never felt its sting and played carefree as ever with her dolls but was heard to scold, "You better be good, baby, or you're gonna get a spankin' too." Bobby was confined to his room without any supper, and when Rita went upstairs later to check on him, she asked, "Do you understand that what you did was very wrong?"

"Yes, Mummy. But we were only trying to cook potatoes."

Rita went to the dresser drawer and took out a pair of pajamas. She chose her son's preferred pair, red print flannels with little boys on bucking broncos, ten gallon hats, pistols, lassoes, cattle, and sheriff's badges. "Please put these on." When he came closer, she winced at the welts on his arms.

"Someone could have been seriously hurt. Do you understand?"

"Yes, Mummy."

"Are you going to do anything like that ever again?"

"No, Mummy."

She sat on the side of the bed and called him to her with a double pat on the mattress. "You're not a bad boy. Why, look what a nice thing you did last week when you brought me those flowers."

Bobby wiped his tears away with a corner of the bedspread. "Daddy gave them to the nice lady, but she told me and Ruth Ann that we should give them to you, Mummy."

"What nice lady?"

"Uh oh, Daddy said it was supposed to be a secret. Please don't tell him."

Rita went into the hallway. *A nice lady. Holy Mother of God.* She picked up the tray just outside Bobby's door and brought back a hush-hush supper for her son, a peanut butter and Marshmallow Fluff sandwich, applesauce, and Oreo cookies, along with a glass of milk. "Be sure to brush your teeth when you're through, and whatever you do, Bobby, don't come out until morning. Good night and God bless you." She closed the door behind her and headed downstairs.

"Bob." Rita found her husband at the kitchen table, going over race results amidst a fog of exhaled smoke, and at the same time snubbing his cigarette butt out in an ashtray, but nonetheless mindful of her presence. "Did you call me, honey?" He looked up.

"Yes. Tell me, just what did you do downtown last Saturday?"

"Last Saturday? That was a week ago, Rit. What's so important about it now?"

"I'm just curious."

He took a pack of cigarettes from his shirt pocket, removed one and tapped the filter-less "smoke" on the table before lighting it.

Frog Pond on Boston Common
An old-fashioned swimming hole
in summer, and the city's favorite
skating rink in winter.

"Let's see . . . first there was headquarters and then the S. S. Pierce stop. The kids wanted to go ice-skating, but by the time we got to the Frog Pond it was getting too cold. Oh, and you'll get a kick out of this. I forgot to tell you they both wanted to know where Jesus and His parents went? You have to admit it's pretty strange to a kid, one minute the Holy Family's there and the next . . . Anyway I said, 'Home to heaven 'til next year,' and that was the end of it."

"Cute." Rita remained standing and folded her arms. "Is there anything else you'd like to tell me about that day?"

"Ya, sure there is. This feels like a goddam interrogation. I'm through."

"According to Bobby there was a 'nice lady' in the picture."

Bob pushed away from the table so forcefully, the scraping chair sounded like the wail of a banshee. "So, there was a nice lady. Why do you always jump to the worst conclusion?"

"I'm not aware of jumping at all. In fact you're the one who moved. Not me. Nervous?"

"I've had just about enough." He grabbed her by the arm. "Enough." Rita shook free from his grasp. "Let's try this on for size, detective. You bought those tulips for someone else, and had the nerve to expose my children to your paramour."

"What the hell are you talking about?"

Their voices were raised now. Bobby cracked the bedroom door open and listened for his name. The girls, playing house in the living room, grabbed their baby dolls and ran upstairs to their bedroom. Rita heard the scurrying footsteps and their obvious fear intensified her anger with Bob. "This is what I'm talking about. We have three kids—ten, nine and four and a half. It's going to be a long time before they're out on their own . . . "

"Jesus, Rita, all of a sudden we're talking 'This Is Your Life?'"

"As a matter of fact, yes. Your life, Mr. Family Man, who thinks he can introduce my children to anyone he goddam pleases."

"It wasn't like that. The kids and I changed our minds about the skating, bought the flowers in a nice floral shop for you, and to tell the truth, I ran into an old acquaintance. I'll admit it wasn't the best judgment to give her the flowers, but it was a spur of the moment kind of situation."

"Oh, that's what we're calling your trollops these days, 'old acquaintance'? You really think I'm going to buy that story? 'Ran into' my foot. That's it, Bob. I'm not putting up with this anymore."

"God Almighty, Rita. Will you please let me explain?"

"No." She pulled a chair out, sat down, lit one of his cigarettes and exhaled. "I'm leaving you, Bob."

He rushed over, crouched down beside her and tried unsuccessfully to take her hand. "Come on honey, this has gone too far."

"You should have thought of that when you gave your 'old acquaintance' the flowers." Rita picked an empty glass up from the table and threw it against a wall. "I don't deserve this and neither do the kids. Their whole lives are going to be disrupted, and for what? So you can be the big shot for a while, enjoy another woman's company whenever you please, and violate our wedding vows."

"Jesus, Rita, watch what you're saying." He gestured his head toward the stairway. "The kids."

"Oh, all of a sudden you're concerned about the kids."

He cut her off. "Let's go see Father Sweeney at Saint Gregory's. He'll help us sort this out."

"Not on your life. There'll be no Father anybody this time. Whenever we go toward the church it's no contest, and you know it."

"Rita, I didn't prearrange anything with her. We just ran into each other. She thought the kids were great. Bobby said, 'My mummy's not feeling good' and that's when she gave the flowers to him. Can I help it if I run into someone?

Jesus, Rita, can I goddam help it if someone I used to know comes across my path? Are you going to hold me responsible for that?"

"I don't know what to believe." She took another drag and tapped the excess embers into the ashtray.

"I gotta tell you, Rit. If we lived in California, there wouldn't be anyone for me to run into. We'd get a whole new start. And I swear on my mother's life nothing like this would ever happen again."

"Oh, now we're back to California." She put the cigarette down, shook her head, and began to cry.

"Come on, Rit. You've blown this whole thing way out of proportion. But maybe it's working out for the best. California's the answer. What do you say, honey?" He tried to take her hand again, but she snapped it away. "Leave me alone, you louse."

"Fine. I will." Bob rumbled down the basement steps, and soon the whir of the punching bag, suspended almost directly beneath Rita's feet, could be heard loud and clear. She went to the stove, put the kettle on, and considered her situation . . . *the rest of my life.* Not since leaving her father's home as a teenager had she felt so alone, so confused, so forsaken. *I need to talk to someone who can help me make this decision. And it's sure as hell not going to be a priest, even if it is that nice Father Sweeney.* The whir of the punching bag intensified.

Rita picked the cigarette up again, put it down, went to a small table at the end of the kitchen counter, rested her hand on the telephone receiver for a minute, took it off the hook, and dialed. Her stomach knotted tighter and tighter with each ring until the other party answered on the fifth. "Hello."

Rita's voice cracked as she addressed the only person in the entire world she trusted completely.

"Hello, Ro."

CHAPTER 45

I remember my mother's prayers and they have always followed me.
They have clung to me all my life.
ABRAHAM LINCOLN

"MOMENTS TO REMEMBER" WAS AT the top of the pop tune charts in 1955. And at the same time, moments to remember were taking place in the two-story, brick, three-bedroom, saltbox home of the Donnelly family. My family.

"It's fortunate spring came early this year," my father said in response to the gas in our home being turned off at his request. The electricity and telephone would be on for one more day. It was March of 1955, the night before our family—parents Bob and Rita; brother, Bobby; sister, Catherine; and myself, Ruth Ann—would leave Boston for the move to California.

All the possessions we would take to our new home three thousand miles away were ready for Allied Van Lines to pick them up the next morning. Large wooden tea crates my father acquired from the Salada Tea Company were packed with soft goods, dishes, pots, pans, silverware, linens, toys, photos, and books. Most of his extensive gun collection had recently been sold to the actor Darrin McGavin, who he met at the Union Oyster House in downtown Boston.

The only furniture taken, other than a console television set, was Bobby's fairly new, solid maple twin bed, nightstand, desk, and chair. It was the newness that saved it. California was a new beginning, and my father was incredibly excited about "starting a new life out there." The rest of the furniture, including a small mahogany wall shelf which held my mother's treasured collection of three Hummel figurines and three miniature Chinese porcelain horses, was given to family and friends. She kept the collectibles. And days before we left, my grandmother was delighted to be given two lamps that had topped the mahogany end tables on either side of our living room couch.

Shortly before we left Boston, a door-to-door photographer took an after-school photo of my brother, sister and me sitting on the couch beneath that shelf. Sealed for all time in a tiny, plastic key-chain telescope and presently safe at home in my jewelry box.

Daddy had phoned Grammy to say we'd be stopping by. "Do you need me to pick up anything? A quart of milk and a loaf of bread? Tell Buddy I'll have something for him too."

Buddy, my father's younger brother, whose keen intelligence belied his helpless physical state of crippling cerebral palsy, still lived with his mother at age thirty-one. Grammy tended to his every need. He was always clean-shaven with combed hair, a pressed sport shirt, and creased khakis. My mother never failed to greet his happy "H-h-h-hi, Riiiitaa!" with "Buddy, you are one spiffy fella."

Grammy's small apartment was on the third floor of a seven-story building adjacent to the sea; two bedrooms, a living room, eat-in kitchen, one bathroom, and a hallway lined with family photographs, she called it "the Ethel Murphy McDonough Museum," parodying one of Boston's most famous and elite cultural attractions, the Isabella Stewart Gardner Museum.

After my grandfather passed away, economic necessity drove Grammy and Buddy's move to Columbia Point's towers of public housing with "an ocean view, no less."

Our family usually took the elevator, although it was extremely slow. My sister, brother, and I raced one another to push the button, but this time our parents didn't have the patience to wait, so all five of us swiftly climbed the three flights of steel and concrete stairs to Grammy's home.

"Oh, there they are!" she exclaimed at the door, her arms opened wide. "There's my pet." That's what she called me, and then she kissed my forehead. "And my only grandson, you're not too big to give your Grammy a kiss now, are you?"

Bobby wrapped his arms around her, threw his head back, and laughed. "No." He pursed his lips for a kiss.

She pretended not to see Catherine, who was hiding behind my father. "Where's the little girl? Did you lose her?"

My baby sister repeated her darling charade for the umpteenth time, peeking out from behind Daddy's trouser legs, she said, "Here I am, Grammy," and ran into her waiting arms. All the while, Uncle Buddy was inside, laughing and calling out in his deliberate, palsied speech, "Is that the-the-the three blind mice I h-h-hear?"

Each of my parents held one of the lamps, and Grammy asked, "What do you two have there?" My father teased, "Well, we've got your groceries and some beer for—"

Buddy called from inside again, "I-I-I heard that Bob. G-g-get in here, w-w-will you?"

As we entered the homey apartment, Mummy said, "Mother, you've admired these lamps for years. I want you to have them."

Grammy replied, "Are you sure, Rita? I wouldn't want you to regret leaving them behind."

"Bob doesn't want to pay the freight, and there's no room in the car. I don't know how we're going to take all that we have now. It's good to know they're going to someone who likes them as much as I do." The whole time she was talking to my grandmother, my mother slowly swayed from side to side as she cradled the lamp in her arms like a baby.

On our second to last morning in Boston, my parents' friends Pat and Bill Connor brought their camping cots to our home. The canvas beds were set up between boxes, luggage, and furniture. A Scotch cooler filled with sandwiches, potato salad,

Uncle Buddy had two positions and stations: prone in his bed at night or seated in a soft armchair by day, where his spastic body writhed endlessly and slowly slid down until Grammy went behind the chair, put her hands beneath his armpits, and pulled him up again.

cold drinks, and a can of evaporated milk was in the kitchen, along with two thermoses—hot tea and coffee—as well as a shallow box lined with a cheery cherry print dishtowel and stocked with hot and cold paper cups, plates and napkins, disposable spoons, knives and forks, potato chips, vanilla sandwich cookies, chocolate Devil Dogs and Twinkies, apples, and one china teacup and saucer.

There was an air of excitement as relatives, neighbors and friends came by to wish our family well. Mrs. Maguire, the mother of four children whose family had the messiest and happiest house on our street, was convinced every family that went to California produced at least one movie star.

"We'll be lookin' for all of ya's in the movies. God knows baby Catherine has what it takes. Wait 'til they see her gorgeous little face."

Mr. Rosen, our across-the-street-neighbor, had his own take on California. "Bob, you'll never have to shovel snow again. What'll you do with all that spare time? Have lunch with Lucy and Ricky?"

Bobby and I loved our weeks at Green Harbor's Camp Cedar Crest for Catholic boys and girls, otherwise known as Mummy's "Godsend," where we went to daily Mass, were driven to the beach in open trucks lined with benches, had a canteen account for candy and ice cream, made lariats and key chains with multi-colored gimp, learned how to shoot a bow and arrow, played any number of games, sang camp songs day and night, pulled pranks, and reveled in the talent shows and giant bonfires.

My father's Uncle Harry Sweeney was slightly envious. "You kids have it made. I wish I'd moved to California. Had a chance, you know. Right after World War I. Could've stayed in San Diego, but your Aunt Peggy was waiting for me here. And God knows her father would have come out there with a shotgun if I didn't marry her. I won't go any further, but let's just say our honeymoon wasn't the first—"

He stopped because my mother gave him "the look" that stopped everyone.

My best friend, Janet O'Neil, wanted to know, "Ruth Ann, do you think you'll see the Mouseketeers? Maybe you could be one. Lucky!"

Janet jumped up on one of the tea crates and off again with her arms in the air, just as we'd done many times from her mother's couch while watching the Mickey Mouse Club on TV. "Hi! I'm Janet!" I jumped up when she came down. "And I'm Ruth Ann!"

My brother's friend, Vincent Pasquali, brought him a packet of Red Sox bubble gum cards. "Hey, Bobby, do you think your parents will let you come back for Camp Cedar Crest next summer?"

The two boys had made their First Communion together and they skipped school for the first time together too. When Mr. Pasquali asked, "So what made you think you could play hooky and get away with it?"

Bobby answered, "Mr. Pasquali, I don't even know how to ice-skate that good." Both families and the two policemen who brought the boys home broke out in laughter.

Mr. Walt Jennings stopped by early on his way home from Boston Police Headquarters, where he and my father had worked together as detectives.

"Eddie Dugan planned on comin', but there's somethin' brewin' in Charlestown. They found two bodies behind a warehouse, and Captain Riley asked for him personally, *mach schnell*. Why a guy named Riley uses German to make his point is beyond me. Ya gotta admit Ed's got some weird kind of radar when it comes to trackin' down the worst of 'em. Anyway, think of us when you tip your glass."

He pulled a box of Four Roses whiskey from behind his back and handed it to my father. "*Go maire sibh bhur saol nua.*" May you enjoy your new life.

Daddy put it next to the thermoses. "Thanks, Walt. I think I feel a thirst coming on. No, better save it for the road. I understand packaged goods stores are few and far between in the South. Thank Eddie for me too, will you?"

Mr. Jennings asked, "Where's Rita?"

"She's in the other room trying to make sense of all this stuff."

Both men walked across the small entry and into the living room, where my mother was folding a blanket.

"Walt, I didn't know you were here. Thanks for coming by," Mummy said as she put the blanket down on a cot and crossed the room with both of her hands reaching for his.

"Mary Alice sends her love, Rita, and she asked me to give this to you." He reached into his suit pocket, took out a small, thin,

May the Sacred Heart of Jesus go before you to guide you, above, to watch over you, behind to encourage you and may His love and peace be with you now and forever. Amen.

Dear Rita & Bob,
God bless your new home. Love,
Mary Alice & Walt Jennings

white-tissue-paper-wrapped package, handed it to my mother, and kissed her on the cheek. "Open it."

She pulled on the green ribbon bow and turned back the tissue to find three holy cards: the first, a portrait of Jesus, His Sacred Heart glowing, with a prayer on the back and a blessing written in Mary Alice's perfect Palmer Method hand. I still have the card.

The second portrayed Saint Rita and told her story of steadfast faith and awe-inspiring miracles. The last held a gold chain and pastel cloisonné medal of the patron saint of safe travel. Mr. Jennings requested, "Rita, turn it over." "Saint Christopher protect us" was inscribed on the back.

My mother smiled. "I kept meaning to buy a Saint Christopher for the trip but got sidetracked because there was so much to do. Please tell Mary Alice thank you and I'll write soon."

My father asked, "Honey, why don't you put it on right now?"

"We don't leave until tomorrow, Bob."

"The sooner the better, honey. It'll look nice."

She gave Mr. Jennings a hug.

We children liked Mr. Jennings because he knew we were there. My parents entertained frequently; there was the adult world, and the kid world, but he always took the time to ask us about school and say how much we'd grown. Now he took the time to say goodbye.

"Okay, you kids, obey your parents, and don't forget to say your prayers." He handed two one-dollar-bills to each of us. "This is for souvenirs," he said as he squeezed my shoulder, shook Bobby's hand, and tickled Catherine's tummy. "God bless you kids. I gotta get going." He headed for the door and stopped. "Better call headquarters and see if Ed left a message for me. Does your phone still work?"

My father said, "Yes. It's in the kitchen. Here let me show you." He immediately returned to us. "Jesus, Rita, would it have killed you to put the medal on for Walt?" Mr. Jennings came back. "Yeah, just what I thought, Riley wants me there too. Do you mind if I use your phone again to call Mary Alice?"

"Of course not, Walt. You should know you don't have to ask."

When he left the room, my father turned to my mother. "Well?"

"I'm not putting it on. Not yet."

Even at age ten I understood why—wearing the medal then would have made everything that was happening too real, too end of the line, too no turning back. It would all come soon enough.

Mr. Jennings announced, "Okay, I'm off," and slipped his hat on. "Hey, Bob, be sure to let us know how things are going out there. He shook my father's hand and held his shoulder. "'May the road rise up to meet you' and all the rest. Bye, Donnelly family."

"Bye, Walt, and thanks for the gifts. You and Mary Alice will have to come out and see us." My father's invitation was more polite than realistic. They had five children, and Mrs. Jennings, like all of our mothers, was a homemaker. On Walt's salary, a trip to California was as close as a trip to the moon.

The sound of Mr. Jennings's keys, closing of his car door, and pulling away resonated with me for years. *God bless you kids.*

Our neighbor Mrs. Bernstein and my mother occasionally shared a cup of tea and rugelach, but more often they enjoyed a slice or two of Drake's raisin pound cake. She arrived right after Mr. Jennings left. Mrs. Bernstein brought a "fresh one" in a new Tupperware container as a going-away gift. "I wonder, Rita, do they have Drake's in California? If not, write me, and I'll mail you one in double waxed paper. So, California, unbelievable that my neighbor should be moving to Hollywood."

"Sylvia, we're not moving to Hollywood. We're moving to San Pedro, and I understand it's not that close to Hollywood. Thank God."

Mrs. Bernstein's last words to my mother as she hugged and kissed her were, "Rita, be happy. For the sake of your children, be happy."

By twilight, it was just the five of us. Everything my parents owned was in perfect order. The cots had been precisely lined up with pajamas across the foot of each one, suitcases beneath. Boxes were stacked just so, and Bobby's disassembled bed was leaning against a wall by the rest of his furniture. The TV was where it had always been, front and center.

I remember Mummy sitting on a small box. She was wearing her standard day clothes, a skirt that came just below her knees, cotton blouse and wool cardigan with the sleeves pushed up, nylons and penny loafers, simple mother of pearl earrings, a wristwatch and wedding rings. She sat with her knees together, pulled toward her for modesty; and wore her stylishly short hair tucked behind her ears with a wisp of bangs. She sat on that box and quietly stared out at nothing in particular. With pen in hand, Daddy was going over the maps he'd picked up at the Automobile Club for our trip. He had them spread out on boxes along with the AAA Travel Log and a half-dollar sized pocket magnifying glass.

I was sitting on a cot rearranging clothes in my Ginny doll's trunk, Bobby was zooming a Matchbox car across a windowsill, and Catherine was trying to weave a red yarn lace through a toy sewing card. She'd just said, "Ruth Ann, help me," when Mummy began crying softly. Then her crying grew louder, and she grabbed the bodice of her blouse and tore it open, sobbing as buttons landed on the hardwood floor like a broken string of pearls. I'd never seen my mother unclothed and was shocked to see her bra.

My father pleaded, "Rita, the kids."

She cried out, tears escaping from her eyes despite their being shut tight, just as her small hands were. "I don't want to move to California. I don't want to leave Boston. My house, my house, my beautiful house."

Daddy pulled Mummy up and led her to the stairway that went to now bare bedrooms. "Jesus, Rita, what are you doing? It's all set, and things are going to be so much better. You're going to love it out there."

In the emptiness of what was once our home, his promising words rang hollow. Bobby and I picked up the buttons. He handed me two and whispered, "Don't lose them." Catherine sat still and sucked her thumb.

"Go upstairs and pull yourself together," my father urged my mother. "I'll find your suitcase and bring you something else to wear."

"I can do it myself," Mummy said with tears in her voice. She went to her cot and stooped down.

Daddy reached past her. "Let me." He pulled the suitcase out and flipped it open. Her beautiful red coat was on top. "Jesus, Mary, and Joseph, Rita!" Holy family names always meant trouble. "We agreed not to take this winter coat out to California." He tossed it on the cot.

"I never said anything of the kind. You did." Mummy pulled a blouse out.

My father closed the suitcase and pushed it underneath again. "Honey," he said in a tone that defied the sweet endearment, "your sister left the coat here because she was moving to Arizona. You. Don't. Need it. You're never going to need it again."

"Yes, I will, Bob!" Mummy picked the red coat up and held it close. "My Mother, Ro, Kay, and I are all wrapped up in this coat, and I'm not going anywhere without it. Not now. Not ever. Let alone California."

"God Almighty, Rita, do you realize how ridiculous this is?"

"I'm taking the coat." She reached in the right pocket and pulled the never used R-monogrammed hankie out just far enough to see it, as if checking for an important document.

My father said, "Mother of God," under his breath. "Okay, fine, Rita. Keep the coat. Now let's get you squared away." He led her to the stairs again, looked back at the three of us children, and motioned with a downward palm that we should remain where we were.

Mummy asked for her cigarettes. He went across the room, opened her pocketbook, and removed a package of Phillip Morris and a lighter. We couldn't see our mother, but we heard her voice. "Thank you," she said, and her footsteps stopped halfway up, then began again.

My father stayed at the bottom of the stairs until she made it to the top. "I'll be there in a minute."

Catherine, Bobby, and I stayed put until he said, "You kids can watch TV. Here let me plug it in. Where are the rabbit ears? You can sit on your coats on the floor. Turn them inside out so they don't get soiled."

He went straight to the kitchen, picked up the Four Roses box, took the bottle out, opened it, and poured whiskey into Mummy's teacup. His feet landed heavily on the stairs, up, up, and then a knock on the bathroom door. "Rita, are you in there?"

Because the door squeaked we knew when our mother opened it, and we heard their hushed tones with her sobs in between. When my parents came downstairs, Mummy was neat as a pin and composed, and she soon served us sandwiches from the cooler, our last supper in the home she loved so much.

"Don't eat yet kids. We need to pray first," she said.

We sat on the edge of the cots, paper cups filled with soft drinks on the floor in front of us, paper napkins spread on our laps, paper plates on top of them and prayed with our mother.

"In the name of the Father, and of the Son, and of the Holy Ghost. Bless us O' Lord, for these Thy gifts which we are about to receive from Thy bounty through Christ our Lord. Amen."

That last day gave birth to two phrases every member of our family would use for the rest of their lives: "Back in Boston" and "After we moved to California."

CHAPTER 46

Your Chevrolet Dealer Presents
Rx for Travel
See New Places
It's the New Motoramic Chevrolet
More than a new car, a new concept of low-cost motoring, a
revolutionary new ride. Only the new Chevrolet has new Glide
Ride front suspension that absorbs road shocks. And new show car
styling lets you travel proudly in the new Motoramic Chevrolet.
TV COMMERCIAL FOR THE NEW 1955 CHEVROLET

DADDY SAT PROUDLY BEHIND THE wheel of his brand new, two-toned, India Ivory and Shadow Gray, 1955 Chevrolet Bel Air, four-door sedan. He was eager to get going. Everything was in place; he'd be with the LAPD, stop by Paramount Studios, say hello to the Hollywood movie director, see if anything was lined up for him or us kids, and get established. He was the first one in the car, at Mummy's insistence. "Your pacing is driving me crazy. I'll take care of the kids."

"Calm down, you three. It's time to get in the car," she insisted as my sister, brother, and I chased each other around the lone tree in front of our house. "We have a long trip ahead of us, and I don't want any shenanigans. Please get in the car now!"

Bobby, Catherine and I jumped in the back seat as ordered and rolled the window down so we could shout goodbye to our parents' friends, Mr. and Mrs. Connor, who'd come to collect their cots, wait for Allied Van Lines to pick up our possessions, and hand over house keys to the next family who would call 97 Standard Street their home.

My parents had cleverly built a makeshift playroom in the back seat of the new car; they placed boxes and suitcases on the floor and tucked a large plaid bedspread in the seat cushion and brought it forward over the floor baggage. We were easily able to play board games, color, read, lie down and nap, or just sit back and enjoy the view, feet straight out in front of us.

I can still picture Mr. Connor shaking his head and grinning as he said to my parents, "Typical Donnellys. You all look like you just stepped out of a bandbox. It's only a car ride for cryin' out loud."

My father laughed and answered, "I know. I know. Give me a break, pal. We're getting ready for a three thousand-mile trip of a lifetime here."

My mother and Mrs. Connor were hugging, and then Mummy got in the car and rolled her window down. "Bye, you two. Thanks for everything. And Pat, if you want those curtains in the rumpus room, you're welcome to them. They weren't part of the deal, and I know you've had your eye on them."

Mrs. Connor winked, leaned in the window, kissed the side of Mummy's head, and said, "I thought you'd never ask. Bye, Rita, take care now."

My mother reached for her hand and didn't let go until Mrs. Connor did. They both had tears in their eyes. Mrs. Connor looked in the back seat. "And you kids behave yourselves." Then she tapped the car door, folded her arms the way women do in situations like that, and said, "Have a good trip, and be sure to let us know you got there safe and sound."

And off we went, down Standard Street, onto Morton Street, up Gallivan Boulevard . . .

My mother had the red coat wrapped around her like a blanket and suggested, "Honey, let's drive through the city one last time, okay?"

466

My father thought it was a great idea. Mummy had another reason for being in town but was biding her time.

We drove past Boston Police Station 3 on Joy Street, up and down a couple of more streets on Beacon Hill, and circled the Common, and who should my father see on Tremont but "Straight Ahead Sullivan," a traffic cop he'd gone to the Police Academy with, who came by that name because of the only directions he ever gave to lost people. Daddy stopped his brand new car in the middle of the intersection.

"Hey, Officer Sullivan, which way to California?"

"Straight ahead, Bob, straight ahead."

Daddy sang, "California here I come!" as we pulled away and the rest of us waved goodbye.

Mummy smiled at him and said, "Sorry to interrupt your sterling performance, Bob, but I want to stop at Filene's. Ruth Ann needs a lightweight jacket for the trip."

"Rita, we're getting a late start as it is. Do we really have to do this?"

"Yes," she answered, her eyes focused on the road ahead. "It won't take that long."

Minutes later my father pulled the car into a no parking zone on Washington Street, got out, opened my mother's door, and entreated, "Please honey, for the love of God, don't shop for anything else. We really need to get going."

Bobby hopped out of the car, opened the backseat door for me, and glanced at my father for recognition.

My mother threw the red coat over her shoulders, grabbed me by the hand, and we dashed into Filene's together for the very last time, into the store where so many of my outfits had been purchased: Easter and Christmas dresses, school uniforms, and summer clothes, purchases that my Grammy kiddingly referred to as "sunken treasure" because most were made in the bargain basement. But that day, Mummy took me straight upstairs on the main store's escalator to the girl's clothing department. Everything happened so quickly.

We immediately spotted a display of spring coats and jackets. My mother politely declined a saleslady's help, and we didn't go into a dressing room but directly to the closest mirror. Mummy held a few coats over her arm, handed them to me one by one, and then hung them on a nearby rack, where she'd pushed back a row of frilly Easter dresses to make room. After I'd tried on every coat, she asked, "Which one do you like best, Ruth Ann?"

"This one, Mummy." I pointed to a light khaki, three-quarter length car coat with richly toned yellow, red, and green striped lining that matched material on the reverse side of the collar.

She agreed. "That's my favorite too. Let's try it on again."

I stepped into the space before the three-way mirror and saw a trio of freckled, skinny ten-year-old girls with light auburn pigtails and bangs that were cut too short, wearing baby-blue, pearlized eye-glasses, tan corduroy pants, white Peter Pan collar blouses, and brown oxfords. But when I put on the stylish new car coat, I saw three Audrey Hepburns. Just the week before, I'd spied the famous movie star on the cover of one of my mother's magazines, and Miss Hepburn was wearing a similar style jacket, the collar pulled up close to her pretty gamine face. "I love it, Mummy. Can I have this one?"

"Yes. It's perfect." She came closer, buttoned every button, tenderly tugging here and there. "It even has a little growing room." My mother smiled but looked sad too. I can't really explain other than to say, Mummy gave me a firm, lingering hug right in the middle of Filene's on that last momentous day in our beloved Boston. I'll never forget it.

She soon motioned to a saleslady, who was at our side within seconds. "We'll take this one, please," my mother said, pointing to the car coat, which I still had on. She paid for it with what she called "my just in case money" put aside in her wallet for unexpected expenses or opportunities. She kept the secret savings folded and tucked behind her Social Security card. I was surprised when Mummy asked, "Could you please clip the tags? My daughter will be wearing the coat out of the store."

She handed the saleslady my navy-blue, wool school coat and said, "This early spring really caught us off guard."

The saleslady pleasantly agreed. "Yes. Well, there's nothing as unpredictable as New England weather. Would you like to take this winter coat out on a hanger, madam, or shall I put it in a bag?"

My mother closed her eyes for an instant, opened them, and slightly moved her head from side to side as she said, "Either. It really doesn't matter. Thank you."

Then my thirty-year-old mother faced me, straightened the shoulders of my new car coat, turned each cuff back precisely, so the striped lining would show, adjusted the collar with care, and pulled it up just like Audrey Hepburn's, the movie star.

What fills the eye fills the heart.
IRISH PROVERB

EPILOGUE

A ND THAT'S HOW THE RED coat came into this family. Its graceful design, an elegant blend of lambswool and crimson, was timeless and covered generations of King women with love.

When Rosemary wore the coat for the very first time, unimagined doors to a new life were opened through the heart of a smitten young man, who one day became her husband.

Kay applied for a job that some said was over her head, which she held a little higher when wearing the borrowed coat during an interview. She got the position.

And a few years later, when Rosemary and Kay's younger sister, Rita, proudly wore the elegant coat into Boston for a Christmas outing with her family, in-town friend Cordelia Parker shockingly recognized the cherished garment as once being her own. The unlikely coincidence proved to be a long time coming, and a blessing in disguise.

The red coat traveled west with Rita when her husband moved their family to California in the 1950s. He never expected she'd need to wear it in the land of endless sunshine. But there was occasion, if only to put her mother's legacy over her shoulders and feel the warmth of home or to stave off chilly winter nights in style.

In the tumultuous sixties, the red coat was a standout garment among tie-dyed shirts, mini-skirts, and bell-bottomed trousers. Rita's eldest daughter, Ruth

Ann, wore it as part of her 1969 bridal going away outfit, and her bridesmaids gave it a name, "the honeymoon coat."

At the turn of the new century, Norah's great-granddaughter Candace sported the red coat with the collar slightly turned up as she walked into a Hollywood film premier party, where admiring men and women inquired of the young television producer, "Where did you ever get that perfectly stunning vintage coat?" And when younger sister, Catherine, had her first child, she asked Candace to please bring the red coat to the baby's christening. "I just want to have it over my shoulders."

Catherine; her husband; her mother, Ruth Ann; her father; sister, Candace; and other family members stood reverently around the baptismal font, and unseen but very present in spirit were Norah, Rosemary, Kay, and Rita gazing over the devoted mother's shoulder as Father O'Neill gently poured holy water on the new baby's head and christened this first child of the next generation.

"In the name of the Father, and of the Son, and of the Holy Spirit, I baptize thee, Grace."

THE ARTIST AND THE AUTHOR IN HIS STUDIO

A special thank you to one of the finest gentlemen in South Boston, Dan McCole! Dan is a renowned watercolorist who kindly agreed to create the cover art for *The Red Coat – A Novel of Boston*. With his great talent and heart for Boston, Dan readily captured the emotion of the story and the beauty of the city while producing this wonderful work of art!

> *"We Irish prefer embroideries to plain cloth.*
> *To us Irish, memory is a canvas—*
> *stretched, primed, and ready for painting on.*
> *We love the "story" part of the word "history,"*
> *and we love it trimmed out with color and drama, ribbons and bows.*
> *Listen to our tunes, observe a Celtic scroll: we always decorate our essence."*
>
> FRANK DELANEY, TIPPERARY

at www.ICGtesting.com

/P

9 780986 223808